Alastair MacNeil. 1960. His family he was six years old and MacNeill returned to Britain in 1985. He became established as an author when he assumed the mantle of Alistair MacLean and wrote seven bestselling novels based on screenplays left after MacLean's death.

ALASTAIR MacNEILL

The Devil's Door

HarperCollins*Publishers*

HarperCollins*Publishers*
77–85 Fulham Palace Road,
Hammersmith, London W6 8JB

This paperback edition 1996
1 3 5 7 9 8 6 4 2

First published in Great Britain by
HarperCollins*Publishers* 1994

Copyright © Alastair MacNeill 1994

The Author asserts the moral right to
be identified as the author of this work

ISBN 0 00 649657 1

Set in Linotron Sabon by
Rowland Phototypesetting Ltd,
Bury St Edmunds, Suffolk

Printed in Great Britain by
Caledonian International Book Manufacturer, Glasgow

THE DEVIL'S DOOR

Eight kilometres to the south of San Salvador, the capital of El Salvador, lies an area characterized by an extensive region of rugged mountain terrain. It was reputed that during the country's lengthy civil war the military and the notorious 'death squads' would dump the bodies of guerrilla fighters, as well as those of so-called 'Communist' sympathizers, in a deep gorge which separates two massive boulders as a gruesome warning to those seeking to try and overthrow the ruling junta.

The area takes its name from the spacious gap which separates the two towering rocks: La Puerta del Diablo . . . The Devil's Door.

ONE

He knew if they found him, they'd kill him.

A pair of headlights swept into view at the end of the street and he instinctively ducked down into the shadows as the car shot past him. False alarm. Shifting uneasily on his haunches, he wiped the sweat from his face then looked across at the dimly lit hotel entrance on the opposite side of the street. He could see into the foyer. It looked empty. That didn't mean anything. They could already be waiting for him in his room. His eyes went to the only illuminated window on the second floor. He knew he didn't have to go back to the room – he was due to meet his contact within the hour and, all being well, he'd be safely over the border by the morning – but his address book was still in the room and it contained the names of all the major contacts he'd made in his fifteen years as an investigative journalist. He couldn't afford to let the book fall into the wrong hands . . .

He scanned the length of the deserted street, then hurried across to the main courtyard and was about to make for the front entrance when he checked himself. No, don't take any unnecessary risks. Not now. Instead he made his way to the alley at the side of the hotel. It was in total darkness. After glancing furtively along the row of empty cars parked in the street, he moved cautiously to the metal stairs which he knew were located at the back of the hotel. Suddenly a hand clamped tightly around his wrist. He cried out in fright and stumbled backwards in terror. The hand held firm. In panic he lashed out with his fist. There was a muffled grunt of pain followed by a dull thud. Then silence. His first instinct was to flee but after several deep breaths he finally managed to steady his ragged nerves. He lit a match and held it up to the face of the unconscious figure slumped at his feet. It was a vagrant. He chuckled nervously to himself then extinguished the match and slowly climbed the stairs to the fire door that led on to the second floor. It was still unlocked, just as he'd left it earlier that evening. Wiping the back of his hand across his clammy forehead, he slipped inside and made his way silently down the deserted hall to his room and crouched down in front of the door. The tiny square of folded paper he'd inserted earlier between the door and the jamb was still there. Nobody had entered the room since he'd been gone. He gingerly opened the door and peered inside. All clear. He made straight for the wardrobe and took the address book from his jacket pocket. It would be too risky to take the book with him. Lighting a match, he touched the flame to the edge of the book and waited until it had caught fire before dropping it into the metal bin at his feet.

Then, sitting on the edge of the bed, he reached for the telephone.

'What a night,' Nicole Auger exclaimed, locking the main doors after the last of the guests had left the restaurant. 'I thought we were never going to get them out.'

'They did spend a lot of money tonight,' Carole Lewis reminded her.

'And the host tried every little trick he knew to try and charm me into his bed,' Nicole replied, rolling her eyes.

'That's what comes of being the partner with the looks,' Carole said with a grin.

'Men,' Nicole snorted good-humouredly. 'All I want to do now is go home, soak in a hot bath, then crawl into bed. Alone. I'm exhausted.'

'It's no wonder, you've been here since early this morning,' Carole said. 'I'll lock up tonight. Go on home and get into that hot bath.'

'Are you sure?'

'Goodnight, Nicole,' Carole said, taking the keys from her.

'I've just got to get something from my office first.'

Nicole crossed to a flight of stairs that led up to her office. She was a petite thirty-two-year-old with short black hair framing an attractive face which was further enhanced by the alluring hazel eyes and the pert, *retroussé* nose. She'd come to Chicago two years earlier, after her divorce had been finalized, to visit Carole Lewis, her best friend since they'd first met as waitresses at a New York diner. She'd quickly taken to Chicago, and when a rundown brasserie had come on the market in the fashionable River North gallery area, they'd decided to go into business together. They'd had the brasserie completely refurbished, and five months later Legends had opened. Now, a year on, it was widely regarded as one of *the* restaurants to be seen at in the city.

She entered her office, switched on the light, then crossed to her desk and sat down. Kicking off her court shoes, she massaged her stockinged feet before reaching for her diary to check on her appointments for the following day. She ran a red manicured fingernail down the page and, satisfied that she didn't have to be at the restaurant before midday, closed the diary again. Her eyes went to the framed photograph of her six-year-old daughter, Michelle, which held pride of place on her desk. She made no secret of the fact that she absolutely doted on her daughter. She picked up the photograph and found herself smiling gently at the freckled face which grinned back mischievously at her. The previous day her ex-husband, Bob Kinnard, had flown in from Washington to take Michelle on a ten-day vacation to Acapulco. Bob had called her that morning to say they'd arrived safely in Acapulco, and that Michelle had already found some children of her own age to play with. Nicole had made him promise that the next time he called he'd have Michelle there with him so that she could talk to her.

'Goodnight, sweetheart,' Nicole said softly, tracing her finger lightly across Michelle's face.

Replacing the photograph on the desk, she slipped on her shoes again, then unhooked her handbag from the back of the chair and crossed to the door. She was about to switch off the light when the telephone rang. Her hand froze over the switch and she slowly looked round at the two telephones on her desk: one was her business line, the other her private line. It was her private phone that was ringing. She'd only given out the number to a selected handful of her closest friends – who would be calling her at the restaurant at one o'clock in the morning? It was with a growing sense of unease that she returned to the desk to answer it.

'Nicole?'

She recognized the voice straight away.

'Yes. What is it, Bob? Has something happened to Michelle?' she asked anxiously.

'Michelle's fine,' came the reassuring reply. 'Look, I've stumbled on to one hell of a story out here. It's guaranteed to put my name on every front page back home. But it's not without its risks. If anything were to happen to me before I got back to the States, I want you to make sure that the story reaches my editor at the *Washington Post*.'

'What do you mean, *not without its risks*?' Nicole shot back, suddenly fearful for her daughter's safety. 'If you've put Michelle in any kind of danger because of some damn story –'

'I told you, Michelle's fine,' Kinnard cut in sharply.

'Then let me speak to her. I want to speak to her, Bob. Now!'

'I swear to you that Michelle's safe. She's not in any . . .'

'Bob, are you still there?' Nicole called out anxiously when Kinnard's voice trailed off. 'Bob?'

'Jesus, someone's trying the door handle,' Kinnard blurted out. 'They must have a key. They're coming in . . .'

Nicole jerked her head away from the handset when Kinnard dropped the receiver at the other end. For a moment there was only silence. Then she heard a man's voice in the background, but she couldn't make out what he was saying.

'I don't know what you're talking about,' she heard Kinnard reply.

'Don't screw with me, Kinnard!' The man was now obviously close to the phone.

'Look, I don't know who you are or what –'

'I want that tape,' the man cut in sharply. 'Where is it?'

Nicole's fingers tightened around the handset as she waited for Kinnard's response. Although she didn't understand what the two men were arguing about, she could only assume that the tape had something to do with the story he'd mentioned. *Give him the damn tape, if only for Michelle's sake, give it to him . . .*

Suddenly a gunshot rang out. She dropped the receiver and stumbled away from the desk, struggling to comprehend what she'd just heard. Then, almost as if in slow motion, she reached out a hand to retrieve the handset. Her heart was pounding fearfully as she slowly put it to her ear again.

'Whoever you are, I know you're still there. I can hear you breathing.'

The soft, menacing voice startled Nicole and she quickly clamped her hand over her mouth to stifle the rising cry in her throat. She cursed herself inwardly for reacting like some frightened schoolgirl. There was nothing he could do to her. Not over the telephone. Although now desperately worried for Michelle's safety, she knew better than to say anything. That would be playing straight into his hands, especially as he didn't know who she was. But what if Michelle was there? She'd never felt so helpless in all her life. If only she could have been sure that Michelle was safe. But there was no way of knowing that . . .

'It won't be difficult to trace this call. Once we know your number, we'll know where to find you. No witnesses, no comebacks.'

Nicole banged down the receiver, reached out a trembling hand and picked up the photograph of Michelle as she struggled to control her ragged emotions. *No witnesses, no comebacks.*

A tear trickled from the corner of her eye, but she brushed it away quickly then reached for the receiver again to call the police.

'Who is it?' Carole Lewis demanded of the two hazy silhouettes who were visible through the rippled glass door.

'It's Detective Andrews,' came the muffled reply. 'I spoke to you earlier on the phone.'

'Do you have any ID?' she asked, opening the door on the chain. A badge was held up for her to see. Satisfied it was genuine, Carole opened the door.

'Mrs Kinnard?' Andrews asked.

'No, I'm Carole Lewis. Nicole's partner. Nicole's through in the restaurant.' Carole put a hand on Andrews' arm. 'She doesn't call herself Kinnard any more. She reverted back to her maiden name after her divorce.'

Andrews gestured to the younger man behind him. 'This is my partner, Sergeant Dobeck.'

'Please, won't you both come through?' Carole said, leading them down the red carpeted foyer and into the dimly lit restaurant.

Nicole, who'd been sitting at one of the tables in the centre of the room, jumped to her feet when the two men appeared behind Carole. 'Detective Andrews?'

'Yes,' Andrews replied, and introduced Dobeck who was hovering at his shoulder.

'Have you found Michelle yet?' Nicole blurted out anxiously. 'Is she safe? Please, I must know. Is she safe?'

'May we sit down?' Andrews asked.

'Of course,' Nicole replied, gesturing absently to the remaining chairs positioned around the table.

'Can I get you coffees?' Carole asked after the two men had sat down.

'Thank you,' Andrews said, and waited until Carole had crossed to the percolator before taking a battered notebook from his jacket pocket and placing it carefully on the table. Only then did he look up at Nicole. 'I contacted the police in Acapulco after we'd spoken on the phone and had them send a car round to . . .' he paused to consult his notebook, 'the Las Brisas Hotel in Acapulco Bay.'

'And?' Nicole implored.

'Neither your ex-husband nor your daughter were registered at the hotel.'

'I . . . I don't understand,' Nicole stammered in bewilderment. 'They must be staying there. Bob rang me this morning from the hotel to say that they'd arrived safely and that Michelle –'

'Miss Auger,' Andrews cut in gently but firmly. 'According to the general manager, they were only due to arrive at the hotel tomorrow. Your ex-husband phoned the hotel yesterday to amend the booking. Wherever he called you from, it wasn't from the Las Brisas in Acapulco.'

'Have you checked the other hotels in the Acapulco area?' Nicole asked in desperation.

'Yes,' Andrews replied, taking the coffee cup from Carole. 'They weren't booked into any of those hotels either. In fact, according to Mexican immigration, there's no record of them ever having entered the country.'

Nicole buried her face in her hands. Carole put a reassuring hand lightly on her shoulder, but Nicole immediately shrugged it off. Her eyes were blazing when she looked up at Andrews. 'What kind of man takes his six-year-old daughter into a situation knowing there's every possibility he'd be putting her life at risk? And for what? Some damn story that would have got his name on the front page of a newspaper. I always knew that Bob had no scruples, but even I wouldn't have believed he could have stooped this low.'

'I know how you must be feeling,' Andrews said gently. 'We're doing everything we possibly can to find them. Interpol have already been alerted, and they're liaising with all the major law enforcement agencies and immigration departments around the world.' He took a sip of coffee. 'Miss Auger, can you tell us anything about the voice of the man you heard arguing with your ex-husband?'

'He's a Londoner,' she replied, reaching for the packet of cigarettes on the table. 'A Cockney.'

'You seem very sure of that,' Andrews said, making a note in his book.

'I am,' came the brusque reply.

'How can you be so sure?' Andrews pressed.

Nicole lit a cigarette and dropped the spent match in the ashtray. 'One of my father's main contacts in Africa was a Cockney. He was the kind of person who'd have slit his own mother's throat if he thought it would have benefited him, but then that's a mercenary for you.'

Andrews and Dobeck exchanged suspicious looks. 'I'm sorry, Miss Auger, you seem to have lost us there,' Andrews said.

'My father was an arms dealer. Most of his business came from the civil wars in Africa. It's where I was raised.'

That answered the question which had been nagging at the back of Andrews' mind ever since he'd first spoken to her on the telephone. The name was unmistakably French, but there was no trace of a French accent. At the time he couldn't place her accent. Now he understood why. It was a legacy of her upbringing in Africa. 'Can you remember what this Cockney said to you on the telephone?'

She recounted his words exactly.

'And you didn't say anything to him?' Andrews asked as he wrote in his notebook.

'No.'

'We have to take this threat on your life seriously,' Andrews told her. 'So until we know exactly what did happen tonight, I think it would be best if Sergeant Dobeck were to stay with you.'

'I appreciate your concern for my safety, Detective Andrews, but you don't need to worry about me,' Nicole replied. 'As a young girl growing up in the androcentric world of professional soldiers, I learnt from a very early age how to look after myself. It was the only way to survive in that kind of environment. You just concentrate on finding Michelle. That's all that matters right now.'

'I've no doubt that you're quite capable of looking after yourself, Miss Auger, but there's no point in taking any unnecessary risks,' Andrews told her. 'We're just as concerned as you are to find your ex-husband and your daughter and, as I said just now, everything possible's being done to trace them. But there's really nothing more we can do from this end. Sergeant Dobeck will take a full statement from you in due course, which will be forwarded on to Interpol along with the information you gave me about the man you heard on the phone.' He closed the notebook and slipped it back into his jacket pocket. 'Do you have any recent photographs of Michelle and your ex-husband that I could fax through to Interpol?'

'There's that photo of Michelle you keep on your desk,' Carole suggested.

'No,' Nicole shot back angrily. She reached out and squeezed Carole's hand gently. 'I'm sorry, I didn't mean to snap at you like that. It's just that that photograph's very special to me.'

'I know,' Carole said.

Nicole stubbed out the cigarette and got to her feet. 'I've got quite a few photos of Michelle up in the office. I'm not sure whether I've got one of Bob though. Not here. I know I've got some at the apartment. Let me go and check for you.'

They watched Nicole cross to the stairs. When she was out of earshot, Carole turned to Andrews, her expression anxious. 'Michelle's her whole life,' she explained. 'She's always been determined to make sure that Michelle wouldn't miss out on her childhood as she did in Africa, and from what she's told me about her own past, Nicole was streetwise long before she was Michelle's age. As she said, she had to learn how to look after herself from very early on.'

'What kind of parents would raise their daughter in that kind of environment?' Dobeck exclaimed with obvious disapproval.

'Nicole never knew her mother. Her father raised her alone. She never went to school but by the time she'd reached her teens she was fluent in English, French and German, as well as being able to get by in several African dialects. He taught her maths, and by the age of sixteen she was already in charge of all the business accounts.'

'He sounds like a remarkable man,' Andrews said.

'I only met Claude Auger once when he came to New York after Michelle was born. I know all the waitresses at the diner where Nicole and I were working at the time were totally besotted with him. He was very good-looking, and had all the Gallic charm to go with it.'

'But you didn't like him?' Dobeck said.

'I could never reconcile myself to what he did. I knew that under the charm lay a very cunning manipulator who would sell weapons to anyone for the right price. It was obvious he had a lot of innocent blood on his hands.'

'Then you could say the same thing about his daughter,' Andrews concluded.

'Nicole and I have our differences,' Carole said matter-of-factly, then indicated the empty cup in front of him. 'Would you like another coffee?'

Andrews shook his head, then got to his feet when Nicole returned to the room. She handed him a colour photograph of Michelle and Kinnard which had been taken on a recent trip to Disneyland. 'Thank you, Miss Auger,' Andrews said, pocketing the photograph. 'You look tired. I know you'll want to wait up for any news, but I do think you should try and get some sleep while you can.'

'Could you sleep if your daughter were missing?' Nicole demanded.

Andrews nodded sympathetically. 'All I'm saying is that it could be a while before we hear anything.'

'I realize that,' Nicole said, taking her car keys from her handbag. She looked at Dobeck. 'I'm parked out back. I'll meet you at the front of the restaurant and you can follow me back to the apartment.'

'I think that under the circumstances it would be better if I were to drive you home, Miss Auger,' Dobeck said. 'We can always have your car sent round to the apartment later.'

'I am capable of driving myself home,' Nicole shot back indignantly.

Andrews was quick to put a restraining hand on Dobeck's arm. 'The sergeant will meet you out front, Miss Auger.'

'Would you like me to come back to the apartment?' Carole asked Nicole.

'No, I'll be all right.'

Carole hugged her tightly. 'OK, but if you want to talk, you just call me. Any time, day or night. Promise?'

'Promise,' Nicole replied with a brave smile, then

disappeared through the double doors leading into the kitchen.

'I think I'd better let you out, sergeant,' Carole said, holding up the restaurant keys. 'Knowing Nicole, she won't wait for you.'

'Somehow I can believe that,' Dobeck retorted, following her from the room.

Although physically exhausted after a gruelling sixteen-hour day at the restaurant, sleep had been furthest from Nicole's mind when she'd returned to her Lincoln Park apartment. Armed with her portable telephone and a fresh packet of cigarettes, she'd retired to the lounge, closing the door behind her. Dobeck hadn't needed to be told that she wanted to be alone. After checking that all windows and doors were secure, he'd made her a coffee and taken it through to the lounge before retreating discreetly to the kitchen. She hadn't said anything to him. It was almost as if she hadn't even seen him . . .

Now, an hour later, the cup remained untouched on the table beside the telephone. Nicole sat motionless in an armchair by the window, her legs tucked up underneath her, with Michelle's favourite soft toy, Kermit, clutched tightly to her chest. Nicole had given it to Michelle for her second birthday and since then Kermit had been Michelle's constant companion through all her childhood adventures. And it showed. A hand was missing and there were several darning scars on the body where Nicole had been called upon to perform emergency surgery with a needle and cotton in front of a tearful Michelle after Kermit had been savaged by a neighbour's Alsatian. And when one of the eyes had come off, Michelle had suggested to her that she sew on a black patch instead of another eye. Nicole traced her finger over the eye-patch and smiled sadly to herself. Michelle had certainly inherited her grandfather's macabre sense of humour . . .

She lit another cigarette, then placed it on the edge of the ashtray which was already balanced precariously on the arm of the chair. Her eyes flickered to the telephone on the table beside her. No news was good news. Only not necessarily in this case, she thought grimly to herself. She'd already accepted the fact that Bob was probably dead. Her father had once told her not to grieve for the dead, but for the children who'd never see them again. It had always struck her as a strange philosophy for someone who dealt in the weapons of death. But in its own way it made sense to her. She knew she would come to grieve for Bob, in time, but her only concern now was for Michelle. She had to believe that Michelle was still alive. It was all that was keeping her going . . .

The sound of the doorbell startled her and she inadvertently knocked the ashtray on to the floor. She quickly retrieved the lighted cigarette, stubbed it out, then got to her feet and hurried out into the hall. Dobeck was already at the front door, revolver drawn. He peered through the spy-hole then reholstered the revolver and opened the door. Andrews entered the hall and his eyes immediately went to Nicole who was hovering uncertainly beside the lounge door.

'Have you found Michelle?' she asked anxiously. 'Have you?'

'I think it's best if we talk in there,' Andrews said sombrely, indicating the lounge behind her.

'What's happened?' Nicole demanded. 'Please, I've got to know.'

Andrews took her arm and steered her into the lounge. He switched on a table-lamp before perching on the edge of the sofa. 'I'm afraid it's bad news,' he said softly. 'Bob Kinnard's body's been found in a hotel room in San Salvador. He'd been shot once through the heart at close range.'

'And Michelle?'

'There was no trace of your daughter. She wasn't with him when he checked into the hotel, but immigration officials at the airport have confirmed that she did enter the country with him yesterday.'

'That means she could still be alive.'

'At this moment in time we have to believe there's every possibility of that, yes,' Andrews told her.

Nicole sat down slowly and looked across at Andrews. 'Where exactly is San Salvador?'

'Central America. It's the capital of El Salvador.' Andrews moved to the window then turned back to Nicole. 'It seems that the detectives investigating the case think that Bob Kinnard may have committed suicide.'

'What?' Nicole exclaimed in disbelief.

'I can only tell you what was in the fax I received a short time ago from the police in San Salvador,' Andrews said, holding up a hand defensively. 'The gun used in the shooting was found beside the body. There were only his fingerprints on it. The hotel manager claims he heard the shot from the reception area, but when he went up to the room he found the door locked. He had to use his pass-key to get in. There was nobody else in the room. The only other way in would have been through a window, but that was latched from the inside.'

'It's obviously a set-up,' Nicole shot back. 'What do they think, that I imagined everything I heard on the telephone? There *was* another man in the room. Damn it, I should know. He made a threat on my life.' It was then that she noticed the uncertainty on Andrews' face. 'You don't believe me either, do you?'

'I believe you heard something, Miss Auger,' Andrews said at length. 'According to the hotel manager, the television was on when he entered the room.'

'You don't honestly think the voices I heard came from the television, do you?'

'It's possible,' Andrews conceded.

'No, it bloody well isn't,' she retorted angrily.

'What I think or don't think is irrelevant, anyway, Miss Auger. The investigation is now officially in the hands of the Salvadorean authorities. They want you to fly out to El Salvador as soon as possible to make a positive ID of your ex-husband. Only then will the body be released for burial.'

'I can do that when I go out there to look for Michelle,' Nicole told him.

'I understand your concern for your daughter's safety, but it's best to leave that side of things to the authorities. They know the country. You wouldn't know where to start looking for her. Not to mention the fact that if you are right and your ex-husband was murdered, you'd be putting yourself in great danger if the killer found out you were there.'

'And what if the authorities are already involved in some way with Bob's death? The police were very quick to write it off as suicide, weren't they?'

'What are you suggesting, Miss Auger?' Andrews asked. 'That there's some kind of government conspiracy going on over there?'

'I'm not suggesting anything. All I know is that Michelle's missing, and as long as there's the slightest chance that she's still alive, then I'll never stop looking for her.' Nicole's voice broke and she clasped her hand over her mouth as she struggled to hold back the tears. 'She's my little girl, and right now she needs me more than ever. Can't you understand that?'

'Yes, I can understand that,' Andrews said softly, then took a slip of paper from his pocket and handed it to her. 'I was told to give you this. It's the number of the American embassy in San Salvador. The Ambassador's already been informed about what happened earlier tonight, and he's asked the Salvadorean authorities to keep him posted on any new developments in their search for your daughter.

Call him before you leave for El Salvador. He'll arrange to have someone meet you at the airport.'

'Thank you, I will,' Nicole replied.

'I think that as an extra precaution Sergeant Dobeck should stay with you until you're safely on board the flight to El Salvador.'

'I'm going to New York first,' Nicole told him. 'There's someone I want to see there before I fly out to El Salvador.'

'I'll arrange to have the NYPD keep an eye on you while you're there,' Andrews assured her. 'It's best not to take any unnecessary risks.'

'You do what you want, but just make sure that they keep out of my way. If they must watch me, then tell them to make sure they do it discreetly. I don't need a chaperon.'

'As you wish,' Andrews replied. 'How long will you be in New York for?'

'That all depends on the person I'm going there to see,' Nicole said, staring thoughtfully out of the window. 'Question is, will he want to see me again?'

TWO

Light snow flurries had been falling intermittently across New York for much of the day, and by late afternoon a biting wind had whipped in from the Atlantic, leaving the city bracing itself for a fourth consecutive night of sub-zero temperatures. Nicole turned up the collar of her blouson as she climbed out of the cab and quickly descended a flight of concrete steps to the bar. A prominent red neon sign in the cracked window read 'Rosewood', above a smaller neon sign advertising Budweiser beer. The drab grey façade was in desperate need of a fresh coat of paint, and when she stepped inside it only confirmed her initial gut feeling – it was a dive. She estimated there to be a couple of dozen people in the room, most of them sitting with their backs to her at the arc-shaped bar counter. Apart from a couple of hookers in one of the booths, one of whom was exceptionally pretty, her features marred though by the excessive make-up she was wearing, all the customers were men; Nicole wasn't sure whether to feel flattered or insulted when their eyes followed her to the bar counter.

'What can I get you?' the barman asked, wiping his hands on a scruffy apron tied around his ample waist.

'I'm looking for Richard Marlette,' Nicole replied. 'I believe he's a regular here.'

The barman shook his head. 'I don't know anybody by that name.'

'This is the Rosewood bar in Greenwich Village, isn't it?' Nicole queried.

'As far as I know, it's the only Rosewood bar in the whole of New York,' came the uninterested reply. 'But that still doesn't mean I know this guy . . . Marley, or whatever his name is.'

'Marlette. Richard Marlette. Most of his friends call him Rich or Richie.'

'I told you, lady, I don't know the guy,' the barman told her firmly. 'Now, if you'll excuse me, I've got customers to serve.'

'Listen, I've flown all the way from Chicago just to see him,' Nicole snapped, grabbing the barman's arm as he turned to leave. 'Brad Casey said I'd probably find him here if he wasn't at his apartment. Brad owns Casey's bar in Soho.'

'I know who Brad Casey is,' the barman said, then glanced at a customer at the other end of the counter who was trying to attract his attention. His eyes flickered back to Nicole and he nodded to himself. 'I guess you are on the level. Brad and Richie go back a long way.'

'So Rick is here?'

The barman gestured to a door at the far end of the room. 'He's through there shooting pool.'

'Thank you.'

'Where do you know Richie from?' the barman asked. 'I've never seen you around here before.'

'I knew him long before he ever started coming here,' Nicole replied, then crossed to the door where she paused to peer into the smoke-filled room. The three pool tables were all in use, but she couldn't see Marlette from where she was standing. It was then she noticed a bearded, over-weight man eyeing her with obvious interest.

'And what can I do for you?' he asked, approaching her.

'I'm looking for Richard Marlette. Richie Marlette?'

The man drank a mouthful of beer from the bottle in his hand, then put an arm around her shoulders. Her first thought was to shove him away from her, but she quickly checked herself and let him lead her to the table furthest from the door. The small cluster of onlookers stepped aside to let them through, and Nicole's eyes went to the figure bent low over the opposite end of the table, his eyes focused on the cue ball. She'd found Richard Marlette.

'You got yourself a visitor, Rich,' the man announced, taking another swig from the bottle. 'And a real cute one at that.'

Marlette raised his eyes slowly without moving his head. He stared momentarily at Nicole before returning his attention to the table and following through with the shot, cracking a yellow ball into the bottom pocket directly in front of her. Only then did he straighten up. He hadn't changed in the six years since she'd last seen him. She knew he would now be thirty-five, and although never conventionally handsome, he had a strong, charismatic face which was given an edge of menace by the faint striae of scars which marked his cheeks. His solid, six-foot frame was lean and muscular under the white vest and tight-fitting jeans and, with his shoulder-length brown hair and gold sleeper in his left ear, he looked more like a member of one of the heavy metal bands he liked so much than one of the most experienced, and respected, mercenaries working out of America.

'This is one classy dame you've got yourself here, Rich,' the bearded man said with a salacious grin when Marlette approached them. 'Where have you been hiding her all this time?'

Marlette pushed the cue into the man's hand. 'I'm winning, Bob. Just see that it stays that way.'

The man eyed Nicole again, then reluctantly turned his attention to the position of the remaining balls on the table.

'Hello, Rick,' she said softly.

'What do you want, Nicole?' came the terse reply.

'Can we talk?'

'So talk.'

She looked around the room. 'Not here. Is there some-where private where we can go?'

Marlette hissed sharply through his teeth when Bob played his shot. The ball struck the cushion, missing the pocket. Bob met Marlette's glowering stare and gave him a conciliatory grin. 'Relax, buddy. I just need a few shots to get my eye in again.'

'I've got twenty-five bucks riding on the game,' Marlette told him. 'You screw up. You pay.'

'Chill out, Rich. I'm in control here.'

Marlette took Nicole's arm and propelled her out into the main bar, where he paused to gesture to an empty table close to the door. 'Is that private enough?'

'Sure,' she said, crossing to the table and sitting down.

'Hey, Richie, everything OK?' the barman called out to him. 'Only the lady said Brad Casey told her where to find you. I know Brad wouldn't see you wrong.'

'It's OK, Ira,' Marlette replied.

'You guys want something to drink?' the barman asked.

'The usual,' Marlette replied.

'And the lady?'

'The usual?' Marlette asked her.

She nodded.

'Bourbon. No ice,' Marlette told the barman, before pull-ing up a chair and sitting down opposite her.

'Smoke?' she asked, extending a packet of cigarettes towards him.

Marlette shook his head. 'I've given up.'

'I never thought I'd see the day when you'd give up cigarettes,' she said with a smile, taking a cigarette from the packet. 'You don't mind if I smoke, do you?'

'No,' Marlette replied irritably.

'Why all the secrecy, Rick?' Nicole asked after she'd lit the cigarette. 'The barman wouldn't even admit that he knew you until I mentioned Brad's name. You're not in any kind of trouble, are you?'

'I didn't know you still cared,' Marlette shot back, then glanced towards the door as he ran his hands through his hair. 'I've got a few problems with some loan sharks, that's all.' He looked up when the barman approached the table with their drinks. 'Put them on my tab, Ira.'

'Let me get them, Rick,' Nicole said, reaching for her purse.

Marlette quickly plucked the chit from the barman's hand, initialled it, and handed it back to him. He waited for the barman to leave, then pushed the ice-cold bottle of Budweiser to one side and rested his arms on the table, his eyes riveted on her face. 'You've got some nerve showing up again after all these years.'

'I can understand your bitterness, Rick,' she said softly.

'Can you?' came the sharp riposte. 'You were the one who walked out on me after two-and-a-half years without even so much as a goodbye. Then three months later I find out from Brad that you'd got married to some hack from the *Washington Post*. You didn't even have the decency to tell me yourself. Jesus, Nicole, didn't the time we spent together mean anything to you?'

'More than you could ever imagine,' she said softly. 'I wanted to tell you but . . .'

'Can't come up with a good excuse?' he shot back sarcastically when her voice trailed off. 'You must be slipping, Nicole. You were always the one with the glib tongue. You could even outdo your father, and that was certainly some achievement.'

Nicole opened her purse and removed the framed photograph that she'd picked up from the restaurant on her way to the airport that morning. She placed it on the table in front of him. 'That's my daughter, Michelle. She's now six.'

'You certainly didn't waste any time in starting a family, did you?' he snapped bitterly.

'She's missing,' Nicole said in a barely audible voice.

Marlette picked up the photograph and stared at the mischievous face smiling out at him. 'What do you mean "missing"?'

She explained what had happened the previous evening. For some moments after she'd finished speaking he didn't reply, turning the bottle around absently on the coaster in front of him. When he finally looked up at her, the harshness had evaporated from his eyes. 'I'm sorry about Kinnard.'

'Bob and I had been divorced for the past two years, but the marriage itself had been over long before that. There was nothing between us any more. I know I'll grieve for him in time, but right now my only concern is to find Michelle.'

'And you want me to find her for you?' Marlette deduced.

'You've worked in El Salvador, Rick. You know the country.'

'How do you know I was out there?' came the suspicious reply.

'I remember Brad mentioning it when I rang him to tell him that I'd got married. He said that you'd gone there to take up a job as a military adviser to the government.'

Marlette drank a mouthful of beer, wiped the froth from his lips with the back of his hand, then banged the bottle down angrily on to the table. 'Brad's got a big mouth.'

'He only told me because I asked after you,' she said, quickly coming to Casey's defence.

'I can't help you, Nicole,' he told her matter-of-factly.

'If it's a question of money, I'll pay whatever –'

'I said I can't help you,' he cut in sharply.

'I understand,' she said, then, stubbing out the cigarette, she replaced the photograph in her handbag and got to her feet. 'If you'll excuse me, I have to reserve a ticket for myself on the next flight to San Salvador.'

'You think I'm doing this out of spite, don't you?'

'It doesn't matter what I think,' she replied. 'If you can't help me find Michelle, then I'll just have to do it by myself.'

He gestured to the chair she'd vacated. 'Sit down, Nicole.'

'I think it's best —'

'Sit down,' he said firmly, and used his foot to push the chair towards her.

She sat down slowly, her purse clutched tightly against her stomach.

'I was deported from El Salvador,' he said at length. 'That's why I can't help you.'

'Why were you deported?' she asked in surprise.

'It's a long story,' he replied. 'I'd only be a liability to you if I were to go back again.'

'But surely the situation's changed now that the civil war's over?'

'Nothing's changed. The people who had me deported are still very active inside El Salvador. In fact, the one who signed the deportation order is now a senior member of the new government. You don't cross those kind of people and expect them just to forgive and forget.' Marlette sat forward and rested his arms on the table. 'If Kinnard has given this tape to Michelle, then she could be in real danger if the wrong people were to get to her first. And from what you've already told me, I think you could be right about there being some kind of cover-up involving the authorities. So you certainly can't trust them to find her. You're going to need outside help. There are a couple of mercs I know who've also worked in El Salvador. They both know the country as well as I do. But I warn you now, they won't come cheap.'

'I'll pay whatever they ask,' Nicole replied without hesitation. 'The money's not important. All I want is to find Michelle and bring her back home.'

'I'll have a word with Brad. He's sure to know where they are. But if they're out of the country, it could prove very time-consuming to try and get them back again. And time isn't exactly something you've got on your side right now, is it? Leave it with me, anyway. I'll do what I can. Where are you staying?'

'The Howard Johnson on Eighth Avenue. Do you know it?'

'Sure I know it,' came the indignant reply. 'I'll be in touch.'

'Thanks, Rick,' she said, putting her hand lightly on his arm.

'If these guys aren't available, then you're on your own out there,' he warned her. 'There's no way I'm going back again. Not for you. Not for the kid. Let's just get that straight right now.'

'I understand,' she said, then got to her feet and moved to the door.

'Nicole?' he called out after her. 'Are you absolutely certain the guy who threatened you over the phone had a Cockney accent?'

'I'm sure,' she replied, then frowned at him. 'Why? Do you know who he is?'

'I'm not sure,' came the hesitant reply.

'I've been straight with you, Rick. I think it's only fair that you do the same with me.'

'I said I'd call you, OK?' he said tersely.

She bit back her anger, then turned sharply and strode out of the bar.

When Marlette returned to the pool room, he found Bob still at the table, now with a new opponent.

'You owe me a beer, Rich,' Bob said, handing Marlette the twenty-five dollars he'd won on the last game.

'Get one from Ira and tell him to put it on my tab,' Marlette replied, pocketing the money.

'So, who's Nicole?' Bob asked, grinning lecherously.

'Just go and get a beer,' Marlette snapped, grabbing his leather jacket off a peg on the wall.

'Come on, Rich, you can tell us,' Bob said, the grin still fixed on his face as he looked at the others who were gathered around the table. 'Nicole? That's a French name, isn't it? I hear these French broads are real good lays. I bet she's a real little tiger in bed.'

Marlette spun round, locked his hand around Bob's throat, and slammed him up against the wall. Bob clawed frantically at Marlette's hand, but the more he struggled, the more the grip tightened around his throat, and within seconds his whole body was shuddering as he desperately fought for breath. 'You ever talk about her like that again, and I'll kill you,' Marlette threatened in a soft, menacing voice. 'Do I make myself clear?'

Bob nodded frantically. Marlette released his grip and Bob crumpled to the floor, his hands clutched to his throat, his breathing ragged and uneven as he gulped down mouthfuls of air. Marlette was already out of the door, flagging down a taxi to take him to Casey's bar in Soho.

In many ways, Brad Casey had been as much Marlette's mentor as his friend. He'd first met Casey while celebrating his eighteenth birthday at a bar in Greenwich Village. At the time, Casey, who was twelve years his senior, had just returned to New York after ten years with the French Foreign Legion. By the end of the evening, Marlette had known he'd wanted to become a legionnaire, and a week later he'd used the last of his savings to fly to the Legion's headquarters at Aubagne in France. He'd been recruited after a succession of gruelling physical tests, and had remained a legionnaire for the next five years, rising to the rank of corporal. When he'd been given the option to sign on for another five years, he chose instead to team up with Casey, who'd since made a name for himself as a free-lance mercenary in Africa. For the next four years they'd travelled around Africa together, seeking out the trouble spots and offering their services to whoever was prepared to pay the most for their expertise.

The lucrative partnership had ended abruptly in Uganda, when a jeep carrying Casey and three government soldiers had struck a land-mine. Casey had been the only survivor, but he'd lost his left leg and his left arm had been amputated below the elbow. He'd returned to the United States where he'd used some of the money he'd accrued over the years to buy a bar in his native New York. Although Marlette had decided to stay on in Africa, he'd returned regularly to New York to visit Casey. He'd even tended bar at Casey's for several months in an attempt to appease Nicole, who'd wanted him to spend more time with her; but over the years Casey's had increasingly become a meeting place for professional soldiers from around the world, and he'd always made a point of distancing himself from fellow mercenaries outside of work. The truth was that there were very few mercenaries he respected, and even fewer he actually liked.

Now Marlette looked up at the Casey's sign in blue neon lights above the door. He couldn't remember the last time he'd been inside the bar. A year? Probably more. He still tried to see Casey whenever he was in New York, usually for a meal at one of their favourite steakhouses on Broadway. He moved to the door and pushed it open. The bar was packed and, as he looked around for Casey, he recognized a number of faces from previous conflicts. He finally spotted Casey playing cards with two men at a table against the far wall.

'Hey, Richie,' Casey called out genially as Marlette approached the table. 'I thought you might show up sooner or later.' He gestured to the men opposite him. 'You know Rhys Evans and Dietmar Rausch, don't you?'

'Rausch and I were in Chad together a few years back,' Marlette replied, acknowledging the German with a curt nod of his head.

'Rhys left the British Paras six months ago to go free-lance. He's just got back from his first tour in Bosnia,' Casey said. 'I thought you two might have bumped into each other over there.'

'We were on different sides,' Evans said, looking up at Marlette. 'I heard a lot about you while I was out there, though. It seems you command quite a bit of respect within the merc fraternity.'

'I need to talk to you,' Marlette said to Casey, then looked at Evans. 'Alone.'

'Will you guys excuse us?' Casey said. He gathered up the cards and replaced them in the box, which he then handed to Evans. 'I'll join you once I'm through here.'

'Sit down,' Casey said to Marlette, indicating the chairs vacated by the two men. 'You want a beer?'

'No, thanks,' Marlette replied, pulling up the nearest chair and sitting down.

'Nicole's been to see you, hasn't she?'

'Yeah,' Marlette replied. 'What did she tell you when she came here?'

'Nothing much. She said she'd been over to your apart-ment in Greenwich Village but that you weren't there. She asked if I knew where she could find you. I told her that you usually hung out at the Rosewood these days.' Casey took a sip of bourbon and replaced the glass on the table. 'She's in some kind of trouble, isn't she?'

Marlette explained briefly what she'd told him.

'There was somebody else here looking for you,' Casey said. 'He'd also been to your apartment.'

'A loan shark?' Marlette asked suspiciously.

'Hardly,' Casey replied. 'His name's Alex Pruitt.'

'Can't say I know the name,' Marlette replied.

'I do. He works for the CIA. He's the DDO at Langley.'

'What the hell's a DDO?' Marlette asked in exasper-ation.

'The Deputy Director of Operations. He's head of the

company's espionage branch which is known as the Directorate of Operations. Not only is the DO responsible for all covert operations outside of the US, it also recruits and runs all agents and double-agents on foreign soil. In other words, Alex Pruitt is a very powerful spook at Langley.'

'Where do you know him from?'

'I've had dealings with him in the past,' was all Casey would venture.

'I might have guessed,' Marlette muttered. 'And you think his being here has something to do with Kinnard's death?'

'It seems too much of a coincidence for it not to be.'

'Well, he's wasting his time. You know as well as I do that I can never go back to El Salvador.'

'I wouldn't be so quick to write him off, Richie,' Casey said, reaching for his glass. 'You're up to your neck in debt right now, and we both know that it's only going to be a matter of time before your creditors finally catch up with you.'

'You let me worry about that,' Marlette snapped defensively.

Casey drained his glass, then sat back in his chair and smiled knowingly at Marlette. 'You've obviously decided to help Nicole, otherwise why come all the way over here?'

'If Nicole's right about there being some kind of cover-up, then she sure as hell can't rely on the authorities to find her kid. And I don't have to spell out what would happen to the kid if Kinnard's murderer was to get to her first.'

'Go on,' Casey prompted when Marlette fell silent.

'There're a couple of mercs who were in El Salvador around the time I was there. They're both good soldiers. If I could contact either of them, I could probably talk them into helping her find the kid – for the right price, of course. That's why I'm here. You know where most of the mercs are hanging out.'

34

'Who are they?'

'The one I'd prefer to speak to is Jim Zilber,' Marlette said.

'Zilber's in Armenia,' came the immediate reply. 'He left about ten days ago. I doubt he'll be back for another three months. I could probably get in touch with him, but it would take some time and even then he might not be willing to come back, unless Nicole was prepared to compensate him for the remainder of his contract out there. It could end up costing her a small fortune in the long run.'

'OK, forget Zilber. What about Jesse Delaney?'

'Jesse's dead, Richie,' Casey replied in surprise, then frowned when he saw the puzzled look on Marlette's face. 'I thought you'd have heard, even out in Bosnia.'

'I didn't hear a thing. What happened?'

'He got back from Africa at the end of last month, and went up to Lake Tahoe for a bit of fishing, as he always did when he returned from a contract abroad. It seems his boat capsized and he drowned. The autopsy revealed that he'd been drinking heavily shortly before his death.'

Marlette exhaled deeply. 'Well, so much for that idea.'

'Which leaves you.'

'No, it doesn't,' Marlette shot back. 'Even if I were to go back, I'd only be a liability to her.'

'You could travel to one of the neighbouring states on false papers and cross the border into El Salvador. You've still got enough contacts there to help you find the kid.' Casey saw the bitterness in Marlette's eyes. 'Forget the past, Richie. The fact of the matter is that Nicole needs you now more than ever before. You're probably her only realistic chance of ever getting her kid back to the States.'

'You don't give up, do you?' Marlette snapped, shaking his head.

'Neither do you. You've never been a quitter. It's a challenge and you've always told me that there's nothing you relish more than a challenge. And if you were to get the kid safely out of El Salvador, it would go a long way to even the score after what happened to you there.'

'I'm not out to even the score,' Marlette retorted disdainfully. 'Just drop it, OK?'

'OK,' Casey replied with a quick shrug, then indicated to the barman that he wanted a refill. 'You sure you don't want a beer, Richie?'

'No,' Marlette replied tersely.

'Are you going to tell me what's on your mind?' Casey asked, pushing his empty glass to the side of the table.

'What do you mean?' Marlette replied suspiciously.

'Something's bugging you, isn't it?'

'Nothing's bugging –'

'Cut the crap, Richie,' Casey interceded sharply. 'I know when something's bothering you. Christ, I should do, after all we've been through together.'

Marlette leaned his elbows on the table, his chin resting on his clenched fists. He stared at the wall for some time before he looked at Casey again. 'Do you remember a merc called Stuart Jayson?'

'Sure I remember him. We worked with him a couple of times in Africa, although I've got to admit I never did quite get the hang of that Cockney accent.' Casey smiled at the memory. 'He was still a good soldier, all the same.'

'He was a fucking bastard, and you know it,' Marlette snorted in disgust.

The barman placed a fresh glass on the table, but Casey waited until he was out of earshot before speaking. 'Why the sudden interest in Jayson?'

'As I said just now, the guy who shot Kinnard also threatened Nicole over the phone. What I didn't tell you was that Nicole said he had a Cockney accent, and that his last words to her were: "no witnesses, no comebacks". Anyone who's ever worked with Jayson knows that that was his catchphrase.'

'And you know as well as I do that Stuart Jayson's dead,' came the blunt reply.

'I heard that he'd been killed,' Marlette corrected him. 'You probably told me.'

'He was killed somewhere in southern Africa. Mozambique, I think. It must be a good four or five years ago now. I don't recall the exact details of his death, but I do remember talking to one of the guys who'd actually been to the funeral in London.' Casey took a sip of bourbon. 'There's got to be some logical explanation to this, Richie, because whoever it was Nicole heard on the phone last night, it couldn't have been Jayson.'

'What if he's not dead . . . ?'

'He's dead,' came the exasperated reply. 'My source was a senior officer in the South African Defence Force. He'd nothing to gain by lying to me.'

'I'm not so sure, Brad,' Marlette said. 'It seems too much of a coincidence. The same accent. The same catchphrase.'

'You said yourself that anyone who's ever worked with Jayson knew that it was his catchphrase. Word gets around. What if another Cockney merc picked up on it? Assuming the guy Nicole spoke to on the phone is one of ours. We don't even know that, do we?'

'This contact of yours in South Africa: is he still with the military?'

'As far as I know,' Casey replied.

'Then get him to check out the exact details of Jayson's death.'

'I think you're way out on this one, Richie,' Casey told him.

'Humour me,' Marlette replied.

'OK, I'll call him,' Casey agreed. 'Then what?'

'Call me at my apartment,' Marlette said. 'If this spook's that desperate to put in an offer for my services, he's sure to go back there again. If nothing else, it should be interesting to find out just what the CIA think I'm worth these days.'

'And if he were to offer you the right incentive, you'd go back to El Salvador?'

'Every mercenary can be bought, Brad,' Marlette replied with a faint smile. 'Hell, you should know that.'

'So why did you turn down Nicole's offer without even waiting to hear her out?' Casey demanded.

'Because I knew she couldn't afford me.'

'You can be a real cold-hearted son-of-a-bitch at times,' Casey snapped.

'I never took you for a sentimentalist,' Marlette said scornfully. 'But then I keep forgetting that you always did have a soft spot for Nicole.'

'She was the best thing that ever happened to you, and you let her slip through your fingers. If you'd shown her the respect she deserved, you'd still be together now, and you certainly wouldn't be in the financial mess you are at the moment. She'd have seen to that.'

'We always come back to this argument, don't we?' Marlette said, then pushed back the chair and got to his feet. 'You're the only person I know who blames me for the break-up.'

'That's because I'm the only person who really knows you.'

'Call me,' Marlette said, tight-lipped, then headed for the door and disappeared out into the street.

Casey knew it bugged the hell out of Marlette that he could read him so well. Nicole had been the only other person who'd ever got close enough to Marlette to see beyond the barriers he'd built up around himself since his early childhood – but then she hadn't seen him in six years. He'd changed since then. He was now even more defensive than ever. He'd also become a lot less tolerant of those around him. Perhaps the most disturbing change Casey had noticed in the past year, though, had been Marlette's growing disillusionment with his work. Casey knew only too well from personal experience that from disillusionment comes indifference. And indifference invariably leads to mistakes. He'd been lucky – he'd survived his mistake. He knew Marlette wanted out, but his greatest fear was that Marlette wouldn't be able to adapt to life outside of soldiering. It was all he knew. Then there were Marlette's outstanding gambling debts. Although Marlette refused to discuss figures with him, Casey knew that he owed a substantial amount of money to several loan sharks across the city. He knew Marlette was having to borrow from one to pay another, and the outstanding interest was obviously mounting with each passing week. He'd offered several times to settle the debts for him, but Marlette wouldn't hear of it. Not that it surprised Casey. Marlette had always prided himself on being totally self-sufficient; accepting charity, even from a close friend, was against his principles. He knew that all Marlette needed was one large contract to clear his debts and get himself back on his feet again. And the CIA were certainly in a position to provide that contract if, as Casey believed, Pruitt had come to New York to recruit Marlette. But would Marlette accept? He knew how bitter Marlette still felt towards Nicole for walking out on him. Yet he knew that somewhere behind those psychological barriers he'd built around himself since her departure, Marlette still cared deeply about her. It was only to be expected after the intensity of their relationship. But if Marlette was going to return to El Salvador, it would be on his own terms. He wouldn't let sentimentality interfere with his decision. He was far too professional to ever let that happen. It would depend solely on any offer Pruitt were to put on the table. If there was an offer . . .

'You in, Brad?'

Casey looked round at Evans, who was now seated with Rausch and three other men at a table close to the door. 'I've got to make a call from my office,' Casey replied. 'I'll join you as soon as I'm through. And just make sure that you leave some money in the kitty for me to win.'

'You just make sure you bring some money with you for us to win,' Evans called back.

Casey manoeuvred his wheelchair to a door adjacent to the bar counter and, pushing it open, made his way down a black and white tiled corridor to another door with his name inscribed on it in gold lettering. He took a set of keys from his pocket, selected one, and unlocked the door. Once inside he wheeled himself to the paper-strewn desk where he picked up a small notebook which was crammed full of the names of all the contacts he'd made over the years. Finding the name he wanted, he wedged the receiver between his shoulder and the side of his face, and was about to dial out when he heard the sound of a door banging in the corridor. He cursed angrily – how many times had he told the barmen to make sure that they locked the back door once they'd dumped the garbage in the side alley? Twice in the last month alone he'd caught vagrants wandering in the corridor, searching for alcohol. The door banged again. He thought about ringing the barman out front to get him to lock the door, but decided against it: the barman was alone on duty. He'd see to it himself, then speak to the barman about it later. Not that it would make any difference. It obviously hadn't in the past. Perhaps he should start fining them if they continued to leave the door unlocked. Hit them where it would hurt most – in the pocket. The idea appealed to him. Yes, he'd do that in future . . .

Casey was still turning the wheelchair away from the desk when he noticed the man standing in the doorway. He was dressed in black leathers with a crash-helmet concealing his face. Casey's eyes went from the helmet's opaque visor to the suppressed 9mm Heckler & Koch P7 pistol hanging loosely in the man's black-gloved hand. In that instant he knew he was going to die.

The man slowly raised the pistol and shot Casey through the heart. Casey was still just conscious, vaguely aware of the man approaching the desk, when a second bullet pierced his heart, killing him instantly.

The man quickly reached out a hand as Casey slumped forward. He pushed the body back into the wheelchair, picked up the address book, leafed through it, then slipped it into his pocket. Unscrewing the suppressor, he pocketed that as well, then unzipped his jacket and replaced the pistol in his shoulder-holster. Zipping up the jacket again, he scanned the length of the deserted corridor, then made his way to the back door and disappeared out into the adjoining alley.

It was already mid-afternoon by the time Marlette got back to his apartment in Greenwich Village. He went straight to the kitchen and took a beer from the fridge, but checked himself as he was about to open it: he would need a clear head to deal with Pruitt. Replacing the beer in the fridge, he went through to the lounge where he slumped down on the sofa, using the remote control to activate the television set in the corner of the room. Selecting the CNN channel, he discarded the remote control and swung his feet up on to the coffee table in front of him. He always made a point of keeping abreast of world affairs, and would sit for hours watching the news bulletins on CNN; such was his intrinsic grasp of international politics that he was often able to predict the outcome of a particular situation well in advance of the so-called 'experts'. He had nothing but contempt for them commenting on events which were taking place tens of thousands of miles away from the comfort of the television studios.

There was a studio discussion underway on the screen, but he quickly found that he couldn't concentrate on what was being said. All he could think about was Nicole – and that really pissed him off. Seeing her again had brought the memories flooding back. The good times. The bad times. Especially the bad times. He could still remember the succession of vitriolic arguments, laced with accusations and recriminations on both sides, which had plagued the last weeks of the relationship. But even then neither of them had wanted to break it off – such was the depth of the feelings between them. Then Nicole had walked out. No warning. No goodbye. He could still vividly remember that afternoon when he'd returned to the apartment to find that she was gone, along with her two suitcases and everything she owned. The note he'd found on the bed had been brief and to the point. The words were still indelibly stamped on his memory. *Rick, I need out – perhaps one day you'll understand why – and this is the only way I can do it. I'll always love you. Yours for ever, Nicole.* Yours for ever ... Three months later she was married. How soon we forget, he thought bitterly to himself. Only he'd never forgotten. Nicole was still the only woman he'd ever truly loved. He'd had several disastrous relationships since then in some forlorn attempt to reproduce the spark that he had once had with Nicole. But he knew he'd only been fooling himself. The spark had gone ...

There was a sharp knock at the front door. Switching off the television set, he got to his feet and went out into the hall, where he paused to retrieve the loaded Beretta he always kept in a desk drawer close to the door. He held the pistol behind him, then moved to the door and peered cautiously through the spy-hole. Nicole was out on the landing with a man he'd never seen before. He estimated the man to be in his late forties with thinning wiry brown hair. He opened the door on the chain and challenged the man to identify himself.

'My name's Pruitt,' came the reply. 'Alex Pruitt. I'm with the CIA.'

'Should that mean anything to me?' Marlette replied.

'It should if your friend Casey told you that I'd been to see him earlier today.'

'Yeah, he told me. You got any ID on you?'

Moments later a wallet was extended through the aperture. Satisfied, Marlette released the chain and opened the door. Pruitt, who was carrying a leather attaché case, gestured for Nicole to enter first. His eyes instinctively went to the Beretta in Marlette's hand as he stepped into the apartment after her.

'You can't be too careful these days,' Marlette said. 'You'd be amazed at the types who come knocking at my door.'

'I can well imagine,' Pruitt replied coldly.

Marlette looked at Nicole, who was standing in the middle of the hall, her arms clasped tightly across her chest, as she slowly took in her surroundings. 'Bring back any memories?'

'It feels like I've never been away,' she said with a nostalgic smile, then gestured to the picture hanging at the end of the hall. 'I see you've still got the Sara Moon print that I used to have in the bedroom. I always thought you hated it.'

'I do, but it's the perfect size to conceal a crack in the wall,' Marlette replied contemptuously. He turned to Pruitt. 'OK, so now you've found me, what do you want?'

'Can we at least sit down?' Pruitt asked.

Marlette led them through to the lounge. 'How did you know where Nicole was staying?' he asked, easing himself down on to the sofa. 'Did Brad tell you?'

'We've been keeping an eye on Miss Auger ever since she flew in from Chicago this morning. I went over to the hotel after I'd spoken to Casey, and introduced myself to her. I thought it best if she were present when I came to see you. After all, this involves her just as much as it does the CIA.'

'In other words, it's got something to do with Kinnard and the mysterious missing tape,' Marlette retorted.

Pruitt nodded. 'I haven't briefed Miss Auger as yet. I thought it best to wait until we got here.'

'Well, now you're here,' Marlette said.

Pruitt placed the attaché case carefully on his knee and opened it. He removed a folder, then closed the case again and deposited it on the floor beside his chair. Finding the document he wanted from inside the folder, he turned to Nicole. 'Miss Auger, your ex-husband worked for the CIA,' he said bluntly.

Nicole looked from Pruitt to Marlette, then shook her head. 'I don't believe it,' she snapped. 'Bob had nothing but contempt for the CIA and the way it operated. I'm sure I don't have to remind you about the scathing articles he wrote on Langley for the *Washington Post* a few years back.'

'Which were all penned at Langley,' Pruitt told her. 'Bob just took the credit for them. It was all disinformation which we backed up with fictitious facts and figures to make it appear genuine.'

'And I suppose you just happen to have the original articles with you?' she shot back.

'That wouldn't prove anything, would it?' Pruitt replied as he handed her the document he'd been holding. 'This is the report Bob filed on you shortly before your marriage. We had to be sure that you weren't going to be a threat to his cover, considering your nomadic upbringing in Africa. We were particularly worried by the fact that you and your father had been known to mix socially with Marxist terrorists in North Africa. I'm afraid you'll find that some of the details in there are of a very personal nature. I'm sorry.'

Nicole read the report in silence. When finally she looked up at Marlette, tears had welled up in her eyes. Tears of anger and betrayal. Her hand was trembling as she held the report out towards him.

'I don't need to read it,' Marlette said, tight-lipped. 'It's obviously genuine, judging by the way it's affected you.'

She crumpled the document into a ball and threw it angrily on to the floor. 'And just how long had he been working for the CIA?'

'He was recruited fifteen years ago,' Pruitt told her. 'I realize that this will have come as something of a shock to you, Miss Auger, but he could never have confided in you about his double life. I'm sure you understand that.'

Nicole lit a cigarette, then got to her feet and crossed to the window. 'The CIA sent him to El Salvador, didn't they?'

'Yes,' Pruitt said. 'But we had no idea that he intended to take Michelle with him. We were as horrified as you were when we discovered that she was missing.'

'Don't patronize me,' she snarled, her eyes blazing. 'You don't give a damn about Michelle just as long as you can get your hands on the precious tape that Bob had with him!'

'Of course we're concerned that the tape shouldn't fall into the wrong hands, but that doesn't detract from the fact that your daughter's safety is of paramount importance to us at the moment.'

'You're good, and if I didn't know any better, I'd almost be inclined to believe you. But I've met your kind before in Africa. CIA. KGB. MI6. The ideologies may be different, but you're all a bunch of lying, treacherous *bastards* when it comes down to it.'

Marlette held up a hand before Pruitt could respond. 'I don't give a shit about the politics of the CIA, or any other intelligence agency for that matter. So far, all you've told us is that Kinnard worked for the company. What I want to know is, what's on this tape that's got Langley in such a flap?'

Pruitt drummed his fingers irritatingly on the cardboard folder, then looked up at Marlette. 'I'm not at liberty to say any more until I know whether you're in or not.'

'In other words, until you know whether I'm prepared to go back to El Salvador to find Michelle and recover the tape,' Marlette said.

'If Michelle even has the tape,' Nicole said from the window.

'It's obvious she's got it,' Marlette retorted. 'Why else would Pruitt be here?'

Pruitt looked across at Nicole. 'We're almost certain now that Bob gave the tape to Michelle sometime yesterday afternoon. It's what happened to her afterwards that we don't know.'

'As I said to Nicole earlier, I'd only be a liability to her if I went back to El Salvador,' Marlette said. 'Hell, I wouldn't even get past customs. I was hoping to recruit a couple of mercs who would have known their way around the country.' He looked grim-faced at her and shook his head. 'No luck there. I'm sorry.'

'Thanks for trying,' she said with a brave smile.

'You wouldn't even get past customs?' Pruitt said with a chuckle. 'I guess that's one way of putting it.'

Nicole looked hesitantly from Pruitt to Marlette. 'Rick, what does he mean?'

'It's not important,' Marlette retorted brusquely.

'Marlette was less than an hour away from a government firing squad when a senior official at the American embassy saved his butt and got him out of El Salvador,' Pruitt said. 'It was made clear to him on the way to the airport that the stay of execution was a temporary one – it would be carried out if he were ever to set foot inside the country again.'

'I think you make a very good case for the defence,' Marlette said sarcastically.

'Come off it, Marlette. You're a pro. One of the best

there is. Our people can smuggle you into El Salvador from one of the neighbouring states, and we've got more than enough contacts inside the country to be able to keep you several steps ahead of the authorities. You're probably the one person capable of pulling this off.'

'I'm flattered,' Marlette retorted.

'I've been authorized to offer you the sum of one hundred thousand dollars in cash for the safe return of the girl and the tape,' Pruitt said, watching Marlette's face for a reaction. There was none. 'I'd say that was a more than generous offer.'

'I'll be the judge of that,' came the reply.

'I don't think you're in any position to turn it down, Marlette. We know you weren't paid for your last tour of Bosnia, and that you're already up to your neck in hock. And I'm sure I don't have to remind you that some of those loan sharks can be very imaginative in their methods of extracting overdue payments, if you get my meaning.'

'I'm quite capable of looking after myself, Pruitt,' Marlette shot back. 'I won't have any trouble getting another contract to help pay off some of my debt.'

'You've heard my offer, Marlette,' Pruitt said. 'Take it or leave it.'

'For God's sake, Rick, take it,' Nicole implored. 'If it's more money you want, I'll make up the difference. I don't care how much you want, I'll pay it.'

'Stay out of this, Nicole,' Marlette snapped without looking round at her. He leaned forward, his elbows resting on his knees, his eyes riveted on Pruitt's face. 'Double it. Two hundred thousand dollars. In cash. Half now, half on completion of the contract. Also, you settle all my outstanding debts before I leave. Those are my terms. It's up to you.'

'You've just priced yourself out of a contract, Marlette,' Pruitt said, replacing the folder in the attaché case. It was then his portable telephone rang. Removing the slimline device from the inside pocket of his jacket, he extended the aerial and answered it. 'Hold on a moment,' he told the caller. He got to his feet and placed his hand over the mouthpiece. 'If you'd excuse me, I'd like to take this call in private.'

'You can use the kitchen. It's at the end of the hall,' Marlette told him.

When they were alone, Nicole stubbed out her cigarette and sat down on the sofa beside Marlette. 'Take the hundred thousand he offered you, Rick. I can probably raise another seventy or eighty thousand at a push. I'm a partner in a very successful restaurant in Chicago. I wouldn't have any difficulty finding a buyer for my share of the partnership. I also have a three-bedroomed apartment –'

'I don't want your money, Nicole,' Marlette interrupted.

'Then why else are you holding out on Pruitt?' she demanded in frustration.

'It's simple. If they want me badly enough, they'll pay. The one thing I've learnt over the years about negotiating contracts is that it's all about bluff and counter-bluff. Believe me, I know what I'm doing.'

'So do I. You're trying to screw the CIA, aren't you? What have they done to make you so bitter towards them?' She noticed the look of uncertainty on his face. 'You never could lie to me, could you?'

He slumped back in the chair and raked his fingers through his hair. 'One of the people responsible for my deportation was a spook at the American embassy in San Salvador. He was reputed to have been the CIA's top man in El Salvador, if not in the whole of Central America. He never did anything without Langley's approval.'

'So in other words this is your way of getting back at them.'

'He'll agree to my terms,' Marlette replied evasively. 'Trust me on this. I know what I'm doing.'

Pruitt appeared in the doorway before she could reply.

He crossed silently to the chair and sat down again, the portable telephone still clutched tightly in his hand. His eyes went to Marlette. 'I'm afraid I've got some bad news.'

'Michelle?' Nicole cried out, clamping her hand over her mouth.

'No, it's not about Michelle,' Pruitt was quick to reassure her. 'The call was from a contact of mine in the NYPD. Brad Casey's been shot and killed at his bar. It happened within the last hour. I'm sorry. I know how close you two were.'

'Oh God, no,' Nicole exclaimed in horror.

'He was found by one of the bar staff in his office. He'd been shot twice through the chest at close range. The only thing that seems to be missing at the moment is the address book he kept on his desk.' Pruitt slipped the telephone back into his pocket. 'It has all the hallmarks of a professional hit. Nobody heard anything and the assassin wasn't seen leaving the building. The police do have one clue though. It's very significant as far as I'm concerned. A few minutes before the body was found, a man came into the bar and asked if Casey was on the premises. Once he'd established he was, he left. The witness couldn't see the man's face clearly because he was wearing a motorcycle helmet with only the visor pulled up. But he is certain that the man spoke with a distinctive Cockney accent.'

'The man on the phone,' Nicole exclaimed, ashen-faced.

'I've read the statement you made to the police,' Pruitt said. 'I think it's very likely that it is the same man.'

'Do you know who he is?' she asked.

'Yes,' Pruitt replied softly.

'It's Stuart Jayson, isn't it?' Marlette said.

'How did you know that?' Pruitt asked in surprise.

'Something he said to Nicole on the phone,' was all Marlette would venture.

'Who is this Jayson?' Nicole asked, lighting another cigarette.

'A merc who was supposed to have been killed in Africa several years ago,' Marlette told her. 'Obviously it was a set-up. So who's he working for now? Langley?'

'We still haven't come to an agreement on the terms of your contract,' Pruitt reminded him. 'I realize that Casey's death may have changed the situation –'

'It doesn't change a damn thing,' Marlette snapped brusquely. 'You know my terms.'

'OK, two hundred thousand dollars in cash. Half up front, half on completion of the contract. But you settle your own debts out of that. And if you fail to bring back either the girl or the tape, you forfeit the balance of the money.'

Nicole bit her lip apprehensively as she willed Marlette to accept Pruitt's new offer.

'Deal,' Marlette said at length. 'Now, answer the question. Is Jayson on Langley's payroll?'

'He was up until about a year ago,' Pruitt replied. 'The CIA faked his death, then sent him to Central America with a new identity and enough money for him to open a business for himself in Guatemala City. He learnt to speak fluent Spanish and Portuguese, and he even married a local girl to add to his cover.'

'What did he do there?' Nicole asked.

'He was obviously an assassin for the CIA,' Marlette snorted contemptuously. 'Jayson doesn't have the brains to do anything else.'

'He was. You'll appreciate that I can't go into details, but what I can say is that Jayson was part of what can only be described as "an illegal programme" which first came to the attention of Warren van Horn, the new Director, when he took over at Langley. I was given the brief to terminate the programme immediately. The individual members of the programme agreed to cooperate with my subsequent investigation, once they realized that Langley would be prepared to prosecute them if they refused. All, that is, except for Jayson. He refused to return to Washington for debriefing, but before I could dispatch a team to bring him back, I received word that he'd disappeared from his house in Guatemala City. All attempts to trace him failed; at one point we even suspected that he might have been murdered in order to silence him. He resurfaced a couple of months later in El Salvador as a security adviser to one of the country's most affluent and influential coffee barons. He's now working for a powerful right-wing cartel who we believe are planning to overthrow the democratically elected government and return the military again to power.'

'And that's what Kinnard was working on when he was murdered?' Marlette asked.

'Yes. Bob had gone to El Salvador to get the evidence we needed to prove to the Salvadorean government that a coup d'état was imminent.'

'You mean to say that the Salvadorean government doesn't know about the coup?' Nicole asked in disbelief.

'Not as far as we're aware. The cartel have kept it carefully under wraps.'

'Then how does the CIA know?' Marlette asked suspiciously.

'We have a mole inside the cartel,' Pruitt replied. 'That's all I can tell you.'

'So why doesn't Langley tell the Salvadorean government what it already knows?' Nicole queried.

'We don't have any proof to back up the allegations, and we're not prepared to blow our mole's cover by having him expose the cartel – because when it came down to it, it would only be his word against theirs. The members of the cartel are some of the country's leading political and military figures, who are all close to the President. He's hardly likely to believe the word of a double-agent over his personal friends, is he?'

'Did Kinnard have the proof you wanted on the tape?' Marlette asked.

'Yes, which is obviously why they sent Jayson to try and recover it,' Pruitt replied. 'The last time I spoke to Bob was yesterday afternoon. He sounded very excited on the phone, but he wouldn't reveal the exact contents of the videotape, except to say that it contained the evidence we needed to prevent the coup from going ahead. He was due to fly back to the States today to deliver the tape to me in person. What happened after he'd called me, up to the time of his death, is still a mystery to us.'

'Did he say anything about Michelle when he rang you?' Nicole asked anxiously.

'No. The first I knew that your daughter was with him was when I received a copy of the fax the Salvadorean authorities had forwarded to the Chicago police. When Jayson reported back to the cartel last night, he told them that he'd searched the hotel room thoroughly, but that there was no sign of the tape. That can only mean that Bob gave it to Michelle after he'd spoken to me, then sent her into hiding with someone he obviously trusted.' Pruitt turned to Marlette. 'You've worked with Jayson before. You know what kind of person we're dealing with here. He can't be allowed to get to Michelle first.'

'He'd kill her, wouldn't he?' Nicole said dully, staring at Marlette's bowed head.

'Remember what he said to you on the phone: "no witnesses, no comebacks",' Marlette replied. 'It's always been the way he operates: why should this be any different?' He looked at Pruitt. 'I assume that you've already booked me on a flight to one of the neighbouring states?'

Pruitt took an airline ticket from the folder and handed it to Marlette. 'Your flight to Honduras leaves Newark Airport at five-fifty tomorrow morning. You'll be met at the other end by one of our people who'll take you on to the border. But a word of warning, Marlette. The CIA can't be seen to be involved in this, so if you are caught inside El Salvador, you're on your own.'

'I wouldn't expect it any other way,' Marlette replied, then snapped his fingers and held out his hand towards Pruitt. 'Aren't you forgetting something?'

Pruitt opened the attaché case and removed a bulky envelope, which he dropped on to the coffee table in front of Marlette. 'There's fifty thousand in there. I'll deliver the other fifty thousand to you later this afternoon.'

'What about weapons?' Marlette asked.

'I can get you whatever you want. If you give me a list, I'll see to it that it's ready for you when you arrive in Honduras.'

'And just where do I fit into all of this?' Nicole asked.

'It's imperative that you still go to El Salvador, Miss Auger,' Pruitt told her. 'As I said earlier, the CIA can't be seen to be involved with this operation in any way, though I have had my secretary book a ticket for you on a flight to San Salvador departing Newark at six-forty tomorrow morning. But as far as the airline's concerned, you booked the ticket yourself over the phone this afternoon and paid for it on your credit card. You agreed to pick up the ticket at the Continental check-in desk a couple of hours before the flight. This way there's no connection between you and Langley. It's as much for your own protection as it is for ours.' He collected together the loose papers and replaced them in the folder.

'There is one other point,' he went on. 'The President of El Salvador is justifiably concerned that this whole incident could have a very damaging effect on his country's tourist trade, especially as the story's already made front-page news in many of the American papers. He wants Michelle found as quickly as possible to dispel the growing tabloid rumours that she's been kidnapped by a group of left-wing terrorists out to undermine the new democracy in El Salvador. For this reason he's asked a personal friend of his to

53

head the investigation into her disappearance. The man's an American who lives there. He was obviously chosen because of the language difficulties you're sure to encounter once you get there. Contrary to what you may read in the guidebooks, very few of the locals actually speak English. He's been told to assist you wherever he can, and to ensure that your stay in El Salvador is as comfortable as possible.' His eyes went to Marlette. 'The American's Peter Dennison.'

Marlette's hands balled into fists at the mention of the name, then he got to his feet and strode angrily to the window.

'Who is this Dennison?' Nicole asked.

'He was the spook I told you about at the American embassy who had me framed and deported from El Salvador,' Marlette replied.

'Dennison was a career diplomat; he never worked for the CIA,' Pruitt said crisply.

'Cut the crap, Pruitt,' Marlette shot back. 'You know as well as I do that Dennison was Langley's main contact with the death squads during the country's civil war.'

'I don't deny that Dennison had links with the death squads,' Pruitt was quick to reply. 'In fact, that was the main reason why he was eventually thrown out of the diplomatic corps. But he was never with us.'

'Have it your way, but I know that Dennison was CIA. Is he also part of this cartel?'

'No. As far as we can tell, he's clean.'

'So what's he doing now?'

'He owns the largest firm of security consultants in El Salvador. It's already made him a millionaire several times over. His clients read like a *Who's Who* of the country's rich and famous, for the simple reason that they're the only ones who can afford his prices. But he's obviously good, otherwise they wouldn't use him.' Pruitt took a photograph from the folder and handed it to Nicole. 'That was taken recently at the wedding of the daughter of one of the country's leading politicians. That's Dennison, to the right of the bride.'

Nicole found herself staring at a tall, commanding figure dressed in a white tuxedo and black bow-tie. With his suave good looks and thick black hair, he reminded her of the archetypal Hollywood hero found in so many of those instantly forgettable B-movies of the thirties and forties. Yet there was something distinctly unnerving about the smile – it never actually reached his eyes. They were cold and intense as he stared at the camera. She felt almost as if he were staring at her. She shuddered and was about to place the photograph on the coffee table when Marlette appeared behind the sofa and plucked it from her hand.

Pruitt removed a second envelope from the attaché case and placed it beside the envelope containing the money. 'There's a false passport for you to use, as well as eighty thousand colónes in cash. That's about ten thousand dollars. That's for expenses. It also contains a list of contacts you can use in El Salvador. Destroy the list once you've memorized the names.' He closed the attaché case. 'You have exactly three days to complete the operation. A helicopter will be at the Devil's Door at precisely nine o'clock on the third night to pick you up. I assume you know where the Devil's Door is?'

'Of course I know where it is,' Marlette countered.

'And a word of warning. The helicopter won't wait for you. If you're not there on time, the pilot will have orders to abort the rescue and leave. All the details are included in the envelope.'

'What's the Devil's Door?' Nicole asked.

'Its Spanish name is "La Puerta del Diablo". It's a mountainous area on the outskirts of San Salvador,' Marlette told her. 'From what I understand it's more of a tourist attraction now, but during the civil war it was common practice for the military and the death squads to dump the bodies of guerrillas there as a warning to others who opposed the regime.'

Nicole shuddered but said nothing.

'I'll bring the balance of the money round as soon as it's delivered to my hotel,' Pruitt said. 'Of course I'll keep you informed of any new developments in the Casey murder.'

'You do that,' Marlette said. 'But in the meantime I'm going down there myself to find out –'

'No!' Pruitt cut in sharply. 'I don't want you to go anywhere near the bar. We still don't know yet why Jayson was there, but if he was trying to get at you through Casey, then there's every chance he could still be watching the place, waiting for you to show.'

'He could just as easily come to the apartment. He must know where I live.'

'Let's hope he does,' Pruitt replied with a faint smile. 'I've got three teams of armed men parked out front. If he makes the mistake of showing his face around there, they'll take him down.'

'It's comforting to know that I'm being protected by the CIA,' Marlette said sarcastically.

'Has Jayson ever seen you before?' Nicole asked.

'No, why do you ask?' Pruitt asked.

'If Jayson is watching the apartment, he'll have seen us come here. That would mean that word would get back to the cartel that I'd been in touch with Rick. It wouldn't take much intelligence for them to realize why I'd flown in from Chicago to see him, would it?'

'It's a valid point, Miss Auger,' Pruitt conceded. 'It's only natural that you would try and recruit Marlette to help you find Michelle. After all, he's worked over there and knows the country well. It's almost certainly the reason Jayson was sent over here in the first place. But officially Marlette already has a contractual obligation to go back to Bosnia in the next couple of days. That's why he had to turn you down.' He gestured to the second envelope on the table. 'There's a more detailed account of the "contract" and your "flight plans" to Sarajevo in there.'

'Those kind of details can easily be cross-checked,' Marlette pointed out.

'A Richard Marlette will be flying out to Sarajevo tomorrow,' Pruitt replied. 'One of our people will be on the flight. He'll return to New York the next day under his own name. But there's such chaos in Bosnia right now that it could take some time for anyone to discover the ruse.'

'Ingenious,' Marlette conceded gruffly.

'There's no guarantee that it'll work, but hopefully it'll give you a bit more breathing space once you've crossed the border into El Salvador. It's the best we could do at such short notice.' Pruitt got to his feet. 'Miss Auger, can I offer you a lift back to the hotel?'

'I'd like to stay here for a while and talk to Rick. Brad's death has come as a deep shock to me. He was a good friend to both of us.'

'I understand,' Pruitt replied.

'She'll take that lift,' Marlette called out after Pruitt, then picked up Nicole's purse and pushed it into her hands. 'I'll see *you* at the airport tomorrow morning.'

'Rick, Brad's dead —'

'And sitting around reminiscing about the good old days isn't going to bring him back again,' Marlette cut in sharply. 'So, if you don't mind, I've still got things to do if I'm going to catch that flight in the morning.'

'I'm sure you have,' Nicole snapped defensively. 'I see some things haven't changed around here in the last six years.'

'And just what the hell's that supposed to mean?' Marlette demanded.

'You never could talk openly about your feelings, could you? It's only natural that you're hurting inside — Brad was your best friend. Not that you'd think so, judging by the way you're bottling up your emotions as if nothing had happened.'

'I'll deal with it in my own way,' Marlette shot back angrily.

'You'll deal with it in your own *destructive* way,' she corrected him, then brushed past Pruitt and disappeared out into the hall.

Pruitt followed her from the room and, moments later, Marlette heard the sound of the front door closing behind them. He crossed to the sofa but didn't sit down; instead his eyes went to a photograph on top of a cabinet in the corner of the room. It showed him and Casey together at the Soldier of Fortune Convention earlier in the year. He'd only gone with great reluctance after Casey had eventually nagged him into it. He'd seen little change since the last convention he'd attended some years back. Admittedly, there had been several interesting seminars where he'd picked up some useful information, but on the whole he felt there was still far too much emphasis on the macho image associated with being a mercenary which, in his opinion, had only served to give the profession a bad name over the years. He'd vowed on the flight back to New York that he'd never attend another convention. He remembered that at the time Casey had just smiled – he'd known that he could probably have talked Marlette into going again. But none of that mattered any more. Brad Casey was dead . . .

Suddenly all the anger that had been building up inside him exploded to the surface. He lashed out violently with his foot, sending the coffee table tumbling across the room. He grabbed it by one of its legs, and was poised to dash it against the wall when an image of Nicole's face appeared in his mind: *You'll deal with it in your own destructive way*. She was right. She was always right. She knew him better than anyone else. What was it Brad had said to him earlier that afternoon? *She was the best thing that ever happened to you and you let her slip through your fingers. If you'd shown her the respect she deserved you'd still be together now . . .*

He sucked in several deep breaths to calm his ragged emotions, then, carefully replacing the table in the centre of the room, he looked across at the photograph. 'You always were a lot smarter than me, buddy. A hell of a lot smarter . . .'

'Did you bring the rest of the money with you?' Marlette demanded when Pruitt returned to the apartment. He purposely kept Pruitt standing on the doorstep.

Pruitt removed an envelope from his attaché case and handed it to Marlette, who tossed it on to the hall table without bothering to count the money. There would be time for that later.

'I've made up a list of the weapons I'll want,' Marlette said, handing the sheet of paper to Pruitt.

Pruitt ran his eyes quickly over the contents. 'You'll have them,' came the brusque reply.

'Any news of Jayson?'

'No. All the airports and harbours have been alerted, but it's my guess that he's already skipped the country. We're dealing with professionals here, Marlette. He probably went straight to the airport after the hit on Casey, and boarded a flight even before the body was found.'

'Then I look forward to meeting up with him in El Salvador,' Marlette said icily.

'You can't afford to allow your personal feelings to jeopardize the operation, Marlette,' Pruitt warned him.

'One way or another, I'll kill him. I don't care whether it's during or after the contract; I'm going to kill him.' Marlette reached for the door handle. 'Well, if there's nothing else, I've still got some packing to do.'

'Actually, there is something,' Pruitt replied as Marlette was about to close the door on him. 'I've got a proposition for you. Once you've heard what I have to say, you'll understand why I couldn't discuss it earlier in front of Miss Auger.'

'What kind of proposition?' Marlette asked suspiciously.

'Could we discuss it inside?' Pruitt asked. 'We're talking about an extra two hundred grand here. A hundred up front, the balance on completion of the job. At least hear me out. After all, what have you got to lose?'

'And you've got the hundred with you?'

'Right here,' Pruitt said, patting the attaché case in his hand.

'Then you'd better come in,' Marlette replied, and stepped aside to let Pruitt into the apartment.

THREE

Nicole had phoned down to the hotel switchboard and asked for a three-o'clock wake-up call before turning in the previous evening. In the event she hadn't needed it. For the second night running she'd barely got any sleep, her mind totally preoccupied by thoughts of her missing daughter. She'd given up trying to get any sleep by midnight and, after flicking absently through the channels on the television set, she'd finally settled for a dated black and white melodrama with a young Carole Lombard as the stoical heroine. If nothing else, it had helped to pass the time. Then, after soaking in a hot bath, she'd ordered a continental breakfast to her room. She'd finished the last of her cigarettes over the second cup of black coffee and, after packing her suitcase, she'd gone down to the reception to check out. The night porter had rung for a taxi; its driver had quickly realized that his friendly banter wasn't going to be appreciated at that time of the morning. On reaching Newark Airport, Nicole had quickly requisitioned a trolley and made her way across the near deserted concourse to the Continental check-in counter. After producing her passport and reeling off the number of her credit card to the ground stewardess on duty, her flight ticket was processed and she was assigned a window seat in the smoking section of the cabin.

She bought herself a carton of Marlboro cigarettes from the duty free shop – it would keep her going for a while in El Salvador – and, after buying a couple of loose packets for the journey and an early edition of the *New York Times* from the newsagent, she went to the cafeteria and paused in the entrance to look around slowly at the occupied tables. There was no sign of Rick. She looked at her watch. It was four-ten. She was early. When he'd phoned her at the hotel the previous evening he'd said to meet him at the cafeteria at four-thirty. She bought a coffee and carried it across to a table close to the entrance. When Rick arrived, he couldn't miss her. Spreading out the newspaper on the table, her attention was drawn to a headline on the front page: JOURNALIST SLAIN IN EL SALVADOR. She read the accompanying text, but it didn't contain anything that she didn't already know.

'You're here early.'

The voice startled her, and she looked up at the figure standing on the other side of the table. For a moment she stared in disbelief at Marlette, then instinctively touched the sides of her head. 'What have you done to your hair?'

'I had it cut,' Marlette replied, brushing his hands over his newly cropped hair. 'El Salvador's still a very conservative country. If I'd gone there looking like Axl Rose, I'd only have drawn a lot of unnecessary attention to myself.'

'You've had long hair ever since I knew you. It just takes a bit of getting used to, that's all.' She nodded to herself as she continued to appraise his short back and sides. 'It certainly gives you a more distinguished look.'

'I'm glad you approve,' Marlette retorted wryly.

'Yes, I think I do,' she said with a grin.

'Have you checked in yet?' he asked.

Nicole nodded. 'You?'

'Yeah.' He looked at his watch. 'My flight's due to be called in the next half-hour.'

'Have you seen this?' She turned the newspaper round to show him, tapping the relevant article with her finger.

'Yeah, I picked up a paper on the way over here.' He gestured to her empty cup. 'You want another coffee?'

'That's already my third cup this morning,' she said, then

took a cigarette from the packet on the table and lit it. 'I think I'll just stick to these.'

'Suit yourself. I'm having one.' Marlette headed off to the self-service counter. When he returned he was carrying a tray containing a coffee and an apple danish. He sat down again, reached into his pocket, and withdrew a piece of paper which he handed to Nicole. 'That's the address of an orphanage in San Salvador. It's run by a Father Bernard Coughlin. I rang him last night. He's agreed to be our go-between. He's been briefed fully on the situation, so you'll be able to talk freely with him.'

'What about the man Pruitt's assigned to be our go-between?' Nicole asked.

'I don't trust Pruitt,' came the brusque reply.

'And you trust Father Coughlin?'

'With my life. In fact, he's the only person in El Salvador I do trust. Naturally we'll still have to work through Pruitt's stooge, if only to allay any suspicions that we're using Coughlin. I'll have to stay with him once I reach San Salvador, but if there's anything important you want to tell me, channel it through Coughlin. Memorize the address, then destroy the paper. If Dennison does have your hotel room searched while you're out, you don't want to give him any reason to suspect that Coughlin's involved in any of this.'

'OK. I assume he'll contact me first?'

'Yeah. I don't know when though. But if you do need to get in touch with me in an emergency, go to that address. He'll be there.'

'How do you know him?' she asked.

'It's a long story.'

'Just like the reason for your deportation. You still haven't told me what you did that led to your deportation.'

'I don't want to talk about it. OK?' Marlette said, then took a generous bite from the pastry, as if to signal an end to the matter.

'Sure,' she replied with a quick shrug.

Having finished the pastry, Marlette took a sip of coffee and looked across at Nicole. 'How's your father doing these days? Is he still arming every warring faction across Africa?'

'He's dead, Rick,' she said softly.

Marlette reached out and touched her arm. 'I'm sorry. I know how close you were to him. What happened?'

'He was in a helicopter which was shot down over northern Sudan. There were no survivors. It was never established who was behind the attack, but as there were several high-ranking army officers in the chopper at the time, the government put it down to rebel forces. I'm not so sure though. I've since heard rumours from some of my father's old contacts in the Sudan that he may have been the target. But they are only rumours. It's been four years now, so I guess I'll never really know the truth of what happened out there.'

'I had a lot of time for your father,' Marlette said after a thoughtful silence.

'It was mutual. You know that. He thought the world of you, Rick. I don't think he ever really forgave me for leaving you. He certainly didn't think much of Bob; that was obvious when he came over for the wedding.'

'Kinnard seemed to have that effect on a lot of people,' Marlette said, but there was no bitterness in his voice. 'Did your father ever get to see your daughter?'

'Yes,' she replied with a smile. 'He came over here when Michelle was still only a few months old. You could see how thrilled he was when he first picked her up. A grandchild of his own. I don't think he ever thought he'd see the day when I'd actually settle down and start a family.'

'I can understand why he'd think that. You were always the feisty, independent one, even after you came back to the States with me. I could never have imagined you with a child. Certainly not when we lived together. But things have obviously changed a lot since then.'

64

'They have,' she agreed with a thoughtful smile.

Marlette finished his coffee, put the cup on the tray and pushed it to one side. 'A word of warning, Nicole. Be very careful of Peter Dennison. Pruitt seemed sure that he wasn't involved in this plot to overthrow the government. I'm not so convinced, though. Not with his track record.'

'Why do you say that?'

'Dennison's been a right-wing zealot for as long as I can remember. He's a member of the Western Goals Institute, a fanatical anti-Communist organization based over in London. It likes to think of itself as a right-wing think-tank. I guess that's one way of looking at it. A past president of the organization was the late Roberto D'Aubuisson, the founder of the Arena party in El Salvador. At the time of its inception Arena was regarded as one of the most openly fascist parties in Central America. D'Aubuisson was also a patron of the death squads. In fact, it was D'Aubuisson who nominated Dennison as a possible recruit for the Western Goals Institute. When I was last in El Salvador, Dennison's best friend was a Major Hector Amaya, a senior officer in the Atlacatl battalion, the élite unit in the Salvadorean military, the National Guard. Amaya was also said to have had close links with the death squads. But in particular he was rumoured to have been the go-between for the military and the notorious UGB, the *Unión Guerrera Blanca* – or the White Warriors Union – which at the time was unquestionably the most feared and hated of the death squads. That gives you an insight into the kind of people we're dealing with here. And from what Coughlin told me last night, Dennison still has close links with the military. Coughlin also claims that at least two directors on the board of Dennison's security firm are former Atlacatl officers who had ties with both Arena and the death squads. I just don't buy Pruitt's story. If a right-wing cartel have hatched a plot to overthrow the government and replace it with a military junta, then

Dennison's got to be in the thick of it. I'd stake my life on that.'

'Why would Pruitt deliberately lie about it?' Nicole asked. 'You don't think the CIA are involved, do you?'

'Anything's possible when you're dealing with Langley,' Marlette replied. 'Just bear in mind what I said about Dennison. Don't be taken in by his charm, because underneath that façade he's the most scheming, cold-hearted son-of-a-bitch I've ever known. He'll stop at nothing to get what he wants. Remember that.'

Their conversation was interrupted by the announcement over the airport intercom system that the American Airlines flight to Tegucigalpa was now ready for boarding.

'That's me,' Marlette said, pushing back his chair and getting to his feet.

Nicole stubbed out her cigarette, then stood up and hugged Marlette tightly. 'You take care of yourself, Rick.'

Marlette just nodded as he picked up his battered hold-all.

'Rick?' she called out as he turned to leave. 'Thanks.'

'Don't flatter yourself, Nicole, I'm not doing this for you,' Marlette was quick to reply. 'I'm only in this for the money. A last throw of the dice so that I can pay off my debts and get the hell out of this damn business once and for all. But don't worry, I'll find your kid for you. I wouldn't want to miss out on the other hundred grand.'

She watched him leave the cafeteria, then slowly sat down again. She'd forgotten how easily he could hurt her with his cutting remarks. It was a side of him that she'd never fully understood. Although she'd tried to talk to him about it when they'd lived together, he'd never ventured an explanation; this had finally led her to reach her own theory — she'd decided that it was a defence mechanism which he resorted to whenever he felt uncomfortable with his own emotions. Did he still have feelings for her, even after she'd walked out on him? The thought caught her momentarily off-guard. Did it really matter? Although she tried to convince herself that it didn't, there was no question that a part of her had never stopped loving him. And when she'd seen him at the Rosewood bar the previous day, those latent feelings had come back to haunt her. She quickly pushed the thought from her mind. It was over between them. Or was it . . . ?

'What?'

She looked up hesitantly at the grey-suited businessman standing beside the table. 'Sorry, did you say something?' she asked him.

The man smiled. 'You said, "Is it over?" as I was passing your table. I wasn't sure whether the question was directed at me or not.'

Nicole felt her face flush with embarrassment as she clamped her hand to her mouth to mute a nervous chuckle. 'I'm sorry. I must have been thinking out loud.'

'Is it?' the man asked. 'Over, that is?'

'I don't know,' she replied with a shrug, then a faint smile touched the corners of her mouth. 'But I hope not.'

Warren van Horn had an obsession. Punctuality. Wherever possible, he arranged his life by the clock. It had cost him two marriages, and even his three children had been forced to adapt to his way of life whenever they brought their families to visit him in Washington. It was an obsession which had stemmed from a distinguished thirty-five-year military career with the United States Army. When he'd finally been coaxed into leaving the armed forces by his close friend, the then DCI, the Director of the CIA, he already held the rank of a three-star general. He was recruited by Langley where he served with the Defense Intelligence Agency, and later as head of the Directorate of Operations; he was promoted to DCI with the advent of a new administration at the White House. It was certainly a controversial appointment: there were many in the intelligence world who felt that he didn't have the necessary experience or skill to take over such a highly sensitive position. A diligent and tireless worker, who made no secret of the fact that he still had much to learn, he'd been in office now for four months, and had yet to provide his critics with any substantial ammunition to use against him.

His eyes went from the wall clock to the red scrambler phone on his desk. The call was late. He returned his attention to the document he was reading. When he'd finished he initialled the last page, slipped the document back in its folder, and placed it in one of the three trays positioned equidistantly from each other on his desk. Military precision. He looked at the clock again. Two minutes late. It wasn't just that the call was overdue. His contact was normally very reliable. Very punctual. So what was keeping him? Had something happened to him? Shifting uneasily in his chair, he drummed his fingers impatiently on the desk, willing the phone to ring. Two-and-a-half minutes. He pulled another folder towards him and opened it.

He looked up when he heard the distinctive buzz of his scrambler line. Closing the folder and recapping his pen, he pushed them to one side, then lifted the handset. His contact identified himself by a code.

'You're late,' van Horn said tersely.

'Only by a couple of minutes.'

'Lost time all adds up,' van Horn replied.

'I'm sorry, it won't happen again,' came the resigned reply.

'Does the name Richard Marlette mean anything to you?' van Horn asked.

'Sure, he was the American mercenary who was deported –'

'Yes, yes,' van Horn interjected irritably. 'Well, it seems he's on his way back to El Salvador. Alex Pruitt was tailed twice to Marlette's apartment yesterday. The first time he

68

went there with Nicole Auger. The second time he was alone.'

'Where does she tie in with Marlette?'

'They were lovers several years back,' van Horn replied.

'Small world,' came the contemptuous reply. 'And you think Pruitt's recruited Marlette to recover Kinnard's tape?'

'I think that's part of it, yes,' van Horn replied. 'But it's my guess that his main reason for bringing in Marlette is to deal with Jayson. As you know, Jayson used to work as an assassin for Pruitt. But now that he's gone freelance, he's a threat to Pruitt. He knows far too much about the "illegal" operations Pruitt's been involved in over the years. So why not use Marlette to kill two birds with one stone? That way Pruitt covers himself. Or so he thinks.'

'It makes sense. When's Marlette due to fly out here?'

'He flew out of New York this morning,' van Horn said. 'Destination: Honduras.'

'Which means he's obviously going to be smuggled over the border into El Salvador. There aren't that many places where he could cross undetected. I can have those areas saturated with my people. He'd never get past them.'

'No, I want you to give him as wide a berth as possible, but just make sure that your people watch him like a hawk. And if he gets himself into any trouble with the authorities, it'll be up to you to get him out of it.'

'That's crazy! How the hell am I supposed to sell them a line like that?'

'I'm sure you'll think of something,' van Horn said. 'It's what you're paid to do.'

'If they ever knew I was working for Langley —'

'They haven't guessed up to now, have they?' van Horn cut in.

'Why are we protecting Marlette, for Christ's sake?'

'Because right now he's the ace up my sleeve,' van Horn told him. 'You know that for the past two months Alex

Pruitt's been the target of a clandestine undercover investigation here at Langley. If Marlette makes the hit on Jayson, it would be exactly the breakthrough we'd need to finally crucify Pruitt. I'm sure we could persuade Marlette to testify against him if it meant the difference between walking, and a twenty-year stretch in San Quentin. I think, given those odds, you'll find that he'd be prepared to see things my way, don't you?'

'You've got it all worked out, haven't you?'

'Not only is Alex Pruitt rotten to the core, but he's already being tipped as future Director here at Langley,' van Horn shot back angrily. 'Can you imagine what would happen if that kind of corruption was allowed to filter up to this level of management? Of course, I don't expect this organization to be squeaky clean, but you have to draw the line somewhere. And I'm damned if I'd allow Alex Pruitt to undermine my authority.'

'I understand, sir.' A moment's pause. 'What if there's more to this than just a hit on Jayson?'

'What are you suggesting?'

'Marlette's a sniper. One of the best, by all accounts. And you said yourself last time we spoke that you suspected Pruitt of being linked in some way to the plot to overthrow this government.'

'If there is a plot,' van Horn reminded him. 'And as for Pruitt's involvement, I'm hoping that the Kinnard tape will give us confirmation of that. But I take your point. With his talents, Marlette would certainly make a good assassin, wouldn't he?'

'Exactly.'

'It can only strengthen the case against Pruitt if he has recruited him as an assassin,' van Horn said.

'And what if Marlette's brief is to assassinate the President? This is my country and I certainly don't want to see it returned to military rule again.'

'Your country?' van Horn snorted contemptuously. 'And

where's your loyal patriotism been hiding while Langley have been depositing regular sums of money in a Swiss bank account for you? You can't have it both ways.'

'This is different,' came the terse reply.

'You work for Langley, and don't ever forget it,' van Horn snapped. 'And if you don't like it, we can always terminate our little arrangement by letting slip to your colleagues that you've been selling them out for the past few years. I'm sure they'd have something to say about that, don't you think?'

'You'd actually be prepared to see this country slip back into anarchy just so that you'd have enough evidence to prosecute Alex Pruitt?'

'I see we finally understand each other,' van Horn said coldly before he replaced the handset in its cradle.

Nicole woke with a start to find a flight attendant shaking her gently. 'We're coming in to land,' he said with a friendly smile. 'Would you fasten your seatbelt and put your seat in the upright position, please?'

'I must have dozed off during the film,' Nicole said, rubbing her eyes sleepily as she unhooked the headphones from around her neck and replaced them in the pouch in front of her.

'You actually dozed off within a few minutes of the lights being dimmed for the film,' the flight attendant told her. 'I tried to unhook your headphones after you'd fallen asleep, but you had your hand on them so, rather than disturb you, I thought it best to just leave them around your neck.'

'Thanks,' Nicole said, snapping the belt around her waist.

'You're welcome,' the flight attendant replied, continuing down the aisle.

Although still tired, Nicole was relieved that she'd finally managed to get some sleep. And how she'd needed it!

Slipping on her sunglasses, she looked out of the cabin window. Small clusters of light, fluffy clouds drifted across the deep cerulean sky, casting their uneven shadows over the segmented countryside which was spread out like some giant green and brown patchwork quilt. It was a breathtaking sight, and Nicole pressed her face closer to the window for a better view. Michelle was out there – somewhere. It was a strangely comforting thought, and she let it linger in her mind as the Boeing 747 made its final descent towards the runway and the pilot executed a near perfect landing. As the aeroplane taxied slowly towards the terminal building, he announced over the intercom that it was currently a dry, humid thirty-five degrees Celsius in San Salvador.

The aeroplane had already reached the main apron in front of the terminal building when a further announcement was made over the intercom, first in English and then in Spanish: 'Would Mrs Nicole Kinnard please make herself known to a member of the cabin staff?'

Nicole identified herself to the flight attendant, and was asked to remain in her seat until everyone had disembarked. Someone would be coming on board to meet her personally, but when Nicole asked who it was, the flight attendant just gave her an apologetic shrug and said that that was all he'd been told. She had a good idea who would be meeting her: Dennison. Who else could it be? Her eyes flickered towards the terminal building. The words EL SALVADOR were displayed prominently on the roof in garish red lettering. Three days ago she couldn't have pinpointed the exact location of El Salvador without the aid of an atlas. Now what she didn't know about its history, economy and politics wasn't worth knowing. She probably knew more about the country than the vast majority of Salvadoreans who'd been on the flight with her. The irony of the situation certainly wasn't lost on her.

She smiled fleetingly at the Salvadorean couple who'd

been sitting beside her as they rose from their seats to take their hand luggage from the overhead compartment. They stared back blankly at her, quickly joining the exodus of passengers heading for the exit. She suddenly felt alone. And vulnerable. Was it a maternal feeling for what she knew Michelle must have gone through in the last couple of days? The thought quickly evaporated from her mind as she noticed the white Mercedes cross the apron and come to a stop alongside the mobile passenger stairs. It was impossible for her to see who sat behind its opaque, dark windows. Nothing happened until the last of the passengers had disembarked, then the driver's door opened and a burly Salvadorean exited. He was dressed casually in an open-necked shirt and flannel trousers. He looked across at the stream of passengers heading towards the terminal building, then opened the rear door of the car. Nicole found herself sitting forward in nervous anticipation. The man who alighted from the car was instantly recognizable as Dennison from the photograph she had seen in Marlette's apartment. He was wearing a loose-fitting white suit, pale blue silk shirt and navy blue tie. He ran a hand over his gelled black hair as he strode to the foot of the mobile passenger stairs. Nicole lost sight of him. She took her bag from the overhead compartment, then sat down on the edge of the aisle seat waiting for Dennison to reappear.

Moments later he entered the cabin, speaking briefly to a flight attendant who gestured in Nicole's direction. Dennison made his way down the aisle to where Nicole was sitting. 'Mrs Kinnard?'

'Ms Auger,' Nicole corrected him. 'I reverted back to my maiden name after my divorce.'

'Of course,' Dennison said with a friendly smile. 'Allow me to introduce myself. My name's Peter Dennison. You may have heard of me.'

'Should I have?' Nicole replied, reluctantly shaking

Dennison's extended hand. Both Rick and Pruitt had told her to feign total ignorance of his existence on first meeting him.

'We have a mutual acquaintance, I believe,' Dennison said. 'Richard Marlette. I thought he might have mentioned me.'

'No,' was all Nicole would venture.

'I see,' Dennison said. 'Well, no matter. The President has asked me to personally assist you in every possible way to find your daughter. He's also asked me to extend his condolences to you at your recent bereavement. I share those sentiments. I knew Bob. He was a good reporter.'

'But a lousy father,' Nicole snapped.

'Don't worry, Ms Auger, we'll find your daughter for you,' Dennison was quick to assure her.

'And how long's that going to take?' Nicole asked curtly.

'We're doing everything in our power to find her, Ms Auger,' Dennison replied. 'Her photograph's been faxed to every police station and every army barracks. I also currently have over a hundred hand-picked men coordinating the search from command centres which have been set up in every major town and city in the country. And on top of that, the relevant authorities in all the neighbouring states have been alerted to your daughter's disappearance. Believe me, Ms Auger, it's only a matter of time before we find her.' He removed an envelope from his pocket and handed it to her. 'I've been asked to give you this. It's a letter from the President just to confirm that I am who I claim to be and that he has asked me to assist you in any way possible while you are out here in El Salvador.'

Nicole opened the envelope and read the note. It was handwritten in English on official Presidential stationery. Once she'd read it she folded it up again and slipped it into her purse. 'Why did you meet me here instead of at my hotel?'

'Unfortunately the press have already latched on to the

story; I don't have to tell you what these journalists can be like when there's an exclusive in the wind. They're already waiting for you in the terminal building, hoping for an interview once you've cleared customs.'

'And if they don't get their interview now, they'll just go to the hotel and wait for me there.'

'That's why I've already taken the liberty of cancelling your reservation at the Sheraton. I have a guest-house that's at your disposal. It's in San Benito, one of the more exclusive areas of San Salvador. I put all my clients – and potential clients – up there when they're in town on business.'

'What is it you do?' Nicole asked.

'I have my own security firm here in San Salvador,' Dennison replied, reaching for the overnight bag on the floor as Nicole was about to pick it up. 'Allow me.'

'What about my other luggage?'

'I've arranged for it to be sent to the house. And don't worry about customs either: I'll see that your passport's validated once you've settled in.'

'How does an American civilian come to be rubbing shoulders with the President of El Salvador?' Nicole asked as she followed Dennison towards the exit.

'I was fortunate enough to make a lot of important contacts while I was assigned to the American embassy here in San Salvador back in the eighties,' Dennison replied. 'I fell in love with the country and decided to stay on when I was offered the chance to further my diplomatic career at another embassy in Europe. That's when I came up with the idea of starting my own security firm. As I've already said, I had the contacts, so the rest was just a matter of selling myself. And I'd certainly had enough practice at that as a foreign diplomat.'

The sweltering heat hit Nicole the moment she stepped out of the air-conditioned cabin and on to the mobile passenger stairs, a sticky, cloying heat that seemed to envelop her whole body. She was already sweating by the time she reached the foot of the stairs. Taking a tissue from her pocket, she dabbed her forehead, then looked round at Dennison as he descended the stairs behind her. 'Is it always this humid?'

'At this time of year, yes,' Dennison replied as he handed the overnight bag to his driver.

'It doesn't seem to affect you,' she said with a hint of envy in her voice.

'I've acclimatized myself to the heat over the years,' Dennison replied as the driver opened the back door for her. 'The car's air-conditioned.'

'Thank God for that,' Nicole replied, climbing into the back seat.

Dennison got in after her and the driver closed the door behind him. He indicated the compact liquor cabinet which had been built into the panel between the front and back seats. 'Would you care for something to drink? A cold lemonade, perhaps?'

'I wouldn't say no to a coffee,' she said hopefully.

'I can't provide that, I'm afraid,' Dennison said with an apologetic smile. 'But they do make a good cup of coffee at the embassy.'

'What embassy?' Nicole asked suspiciously as the car pulled away from the aeroplane.

'I'm sorry, I meant to tell you. The American Ambassador has asked to meet with you once you arrive in San Salvador. Of course, I can have my driver take you to the house if you'd prefer to freshen up first, but I doubt that your luggage will be there yet. Unfortunately the baggage handlers here aren't quite as efficient as they are at JFK or LaGuardia.'

'I'm quite happy to go to the embassy first,' Nicole told him.

Dennison gave his driver orders in Spanish to take them to the American embassy on the Avenida Norte in downtown San Salvador; then, after securing the dividing panel

76

between the front and back seats, he took a folder from the attaché case at his feet. 'There still aren't any definite leads in the search for your daughter, but I'm confident that it won't be too long before we get the breakthrough we're after.' He opened the folder before turning to Nicole. 'But in the meantime, let me brief you on what we've uncovered so far.'

'The Ambassador will see you now.'

Dennison nodded in acknowledgement to the secretary, then crossed to the door which led into the Ambassador's inner office. Pushing it open, he gestured for Nicole to enter before following her inside, closing the door again behind him.

A man in his early sixties, with silver-grey hair and a neatly trimmed white moustache, got to his feet and came round from behind his desk to greet them. 'Good to see you again, Peter,' he said, pumping Dennison's extended hand.

'And you, sir. Allow me to introduce you to Ms Nicole Auger,' Dennison said, then turned to Nicole beside him. 'This is Ambassador Maxwell Hersch.'

'How do you do?' Hersch said, shaking her hand gently, but firmly. 'My condolences to you on your recent loss.'

'Thank you,' Nicole replied.

'Please, won't you sit down, Miss Auger?' Hersch said, gesturing towards one of the two leather armchairs in front of his desk.

She sat down and watched Hersch return to his chair. 'Did you know my ex-husband?'

'I met him a couple of times when he was a political correspondent on Capitol Hill, but I'd hardly say that constitutes knowing him as such,' Hersch replied with a smile. He opened a silver cigarette box which was divided into two sections and held it out towards her. 'The milder cigarettes are on the left,' he said, and was surprised to see that

Nicole took a cigarette from the right-hand compartment.

'I first started smoking when I was fifteen,' she said, noticing the look on Hersch's face. 'I was living in North Africa at the time. My father used to buy his cigarettes from a black marketeer in Libya. They were hand-rolled and I remember that they used to taste like tar. But knowing nothing else, I quickly acquired a taste for them. That's why I'll only smoke strong brands now.'

'From what I've read about your father, he was something of a legend amongst the tribesmen of North Africa, wasn't he?' Dennison said, lighting the cigarette for her.

'I guess he was,' Nicole replied, as if she hadn't really thought about it before.

Hersch closed the box again and replaced it on the desk. 'I've read through the statement you made to the Chicago police on the night that Bob Kinnard died, Miss Auger. You seem very certain that he was murdered.'

'He was,' she retorted.

'Even though all the evidence points to it being a suicide,' Hersch continued.

'I know what I heard on the telephone,' she said firmly.

'And I believe you,' Dennison said, taking a packet of cheroots from his jacket pocket. He lit one, then looked across at Hersch. 'I also know that the local police are beginning to come round to that way of thinking as well. It makes no sense that an experienced journalist like Bob Kinnard would bring his daughter out here at a moment's notice, send her into hiding without telling anyone, then kill himself.'

'Why wasn't I informed that the police are now treating the death as suspicious?' Hersch demanded.

'You have to understand that this is an ongoing investigation, Ambassador. Naturally I'll see to it that you receive word of any new evidence as soon as it comes to light.' Dennison turned to Nicole. 'Last night the President instructed the head of his own security team to take over the investigation into Bob's death and, having spoken to him earlier this morning, I know that he's now treating your statement a lot more seriously than his predecessor did. In fact, he's asked to meet with you later today. Would that be convenient?'

'Sure,' Nicole agreed. She was at a loss to understand Dennison. If Rick was right, and Dennison was part of a cartel, then surely it was in his interests to make sure that the police continued to treat Bob's death as suicide? If the police were to launch a murder hunt, then surely there was a chance that the trail could lead back to Jayson. And that could only do irreparable harm to the cartel in the long run. It made no sense, unless Dennison wasn't a part of the conspiracy. But she knew that Rick's hunches were rarely wrong, and all her own instincts told her that he was right. Dennison's whole life had been devoted to furthering the cause of fascism. It had almost become an obsession with him. Then another thought came to her as she drew deeply on the cigarette. Was Dennison testing her to see if she knew anything about Jayson? It was a possibility, especially if he already knew that she'd gone to see Rick the previous day. Dennison would know from Jayson that he'd worked with Rick in Africa. And if he also knew what Jayson had said to her over the telephone, then it would be safe to assume that he'd already have guessed that Rick would know that Jayson had killed Bob. She knew she'd have to tread very carefully if she wasn't to give anything away. One slip, that's all it would take . . .

'Ms Auger?'

Nicole turned sharply to Dennison and gave him a rueful smile. 'I'm sorry, I was miles away.'

'So I noticed,' Dennison replied. 'Something on your mind?'

'I was just thinking about the voice I heard on the telephone,' she was quick to improvise, cursing herself silently for allowing her mind to wander so easily. 'Have the police come any closer to identifying the man?'

Dennison just shook his head.

'Surely there can't be that many Cockneys here in El Salvador?' Nicole said, her eyes never leaving Dennison's face as she leaned forward and tapped the end of her cigarette on the rim of the ashtray on Hersch's desk.

'It's always possible that he was a contract killer brought in from abroad,' Dennison replied. 'All flights to and from El Salvador over the last month are currently being checked by the police.'

'So you think Bob was silenced because he'd stumbled on to a story out here?' she asked.

'It's possible,' Dennison replied.

'It seems pointless to speculate right now on the circumstances which led up to Bob Kinnard's untimely death,' Hersch said, breaking the silence. 'We'll only know the truth once the police have pieced all the facts together.'

'And I have every confidence that they'll do just that,' Dennison added, staring at the ash glowing on the tip of his cheroot.

Hersch opened the folder in front of him, then looked up at Nicole. 'There is actually a reason why I've asked you over here this morning, Miss Auger. It has been brought to my notice that some years back you and a mercenary called Richard Marlette were . . . how can I put it, close?'

'We were lovers, if that's what you're trying to say,' Nicole said bluntly.

'Quite,' Hersch replied uncomfortably. 'I assume you know that he was once under contract to train government troops here in El Salvador?'

'Yes, he told me.'

'Did he also tell you that he was deported within six months of taking up that contract?' Hersch continued.

'Yes.' Nicole stubbed out her cigarette, then sat back in

the chair, her arms folded defensively across her chest. 'Is there a point to any of this?'

'The point being, Ms Auger, did you hire Richard Marlette to help you search for your daughter?' Dennison said.

'No,' Nicole retorted sharply. Pruitt had warned her to expect to be questioned on her relationship with Rick, but he hadn't tried to tell her what to say – that was down to common sense. She would have to play it by ear. Under the circumstances, it was all she could do.

'Did you see him while you were in New York?' Dennison asked.

'What's that got to do with you?' she asked indignantly.

'Please bear with us, Miss Auger,' Hersch said. His tone was placatory.

Nicole opened the silver box on the table and helped herself to another cigarette. 'Yes, I saw him,' she said at length, knowing that she had no choice but to admit to it in case she had been seen at the apartment. 'And yes, I did try to recruit him to help me find Michelle. He wasn't interested – not even for the kind of money I was prepared to pay him. That's when he told me that he'd been deported from El Salvador. He didn't tell me why he'd been deported though.'

'I can't say I'm surprised,' Hersch said contemptuously.

'And just what's that supposed to mean?' she demanded.

Dennison looked from Hersch to Nicole. 'If Marlette chose not to tell you, then I don't think it's our place –'

'What the hell happened?' she demanded impatiently. 'I'm fed up with being given the run around.'

'I think Miss Auger has the right to know,' Hersch said to Dennison. 'You were here when he was deported. It's best if you tell her what happened.'

Dennison got to his feet and crossed to the window. He turned back to face Nicole. 'As you already know, Marlette came out here to train government soldiers. At least, that's what was stipulated in his contract. I actually met Marlette

81

several times while he was here, and he always struck me as a damn good soldier. But psychologically he was all screwed up. He was drinking excessively and he was also doing drugs. Soft drugs, admittedly, but drugs all the same. I guess it was inevitable that he would be enticed into the shadowy world of the death squads. Many foreign mercenaries had fallen into the same trap. The pay was usually three or four times as much as they would get from the government to train National Guard troops. The wealthy land-owners, who were protected by these death squads, were more than happy to pay those kind of inflated wages to give themselves peace of mind. He fell in with a couple of other American mercenaries who were out here training the various death squads at the time. Marlette seemed to be under the impression that because the country was at war he was somehow above the law. His drinking became steadily worse. It finally came to a head one night when he went to a party. He raped a twelve-year-old girl. The two Americans tried to stop him and he shot them. They were both killed instantly. Then he turned the gun on the girl and shot her as well. The girl was the daughter of one of the most influential coffee barons in the country. Marlette had been assigned to protect her after the family feared that she was a possible kidnap target for the FMLN, the main Marxist guerrilla group here in El Salvador. He was arrested but the government were reluctant to put him on trial in case it came out in court that he'd been simultaneously training the National Guard and the death squads. I don't know how much you know about the civil war in this country, Ms Auger, but the government always insisted to the international press that they never had any links with the death squads. Of course it wasn't true, but that was the pretence they put up at the time. It was decided to execute Marlette quietly. Well, we got to hear of this at the American embassy, and of course we threatened to create an international incident out of it if Marlette wasn't given a fair trial. That's when a compromise was reached. Marlette was deported back to the US and told that if he were ever to set foot inside El Salvador again, he would be put on trial for the girl's murder.'

'It was actually Peter who intervened on Marlette's behalf,' Hersch pointed out, gesturing to Dennison. 'Marlette was quite literally an hour away from being executed by one of the death squads when Peter got him out of the country.'

Nicole looked from Hersch to Dennison, then slowly shook her head in total disbelief. 'Do you honestly expect me to believe that Rick raped then murdered a twelve-year-old girl? I'm the first to admit that Rick could be a complete bastard at times, but I also know he could never have done anything like that. Never.'

Hersch tapped the folder in front of him. 'In here are statements from over a dozen witnesses who were at the party that night.'

'I don't care if you've got a statement from the President himself, I know Rick isn't capable of anything so despicable,' Nicole cut in sharply, her eyes blazing. 'It was obviously a set-up from start to finish, and I can't believe that the American embassy could have been so gullible as to believe any of it.'

'I can assure you it did happen, Miss Auger,' Hersch bristled indignantly.

'Drink and drugs can be a very dangerous cocktail, Ms Auger,' Dennison pointed out. 'And when Marlette was tested, both were found to be in his bloodstream.'

'I know what Rick's like when he drinks. He gets mellow, not violent. I also know what he's like when he's stoned. Christ, we did enough cannabis together for me to know the effect it had on him, and it certainly didn't turn him into some psychopathic rapist.'

'The issue here isn't whether he's guilty or not,' Hersch replied, and held up a hand to silence Nicole before she could say anything. 'It's whether Marlette would be foolish enough to return to El Salvador again after what happened five years ago. If he does choose to return, then he's on his own this time. The American embassy would be powerless to intervene if he were arrested. He'd be at the mercy of the courts. And God help him if he were ever to fall into the wrong hands. It's said that the girl's father still has a contract out on Marlette. And there are more than enough takers for that kind of money.'

'I've already told you, Rick wasn't interested in my offer,' Nicole replied, hoping the anxiety knotted in the pit of her stomach hadn't filtered through to her voice.

'For his sake, Miss Auger, I hope you're right,' Hersch said, then closed the folder on the desk and got to his feet. 'Well, thank you for coming over here today at such short notice. And of course it goes without saying that if there's anything you should need while you're out here, please don't hesitate to call me here at the embassy. We're just as concerned as the Salvadorean authorities are to see that you're reunited with your daughter as quickly as possible.'

'I'm sure you are,' Nicole said without much conviction, and reluctantly shook Hersch's extended hand.

'Peter, could I have a word before you leave?' Hersch called out as Dennison led Nicole to the door.

Dennison waited until Nicole had left the room, then closed the door behind her and turned back to Hersch. 'Well?'

'What do you make of her?' Hersch asked, resuming his seat.

'Smart,' Dennison replied without hesitation.

'Do you think she was on the level about Marlette?'

Dennison thrust his hands into his pockets and crossed again to the window. 'I've got a feeling she was,' he said at length. 'She didn't need to tell us that she'd been to see Marlette in New York. It's not as if we could have known that beforehand.'

Hersch cupped his hands over his nose and mouth as he stared thoughtfully at the door. He finally lowered his hands and looked across at Dennison. 'I'm not so convinced. From what I've read on Marlette, this is exactly the kind of contract he'd be likely to take on. He seems to survive by living on the edge. This would be a great challenge to him, especially if he were able to get the girl safely out of the country. He'd see it as a personal victory, wouldn't he?'

'He'd be very stupid if he were ever to come back,' Dennison said. 'He knows what would happen to him.'

'I'd say that all depends on who got to him first.'

Dennison turned towards Hersch, his face creased in a frown. 'Meaning?'

'If he were arrested by the authorities, it's more than likely that he'd be deported again. They wouldn't want to dredge up the past, especially as any court case would be seen by the international press to be supporting, even if only indirectly, the illegal actions of the previous military juntas.' Hersch got to his feet and moved to where Dennison was standing, the contempt now evident on his face. 'I've never made any secret of the fact that I dislike you intensely, but the President's chosen you to work on this case, and that's something I'll just have to accept. A word of warning though. Should Marlette return to El Salvador, you'd better personally see to it that nothing happens to him, because if he should turn up dead in some back street, I'll make sure that you're implicated in the murder. I don't think that would go down very well with the President or any of the other influential friends you've made in the government. It also wouldn't be very good for business, would it? Don't get me wrong, I despise Marlette for what he did, but I despise you and your kind even more. So I'd have a quiet word with your fascist colleagues around the country in case any of them should get the sudden urge to take the law into their own hands.'

A faint smile touched Dennison's mouth, but it never reached his eyes. They remained icy in their piercing intensity. 'Thanks for the warning, Ambassador. I'll be sure to take it on board, should the need ever arise.'

Hersch watched Dennison cross to the door. 'I actually hope Marlette does turn up dead in some back street, because then I'd finally have got something on you. You may have managed to charm your way into government circles, but then none of those politicians have ever seen the file that Langley have compiled on you since you first arrived in this country.'

'And they're hardly likely to see it either, are they?' Dennison snorted. 'I believe it's deemed so sensitive that it's actually been classified top-secret. That's because part of the file also contains the ultra-sensitive material relating to the clandestine operations I carried out both for Langley and for the Pentagon while I was stationed out here. Certainly sensitive enough to seriously damage the CIA if it were ever made public. So don't muddy the waters, Ambassador, it wouldn't be appreciated back home.' He reached for the door handle, then looked back at Hersch. 'I know you'll have a tape recorder running somewhere in the room. I think it would be in your best interests if you were to erase our little conversation here today. I don't think Langley would be too pleased if it were to fall into the wrong hands, do you?'

FOUR

The exclusive residential suburb of San Benito lies on the slopes of El Boqueron, the dormant twin-peaked volcano which towers over the city of San Salvador, dominating the skyline. It's an affluent area lined with stylish boutiques carrying the latest designer clothes fresh from the catwalks of Europe, expensive restaurants catering for all tastes of international cuisine, and glitzy nightclubs where the rich and famous can dance through the night until the early hours of the morning. The majority of the suburb's sumptuous mansions are protected by closed-circuit television cameras concealed behind high brick walls, which are topped with layers of barbed wire and, in some cases, electrified fencing. Few would dare to be seen without the latest model of Mercedes, BMW or Porsche in the driveway.

Yet on the periphery of San Benito lie some of the city's worst *mesónes*, the shanty-town slums, where rows of rickety houses constructed from rusted sheets of zinc and warped plywood boards are held together with little more than a prayer. These wretched structures are piled on top of each other, like a ramshackle colonnade of grotesquely disfigured sentinels watching over the splendour of their more fortunate and opulent neighbours.

The irony of these stark contrasts wasn't lost on Nicole as the chauffeur-driven Mercedes wound its way through the tranquil streets of San Benito.

'Most of the residents of San Benito choose to ignore the slums,' Dennison replied when she raised the subject.

'It's one of the main reasons why the security measures have remained intact around here even though the civil war has officially come to an end. There's a new menace in society now. Crime. And as it is in any community anywhere in the world today, those who "have" will go to any lengths to keep it that way. They don't want the poor encroaching on their territory. So they take the necessary precautions to protect themselves. Most of these properties are patrolled around the clock by armed guards.'

'Supplied by your security firm?'

'Many of them do work for me, yes,' Dennison conceded with a nod. 'Most are ex-soldiers who were only too glad of the work after the military was almost halved when the ceasefire was signed.'

'You make it sound as if you don't approve of what happened to the military,' Nicole said, casting a sidelong glance at Dennison.

'The National Guard recruited many of the soldiers straight from school. It was the only life they knew. Then when the military was decimated by a bunch of politicians at the negotiating table, these young men were thrown out into the street with little or no money, and no real prospect of ever holding down another job. There's a lot of resentment in this country about how the armed forces conducted themselves during the civil war. Sadly most of this resentment has been fuelled by unsubstantiated allegations from left-wing politicians of so-called military atrocities which were supposedly carried out against the civilian population; unfortunately these prejudices have now been allowed to spill over into the employment arena as well. It's a disgrace that these young men should be treated like this after all they've done for their country.' Dennison gave Nicole a rueful smile. 'It's just that I've heard the same story so many times from my employees. These men are very bitter towards the government.'

'It sounds as if they've got every right to be,' Nicole said, finding herself agreeing with him before she could stop herself.

'The house is just up ahead,' Dennison announced. 'I'm sure you'll like it.'

When the Mercedes came to a halt in front of a pair of black wrought-iron gates, a guard dressed in khaki fatigues and a brown peaked cap emerged from a small hut inside the property and peered suspiciously at the car through the gates, his hand resting lightly on the Uzi sub-machine gun which was draped menacingly across his chest. The driver activated his window and shouted to the guard, who acknowledged him with a wave then unhooked a remote control from his belt and used it to activate the gates. The guard snapped to attention and saluted as the car drove past, using the remote control to close the gates again before disappearing back into the hut.

The Mercedes continued up the tree-lined driveway for another fifty metres before turning off on to a spacious gravel courtyard. Beyond the courtyard lay an imposing Spanish-styled double-storey mansion, with a red-brick roof and whitewashed exterior walls which contrasted vividly with the open black louvred shutters on all the windows. The driver brought the car to a halt in front of the portico, switched off the engine, then got out and opened the back door for Nicole. A uniformed maid, whom Nicole estimated to be roughly the same age as herself, emerged from the house and crossed the portico to greet her warmly in Spanish.

'This is Manuela,' Dennison said, indicating the maid. 'She's the housekeeper. I'm afraid she doesn't speak any English. She lives on the premises with her husband. He's the resident chauffeur. His name's Raoul. He's already gone to the airport to collect your luggage. He should be back shortly. Unfortunately he doesn't speak any English either but, should you want to go anywhere, just write the address down and give it to him. He'll get you there.'

'I will, thank you,' she replied.

'So what do you think?' Dennison asked, gesturing towards the house.

'I like it, I really do,' she replied truthfully. 'I can imagine that your clients must be pretty impressed with it as well.'

'They're more impressed with not having to pay for any hotel accommodation while they're in town,' Dennison replied with a smile, then led her towards a wooden gate at the opposite end of the courtyard. He unlocked it, then stepped aside and gestured for her to enter.

She stepped tentatively through the door and whistled softly to herself as she slowly took in her decorative surroundings. An ornately paved pathway led off from the covered patio at the back of the house, and wound its way intricately through myriad small, multicoloured flowerbeds to a diamond-shaped swimming pool in the centre of the lush green lawn. A gardener, stripped to the waist, was sweeping the tennis court at the other end of the garden. As soon as he noticed Dennison, he immediately gave him a respectful bow.

Dennison acknowledged him with a quick wave, then moved to the umbrella-shaded table next to the swimming pool and sat down. He watched as Nicole crouched down beside the pool and trailed her fingers lightly through the shimmering water. 'Do you swim?' he asked.

'When I can,' Nicole replied. 'But it's Michelle who really loves swimming. Her favourite beach's the Oak Street Beach on the Gold Coast. Unfortunately it's also the busiest of the beaches around the Chicago area, especially on the weekends. But you know what kids are like. The more people there are around them, the more fun they seem to have. Personally, I'd rather . . .' She trailed off with a sheepish smile. 'Listen to me. All you did was ask a simple question and I end up giving you a guided tour of Chicago's beaches.'

'On the contrary,' Dennison replied. 'I'm grateful for

any insight you can give me into Michelle's character. At the moment all I have to go on is a face in a photograph. I'd certainly like to know more about her.'

'You've certainly come to the right person,' Nicole replied as she continued to brush her fingers in the water. 'I wish I'd brought a swimming costume with me now. I guess I'll have to go into town and buy one.'

'No need. There're plenty of costumes in the house,' Dennison told her. 'I throw a lot of pool parties here for the simple reason that there's more pool space than I have at my own house. I'm sure you'll find a costume that fits.'

'I may take you up on that,' she said, then crossed to the table and sat down opposite Dennison. 'Where do you live? Here in San Benito?'

Dennison nodded. 'My house's not five minutes' drive from here. I'd be glad to show it to you. Perhaps you'd like to come round for dinner tonight? Then we could talk more about Michelle.'

For a moment Nicole was caught in a dilemma. If Dennison was part of the conspiracy to overthrow the government, then she'd be a fool to venture any information that could aid him and his co-conspirators in their search for Michelle. But what if Rick was wrong about Dennison? What if he had nothing to do with the conspiracy? She knew that her gut feeling was still to trust Rick's instincts, but at the same time she was only too well aware that Michelle was still somewhere out there, probably very frightened and alone . . .

'Ah, refreshments,' Dennison announced, clapping his hands together as Manuela emerged from the kitchen with a tray.

Nicole was grateful for the distraction. She watched as Manuela carefully filled the two glasses with the cold mixture from the jug, which she then left on the table before returning to the house. Nicole picked up the glass in front of her. 'Is this some exotic Salvadorean drink?'

'It's nothing more exotic than fruit juice, I'm afraid,' Dennison replied. 'But it's very refreshing on a day like this.'

Nicole took a sip. Mango juice. And it was refreshing. She proceeded to drink down half the contents of the glass, then sat back in her chair. 'I could get used to this,' she said, stretching out her bare legs to catch the rays of the sun.

'I already have,' Dennison replied with a smile. 'I couldn't ever imagine living anywhere else. Not now. The only reason I still carry an American passport is to make it easier when I travel abroad. Apart from that, I consider myself a Salvadorean.'

'Some say that the only way to judge true patriotism is if you'd actually be prepared to die for your country,' Nicole said, swilling the remainder of her drink around in her glass. 'Or, as in your case, your adopted country. Would you die for this country?'

'Gladly,' Dennison replied without hesitation. 'Perhaps they should apply that rule to the endless number of immigrants who flood into the United States every year. It might just help to weed out the parasites from the genuine cases. But then I'm sure the human rights activists would have something to say about that. The strange thing is, I've never heard any of them complaining when American citizens lose their jobs to these so-called political refugees.'

'And what would you do with all those immigrants who didn't conform to your rule?' Nicole asked, holding Dennison's stare. 'Send them back home to face possible torture and death at the hands of some autocratic regime?'

'What is a political refugee other than a troublemaker in his home country?'

Nicole shook her head slowly to herself. 'I think we'd better just agree to disagree on this and leave it at that.'

Dennison chuckled. 'As you wish. But to get back to

your original point, what country would you be prepared to die for? From what I understand, you grew up in Africa of French parentage, and now live in the United States. It's an interesting equation, isn't it?'

'I'm nomadic,' Nicole replied. 'I have been since childhood. And there's no place for patriotism in a nomadic environment. My only loyalty is to my daughter.'

'That's very admirable,' Dennison said. His eyes flickered past Nicole to a figure who had appeared at the gate. Dennison beckoned the man towards them, then got to his feet and welcomed him with a firm handshake. As Nicole studied the man she could swear that she'd seen him somewhere before. He was in his early forties, with a neatly trimmed black moustache and thinning black hair, which was combed back carefully over his head to best conceal the bald spot. She continued to stare at him as the two men spoke together in Spanish. She was now absolutely certain that she knew the face. But from where?

Dennison turned to her. 'This is the man I told you about at the embassy – he's the head of the President's élite bodyguard who's now officially in charge of the investigation into Bob Kinnard's death. Ms Nicole Auger, Colonel Hector Amaya.'

Suddenly Rick's words came back to her: *When I was last there Dennison's best friend was a Major Hector Amaya, a senior officer in the Atlacatl battalion, the élite unit in the Salvadorean military . . . Amaya was also said to have had close links with the death squads . . .* It was then she realized where she'd seen him. He'd been standing beside Dennison in the wedding photograph that Pruitt had shown her at the apartment the previous day.

'You look as if you've just seen a ghost,' Amaya said to her.

'I'm sorry, I just suddenly felt very light-headed,' Nicole replied, furious with herself for letting down her guard that easily. She instinctively rubbed her temple gingerly, hoping

93

it hadn't looked too theatrical. 'I guess I'm just not acclima-tized to this heat yet.'

'You look as if you could do with a few hours' rest,' Amaya said, pulling up the vacant chair and sitting down.

'I think that would be a good idea,' Dennison agreed. 'It certainly wouldn't do you any harm. And if we were to hear anything about your daughter, we'd be sure to wake you straight away.'

'I'll be fine, thanks,' she replied, without taking her eyes off Amaya. 'Where did you learn to speak English?'

'At a night school here in San Salvador, while I was still a junior officer in the National Guard. I was also privileged to have trained with the 82nd Airborne at Fort Bragg in North Carolina. That's where I picked up some of your more colourful expressions. If nothing else, American ser-vicemen certainly know how to express themselves.'

'Don't I know,' Nicole said with a smile.

'Marlette was never in the American army, was he?' Dennison asked.

Nicole shook her head. 'No. He spent five years with the French Foreign Legion then left to team up with Brad Casey in North Africa.'

'I know Casey well,' Amaya said. 'He was my main contact in the States when I was in charge of recruiting foreign nationals to help train the National Guard. Do you see anything of him these days?'

You scheming bastard, she thought angrily to herself, but she quickly put her emotions in check before she spoke. 'Brad's dead. He was shot yesterday at his bar in New York.'

'That's awful,' Amaya replied. 'Do the police have any idea who did it?'

'I believe they've got a few leads,' she lied. Neither showed any alarm. Not that it surprised her. These were cold, calculating professionals.

94

'Talking of leads, how's the investigation coming on?' Dennison asked Amaya.

'We're still working on this Cockney angle. It's the best lead we've got up to now. Or perhaps I should say it's the *only* lead we've got up to now. So far we haven't come up with anything from the passenger records at the airport, but if, as I suspect, he was travelling on a false passport, then it could take some time to eliminate all the possible suspects. We're already liaising with Interpol to help clear the backlog of names.' Amaya gave Nicole a despondent look. 'I'm sorry it looks so bleak at the moment, but I can assure you that we will find this man. And when we do, he'll be brought to justice.'

'Right now I'm more concerned about finding Michelle than I am about bringing Bob's killer to justice.'

'As I am,' Dennison assured her.

I bet you are, Nicole thought caustically to herself.

Amaya looked at his watch. 'You'll have to excuse me. I've got to get back to headquarters for a briefing. Ms Auger, I'll need you to formally identify the body at the mortuary. Would it be convenient for me to pick you up here at, say, four o'clock this afternoon and take you there?'

'Yes, that would be fine,' Nicole replied sombrely.

'Thank you,' Amaya said, then pushed back his chair and stood up.

'You'll have to excuse me as well,' Dennison said, draining his glass and getting to his feet. 'I still haven't been in to my office today, and when I last rang my secretary she said that the messages were already piling up on my desk. I assume that we're still on for dinner this evening?'

Nicole had forgotten about that. Not that she'd given him a reply one way or another. But what could she say? She could hardly turn him down. 'Yes, of course,' she replied, desperately trying to inject some enthusiasm into her voice.

'Good. I'll have my driver fetch you at eight.' Dennison turned to Amaya. 'You're most welcome to join us.'

'Unfortunately I've got a meeting scheduled with the President for seven-thirty this evening,' Amaya replied. 'He wants a complete update on the investigation so far.'

The two men left Nicole by the swimming pool and walked to the wooden gate at the end of the garden.

'What do you make of her?' Amaya asked, switching to Spanish as he closed the gate behind them.

'Feisty's the word that springs to mind. I took her to see Hersch at the embassy before we came here. She knew that Marlette had been deported from El Salvador, only she didn't know why, so Hersch in his wisdom decided that she should be told. She didn't believe a word of it. She even told Hersch that the embassy must have been gullible to have believed the story in the first place. And the more Hersch tried to defend the embassy, the more she laid into him.' Dennison chuckled to himself. 'You should have seen his face. I think he was glad to see the back of her.'

'What did you find out about Marlette?'

'She admitted that she went to see him in New York yesterday, but said that he'd refused to help her.'

'Do you believe her?' Amaya asked as they reached Dennison's Mercedes.

Dennison dismissed his driver with a curt flick of the hand when he hurried forward to open the back door for him. He waited until the driver was out of earshot before answering. 'No, I don't,' was his blunt reply.

'So you think he's already in El Salvador?'

'I think there's every possibility of it, yes,' Dennison replied, leaning back against the side of the car and folding his arms across his chest.

'Word amongst the mercenary fraternity in New York is that he's already left for Bosnia,' Amaya said. 'There's even a booking in his name on a flight which left for Sarajevo earlier this morning.'

'It's too much of a coincidence. My guess is that it's a decoy to try and throw us off the scent. It's exactly the sort of thing Marlette would do. He knows what would happen to him if he were ever caught inside El Salvador again.'

'Have you already given the order for him to be shot on sight?' Amaya asked.

'No, I want him taken alive,' Dennison replied to Amaya's surprise, then went on to explain what Hersch had said to him in private at the embassy.

'If Marlette were to retrieve the tape first, the whole coup would be in jeopardy,' Amaya said in dismay once Dennison had finished speaking.

'I've got over a hundred of my men combing the length and breadth of the country for that kid. They've all been specifically assigned to particular regions because they know those areas like the backs of their hands. And you're worried that Marlette, who once spent less than six months here in San Salvador, is going to find her by himself?'

'Don't underestimate Marlette,' Amaya warned.

'I've no intention of underestimating him,' Dennison replied. 'But Marlette will need contacts here in El Salvador if he's going to have any chance of getting his plan off the ground, and you can be sure that my men will pick up on any unusual activity in the districts. Don't worry, Hector, the situation's well under control. The coup will go ahead as planned in two days' time.'

'For your sake, I certainly hope so.'

Marlette knew of the perilous dangers facing the big jets on their final approach to Tegucigalpa's Toncontin International Airport, even though it was the first time he'd been to Honduras. He'd worked with several mercs who'd all told him the same story about Tegucigalpa – the city is hemmed in on all sides by a sea of hills which means that a pilot has to wait until the very last moment before making an extremely fast descent on to the short runway, where he then has to call on all his guile and experience to bring the aeroplane to a halt. Each year there were fatal crashes on the approach to the airport, with the result that more and more flights were now being rerouted to San Pedro Sula's Ramon Villiera Morales Airport in the north of the country. Marlette had never been the best of flyers to begin with, and although he'd have preferred the safer approach of San Pedro Sula, the fact remained that Tegucigalpa, situated in southern Honduras, was barely an hour's drive to the border with El Salvador. And that was what really mattered . . .

Marlette had, as usual, chosen an aisle seat, and although he'd kept his eyes fixed firmly on the seat in front of him as the jumbo jet made its final, sharp descent towards the runway, he couldn't seem to shake the disturbing thought that the slightest pilot error could leave him as just another statistic on some future IASA report. What a way to be remembered! In the event Marlette's worst fears were unfounded when the pilot executed a faultless landing and taxied the aeroplane to the apron in front of the terminal building. Marlette was one of the first passengers to disembark. As he emerged out into the fierce sunlight, he slipped on his dark glasses. He'd forgotten just how sticky the weather could get in Central America, and was grateful to enter the cool terminal, where he joined one of the lengthening queues waiting to pass through immigration control.

The official eyed Marlette suspiciously when he finally approached the booth. Marlette removed his sunglasses and greeted the man cordially in Spanish as he slid his flight ticket, false passport and visa through the narrow aperture at the foot of the glass partition. He'd heard stories about Honduras being one of the more difficult countries in Central America for a foreigner to enter. He knew of one merc who'd been turned back because he didn't have a return ticket, and another who'd been refused entry because he had a Libyan immigration stamp in his passport. But Marlette felt completely at ease as he watched the official slowly page through his passport – he knew that the CIA would have done their homework and all the validated 'stamps' would be of countries which already had diplomatic ties with Honduras. They couldn't afford any slip-ups. When the official tried to question him in broken English about his intended movements once he entered Honduras, Marlette was quick to tell him that he could understand Spanish. He could see that this put the official at ease, and he knew then that half the battle had already been won. He had to produce evidence of where he would be staying, as well as of the amount of money he was bringing into the country. Once the official had established these details, he flicked through Marlette's passport and his flight ticket again before finally reaching for his stamp. He selected a clean page in the passport, stamped it, then returned the documents to Marlette.

Marlette found his way to the baggage carousel, where he collected his single suitcase before making his way out into the main concourse.

'*Señor* Graves?' a voice queried beside him.

Marlette recognized the man from the photograph which Pruitt had left with him at the apartment. He nodded, then, as agreed with Pruitt, he produced his passport and gave it to the man who opened it, checked the photograph, then returned it and gestured for Marlette to follow him. The man waved aside the taxi-drivers who hovered hopefully outside the main doors, and led Marlette to a green Peugeot in the car park. Within minutes they had left the airport and were heading south on the Pan American Highway towards the border with El Salvador. The man turned out to be one of those infuriatingly loquacious types and, even though Marlette made it obvious from the start that he was in no mood for small-talk, the man was quite happy to carry the conversation by himself.

Fifty minutes later they turned off the highway close to the border town of Goascoran, continuing for another few kilometres until they reached an abandoned gas station. Here they pulled up behind a battered white Ford pick-up truck. Marlette watched as his driver approached the Ford driver's window, but couldn't hear what he said to the lone occupant in the cab. Finally he beckoned to Marlette, who got out of the passenger seat. As Marlette was reaching for his suitcase on the back seat, the truck door opened and the driver jumped out. It was a woman in her twenties. A deep scar ran from her left earlobe to the base of her neck. She stabbed her thumb impatiently towards the truck.

Marlette nodded, quickly transferring a few clothes from his suitcase to the hold-all. He left the suitcase in the car – it would be placed in a locker at the airport for him to pick up again on his return to Tegucigalpa. He crossed to the Ford, tossed the hold-all into the back of the truck, then climbed into the passenger seat. Wordlessly the woman started up the truck and pulled away from the Peugeot in a cloud of dust. Once clear of the gas station, she pointed to a rucksack on the floor at Marlette's feet. He placed it carefully in his lap and unfastened the straps. Inside were the weapons on the list he'd given Pruitt in New York. Like so many of his fellow professionals, he swore by the Heckler & Koch brand name. Their weaponry had certainly saved his life on several occasions in the past. The rucksack contained a P9S automatic pistol with five spare nine-round magazines and an MP5 sub-machine gun with five thirty-round boxes. Also included were a set of camouflage army fatigues, a Buckmaster survival knife with a twenty-centimetre serrated blade, and a pair of powerful Zeiss binoculars. There were holsters for both the pistol and the knife. It was all there. He replaced the rucksack on the floor, then asked the driver how far they were from the border. She replied by opening and closing her hand twice in succession. Ten kilometres? She nodded, pointing to her mouth. It was then that Marlette saw to his horror that her tongue had been cut out.

The dirt road seemed to go on for ever without them coming across another living soul – obviously the reason why it had been chosen in the first place – and although Marlette couldn't be sure of when exactly they had crossed the border into El Salvador, an educated guess was when the woman began to weave the truck between a succession of land-mine craters in the road. Then, as the truck turned into another corner, he saw the rusted, burnt-out shell of a military transport vehicle which had long been abandoned in a ditch at the side of the road. The letters 'FMLN', now faded from the incessant exposure to the elements, had been daubed across the side of it in red paint. He knew then that they were finally in El Salvador. The initials stood for *Farabundo Marti Frente de Liberación Nacional*, the Farabundo Marti National Liberation Front, by far the most popular and powerful of the Marxist guerrilla movements during the country's lengthy civil war. At the ceasefire negotiations, the FMLN had agreed to disband the armed wing of their organization if the government agreed to cut their own armed forces by half. They had also agreed to drop their long-standing demand to be a part of any future coalition government. Both these resolutions had proved invaluable to the signing of the final ceasefire on 1 January 1992. Although Marlette had heard rumours that a hard core of FMLN guerrillas had refused to lay down their arms after the ceasefire, and had regrouped in the north of the country where many of the locals were still sympathetic to their cause, he had yet to see any tangible proof of these allegations. Not that it bothered him unduly. As far as he was concerned, the civil war was now officially over. He wasn't being paid to be a part of the fight against the rebels. Not any more.

A sharp tug on his sweat-soaked sleeve brought him out of his reverie. He saw that the woman was pointing to a village in the distance. The dirt road led straight into the town square, and she brought the truck to a shuddering halt in front of the steps of the red-brick church which dominated the rest of the settlement. He took in the solid oak doors which led into the sanctuary of the church, then his eyes went to the bullet-holes which pock-marked the walls on either side of the door – a reminder that over the years the civil war had reached every corner of this small country. Tiny hands grabbed at Marlette as he got out of the truck, and he looked down at the grinning faces of the children who clung on to his arms as if he were their own father. He noticed that many of them were wearing an array of flattened bullets, which had obviously been dug out of the church wall, on pieces of string around their necks. It angered him to see just how much the civil war had destroyed the innocence of youth. He crouched down in the centre of the milling children and beckoned the nearest child towards him. The boy hurried forward, and Marlette brushed his fingers across the boy's ear. When Marlette opened his hand he had a shiny fifty-centavo coin in his palm. The boy instinctively patted his ear, a look of amazement on his face, then he giggled delightedly and quickly plucked the coin from Marlette's hand. Marlette then pulled a handful of change from his pocket and tossed the coins on to the ground. He left the children squabbling over the money and, slinging a strap of the rucksack over his shoulder, he grabbed his hold-all from the back of the truck, giving the driver a thumbs-up sign as he did so. She started up the truck, engaged gears, and did a U-turn before driving away.

Marlette heard a noise behind him. When he looked round he saw a young priest standing on the steps of the church. '*Padre* Lorenzo?' he enquired of the man.

'*Sí*,' came the reply.

'I assume that Father Coughlin told you I was coming?' Marlette asked in Spanish.

Lorenzo nodded. 'Yes, he told me. When I heard you were on your way from the airport I radioed the news through to him. He said he would arrange for a car to come and pick you up. It should be here within the next hour.'

'Thank you.'

'I don't want your gratitude,' Lorenzo said tersely. 'I just want you out of my village as soon as possible. Believe me, if it wasn't for Father Coughlin I would never have agreed to any of this. I heard about what you did to that girl in San Salvador. You and your kind have no place here.'

'You shouldn't believe everything you hear, Father,' Marlette replied tetchily. He wiped the sweat from his forehead with the back of his hand. 'May I wait inside until the car gets here?'

'What do you have in those bags?' Lorenzo demanded. 'Guns?'

Marlette looked down at the boy who'd appeared beside him, the shiny new fifty-centavo coin still clutched tightly in his hand. He ruffled the boy's hair then looked up at Lorenzo again. 'I think you know the answer to that question already.'

'Then you leave the bag out here. I will not have any guns in my church.'

'You want me to leave them out here for these kids to find?' Marlette asked. 'You know as well as I do how inquisitive they can be at their age.'

Lorenzo watched the children playing in the square behind him. 'Come inside,' he said abruptly, then disappeared back into the church. Marlette picked up his hold-all and went after the priest. The boy was quick to follow him up the stairs and into the church.

'*Padre, Padre!*' a voice shouted anxiously behind them. Marlette looked round to find a teenage girl running towards the church.

Lorenzo, who had been alerted by the tone of the girl's

voice, brushed past Marlette and hurried down the steps, where he had to grab her as she almost collided with him.

'*Soldados*,' she said breathlessly, gesturing excitedly towards the approach road.

Soldiers. Marlette cursed under his breath. It was all he needed. What if they'd intercepted the driver outside the village? How long would she last under interrogation? And where would that leave him?

Lorenzo looked up at Marlette. 'Are the soldiers looking for you?'

'It's possible,' Marlette admitted.

Lorenzo told the girl to round up all the children and take them down to the river. At least they would be out of harm's way if the soldiers decided to search the village. He then hurried up the stairs and, grabbing Marlette's arm, propelled him through the door and into the church. 'I don't know why you've come to El Salvador, and frankly I don't care, but right now your very presence here could be putting the lives of all the villagers at risk. That I do care about.'

'So what do you intend to do? Hand me over to the soldiers when they get here?'

'I promised Father Coughlin that you'd be safe here until the car arrived to take you to San Salvador. I intend to keep my word,' Lorenzo replied. 'There's an outhouse at the back of the church. You can hide in there until they've gone.'

Marlette followed Lorenzo round the side of the church to a wooden outhouse situated close to the vestry. Lorenzo pulled open the door and beckoned Marlette inside. Marlette entered the room and looked around him slowly. Two broken wooden crates stood in one corner, and half a dozen sacks of maize had been dumped against the far wall. One of the sacks was torn and maize lay scattered across the floor. The floorboards creaked as Lorenzo crossed to the nearest sack and, gritting his teeth, he dragged it aside to reveal a trapdoor underneath. As he opened the door, Marlette peered cautiously into the aperture. He couldn't make out anything in the darkness below.

'What's down there?' he asked suspiciously.

'It's part of the old sewer,' Lorenzo told him. 'Now hurry up before the soldiers get here.'

Marlette tossed the hold-all through the aperture and heard it land with a thud on the ground. 'Put the torn sack over the trapdoor and throw some maize on the floor around it. That way it'll look less suspicious.'

'OK. Now *go!*' Lorenzo urged him anxiously.

Marlette descended the rusted ladder and grimaced as his fingers brushed against the intricate network of spiderwebs which were laced between the rungs of the ladder. When he reached the foot of the ladder, he could feel the hard ground underneath his feet. As Lorenzo closed the trapdoor above him, he was enveloped in darkness. He heard the sack being dragged back over the trapdoor followed by the rattling sound of maize being scattered across the floor. He heard Lorenzo's footsteps as they crossed to the door – then silence.

Easing the rucksack off his shoulder, Marlette crouched down on his haunches. What he'd have given for a lighter. Or a box of matches. For the first time since he'd kicked the habit, he regretted having given up smoking. Pushing the thought from his mind, he knew that he'd need to be armed in case he was discovered. He certainly wouldn't have any qualms about killing any of the soldiers – not if it meant coming out of this alive. He felt for the rucksack at his feet and managed to open the straps. When he found the pistol he slipped it into the back of his trousers. Suddenly he heard voices. Moments later came the sound of footsteps on the floorboards above him. Although the voices were now directly above him, they were too muffled for him to hear what was being said.

Then came the sound of a maize sack being dragged

across the floor. Marlette pushed the rucksack behind him, then eased the automatic from his belt and shrank back against the ladder. The trapdoor was pulled open and a powerful torch beam was played down into the narrow corridor. Using the light from the torch he was able to assess his surroundings. Quickly he ducked down behind the ladder; now he was completely out of sight of the aperture above him. The sweat stung his eyes mercilessly, but he knew he couldn't move for fear of casting a shadow across the corridor walls. The beam arced across the crumbling brick wall opposite him and, as he shrank further away from the light source, he suddenly felt something on the side of his neck. He realized it was a spider and, as the tips of its legs slowly probed his skin, with every tentative step he struggled to fight back the urge to brush it off. Then came the sound of a thick-soled boot being stamped down on to the first rung of the ladder. The bastard was coming down for a closer look. Gripping the automatic more tightly in his hands, he slowly raised the barrel until it was trained on the ladder above him.

'What are you doing here?' a voice demanded above him and for a horrifying moment Marlette thought he'd been discovered.

'Are you looking for someone?' came the reply.

Marlette could feel the relief flood through him. It was the boy's voice.

'Yes. A *Yanqui*. He's about six foot tall and he speaks good Spanish. Have you seen him?'

Marlette held his breath. All the kid had to do was tell the truth. And weren't kids so good at that at all the wrong times?

'No,' came the reply.

'What's that you've got there?'

'Fifty centavos,' the boy replied.

'And where does a boy like you get a shiny new fifty-centavo coin?' the voice demanded. 'Did you steal it?'

'No,' the boy replied nervously.

'Then who gave it to you?'

'I did.'

For a moment the new voice caught Marlette by surprise. Then he recognized it as Father Lorenzo's.

'I got it as part of my change when I was last shopping in San Miguel,' Lorenzo continued. 'You don't find many new coins around here, so I thought it would be nice to give it to Eduardo. Is there a problem with that?'

The man snorted in disgust, then climbed back up into the room and slammed the trapdoor shut behind him. Marlette waited until the voices had faded into the distance, then brought his hand down savagely on to the spider which had already reached the corner of his mouth. Quickly brushing the sticky remains off his cheek, he ducked out from under the ladder and took a handkerchief from his pocket, gratefully wiping away the intricate mesh of cobwebs plastered to his sweating face.

Suddenly the trapdoor opened above him, flooding the narrow corridor with light. Marlette instinctively swung the automatic upwards, his finger already curled around the trigger. It was the boy. Marlette cursed inwardly and immediately lowered the pistol, but he could see from the fear in the boy's eyes that the damage had already been done.

'The soldiers have gone,' the boy said, then lowered the trapdoor back on to the floor and disappeared from sight.

Marlette replaced the pistol in the rucksack, which he slung over his shoulder, then, picking up the hold-all, he climbed back up the ladder and crossed to where the boy was standing at the door. 'I didn't mean to frighten you,' he said, crouching beside the boy. 'I thought you were one of the soldiers. I'm sorry.'

'They were not soldiers,' the boy said as he walked off.

Marlette hurried after him. 'Hey, Eduardo, wait up.' The

boy stopped abruptly, surprised that the stranger knew his name. 'What do you mean, they weren't soldiers?' Marlette asked.

'They did not look like soldiers,' the boy replied.

'Eduardo's right, they weren't regular soldiers,' Lorenzo said, appearing at the vestry door. 'It's my guess they were ex-soldiers. It was obvious from the way they searched the area around the church that they had some kind of military training. Most probably in the National Guard. But these men were all unshaven and the army fatigues they were wearing were torn and unwashed. One of them even had long hair. Also, the jeep they were driving bore no military insignia at all. Whatever else is wrong with the army in this country, they always pride themselves on their appearance. That's why I'm so sure they weren't serving soldiers.' He looked at his watch. 'Your transport should be here within the next twenty minutes. You can wait in the church until it arrives.'

'You said earlier that you have a radio set. Can you put me through to Coughlin? I need to talk to him before I leave.'

Lorenzo gestured to the vestry behind him. 'The radio's through there. I'll see what I can do.'

Marlette was about to thank him, but he thought better of it and followed him silently into the vestry. He dumped the rucksack and hold-all in the corner of the room, then stood by the door, his arms folded across his chest, as Lorenzo tried to contact Coughlin at the orphanage in San Salvador. When he finally got through, the call was answered by one of Coughlin's staff, who told him that the priest was busy teaching a class in another room. 'It's imperative that I speak to Coughlin,' Marlette told Lorenzo, and Lorenzo passed on the message.

'They're going to fetch him,' he assured Marlette, then got to his feet and gestured to the chair he'd just vacated. 'I assume you know how to operate the radio?'

Marlette sat down and slipped the headphones over his ears. 'I'll be fine, thank you, Father.'

Lorenzo left the vestry. Marlette was still waiting for Coughlin when Eduardo entered, carrying a tray. It contained a mug of black coffee and a half a dozen piping hot *pupusas*, small corn tortillas which can be stuffed with a variety of fillings and are widely regarded as the national dish of El Salvador. These *pupusas* were filled with melted cheese.

'My mother made them,' the boy announced proudly. 'She let me bring you these.'

Marlette thanked the boy and helped himself to one. He'd forgotten how good they tasted. He washed it down with a mouthful of coffee. It had always amazed him that for a country whose chief export was coffee, the local brand was consistently weak and lacking in flavour. Obviously the best was exported for foreign consumption.

'Hello, this is Father Coughlin,' a harassed voice announced in Spanish over the radio.

'And this is your favourite rock 'n' roll mercenary,' Marlette replied with a grin.

'Richie?' Coughlin said in surprise.

'The very same. I had Father Lorenzo patch me through to the orphanage, although I get the distinct feeling that he doesn't exactly approve of me.'

'He's a good man at heart.'

'I doubt he'd say the same about me,' Marlette replied dryly. 'I just wanted to know whether Nicole had arrived safely in San Salvador.'

'She got in a couple of hours ago. Dennison was at the airport to meet her. But there's a problem, Richie.'

Marlette slowly lowered the *pupusa* he was about to ingest and replaced it on the plate. 'What sort of problem?' he asked suspiciously.

'I've heard from a contact of mine that Dennison cancelled Nicole's reservation at the Sheraton.'

'Where's she staying now?'

'I don't know yet, but what I do know is that she hasn't been booked into any of the other major hotels in the city,' Coughlin replied. 'It's my guess that Dennison's put her up at his guest-house in San Benito. And that's where the real problem lies. The place is like a fortress. If she is staying there, I won't be able to get anywhere near it, not without Dennison knowing.'

'Which is obviously why he did it in the first place. Only he expected me to contact Nicole once I reached San Salvador, so the more he disrupts my operation, the more chance he'll have of recovering the tape first.'

'So you think he already suspects that you're in the country?' Coughlin asked.

'Of course he does,' came the disdainful reply. 'There's already been a deputation here looking for me since I arrived. I didn't see them, but Lorenzo said that they weren't National Guard. They're more likely to have been ex-soldiers.'

'That makes sense. Apart from the regular army and the police, Dennison's also brought in over a hundred of his own men from his security firm to spearhead the search. They're all ex-soldiers, many of them Atlacatl veterans, and each team is being led by an experienced tracker.'

'It's just as well then that I'm getting out of here. I'll speak to you again once I reach San Salvador. Hopefully you'll have been in touch with Nicole by then.'

'If she is at Dennison's guest-house, then she's going to have to make contact first. I just hope she realizes that.'

'She will,' came the assured reply. 'You can be sure of that.'

FIVE

Nicole decided against going for a swim after Dennison and Amaya had left the house. Instead she went up to her bedroom, where she found that her luggage had been placed neatly at the foot of her bed. She stripped off her travelling clothes then went through to the bathroom and switched on the shower. She adjusted the temperature of the water until it was hot, then stepped into the cubicle and closed the door behind her. Tilting back her head, she closed her eyes and felt her body relax as the concentrated jet of steaming water massaged her tired, aching limbs.

Her mind, however, remained alert as she thought back over the hours since her arrival in San Salvador. She knew there was no way of proving whether there had been any reporters waiting for her at the airport, but the fact still remained that Dennison now held the upper hand. She was isolated on his territory, playing by his rules. It was going to be that much harder to make contact with Rick. She was still confident she could do it without alerting Dennison, but first she would have to get in touch with Coughlin. Again, it would be difficult now that Dennison had changed the rules to suit himself. Or should she say Dennison and Amaya? It had caught her by surprise when Amaya had arrived at the house. This was the same man who'd once been the military's liaison with one of the most notorious death squads in the country, a man who was now the head of the Presidential élite bodyguard. But what was even more disturbing was how he'd managed to inveigle his way into taking charge of the investigation into

Bob's death. Or had Dennison had a quiet word with the President on his behalf? Did Dennison really wield that kind of influence within government circles? It was certainly a frightening thought. But whatever they'd done, it had certainly worked to their advantage. She was convinced they were involved in the plot to overthrow the government – and now that they were both in a position of supreme authority, it would make it that much easier for them to recover the tape that had ultimately cost Bob his life. And where would that leave her? But more worrying, where would it leave Michelle? Suddenly, those harrowing words came back to haunt her again – *no witnesses, no comebacks* . . .

She opened her eyes abruptly as the fearful thought flashed through her mind, then, switching off the hot water, she activated the cold tap and grimaced as an icy jet of water cascaded down on to her. Thirty seconds later she turned off the tap and stepped out of the shower. After drying herself she slipped on the white towelling robe which was hanging behind the door. When she returned to the bedroom, she found that her dirty clothes had been removed from where she'd discarded them. On further investigation she also discovered that her suitcase had been unpacked and her clothes arranged neatly in the wardrobe. The photograph of Michelle that she'd brought with her had been placed carefully beside the telephone on the bedside table. An Avis street map of the city had also been left for her convenience on the table. It certainly beat staying in a hotel, she thought to herself as she selected a pair of baggy jeans and a white blouse to wear. She dressed quickly and, after running a comb through her damp hair, slipped on a pair of plimsolls and grabbed her purse off the chair on her way to the door. She'd descended the stairs and was making her way to the front door when Manuela emerged from the kitchen at the end of the corridor and called out to her in Spanish. Nicole shrugged helplessly, not understanding what she'd said. Manuela smiled and repeated herself, this time more slowly. Not that it helped. Nicole still didn't understand a word of it.

'Raoul?' Manuela said, pointing to the door, then made as if she were holding a steering wheel.

'No, I'm just going out for a walk,' Nicole replied, using two fingers to simulate a walking motion.

Manuela dug her hand into the pocket of her housecoat, removed a key and handed it to Nicole. She indicated the front door, then said something else in Spanish which Nicole didn't understand. Nicole tried the key in the door. It worked. '*Gracias*,' she said, slipping the key into her purse.

Manuela waited until Nicole was clear of the portico before closing the door. She crossed to the nearest telephone and dialled a number she'd long since consigned to memory – Dennison's private line at his office on the Boulevard de los Heroes.

'*Hola?*' came the brusque reply.

'This is Manuela, sir,' she said in English. 'The woman has just left the house. On foot.'

'Tell Raoul to keep an eye on her,' Dennison replied. 'I want to know where she goes and who she sees.'

'I will tell him, sir.'

'Are the taxis in place?' Dennison asked.

'Yes, sir. There is one parked at each end of the street.'

'She's no fool. She'll more than likely change cabs at some stage. Unfortunately my influence doesn't extend to every taxi-driver in this town, so it's imperative that Raoul keeps close tabs on her. But she mustn't suspect for a moment that she's being tailed.'

'She will not suspect anything, sir,' Manuela replied confidently.

'Have you had a chance to go through her luggage yet?'

'I have been through everything, sir. There is nothing there to suggest any links with Marlette.'

'I can't say I'm surprised,' Dennison said. 'See that I'm kept posted on any new developments.'

'I will, sir,' she replied, but the line had already gone dead.

Once clear of the main gates, Nicole used the street map to get her bearings as she made her way towards the Zona Rosa, San Benito's fashionable and expensive shopping precinct, which was situated a few hundred metres from the house. It seemed the most likely place to find a cab. In the event she came across a battered yellow Acacya taxi parked at the side of the road close to the roundabout on the Boulevard del Hipódromo. The driver was sitting behind the wheel reading a copy of *La Prensa*, the most popular of the city's daily newspapers.

When Nicole appeared at the window, the driver was about to tell her that the taxi wasn't for hire, as he'd already told two other potential customers within the last hour, when he realized she was the woman in the photograph that he'd been given earlier by one of Dennison's men. He folded over the newspaper, discarded it on the dashboard, then climbed out and opened the back door for her. When he got back behind the wheel, he noticed that she was already paging through a phrasebook which she'd taken from her purse. 'I speak little English,' he said with a nicotine-stained smile. 'Where you want to go, *Señorita*?'

'The Metrocentro,' she said.

'You go to buy souvenirs?' the driver asked, starting the taxi. 'There are plenty shops there.'

'Yes,' she lied. 'How much will the fare be?' she added, remembering how Rick had told her that the taxis had no meters and it was essential to negotiate the fare before setting off.

'*Veinte colónes*,' the driver replied, pulling away from the kerb. 'Twenty colónes.'

Rick had estimated that it would cost around twenty or twenty-five colónes for a one-way trip within the confines of the city.

'You are American, yes?' the driver asked, glancing at her in the rearview mirror.

'Yes.'

'Where you from? New York?'

'Chicago.'

'Gangsters,' the driver said with a grin.

Nicole nodded in agreement, then turned her attention to the passing scenery, hoping the driver would take the hint and concentrate on the driving, leaving her to her own thoughts. It worked. Ten minutes later the taxi pulled up in front of the Metrocentro, the largest shopping mall in Central America. After paying the agreed fare, she entered the air-conditioned mall and spent the next twenty minutes window-shopping. Once she was satisfied she hadn't been followed, she left the mall, flagged down a passing taxi and told the driver to take her to the central square on the Avenida Cuscatlan. It took less than five minutes to reach the square. She waited until the taxi had pulled away before looking around to get her bearings. To her left was the Metropolitan Cathedral, and ahead of her, on the opposite side of the square, was the National Palace. Both buildings were in a state of disrepair. The main doors of the cathedral were boarded up and, despite the fact that the plaza was teeming with locals, the area still seemed to be haunted by an uneasy air of dereliction.

She walked the two blocks to the Mercado Cuartel, one of the city's two main markets, pausing occasionally in front of a shop window on the pretence of looking at the goods on display. There was still no sign of anyone following her. On reaching the market she spent another ten minutes browsing through the stalls, her eyes continually alert behind her dark sunglasses. She bought a T-shirt for Michelle, then made her way down a side street at the back of the market which brought her out into the heart of a small shanty town. The air was filled with the sickly stench of overripe fruit on sale outside many of the tin shacks which lined the dirt road. An old, rusted cattle truck hooted at her as it rumbled past, forcing her to step back on to the cracked sidewalk. She stared into the frightened eyes of the cows crammed into the back of the truck, their bodies rocking from side to side as the driver weaved the vehicle between the potholes in the road. Then the truck was gone, lost around a sharp bend in the road. A hen suddenly darted out from the doorway behind her and disappeared into the undergrowth on the other side of the road. An obese woman emerged from the hut, brandishing a machete, and pushed Nicole aside in her rush to pursue the fleeing animal. Nicole grimaced at the stink of stale sweat which lingered uncomfortably in the woman's wake. How could these people live in such squalor? she thought to herself as she waved away a fly which was buzzing around her face. But she knew they weren't living there by choice. In a city where unemployment ran at almost fifty per cent, most of the people around her would probably never hold down a steady job. And that included the children. What future in this new democracy?

The woman emerged from the undergrowth, now carrying the squawking, wriggling hen upside down by its legs. She said something to Nicole in Spanish, then laughed out loud and disappeared back inside the tin shack. Nicole smiled sadly after her, then, dabbing her sweating forehead with her handkerchief, she followed the contours of the road until she came to a junction. Turning left, she continued for another fifty metres. At this point the road branched off in three different directions. She consulted the map but wasn't surprised to find that these back roads weren't included on a map which was obviously geared towards the tourist trade. She approached a man sitting in the shadow of an overhanging tree. 'Hello,' she said with a smile, unsure of how he'd react to her. 'I'm looking for Father Coughlin's mission.' Nothing. 'Father Coughlin? *Padre* Coughlin?'

'*Padre?*' the man said, responding to the only word he'd understood. '*Yanqui padre?*'

'*Sí,*' she replied, nodding quickly.

The man gestured with a wave of his hand to the nearest road, a cul-de-sac, and said something in Spanish. She exhaled deeply, but knew it would be pointless to ask him to repeat himself. He didn't speak English. She didn't speak Spanish. Communication breakdown. She thanked him, then set off down the road she thought he'd pointed out, still not sure whether she was even headed in the right direction. A tourist wandering aimlessly around the back streets of a shanty town: she knew she was asking for trouble. But what choice did she have? She looked behind her. A couple of children kicking a plastic football in the road; a woman carrying a wicker basket; a man tinkering with the engine of a rusted Buick. At least there was one consolation – she would be able to see if there was anyone following her . . .

The three youths ghosted out from a narrow alleyway a short distance ahead of her. She guessed they were in their late teens and, judging by the flashy clothes and the catchpenny jewellery draped around their necks, they weren't from the shanty town. As they advanced towards her, the one in the middle pulled a flick-knife from his pocket and sprung the blade inches from his leg. He ran his eyes the length of her body and his mouth curled in a salacious grin. Her first thought was to run. But where? And how far would she get before they caught up with her? The one in the centre held up his hand and his two colleagues stopped in their tracks. He approached her alone. Time for diplomacy, she decided, extending her purse towards him. He grabbed it from her hand, but tossed it without interest to one of his colleagues. He continued to advance towards her. So much for diplomacy, she thought to herself. She knew the best way to lull him into a false sense of superiority was to play the helpless female. She slowly raised her hands, as if in a pleading gesture, and the youth laughed callously at her apparent fear. He called out something in Spanish which brought more laughter from his colleagues. *Come on, you bastard*, she urged silently to herself. She waited until he was within range, then suddenly swung her left arm down on to his right wrist, deflecting the knife away from her. Before he could react, she brought her knee up savagely into his groin, and at the same time slammed the heel of her right hand up against his chin. The force of the blow knocked him off his feet, and he fell heavily to the ground. The knife spun from his hand and landed close to the other two youths. One of them instinctively reached down to pick it up, then cried out in pain and fell to the ground, clutching painfully at his legs. It was only then that Nicole saw the man who'd stolen up silently behind the youth and caught him across the back of the legs with a baseball bat. He was in his mid-fifties, with cropped brown hair and the kind of ingrained tan that could only have come from years under the blistering sun. The man picked up the flick-knife, retracted the blade, and slipped it into his pocket. The fury was evident in his voice when he turned on the two youths and bellowed at them in Spanish. They hurried over to their colleague who was moaning in agony on the ground, his hands clutched tightly over his groin, and hauled him unceremoniously to his feet. Ignoring his desperate cries, they dragged him back down the alley.

The man retrieved the purse from the ground. 'You're Nicole Auger, aren't you?'

'How do you know . . . ?' Nicole trailed off as she took the purse hesitantly from him. 'Father Coughlin?'

'Yes,' he replied. 'Are you all right?'

'I think so,' she said. 'Thanks for showing up when you did. You certainly saved my skin.'

'I'd say you had the situation pretty well under control before I got here.' Coughlin shook his head. 'Who taught you to handle yourself like that? Richie Marlette?'

'My father,' she replied. 'I was learning the finer points of self-defence when most girls of my age were taking ballet classes.'

'Your father? I should have guessed. Richie told me a lot about him. And from what he said, he obviously thought a lot of him.'

'It was mutual, believe me. My father never forgave me for leaving Rick.'

'And neither did Richie,' Coughlin said with a faint smile.

'How did you know who I was?' she asked.

'You were all Richie ever talked about when he was out here,' Coughlin told her. 'And after a few drinks, he'd invariably bring out photographs. I must say, though, you've certainly changed since those photos were taken.'

'For the better, I hope?'

'Definitely for the better,' Coughlin replied good-humouredly.

'Who were those creeps anyway?' Nicole asked, jabbing her thumb towards the alley. 'I would have assumed from their clothes that they weren't from around here.'

'No, they're not,' Coughlin replied as he led the way towards the orphanage at the end of the street. 'They run a numbers racket here in the shanty town. I've tried to dissuade these people from betting money they can ill-afford to waste, but they won't listen to reason, though in a way I can understand why. One lucky number and they'd have enough money to buy their way out of here. I guess they feel it's a chance worth taking.'

'You won't have any trouble with those guys after what happened here, will you?' Nicole asked.

'Don't worry about them. I've been here for eight years now, and it'll take a lot more than a few uncouth louts to frighten me.' Coughlin paused as they reached the perimeter fence which enclosed the orphanage. 'I was sorry to hear about Bob Kinnard's death.'

'Thank you,' Nicole replied softly.

'You were divorced, I believe?'

'Yes. Two years ago. Once the divorce came through, I only ever saw Bob during the school vacations when he came to fetch Michelle. She used to stay with him in Washington for a couple of weeks every year.' Nicole followed Coughlin through the gate and down a narrow concrete path towards the red-brick building. 'You're certainly not how I imagined you'd be.'

'You thought I'd be a drunken old Irish priest dressed in a dirty, unwashed cassock,' he said with a faint trace of sarcasm in his deep Bronx voice.

'You forgot the glasses,' she said with a sheepish grin.

'They're in here,' Coughlin said, patting his breast pocket. He showed her into a small office, then removed a pile of folders from a chair and gestured for her to sit down. 'Would you like a coffee?'

'That would be nice,' she replied.

She watched him fill an old kettle from the tap before placing it on a small gas stove in the corner of the room. 'I'm afraid it's all a bit primitive around here,' Coughlin said, lighting the plate. 'We do have electricity, when the generator decides to work. Unfortunately it's a temperamental old thing but it's what I inherited from the priest who was here before me. Come to think of it, so was he.'

Nicole put her hand to her mouth as she chuckled to herself. She'd only known Coughlin for a few minutes, but already she felt completely at ease with him. In many ways he reminded her of her father, and although she regarded that as the finest compliment she could have paid to anyone, she doubted whether Coughlin would necessarily agree with her. She took a packet of cigarettes from her pocket and extended it towards Coughlin.

'I don't, thank you,' Coughlin replied.

'Do you mind if I smoke?'

'Not at all,' Coughlin said, handing her an ashtray.

She lit a cigarette and discarded the match in the ashtray. 'Have you heard anything from Rick?'

'He contacted me earlier this afternoon,' Coughlin replied.

'So he's already in El Salvador?' she asked.

'Yes, and God willing he should be on his way to San Salvador by now.'

Nicole nodded. 'I assume you have a number where you can contact him here in San Salvador?'

'Yes, he gave me a number to use in case of an emergency, but he'll contact me first once he gets here.' Coughlin placed a steaming mug of coffee on the small table beside her. 'Do you take milk and sugar?'

'Just milk, thanks.'

'I'm afraid I've only got powdered,' Coughlin said, holding up the jar. 'If you'd prefer fresh milk, I can send one of the children to the shop to get some.'

'No, powdered milk's fine,' she replied, helping herself from the jar.

He took a sip of coffee then sat back and smiled to himself. 'It'll be good to see Richie again after all these years.'

She took a long drag on her cigarette. 'How did you two first get to know each other? A priest and a mercenary? It certainly seems like an uneasy alliance.'

'I've only been a priest for the last eight years,' Coughlin told her. 'I was in the Foreign Legion for fifteen years before that. That's where Richie and I first became friends.'

'You used to be a mercenary?' she said in surprise.

'A legionnaire,' Coughlin corrected her. 'There is a difference.'

'What made you turn to the priesthood?'

Coughlin turned the cup around thoughtfully on the table before answering. 'I killed a child while I was serving in the Lebanon. I was riding shotgun on a night patrol in central Beirut when a boy darted out from an alley and ran towards the truck. He had something in his hand, but in the darkness I couldn't make out what it was. My first thought was that it was a hand-grenade, so I shot him. He died instantly. Then when I got out to investigate, I discovered to my horror that it wasn't a hand-grenade at all. It was an apple. A gesture of friendship from an innocent child. A subsequent investigation exonerated me of any blame, but I still couldn't come to terms with what I'd done. I would have gone to pieces had it not been for our chaplain. He was a rock. He guided me through the worst of it. That's how I came to find religion. I know that sounds really corny, but it worked. So much so that I probably wouldn't be alive today if I hadn't had my beliefs to hold me together.'

'Did you specifically ask to work with children when you were assigned your field duties?' Nicole asked.

'It was the only way. A catharsis, if you like. Having joined the Legion as a teenager, I'd never really had much to do with kids, so it was certainly something of an eye-opener for me when I first arrived here. My Spanish was very basic and I had no real experience in dealing with kids, let alone orphans. But they say the best way to learn is to be thrown in at the deep end. You either survive, a stronger person for it, or else you drown in self-pity. I've been offered the chance to travel to Africa and the Far East but I could never leave here. Not now. This is my home. These are my children. I really couldn't imagine what my life would be like without them around me.'

'That's exactly the way I feel about Michelle,' she said softly.

'I'd like very much to see what she looks like,' Coughlin said. 'Do you have a picture of her with you?'

'Yes,' Nicole replied, opening her purse. She handed Coughlin a snapshot she'd taken of Michelle when they'd gone to the circus the previous year. 'As you can see by the scowl on her face, she wasn't too thrilled about having to wear that dress. I'm sure you can understand why just by looking at it. It's covered in frills and bows, hardly the sort of dress you'd expect a child to wear. Bob's mother gave it to her as a birthday present, and as she was staying with us at the time, I insisted that Michelle wear it to please her. She's never worn it since.'

Coughlin chuckled at Michelle's expression as she pouted grumpily at the camera. 'How old was she when this was taken?'

'That was taken a couple of days after her fifth birthday,' Nicole replied.

'She's the spitting image of her mother, isn't she?' Coughlin said, looking up at Nicole.

'Not when she pulls faces like that, she isn't,' she was quick to point out.

Coughlin handed the photograph back to Nicole. 'I hope I'll get to meet her sometime in the near future.'

'You can count on it,' Nicole promised.

Coughlin took a sip of coffee, then replaced the mug on the desk. 'I believe you're staying at Dennison's guesthouse in San Benito?'

'Not by choice, believe me. He already had it all worked out by the time I arrived here. He cancelled my reservation at the Sheraton, claiming that if the press didn't corner me at the airport, then they'd certainly track me down to the hotel. To be honest, I don't even know whether there were any journalists waiting for me at the airport. I just had to take his word for it.'

'The story's already received wide coverage in the press

over here, so I'd say it was safe to assume that you'd have been tracked down eventually to the hotel,' Coughlin replied. 'But it's still worked out well for Dennison. He knows that Richie won't be able to get near you as long as you're staying there, certainly not without advertising his presence here in El Salvador.'

'How well do you know Peter Dennison?' Nicole asked.

'I've met him a couple of times over the years,' Coughlin replied with obvious contempt. 'He likes to portray himself as a philanthropist. He regularly donates substantial sums of money to local charities but, contrary to what he likes everyone to believe, it's certainly not out of any kind of altruism on his part. There's always an ulterior motive to everything he does. And it's invariably dishonest into the bargain.'

'So how has he managed to weasel his way into the affections of the new government if he's that corrupt?' Nicole asked.

'Money, of course,' Coughlin replied, rubbing his thumb and forefinger together. 'Although he's still officially a US citizen, Dennison was quick to latch on to the Arena party at the last elections. I don't know how much he donated to the party, but the rumours put it at something in the region of a million dollars.'

'A million dollars?' Nicole repeated in amazement.

'And from what I've heard, it wasn't all in the form of donations, if you get my meaning? After all, he does have the largest security firm in the country and, as a shrewd businessman, he'll obviously want to keep it that way. Let's just say he wouldn't want a rival firm fishing for his clientele.'

'Bribes, in other words,' Nicole deduced.

'I didn't say that,' Coughlin said with a smile. 'I'm only going on the rumours that circulate around town. There are other security firms here in El Salvador, but none of them are anywhere near as large or powerful as his company. He provides over ninety per cent of all security personnel for the *fincas*.'

'*Fincas?*' Nicole said with a frown.

'The coffee plantations, which are owned by some of the wealthiest men in the country. And there you have yet another way to win over the affections of any conservative government. Befriend the country's financial élite, and you'll find that it opens so many new doors to you.'

'In the same way as it did for Hector Amaya?' Nicole said contemptuously. 'From army officer to the head of the President's security team. That's quite a leap, isn't it?'

'Let's just say his close friendship with Dennison didn't do him any harm when his name was forwarded as a candidate for the vacancy.'

'I met him at the house this afternoon. He's been put in charge of the investigation into Bob's death.'

'When did this happen?'

'Last night. At least that's what Dennison told me. It's obviously another move on their part to further isolate the police from the investigation into Michelle's disappearance so that they can recover the tape before Rick can get to it.'

'So you believe this theory about there being a coup planned to overthrow the government?' Coughlin asked.

'Don't you?' Nicole countered.

'I've lived here long enough to know that anything's possible in El Salvador. Nothing surprises me any more. Richie briefed me on what Pruitt told you in New York, but to be perfectly honest with you, I wouldn't trust Langley any more than I would Dennison or any of his fascist cronies. One's as bad as the other. I can remember a time when the CIA were supporting the military junta here in El Salvador. It was a standard joke in San Salvador at the time that the Sheraton Hotel was a second Langley for the CIA. It just seems strange to me that the CIA are now suddenly concerned about a right-wing takeover when not so long ago they would have gone out of their way to actively encourage it.'

'What are you suggesting? That the CIA could be somehow involved in the coup?'

'As I said just now, nothing surprises me any more,' Coughlin said, sitting back in his chair and clasping his hands behind his head.

Nicole crossed to the door, where she watched a group of children laughing and shouting excitedly amongst themselves as they played a game of football on a barren patch of waste ground between Coughlin's office and an adjacent building.

'What's bothering you, Nicole?' Coughlin asked.

She dropped the cigarette on to the concrete step outside the door and crushed it underfoot before looking round at Coughlin. 'Can I ask you something, Father? About Rick, that is?'

'Of course,' Coughlin replied.

'When we were in New York, I asked him why he'd been deported, but he refused to talk about it.'

'And you want me to tell you?'

'I've heard the official version,' Nicole told him. 'The American Ambassador went to great lengths to spell it out to me in nauseating detail when I met with him at the embassy earlier this afternoon. That he raped and murdered the twelve-year-old daughter of a wealthy coffee baron. I don't believe it for a moment. Not Rick. Do you know what really happened?' She noticed the hesitation in his eyes. 'You obviously know the truth, Father, because it would go against all your Christian beliefs to help Rick if he had been guilty of those charges. I just want to know what really happened, that's all.'

Coughlin remained silent for some time, then slowly got to his feet and came round to the front of his desk. He pushed aside a pile of folders and perched on the edge of it. 'You're right, I do know what happened that night. In fact, I'm probably one of the few people still alive who does know the truth. But that doesn't mean I'll tell you what happened. When Richie told me it was in the sanctity of the confessional. I could never betray that trust.'

'You know as well as I do that Rick's not a Catholic,' Nicole replied in surprise. 'His father was a fire-and-brimstone preacher in Alabama. Rick's despised all forms of religion from an early age.'

'I'm well aware of Richie's views on religion,' Coughlin said wryly. 'We had more than enough arguments about the merits of religion in this very room. And in particular the Catholic faith. But that doesn't detract from the fact that he spoke to me in confidence. I must respect that, Nicole. I'm sure you can understand that. The only person who can tell you is Richie. And frankly, I doubt he will. Not under the circumstances.'

'What do you mean, *not under the circumstances*?'

'I'm sorry, I can't say any more than that,' Coughlin said with a sympathetic smile.

Nicole pushed her hands deep into the pockets of her baggy jeans. 'I appreciate your situation, Father. I know I'd be pretty pissed off if the roles were reversed and you told Rick something that I'd said to you in confidence.'

'Would you like another coffee?'

Nicole looked at her watch. 'I'd better be making tracks. Amaya's taking me down to the mortuary later this afternoon. He needs me to identify Bob's body so that it can be released for burial.'

'Would you like me to arrange for someone to be with you at the mortuary? A priest? A chaplain? Whatever you'd prefer. I know only too well how traumatic it can be when it comes to identifying the body of a loved one.'

'Thanks, but I'll be fine,' Nicole said, then crossed to the table and picked up her purse. When she turned round there was a fierce anger burning in her eyes. 'Right now I don't feel any grief whatsoever over Bob's death. Not after what he's put Michelle through. And for what? Some damn story that would have got his name splashed across the front page of a newspaper back home? You probably think I'm being cold and insensitive, but right now it's the way I feel, and I was taught from an early age to always speak my mind. My father used to say that that way there could be no misunderstandings.'

'I can understand the anger you're feeling, Nicole,' Coughlin said softly.

'No, I don't think you can, Father,' Nicole retorted sharply. Suddenly the tears welled up in her eyes, but she made no move to brush them away as they rolled down her face. She sat down slowly on the chair and her voice was a mixture of anger and anguish when she spoke. 'I keep saying to myself that Michelle's somewhere out there waiting for me to find her and take her home. Sure, she'll be frightened and alone, but at least she'll still be alive. But the fact of the matter is, I don't even know that, do I? For all I know she could be . . .' She wiped her palm across her cheeks. 'She could already be dead, couldn't she?'

'You have to think positively, Nicole.'

'And even if she is still alive, what will happen to her if Dennison's thugs get to her first?' Nicole continued, ignoring Coughlin's attempt to placate her. 'Or that bastard Jayson. "No witnesses, no comebacks." That's his sick catchphrase, isn't it? And Michelle's a witness. An innocent child but still a witness. And you honestly expect me to grieve for the man who's put her life at risk for the sake of some exposé? As far as I'm concerned, he can burn in hell. And if there is any kind of justice in the afterlife, then that's exactly where he'll be going. Straight to hell.'

Coughlin handed her a handkerchief, then crouched down beside the chair. 'Your father was right. It is good to speak your mind. That purges the soul. But it's even better to cry. That cleanses the soul. And you always feel so much better for it afterwards.'

Nicole dabbed her eyes with the handkerchief. 'When I first went into labour I couldn't believe that anything, or anyone, was worth that kind of pain. Then suddenly there she was. I remember my first thought on seeing her was that she reminded me in so many ways of the foals I'd delivered when I was a teenager in Africa. Those little blotchy, bedraggled creatures who were totally dependent on their mothers. I had this sudden urge to wrap her up in a blanket and hold her in my arms for ever so that I could protect her against all the injustices of the world. I didn't want her to grow up. I always wanted her to be a little blotchy, bedraggled creature who would be totally dependent on me. I just wish I had that chance over again. Only this time I would make sure that I never let her go. I can't stop thinking that I should have been there for her when she needed me most.'

'I know you'll always be there for her, Nicole, and I've got a feeling she knows that as well,' Coughlin said. 'And you can be sure that, wherever she is right now, that thought alone will be more than enough to keep her going until she sees you again.'

'*If* she sees me again,' Nicole said, returning the handkerchief to Coughlin.

'You're forgetting one important factor here,' Coughlin said, holding up a finger. 'Richie Marlette. It doesn't matter how long it takes, I know he'll find Michelle for you. I'd be prepared to stake my life on that.'

'Money's always been a strong persuader as far as Rick's concerned,' Nicole said, getting to her feet.

'It's got nothing to do with money,' Coughlin replied as she crossed to the door. 'Richie's still in love with you.'

Nicole looked round at Coughlin. 'Did he tell you that?'

'Remember you asked me when we first met in the street how I knew who you were? I've been over to New York to see Richie a few times in the last five years, and on two of those visits I was introduced to two different women that he was dating. I've since heard from several reliable sources that he's never had another serious relationship since the two of you broke up.'

'That doesn't mean he's still in love with me,' Nicole countered.

'The two women were the spitting image of what you looked like in those photographs he had of you when he was last in El Salvador. It's patently obvious that he's never got over you.' Coughlin wagged a finger of warning at her. 'And you heard that in complete confidence.'

She kissed Coughlin lightly on the cheek. 'You're a rogue, do you know that?'

Coughlin smiled, then followed her to the door. 'All being well, Richie should get into San Salvador within the next couple of hours. Can you contact me again either later tonight or first thing tomorrow morning? I should have heard from him by then.'

'I'll call you this evening. There's sure to be a pay-phone near the house.'

'Be careful, Nicole. They're bound to be watching you.'

'I will,' Nicole assured him. She slipped on her sunglasses and walked down the narrow path towards the main gate. She looked round when she reached the gate but Coughlin was nowhere in sight. Was Rick still in love with her? She pondered the thought for a moment, then pushed it from her mind, but there was a fresh spring in her step as she went in search of a taxi to take her back to San Benito.

Dennison was on the phone in his penthouse office when the intercom buzzed on his desk. Placing a hand over the mouthpiece, he pressed a button on the machine. 'Yes, what is it?' he demanded tersely.

'Colonel Amaya is here to see you, sir,' his personal secretary announced from the outer office.

'Show him in,' Dennison replied, then cut the connection before resuming his conversation on the phone. The door opened and his secretary led Amaya into the room. Dennison pointed to the leather armchair in front of his desk, and Amaya sat down as the secretary left, closing the door again behind her. Dennison spoke for another couple of minutes on the phone, then hung up and reached for the packet of cheroots lying on the desk. He took the last one from the packet and lit it before crumpling the box and discarding it into the bin beside the desk. Only then did he look across at Amaya. 'Have you been to the mortuary yet?'

Amaya nodded. 'The Auger woman made a positive ID. I've already arranged for the body to be released into the care of the American embassy. They can sort out all the details with his family and get the body shipped back to Washington. She's a cool one, though. She didn't even flinch when she saw the body. Hell, she could have been identifying a lost shirt for all the emotion she showed.'

'You're forgetting that she grew up in Africa with civil wars raging all around her. She's probably seen more dead bodies than you and I put together. And you know as well as I do that you become immune to it after a while.'

'But still, the guy was her ex-husband,' Amaya replied. 'The father of her daughter. You'd think that would have counted for something.'

'He's also the guy who was supposed to have taken her daughter on holiday to Acapulco. Instead he drags her out here at a moment's notice, then dumps her somewhere without even telling anyone first. Some father.'

Amaya just shrugged. 'Well, it's done. The embassy can deal with the paperwork now.'

Dennison paused for a moment, then said, 'By all accounts Nicole Auger's been pretty busy these last few hours. Manuela rang me shortly after we'd left the house to report that Auger had gone for a walk. I certainly appreciate you bringing Manuela to my attention last year. She's damn efficient and really hard-working. I couldn't imagine having anyone else now to run the house for me.'

'She's ex-military. What do you expect? I couldn't believe it when they let her go as part of the cutbacks. An officer who speaks fluent English. There certainly aren't too many of those in the National Guard.'

'Their loss is my gain,' Dennison said with a satisfied smile.

'So where exactly did she go after she left the house?' Amaya asked.

'She took a taxi to the Metrocentro and spent the next twenty minutes checking to see if she'd been followed from the house. Then she took a second taxi downtown to the Cuartel Market, where she again checked to see if she'd been followed by pretending to browse through the stalls.'

'Do you think she spotted Raoul?' Amaya asked.

'Raoul only followed her as far as the Metrocentro. It was obvious that she was on the lookout for a tail. I thought it best to send him a couple more men as additional backup. Both are ex-military scouts and, from what they told me, they had to be on their toes all the time to make sure that they weren't seen. But she can't have spotted them, otherwise I'm sure she'd have aborted her plan and returned to the house.'

'Did she meet someone at the market? Was it Marlette?' Amaya asked excitedly.

'Wishful thinking,' Dennison retorted. 'No, she went into the shanty town behind the market and met with Father Bernard Coughlin. It makes sense, though, when you think about it. He and Marlette go back a long way. They served together in the Foreign Legion. Marlette's obviously using Coughlin as a go-between while he's in the country.'

'So what happens now?' Amaya asked.

'We pay a visit to Coughlin. Who knows, we might even be able to persuade him to tell us where we can find Marlette.'

'When are you going to see him?'

Dennison looked at his watch. 'It's gone five already. I've got an appointment with a client at six. I would have cancelled it, but he's flying in specially from Santa Ana to see me. I doubt I'll be able to get away before seven at the earliest.'

'Count me out. As I told you this afternoon, I'm due to meet with the President at seven-thirty to brief him on the latest developments in the case. And don't forget, you're supposed to be entertaining the Auger woman at your house tonight.'

'I've already spoken to her about that. I told her that something had cropped up unexpectedly here at the office so I wouldn't be able to make it tonight.'

'Are you going to go and see Coughlin by yourself?' Amaya asked.

'I'll take Jayson with me. It'll do him good to get out of the house. He's been stuck in there ever since the last hit.'

'Do you think that's wise?' Amaya asked. 'Every policeman across the country's been alerted to be on the lookout for a foreigner with a Cockney accent.'

'It's not as if the police have even got a description of him,' Dennison replied.

'Unless Coughlin tells them,' Amaya retorted. 'Then where would that leave us? I say it's too risky to use him at the moment, Peter.'

'I really wouldn't worry about Coughlin going to the police,' Dennison said, then sat back in his chair and smiled faintly to himself. 'As Jayson would say: "No witnesses, no comebacks."'

SIX

It was policy at the orphanage for all the children under the age of ten to be in bed by eight o'clock. The older children were allowed to stay up longer, and most would eagerly congregate in the lounge to watch the evening film on the new colour television set which had been donated to the orphanage by the mayor's office. Coughlin, who in the past had invariably retired to his quarters after reading a story to the younger children before they went to bed, now found himself spending more time watching television. He especially loved the old Westerns, and always got a kick out of seeing someone like John Wayne or James Stewart talking fluent Spanish.

But that night he had other things on his mind and, after switching off the lights in the dormitory, he left the main building and made his way briskly along the narrow pathway which led through a grove of trees to a small outhouse at the far end of the compound. The outhouse had been little more than a derelict shell when he'd first arrived at the orphanage, but the children had all pitched in to help him convert it into habitable lodgings and, although he still spent most of his time either in the main building or in his office, he always knew he had a retreat of his own to retire to at the end of the day. . .

The door creaked as he pushed it open. The hinges had been squeaking for the past week, and every night he'd promised himself that he'd see to it the next day. And he never did. *Make a note of it*, he said irritably to himself as he switched on the single light in the corner of the room.

He froze in the doorway when he saw the man sitting in the armchair against the opposite wall. The face was all too familiar.

'Please come in, Father,' Dennison said, gesturing Coughlin into the room. 'The door was open so we let ourselves inside. I hope you don't mind?'

Coughlin ignored Dennison's sarcasm and, as he stepped away from the door, he noticed a second man seated on the bed. The man was in his late thirties with straggly, unwashed blond hair which hung untidily on his square shoulders. The skin around his neck and on the back of his hands was peeling from too much exposure to the sun.

'It's been a long time, Coughlin,' the man said in a distinctive Cockney accent. 'Hell, it must be a good ten years now.'

Dennison's eyes flickered between the two men before settling on Coughlin again. 'I see you already know Stuart Jayson.'

'Oh yes, I know him,' Coughlin replied, the revulsion he felt for Jayson evident in his voice. 'Chad. Twelve years ago.'

'Is it really that long ago?' Jayson said with affected surprise. 'You were still with the Foreign Legion then, weren't you? Your lot were supporting the government forces. I was acting as a military adviser to the Libyan-backed rebels.'

'An adviser?' Coughlin shot back contemptuously. 'I think a butcher would be a better description of what you did. I saw your work at first hand, Jayson, and it's something I'll never forget for as long as I live. An entire village wiped out on your specific orders. Women and children gunned down in cold blood as they tried to flee their burning homes.'

'There are other ways of destroying your enemy than just by pointing a gun at them and pulling the trigger. You get inside their heads and fuck with their minds. You demoralize them. You dehumanize them. And what better way of doing that than by systematically raping their women and killing their children. It's psychological warfare, Coughlin, and believe me, it works every time.'

'You should have been tried as a war criminal,' Coughlin hissed furiously.

'So the Foreign Legion seemed to think after I was captured, but for some reason your commanding officer couldn't seem to find any witnesses to testify against me,' Jayson sneered.

'That's because they were all dead,' Coughlin retorted.

'No witnesses, no comebacks,' Jayson said with a chilling smile. 'It's the only way to survive in this business, Coughlin.'

'Come inside and close the door,' Dennison instructed Coughlin, gesturing him impatiently into the room.

'What do you want?' Coughlin snapped as he closed the door behind him.

'Nothing more than a simple answer to a simple question,' Dennison replied. 'Then we'll leave you in peace.'

Coughlin felt a nervous apprehension clawing at the pit of his stomach as he waited for Dennison to continue. Dennison must have had Nicole followed from San Benito. It seemed the only logical reason to explain why Dennison would have come to the orphanage at that time of night. With this in mind he'd already anticipated Dennison's question even before he asked it.

'Where can we find Richard Marlette?'

Coughlin perched on the edge of his desk and shrugged his shoulders. 'In New York as far as I know.'

Dennison's eyes narrowed fractionally in anger, then he smiled fleetingly before getting to his feet and crossing to the door. He stared thoughtfully at the carpet, then turned back to Coughlin. 'I can understand your reluctance to turn Marlette in. After all, you two go back a long way.

But the fact remains that Marlette is officially regarded as *persona non grata* in this country, and anyone caught shielding him would be guilty of aiding and abetting a wanted criminal. Of course, if someone who'd helped him in the past were to deliver him into my custody, I'd be more than happy to overlook their – shall we say – indiscretion.' He took a sheet of paper from his pocket and extended it towards Coughlin. 'These orders were issued to me by the President himself. As you can see, it bears the President's official letterhead, as well as his personal signature. My brief is very simple. Find Marlette at any cost. Please, feel free to read it.'

'Orders can easily be forged,' Coughlin retorted sharply.

'That's a serious accusation to make,' Jayson shot back, but when he got to his feet Dennison was quick to gesture him to sit down again.

'If Richie is in El Salvador then I certainly don't know about it,' Coughlin said, holding Dennison's cold stare.

'And I suppose you also deny having met with Nicole Auger in your office this afternoon?' Dennison said.

Coughlin knew he'd have to tread very carefully through the minefield Dennison was laying out in front of him. One mistake. That's all it would take to condemn Richie. And without him, what chance would Nicole have of ever finding her daughter? 'Nicole did come to see me this afternoon,' he admitted at length.

'Now we're finally getting somewhere,' Dennison said, and a smile flashed across his face. Coughlin noticed that his eyes remained cold and impassive.

'Richie phoned me from New York last night and told me that Nicole was coming to El Salvador to look for her missing daughter. He asked if I knew of anyone who could act as an interpreter for her. Obviously at the time neither of them knew that the President had assigned you to head the official investigation into her daughter's disappearance. That's what Nicole came to tell me this afternoon. She said that she'd tried to recruit Richie in New York, but that he wasn't interested in coming out here. He'd already signed up for another tour of Bosnia. She'd even offered to double the money, but he would have known that if he was arrested he could spend the rest of his life in a hell-hole like the Mariona prison here in San Salvador. That's hardly an incentive to return, is it?'

Dennison slowly clapped his hands together. 'That's good, Father. Really good. And you know something, if I didn't know better, I'd almost be inclined to believe that story.'

'Look, I've told you –'

'A pack of lies, and you've also just exhausted my patience,' Dennison cut in sharply, his finger levelled accusingly at Coughlin. 'We already know that Marlette's in the country. What we don't know are his present whereabouts. The woman who met him at the border was picked up a few hours ago by a patrol in the north of the country. She's a known member of the FMLN. She was a mute, but I'm told that she turned out to be very communicative in the end. It seems that she dropped Marlette off at a church run by one of your colleagues. A Father Lorenzo. Had we known this earlier, we could have intercepted him there and saved Lorenzo a lot of unnecessary pain. As it is, Lorenzo claimed that all he knew about Marlette was that he was headed for San Salvador, where he was going to make contact with you. Personally, I think he was telling the truth, because I can't believe that anyone would have willingly endured that kind of torture to protect a man he hardly knew.'

'You bastard,' Coughlin snarled, lunging at Dennison.

Dennison side-stepped the clumsy challenge and, when Coughlin spun round to face him, he found himself staring down the barrel of a Beretta. 'Sit down.'

Coughlin sank dejectedly on to the edge of the armchair. 'Where's Father Lorenzo now?'

'I'd say that all depends on whether you believe in the afterlife or not,' Dennison replied coldly.

Coughlin buried his face in his hands. None of this should have happened – it had all gone so horribly wrong. He'd given Lorenzo his word that no harm would come to him or his parishioners if he provided Marlette with temporary shelter until the transport arrived to take him on to San Salvador. But the truth of the matter was that he'd used Lorenzo as a patsy to help get Marlette into the country, knowing only too well the dangers involved. Only he hadn't warned Lorenzo of those dangers. He'd lied to him. As far as he was concerned, his word now meant nothing. How could it after what he'd done . . . ?

'Where's Marlette?' Dennison demanded.

Coughlin looked up slowly at him. 'I told you, I don't know,' he hissed through clenched teeth.

'That's a pity,' Dennison replied, then looked across at Jayson. 'Show him.'

Jayson pulled out a dirty blue hold-all from under the bed and opened it. He reached inside and withdrew a fragmentation grenade. He held it up for Coughlin to see, then removed the safety pin and clamped his thumb tightly over the lever. 'I don't have to tell you how destructive these little beauties can be in a confined space.'

Coughlin knew that he was in no immediate danger as long as they believed he could lead them to Marlette. 'And I suppose the President also authorized you to threaten anyone who might know of Richie's present whereabouts?'

'What the President doesn't see, he doesn't have to know about,' Dennison replied. 'Believe me, Father, I'll resort to any means at my disposal to find Marlette. And if that means resorting to threats and violence, so be it. If it results in Marlette's arrest, then the end has justified the means.'

'I don't buy that. There's more to this than you're letting on, isn't there? Why are you so desperate to find Richie?'

Coughlin asked, forcing himself to go back on to the offensive. He certainly couldn't let on that he knew anything about the missing tape or the planned coup d'état. He had to make out that he didn't know anything, and that meant he would have to act suspicious. Dennison would expect it of him. And it was essential that he stayed in character. It was all he had left going for him now.

'Where's Marlette?' Dennison snapped furiously. 'I won't ask you again.'

'Or what?' Coughlin shot back. 'You'll lock me in here and blow me up? I would have thought I'd be more important to you alive right now.'

'You are,' Dennison was quick to agree in an equanimous tone. 'If I'd wanted to kill you I could have already shot you. It would have been so much easier, and certainly a lot less theatrical than using the grenade. No, the grenade has another purpose. Tell me, Father, how many children are there sleeping in the dormitory right now?'

Coughlin stared ashen-faced at Dennison as the realization of what he was planning slammed into him like a punishing blow to the body. He slumped down in the chair and shook his head in disbelief, but when he tried to speak he found that his throat was dry and the words refused to come.

'I see I've finally touched a raw nerve,' Dennison said with evident satisfaction. 'Imagine the carnage if Jayson were to throw the grenade through the dormitory window. You'd be burying the dead for the next week. And of those who did survive, many would certainly be left maimed for life. Is that what you want, Father? Surely those little children have suffered enough tragedy in their short lives? Personally, I'd hate to see anything happen to them because of your stubborn obstinacy. But it's entirely up to you. It's really a very simple choice – give me Marlette or start digging those graves.'

'I don't know where Marlette is,' Coughlin said softly in a hollow, emotionless voice.

'Do it,' Dennison snapped at Jayson, who got to his feet and crossed to the door.

'Wait!' Coughlin shouted desperately after him.

Dennison held up his hand to stop Jayson as he was about to leave the room. 'You were saying, Father?'

Coughlin knew there was no way out. If he didn't cooperate, Jayson would see to it that as many children as possible were either killed or maimed by the grenade. It was exactly the sort of cowardly attack which had gained him such notoriety when he'd first come across him in Chad. And if he did cooperate, he had no doubt in his mind that Marlette wouldn't see out the night. And with his death would go Nicole's one realistic chance of ever reaching Michelle before Dennison's thugs could get to her. He already knew that either way he was going to die. But that didn't bother him any more. If anything, he'd be grateful for the release from the overpowering guilt which had taken root inside him like some insidious and malignant disease . . .

'Where's Marlette?' Dennison snapped, then glanced across at Jayson who was standing by the door, his hand curled around the handle, a twisted grin on his face as he waited eagerly for the order to dispatch the grenade into the children's dormitory.

'I swear I don't know where Marlette's staying, but he did give me a telephone number here in San Salvador where I could contact him in case of an emergency,' Coughlin said in desperation. 'I'll give you the number. Just get that bastard away from the door.'

Dennison gestured for Jayson to return to the bed. The smile faltered on Jayson's face, then he reluctantly crossed to the bed and sat down again.

'Write the number down,' Dennison ordered, then levelled the automatic at Coughlin when he got to his feet.

'Remember, Father, you're not a soldier any more. Try anything stupid and I'll kill you. Then where would that leave your precious little orphans?'

Coughlin said nothing as he took a sheet of paper and pen from the desk drawer and wrote down the telephone number he'd already committed to memory. There was no fight left in him any more. Only regrets . . .

Marlette wiped his hand across his sweating face, then eased the Heckler & Koch automatic from the holster secured at the back of his camouflage trousers. He still didn't know what to make of the phone call he'd received thirty minutes earlier. Coughlin, who'd clearly sounded agitated, had told him that Nicole was in trouble but had refused to go into details over the telephone, except to say that Dennison had already had her taken into custody. He'd been told to meet Coughlin at the orphanage. Then the line had gone dead. Had the call been genuine? Or had it been made under duress? All Marlette's instincts told him that it was a trap. But what if Coughlin had been on the level? What if Nicole had been taken into custody in an attempt to force him out into the open? Although Marlette still suspected a trap, he also knew he couldn't ignore the possibility that Nicole was in danger.

He'd driven to Cuscatlan Square in the car which Pruitt had had left for him at the safe house, then continued on foot into the shanty town. Dressed in camouflage fatigues, his presence had been regarded with suspicious, and even nervous, glances from the *tugurios*, the inhabitants of the shanty town, many of whom could still remember the days when foreign mercenaries, under contract to the wealthy coffee barons, had teamed up with the death squads during their murderous raids on the city's shanty town communities. But nobody had tried to challenge him as he'd made his way to the orphanage, either out of fear or just common sense.

He pulled an olive green bandanna from his jacket

pocket and secured it tightly around his head before easing open the main gate and stepping cautiously into the deserted grounds. He noticed a couple of lights on behind the drawn curtains in the main building, but Coughlin's office was in total darkness. He ran, doubled over, to the office and tried the door. It was locked. He dropped down on to one knee, the automatic gripped tightly in his hands, and slowly took in his surroundings. Everything seemed quiet. It was almost as if he could feel the net closing in on him. But there was no turning back, not when there was the slightest chance that Nicole could be in some kind of trouble. He'd never be able to live with himself if he allowed anything to happen to her.

He scanned the trees beyond the main building, but from where he was crouched he couldn't see the outhouse. He lost count of the number of times he'd sat in there with Coughlin, a beer in one hand, a cigarette in the other, discussing world affairs. Like himself, Coughlin had a keen understanding of international politics, and their vociferous arguments would often drag on through the night until the first rays of dawn broke across the city.

Marlette quickly pushed the past from his mind and, glancing around furtively, he broke cover and sprinted across the open ground until he reached the trees. He paused to catch his breath, squinting into the darkness beyond the trees. He could now just make out the silhouette of the building, but there was no light emanating from behind the curtains which were drawn across the single window. He threaded his way cautiously through the trees, then dropped to his stomach and crawled the last twenty metres to the building. He straightened up out of sight of the window and, keeping his back pressed against the side of the building, moved stealthily towards the closed door. He was only a few metres away from the door when he stepped on a pile of twigs. The sound was deafening to him. A fine layer of brittle twigs had been laid out carefully on the caked ground around the door to warn anyone inside of his impending approach. So much for the element of surprise, he thought grimly. He stepped gingerly across the ground and curled his fingers around the door handle, ready to push open the door and dive low into the room.

'Richie?' a voice hissed from inside the building. 'Richie, is that you?'

Marlette recognized Coughlin's Bronx brogue straight away.

'Richie, the orphanage is being watched. That's why I've had to switch off the lights. Hurry up and come inside before they see you.'

Marlette swallowed anxiously, then eased down the handle and pressed himself flat against the wall as he pushed open the door. Nothing. He launched himself low through the doorway, coming up fast on one knee, the automatic clenched tightly at arm's length. It took his eyes a few seconds to adjust to the darkness, but by then it was already too late. His body stiffened when he felt the cold barrel of a pistol pressed against the back of his neck. A moment later the light was switched on.

Coughlin was sitting in the wooden chair in front of the desk. His hands and feet were bound with rope and there were several discoloured bruises on his face. Jayson stood behind him, the fragmentation grenade in one hand, the Sig Sauer P226 automatic in the other trained on the back of Coughlin's head. Marlette inclined his head slightly to look up at the man standing over him. He wasn't surprised to find it was Dennison.

Dennison plucked the Heckler & Koch from Marlette's grasp and nodded his approval as he appraised the automatic in his gloved hand. 'I certainly can't fault you on your choice of weapon. Now get to your feet. And do it very slowly.'

'Are you OK?' Marlette asked Coughlin after he'd stood up.

'I'm OK, Richie,' Coughlin replied dejectedly. 'I'm sorry. I had to get you here. If I'd refused, Jayson would have thrown the grenade into the orphanage. I'm really sorry, Richie, but I had to do it for the children. You must understand that.'

'I understand,' Marlette replied absently as his eyes went to Jayson. 'How was New York?'

Jayson frowned, then gave a quick shrug. 'New York? I don't know what you're talking about?'

'You know damn well what I'm talking about,' Marlette snarled furiously.

'I hate to break this up but there's work to do,' Dennison snapped at Jayson, then shouted over his shoulder in Spanish. A man appeared in the doorway. He was also armed with an automatic. Dennison gestured for the man to close the door, then Jayson untied Coughlin's hands and feet and stepped out from behind him.

Dennison moved away from Marlette and pocketed his own Beretta. 'You can count yourself a very lucky man, Marlette. The President's taken a personal interest in the case, which means that I'll have to play it strictly by the book. My instructions were to take you alive, so all I can do now is arrest you on suspicion of murder and leave you to the mercy of the courts.'

'And just who exactly am I supposed to have murdered?' Marlette retorted disdainfully.

Dennison raised Marlette's Heckler & Koch and shot Coughlin twice through the heart. Coughlin was punched backwards and the chair toppled back against the desk, spilling his lifeless body on to the threadbare carpet. Marlette was still lunging at Dennison when Jayson caught him squarely behind the ear with the butt of his automatic. He fell to his knees, and by the time he'd managed to clear his head he found that he had three automatics trained on him.

'It seems as if we got here just too late to prevent you

from killing Father Coughlin,' Dennison said as he crouched beside Coughlin to check for a pulse. Satisfied that the priest was dead, he straightened up and turned back to Marlette. 'Fortunately we do have the murder weapon, and when it's sent to forensics they'll find your prints on it. That makes it first-degree murder, Marlette. The prosecution will also have two reliable witnesses to testify against you in court. We wouldn't want to involve Jayson – it would only throw up a lot of awkward questions. I'd say it was an open-and-shut case, wouldn't you?'

'And what's to stop me from telling the truth when I get into court?' Marlette shot back as he gingerly massaged the bruise behind his ear. 'Not only could I finger Jayson as Kinnard's murderer, I could also link him with you. What would that do to your so-called reputation?'

'It would be your word against mine,' Dennison replied. 'And with your track record here in El Salvador, who do you think the jury would be inclined to believe?'

'I see you've got it all neatly worked out, just like you did five years ago.'

'Only this time around the American embassy won't be able to bail you out,' Dennison said. Gesturing the other man forward, he ordered him to take Marlette to the car which was waiting outside for them.

Marlette had already guessed that he'd never live to stand trial. He would be handed over to Dennison's goons to find out just how much he actually knew about the missing videotape. Then he would be executed. The President would doubtless be informed that he'd been murdered by fellow prisoners while in custody. And if the coup d'état was successful, the new President would certainly welcome the news of his death as a personal triumph for the military regime. However he looked at it, his situation appeared bleak. But hope can be a powerful weapon, especially in the hands of a desperate man, and a plan was already beginning to take shape in his mind. He called it a plan, whereas in reality it was little more than a wing-and-a-prayer attempt to extricate himself from an ever worsening situation. He knew only too well that if it backfired on him, he'd be dead. But it wasn't as if he had much choice.

'I can get up by myself!' Marlette snarled angrily when the man tried to haul him to his feet. He caught Jayson's eye. 'Call him off, for Christ's sake. It's not as if I can go anywhere with all this artillery pointing at me.'

'Take away a man's dignity and you take away the very essence of his soul,' Jayson said. 'That's what my old man always used to say.'

'Wise words,' Marlette said, struggling to his feet.

'He was a wise man,' Jayson replied, taking a step towards Marlette.

Come on, you bastard, Marlette urged Jayson, *just come a bit closer. Just a bit closer . . .*

'Get him out of here,' Dennison snapped at Jayson.

The man opened the door and stepped outside, the automatic still trained on Marlette. Marlette moved to the door and saw a white Ford parked close to the trees. He stopped abruptly in the doorway to look back at Coughlin's body. Jayson, who'd been following closely behind him, was caught off-guard and almost walked straight into him.

'Say a prayer for him on the way to the station,' Jayson sneered, and jabbed the automatic menacingly at Marlette.

Marlette knew he had to take his chance. He feigned to turn away, then deflected Jayson's gun hand with his left arm and simultaneously chopped his right hand down viciously on Jayson's other wrist. Jayson cried out in pain; the grenade tumbled from his hand and rolled across the carpet. Marlette shoulder-charged the man outside the door, knocking him to the ground; he was still sprinting towards the car when the driver unholstered an automatic and pushed open the door. Without breaking his stride, Marlette slammed the sole of his boot against the door. The driver screamed in agony and dropped the automatic as he was crushed between the door and the chassis. Marlette was still reaching for the fallen gun when the building exploded, spewing out a barrage of lethal projectiles in all directions. The force of the blast knocked Marlette off balance and, as he stumbled forward, he caught his leg painfully on the fender of the car, forcing him to drop down on to one knee. A bullet slammed into the side of the car, inches from his head. He hurled himself sideways, then scrambled to his feet. As he ran, doubled over, to the temporary sanctuary of the trees, he noticed that dozens of children had spilt out from the orphanage and were now huddled together in a protective group, most of them in their nightshirts, as the flames danced uneven shadows across their innocent faces. They were like a sea of ghosts, the hems of their nightshirts rippling in the gentle evening breeze, staring in eerie silence at the burnt-out shell of what had once been Coughlin's quarters.

A second shot echoed across the night and suddenly Marlette felt a sharp burning sensation in his neck. For a horrifying moment he thought he'd been badly hurt, but when he put his fingers gingerly to his skin, he realized that it was only a flesh wound. It stung mercilessly as the sweat mingled with the blood that was streaming down his neck and under the collar of his tunic. It had been that close. Third time unlucky? The hell he was going to stick around to find out. A third shot rang out as he zig-zagged his way across the open ground to the main gate, but the bullet passed wide of him.

He was aware of Dennison's raised voice somewhere behind him. 'I want him taken alive. Do you understand . . . ?' He didn't hear the rest of the sentence as he pulled open the gate and darted out into the road. He could see that several curtains inside the tin shacks had been tweaked aside as residents peered out inquisitively at him, but nobody ventured outside to investigate the explosion. Marlette knew only too well that the inured inhabitants of the city's numerous shanty towns had lived in abject terror during those long years of the country's pernicious civil war. Then they had been ever fearful of being dragged from their homes for no other reason than to make up the numbers for one of the summary executions which had been carried out nightly – either by militia or by one of the infamous death squads – in retaliation for the death of one of their own at the hands of the FMLN guerrillas. They had been trained from an early age not to get themselves involved in any kind of trouble outside the confines of their own home. Old habits die hard . . .

He heard the sound of an approaching vehicle; moments later an army jeep appeared at the end of the street. The soldier in the passenger seat strafed the ground in front of Marlette, ordering him to stay where he was. Marlette glanced behind as the jeep sped towards him. He saw that Jayson had already reached the main gate, the Sig Sauer automatic in his hand. Jayson's face was momentarily illuminated in the jeep's headlights, and Marlette noticed with some satisfaction the deep laceration across his right cheek. The sight of the blood streaming down Jayson's face gave Marlette the lift he needed and, as the jeep closed in on him, he ducked into the alley alongside. A fusillade of bullets peppered the side of the shack closest to the alley, and Marlette heard Jayson yell furiously in his accented Spanish at the soldier to stop firing. Marlette ran the short distance to where the alley was dissected by a narrower tributary. He knew all about the maze of alleys and roads that intersected each other in every shanty town across the country. He'd been involved in enough follow-up operations when he was working with the military to know just how easy it was to get hopelessly lost in even the smallest shanty town. And to add to the military's problems, the guerrillas had always seemed to know their way around the shanty towns, often luring a younger, more inexperienced soldier into a cul-de-sac where he would be silently dispatched with a single stroke of a razor-sharp knife across the throat. And by the time his colleagues had found him, the assassin had disappeared, usually with the help of locals sympathetic to the cause. Then followed the inevitable midnight raids by the military to punish the community for aiding and abetting those regarded as enemies of the state. It had been a continuous, and bloody, stalemate . . .

Marlette heard the sound of approaching feet and, as he ducked into the shadows, he saw one of the soldiers arrive at the intersection of the two roads. The man wiped his sweating face, looked left, looked right, then continued straight ahead. Marlette waited a few seconds before emerging from his hiding place. He was well aware that Jayson and the other soldier were still out there in the darkness. Possibly Dennison as well. What if Dennison had already called in for reinforcements? It was imperative that he find his way out of the shanty town as quickly as possible, otherwise he could be moving around endlessly in circles while the military slowly closed in on him. But he couldn't double back the way he'd come for fear of running into the army patrol. Marlette decided to take the left fork.

He'd barely travelled a few tentative metres when he caught sight of a shadowy movement out of the corner of his eye. His heart missed a beat when a snarling Alsatian loomed up on its hind legs from behind a wire fence and began barking furiously at him. Marlette scanned the length of the deserted alley, half expecting to see a posse of soldiers bearing down on him. Another dog began to bark in the distance. Then another – and within seconds there was a cacophony of sound as more dogs responded to the chorus of incessant barking that echoed around the confines of the shanty town. It was the perfect cover – not only would the soldiers be unable to hear his footsteps above the noise, it would also disorientate them when they tried to pinpoint the original source of the barking. He willed the noise to continue as he hurried through the shanty town, pausing only at the mouth of each road to check for any sign of the opposition. Although he'd managed to evade capture so far, his worst fears were being realized the deeper he ventured into the shanty town: he was becoming hopelessly lost. Exactly what he'd been wanting to avoid.

Suddenly a pair of headlights appeared at the end of the street. Hurriedly he ducked down out of sight behind a couple of steel drums. They were overflowing with garbage and the putrid stench was almost unbearable, but he didn't move as the headlights came closer. He peered cautiously through the aperture between the two drums as the car drove past him. It wasn't a military vehicle. Probably a local resident, judging by the car's battered appearance. The car turned into a side street further down the road, and he waited until the sound of the engine had faded into the distance before slowly straightening up again. Where the hell was he? More to the point, how was he supposed to find his way out of this mess? He moved cautiously along another road, but it was only when he'd neared the other side that he realized he'd inadvertently entered a cul-de-sac. As he turned he was illuminated by a pair of powerful headlights. He looked round desperately for somewhere to flee, but realized that he was now hopelessly trapped. The car edged forward and he shielded his eyes as he tried to make out the occupants behind the glare of the headlights. It was the same car which had passed him earlier. Only this time he didn't dismiss it simply as a local resident. What if they were Dennison's men? That would be even worse than being picked up by a regular military patrol. He could just disappear without the authorities ever knowing about it. He scoured the ground around him for a weapon. A piece of wood. A length of pipe. Anything that could be used to defend himself. There was nothing. Play it by ear, he said to himself, as the car pulled up in front of him.

The passenger door opened and a woman climbed out of the car. She was dressed in loose-fitting olive green fatigues and her face was partially obscured behind a red bandanna. She was armed with an AK-47 assault rifle. Both the clothes and the weapon were standard issue of the FMLN guerrilla movement. Not that it meant anything. It could be a trap.

'Who are you?' Marlette demanded.

'You're looking for the Auger girl, aren't you?' came the sharp riposte.

Marlette said nothing.

'We know who you are and that you've come out here to find the girl,' she continued. 'One of our comrades spoke to Bob Kinnard the day before he was murdered. He knows where the girl is. We can take you to him.'

'I'm not going anywhere with you until I know who you are,' Marlette retorted defiantly. 'Are you FMLN?'

'Dennison has already called in for additional backup to seal off the shanty town,' she said, ignoring his question. 'We monitored the call over the police radio we have in the car. As I speak there are probably a dozen military vehicles on their way here. If we were caught by one of Dennison's vigilante patrols, we'd be executed on the spot. So either you come with us now, or else you can try and get out of here on your own. It's your choice, Marlette.'

'How do I know that you're not really working for Dennison?' Marlette asked quickly.

'Do you think we'd have offered you the chance of getting into the car voluntarily if we were a couple of Dennison's thugs?' came the sarcastic response. 'We can't stay here any longer. Those patrols will be arriving within the next few minutes to seal off the whole area. This is your last chance, Marlette. Are you coming or not?'

Marlette knew there wasn't time to weigh up the situation. Was it all some elaborate trap by Dennison's men to lure him into the car? If not, was she with the FMLN? Why would they want to help him? But more importantly, could she really lead him to Michelle? He knew only too well that his chances of finding Michelle had all but disappeared after what had happened at the orphanage. And even if he were to slip through the cordon that would be thrown around the shanty town, he'd already guessed that Dennison would see to it that his face appeared on the front page of every national newspaper the following day in connection with the murder of Bernard Coughlin. A wanted man. Then what use would he be to Nicole? Although he was loath to admit it, he had very little choice but to get in the car, especially while there was even the slightest chance that she was telling the truth about Michelle.

Marlette reluctantly walked to the car. He looked into the front seat and noticed that the driver's seat was now empty. The woman in the passenger seat was fidgeting with something on the floor and, although she'd removed the red bandanna, he still wasn't able to see her face. Then she suddenly sat up and looked directly at him. For a moment he stared back in disbelief at the face before a sharp blow caught him behind the ear. He was already unconscious before he crumpled to the ground.

Amaya watched in silence as the paramedic zipped up the body bag and gestured for his two colleagues to bring over a stretcher. Coughlin's body was lifted on to the stretcher and taken to the waiting ambulance.

'I see you managed to tear yourself away from the President's little soirée to join us,' a voice said behind Amaya.

Amaya swung round to face Dennison, his eyes blazing. 'Only after the President ordered me to have a full report of what happened here tonight on his desk first thing in the morning.' He grabbed Dennison's arm and propelled him out of earshot of the forensics team which was busy sifting painstakingly through the ruins of the gutted outhouse. 'The only reason the Military Council agreed to sanction this plan in the first place was because of your personal assurances that you could lure Marlette into a trap and kill him without alerting the authorities. A foolproof plan, you called it. What the hell went wrong?'

'OK, so it didn't go exactly to plan, but at the end of the day there's no real harm done,' Dennison replied with a dismissive shrug as he lit a cheroot.

'What?' Amaya retorted in disbelief. 'Coughlin's dead, Marlette's escaped and I've got over forty kids who witnessed a firefight outside the orphanage tonight. And you say there's no real harm done? The members of the Military Council are convening an extraordinary meeting at its headquarters at eight o'clock tomorrow morning. You *will* be there to explain what happened here tonight. Jayson is also to attend. Talking of Jayson, where is he?'

'He needed medical attention. He was hit by flying glass when the grenade went off. I sent him to a doctor I know in San Benito. He'll patch him up, no questions asked.'

'And what do you intend to do about Marlette?' Amaya demanded. 'I heard on the police radio a few minutes ago that so far he's managed to run rings around your people. Then again, judging by the fiasco that preceded his escape, I'd say there was every chance of him outsmarting them. It doesn't seem to be very difficult, does it?'

Dennison's jaw hardened as he glared furiously at the ground. When he looked up at Amaya again he'd managed to regain his composure. 'It's of little consequence whether Marlette escapes or not. I have the murder weapon in my possession. His gun with his prints on it. I've also already arranged to have his face splashed across the front pages of tomorrow's editions of *La Prensa*, *Diario de Hoy* and *El Mundo*. The reward I've offered for any information leading to his arrest is twenty times the national wage. He won't be able to show his face anywhere without the locals reporting his movements to the nearest precinct. Believe me, Marlette's now effectively out of the picture, and that's what the Military Council wanted, wasn't it?'

'What they didn't want was forty potential witnesses who could place Jayson here at the orphanage tonight. What am I supposed to tell the President in my report?'

'Pass him off as one of my men,' Dennison replied quickly.

'And just how many Salvadoreans have you ever seen with pale, blotchy skin and shoulder-length blond hair?' Amaya retorted contemptuously. 'I warned you not to use Jayson, but you wouldn't listen, would you?'

'You're in charge here. Use your authority to sit on those kids' statements. It shouldn't be too difficult, considering the overwhelming evidence you've already got against Marlette. If it were ever to go to court, any jury would convict him.'

'And just how long am I expected to "sit" on these statements?' Amaya demanded.

Dennison clamped his hand around Amaya's arm and pulled him towards him. 'The coup d'état's less than forty-eight hours away. I'm sure you can find a way to accidentally "misplace" those statements until then, can't you? You know as well as I do that Jayson has an integral part to play if the coup's to be a success. After that, you can do what you like with him for all I care.'

'So much for loyalty,' Amaya snorted.

'He's a hired gun, that's all,' came the disdainful reply. 'His kind don't give a damn about the politics of this or any other country. The only reason he wants the coup to succeed is because then he'll be paid the balance of the money owed to him. But if someone else were to offer him a lucrative contract to turn his gun on me, he'd do it without a second thought. So don't expect me to feel any loyalty towards him.'

Amaya traced the tip of his finger thoughtfully across

his lower lip as he watched the forensics team at work. 'Why did you let Marlette escape?'

'What are you talking about?' Dennison shot back.

'I've already spoken to the two men who accompanied you and Jayson here tonight. They both told me that you had more than enough time to kill Marlette, but that you chose instead to turn the gun on Coughlin. I can understand your reasons for wanting to silence Coughlin, but they also said that when Jayson tried to shoot Marlette as he was fleeing the orphanage, you told him that you wanted Marlette taken alive. When you presented your plan to the Military Council earlier this evening, you assured them that you would kill Marlette at the first opportunity you got. Why did you lie to them?'

'I didn't lie to them, and I didn't let Marlette escape,' Dennison responded quickly. 'I had my reasons for wanting him alive.'

'Which were?' Amaya pressed when Dennison fell silent.

'As I said when I presented my initial plan to the Military Council, the only way I knew of getting to Marlette was through Coughlin. I thought that with the right pressure I could persuade Coughlin to lead us to Marlette. But as it turned out, Coughlin didn't know where Marlette was hiding out. He only had a telephone number that he was to use to contact Marlette in case of an emergency. I had the number run through the police computer to match it up against an address here in the city. It was my intention to go to that address and deal with Marlette there. It would certainly have been a lot easier than having Coughlin lure him to the orphanage.'

'So why didn't you?' Amaya asked suspiciously.

'The number checked out to a house in the La Floresta area in the south of the city. Only I know the house. I'd actually visited it several times while I was with the American embassy here in San Salvador.'

'I don't understand,' Amaya said with a puzzled frown.

'It used to be a CIA safe house back then and, for all I know, it probably still is. And if the CIA are still using it, then you can be sure that it'll be well protected. It certainly was when I was last there. Security lights, trip-wires, and infrared scanners on every door. Standard company stuff. We wouldn't have got near the house without alerting Marlette. That's why I had to lure him out here instead. If that is still a CIA safe house, then that would imply that they're pulling his strings while he's here. That's why I wanted him alive. We need to find out exactly why Langley sent him here.'

'To recover the videotape, surely?' Amaya replied.

'What if there's more to it than that?' Dennison asked.

'What exactly are you getting at, Peter? That Langley already know about the coup?'

'It has to be a possibility,' Dennison agreed.

'You said yourself that you'd made several discreet enquiries at Langley after Kinnard's death, and that all your contacts had come back to you with the same story – that the CIA knew about the existence of the videotape but that Kinnard had refused to disclose what it contained until he was safely back on US soil.'

'That's what they told me at the time,' Dennison agreed. 'But who's to say that wasn't just disinformation put out by Kinnard's handler? After all, disinformation can be just as effective against your own side when you're trying to protect an operative abroad.'

'Are you suggesting that the CIA have a mole inside the Military Council who's been feeding information back to Langley?' Amaya demanded.

'It's a possibility,' Dennison replied.

'That's a serious accusation to make, and one totally without foundation. You know as well as I do that everyone in the Military Council is completely above suspicion.'

'Can we afford to take that chance?' Dennison retorted.

He drew on his cheroot and exhaled the smoke out of the corner of his mouth. '*If* there is a mole in the Military Council, then it's possible that Marlette may already know his identity. That's why it's so imperative that he's taken alive.'

'So that you can interrogate him, or protect him?' Amaya retorted.

For a moment Dennison looked puzzled, then a slow smile spread across his face when he realized what Amaya was implying. 'Do you think that I'd have mentioned any of this to you if I was the mole?'

'It's your theory, Peter, not mine,' Amaya replied. He looked at his watch. 'You'll have to excuse me. I've still got a long night ahead of me.'

Dennison turned to leave, then paused to look back at Amaya. 'If there is a traitor in the Military Council, I'll weed him out. You can be sure of that.'

'A word of advice, Peter,' Amaya called out after Dennison. 'Make sure you get there on time tomorrow morning. You've already infuriated the Military Council with this fiasco here tonight. Don't make things any worse for yourself than they already are.'

Dennison bit back his anger as he strode briskly to where his car was parked at the main gate.

'Get up!'

Marlette opened his eyes slowly and grimaced at the intensity of the naked bulb hanging from the ceiling but when he tried to sit up, a sharp pain speared through his head. Gingerly he lay back on the palliasse and closed his eyes again.

'I told you to get up!' This time the order was accompanied by a sharp and painful kick to his ribs.

Marlette struggled into a sitting position and, using his hand to shield his eyes from the light, he squinted up at the woman standing over him. She was in her late thirties with long black hair which was pulled back tightly from her thin face and secured in a ponytail at the back of her head. She was still dressed in the green fatigues that she'd been wearing earlier at the shanty town. The Russian T-33 pistol in her hand was trained on his chest.

'You know who I am, don't you?' she said in Spanish. 'That much was obvious from your expression when you saw me in the car.'

'Is that why I was knocked out?' he snapped, struggling to his feet.

'We couldn't be sure how you'd react when you realized who I was.'

'Anna Chavez,' Marlette said. 'Head of the FMLN's propaganda machine in the last years of the civil war. I could hardly not have known who you were. Your face was on every other wanted poster across the country.'

'It still is,' she replied proudly. 'Only now I'm the deputy leader of the movement.'

'And here I thought the FMLN was supposed to have been disbanded after the ceasefire was signed,' he said sarcastically.

'For the most part, it was,' she replied.

'Yeah, I heard rumours that there was still a hard core of militant Marxists who'd refused to recognize the new government of the country. I suppose it doesn't matter to you that this government was democratically elected by the people?'

'You've seen for yourself the poverty and misery that still exists in the shanty towns. This government made electoral promises to rehouse these people and tackle the chronic levels of unemployment that still exist throughout the country. They haven't. And they won't. The civil war may now be officially over, but the fight must go on if we're ever to eradicate the blatant and unjust class system that still exists in El Salvador.'

Marlette had met her kind before – unable to accept the

fact that those who had once supported them had chosen another path. All that was left for them was to continue fighting their own little war in some corner of the country. And like her colleagues, she still believed that she was on the side of justice and equality. He knew it would be pointless to argue with her . . .

He touched the bruise behind his ear as he looked around him slowly. The room was small; the furnishings spartan. A chipped washbasin, a wooden table, a cane chair and a threadbare palliasse. The single window was protected by a rusted iron grille but he couldn't see anything beyond the frosted glass. 'Where am I?'

'Safe,' came the sharp riposte. 'If we'd left you in the shanty town, Dennison's men would have tracked you down and killed you. We saved your life.'

'I'll be eternally grateful,' he retorted sarcastically.

'Do you know why I joined the FMLN, Marlette?'

'I'm sure I could guess –'

'To avenge my brother's death,' she cut in savagely. 'He was a social worker who helped families in the shanty towns of San Salvador to come to terms with the loss of loved ones during the civil war. One night he was comforting a woman who'd lost both her sons when three men suddenly burst into her home, dragged him outside, and shot him through the head. It turned out that his death was in response for the murder of one of their own earlier in the day. Only they weren't soldiers. They were part of a death squad which was touring the shanty town, executing civilians at random. My brother just happened to be in the wrong place that night.'

'I'm sorry,' Marlette said. 'I had no idea.'

'It wasn't just any death squad though. It was the UGB.' She pressed the barrel of the pistol against Marlette's forehead. 'You trained members of the UGB, didn't you?'

'It was part of my contract,' Marlette replied, holding her icy stare. 'Had I known –'

'Spare me the remorse,' she snapped. 'How do I know that you didn't help to train the men who murdered my brother? And if you did, it would make you an accomplice, wouldn't it?'

'If that's what you think, then you'd better pull the trigger.'

'You're very sure of yourself, aren't you?' she said, her finger curled around the trigger. 'You don't think I'll kill you, do you?'

'If you'd wanted to kill me, you'd have done so in the shanty town. You wouldn't have told me that you could take me to see someone who knew the whereabouts of the girl, and neither would you have risked your life by smuggling me out of there from under the noses of Dennison's men. You obviously wanted me alive. The question is, why?'

'And here I thought you had all the answers,' Chavez replied sarcastically, then she pushed the pistol back into her belt and crossed to the door where she paused to look round at him. 'Come with me!'

The bare floorboards creaked under his weight as he followed her to an illuminated doorway at the end of the corridor. It led into a kitchen. There was a table in the centre of the room with four chairs positioned around it. Chavez sat down in the chair facing the door. Although Marlette didn't recognize the slimly built man seated beside her, he assumed it was the driver of the car who'd slugged him earlier in the shanty town.

'Sit,' Chavez said, pointing to the chair opposite her. Marlette pulled out the chair and sat down slowly. 'Are you thirsty? We've just made a fresh brew of coffee.'

'I could use a coffee,' Marlette agreed.

The man pushed back his chair and used a cloth to hold the handle of the kettle as he poured out the coffee into a mug. He replaced the kettle on the stove and handed the mug to Marlette before retaking his seat beside Chavez.

Marlette took a sip of the piping hot coffee. It was bitter, but welcome.

'This is Miguel,' Chavez said, indicating the man beside her. 'That's all you need to know about him.'

'Well, now that the pleasantries are over, perhaps we can get down to business,' Marlette said. 'Where's Michelle Auger?'

Miguel's mouth flickered with a faint smile. 'It's not that easy, my friend.'

'Somehow I didn't think it would be,' Marlette replied, and placed the mug on the table. 'OK, so what's the deal?'

Chavez pulled a dog-eared photograph from the top pocket of her tunic and pushed it across the table to Marlette. 'Do you know who that is?'

Marlette picked up the photograph. It depicted Chavez and a bearded man standing in front of an abandoned government tank. He handed the photograph back to her. 'Guillermo Ruiz. Your former lover. He was the leader of the remnants of the FMLN until his death earlier this year.'

Miguel chuckled to himself, taking a packet of cigarettes from his pocket. He used his lips to pull one from the packet, then struck a match against the sole of his boot. He lit the cigarette and discarded the match on the floor. 'One right. Two wrong. You're right – it is Guillermo Ruiz.'

Marlette looked at Chavez. 'There was an article in *Time* magazine reporting that Ruiz had been killed when a bomb went off in a room where he was meeting with a team of his military advisers. There were said to have been no survivors.'

'There was one survivor,' Chavez replied. 'And it's taken Guillermo five months to recover from his injuries.'

'And where exactly does he fit into this?' Marlette asked.

'I told you that one of our comrades had met with Kinnard the day before he was murdered,' Chavez replied. 'It was Guillermo.'

'Kinnard met with Ruiz?' Marlette shot back in amazement. 'Why?'

Chavez sat back in her chair. 'All Guillermo would say about the meeting was that Kinnard had promised him a copy of a tape which he claimed contained insurmountable proof that there was a plot by members of the military to overthrow the present civilian government. I assume that you already know of the existence of this tape?'

'I've heard about it,' Marlette replied vaguely.

'Guillermo knew that we could use the tape not only to prevent the coup d'état from taking place, but also to press the government for further economic reforms,' Chavez continued. 'I think they'd be prepared to listen to reason if we had that kind of information to bargain with.'

'Blackmail, in other words,' Marlette retorted.

'If you like, yes,' Chavez replied with a quick shrug. 'In return for a copy of the tape, Kinnard asked Guillermo to ensure the girl's safety until he was ready to leave the country.'

'So where is Michelle now?' Marlette asked.

'I don't know,' Chavez replied. 'Her exact whereabouts are known only to those who are directly involved in protecting her. Guillermo refused to tell me any more than that in case the military found out about the tape. And, as it turned out, his fears were realized when Jayson murdered Kinnard.'

'How do you know about Jayson?'

'We have our sources,' Miguel replied vaguely.

'I assume that Ruiz knows of Michelle's whereabouts?' Marlette asked Chavez.

'He must do, he arranged it,' came the reply.

'So what's the catch?' Marlette asked suspiciously.

Chavez reached behind her for a copy of the morning edition of *La Prensa*, which was lying on the fridge. She pushed it across the table to Marlette, who picked it up and read the article which had been circled in red pen.

When he'd finished, he dropped the newspaper on the table and frowned at her. 'All it says here is that two unidentified men found in an abandoned car on the outskirts of the city late last night had been shot through the head at close range. What has this got to do with Ruiz?'

'They were Guillermo's personal bodyguards. He'd been on his way to a meeting in a village about twenty kilometres north of the city. Only he never arrived. My first thought on hearing this was that he'd been arrested by the police, but all my subsequent enquiries drew a blank. It was through one of Miguel's contacts that we finally discovered the truth earlier today. Guillermo's being held at a farmhouse on the outskirts of the city. It used to belong to the military but, like most of their safe houses, it was sold by the government after the ceasefire to raise additional money for the beleaguered treasury.'

Marlette took a sip of coffee. 'Let me guess. You want me to get Ruiz out of there for you. Am I right?'

'You catch on quickly, my friend,' Miguel said with a smile.

'When it comes down to it, Marlette, you've just as much to gain by getting Guillermo out of there as we do,' Chavez said.

Marlette sat back in his chair and folded his arms across his chest. 'None of this makes any sense. You know as well as I do that your own people could spring Ruiz from the safe house, yet you took one hell of a risk tonight by smuggling me out of the shanty town. Question is: why take that risk unless there's more to this than meets the eye?'

Chavez stubbed out her cigarette in the ashtray, then got to her feet and moved to the window. 'You're right, we could have used our own people, except that, apart from Miguel, myself and the two senior council members whom Guillermo was on his way to see last night, nobody else in our organization knows he survived the explosion. As far as the rank and file are concerned, he's been dead for the past five months.'

'Why?' Marlette asked in bewilderment. 'Surely it would have been a great boost to their morale if they knew that Ruiz had survived?'

'Two reasons. We believe that the bombing was ordered by someone in our organization. Someone in a senior position. We'd hoped that this person would have tried to make a move on the vacant leadership if he thought that Guillermo was actually dead, but so far nobody has come forward to challenge me since I took over as the acting commander-in-chief. We were going to hold a rally next month to elect a new leader in Tejutla, an FMLN stronghold in the north of the country. We'd already decided that Guillermo should appear there unannounced. It would have been a great coup for him and the organization as a whole. All the national newspapers would have splashed us across their front pages. It would have been the kind of publicity we could only have dreamed of before.'

'You say all this in the past tense,' Marlette pointed out.

'Guillermo's greatest strength has always been his negotiating skills. He was, after all, one of the organization's senior representatives at the original UN-backed peace talks which were held between the government and the FMLN in New York and Geneva in the early nineties. It was only after his colleagues sold out unconditionally to the government by agreeing to suspend all attacks against non-military targets and by proposing future negotiations with the government representatives to further erode the democratic rights of our organization that he walked out of the talks and returned home to resume the armed struggle.

'But if we're to use this tape to negotiate new terms with the government – terms acceptable to us and to our supporters – then we'll need Guillermo to lead our delegation. His reappearance would still generate great media interest, although not on the scale that it would have if it had been in front of his own people.' Chavez helped herself to another cigarette. 'Perhaps now you can understand why we took those risks to get you out of the shanty town. We don't have to like each other, Marlette, but right now we do need to work together.'

Marlette had to admit reluctantly to himself that she was right, but at the same time he recognized that it was an alliance born out of necessity and more than just a hint of desperation – on both sides. They needed each other to achieve their own ends. But that didn't mean he would venture any information that they didn't already know. No mention of the CIA or the fact that he was just as keen as they were to get his hands on the tape. It would only complicate an already convoluted situation . . .

'OK, so you've told me why you can't use your own people to spring Ruiz, but that still doesn't answer my question. The two of you could have done the job yourselves. Why bring me in on it?'

'Because right now we're the two most senior members of the organization. If something were to go wrong and we were caught, not only would it be a great coup for the government, but it would also be a serious blow to the future of the movement as a whole.'

'In other words, I'm going in alone,' Marlette retorted.

'No, you'll be working with Miguel.'

'Working with him, or taking orders from him?'

'You're a professional soldier, Marlette,' Chavez replied. 'Your experience and expertise will prove invaluable during this type of operation. You will lead the assault. Miguel will follow your orders. Satisfied?'

'So what do you say, my friend?' Miguel asked, breaking the sudden silence. 'Are you in or out?'

'What can you tell me about this farmhouse?' Marlette asked Chavez.

'You didn't answer my question,' Miguel said, leaning forward, his eyes riveted on Marlette's face.

'Of course he's in,' Chavez snapped as a faint sneer touched the corners of her mouth. 'After all, it's not as if he's got much choice. Show him the diagram.'

Miguel removed a sheet of paper from his pocket and handed it to Marlette. It was an architect's blueprint of the farmhouse. The points of entry had been highlighted in red pen.

'I managed to get the blueprint earlier today from a sympathizer who works at the city hall,' Chavez said. 'And from what I could gather from the clerk, the farmhouse was bought by a senior military officer who was retired from the National Guard after the new government came to power. He died a year ago, and it seems that the farmhouse has been deserted since his death. The perfect place to hold someone like Guillermo without raising any suspicion.'

Marlette studied the diagram. 'How many guards are there stationed in and around the farmhouse?'

'I don't know,' Chavez replied.

'Surely your contact must have a rough idea.'

'He doesn't,' Miguel replied. 'He only heard about Guillermo by chance when he bumped into a colleague of his at a bar last night. It turns out that this colleague had been involved in Guillermo's abduction. He plied his colleague with drink, hoping to find out more, but he never did discover the man's exact role in the whole affair, other than that he knew where Guillermo was being held.'

'Who was this other man? A soldier?' Marlette asked.

'An ex-soldier,' Miguel told him. 'And from what my source could determine, it seems that the military weren't involved in the incident last night. Both men work for Peter Dennison.'

'Dennison,' Marlette snorted in disgust. 'I might have guessed that he'd be mixed up in this.'

'But that raises the question, why would he want to abduct Guillermo?' Chavez continued.

'Unless he found out about the meeting between Ruiz and Kinnard,' Marlette replied. 'Ruiz could lead him to Michelle Auger – and this tape that everybody wants to get their hands on so badly.'

'Including you, my friend?' Miguel asked.

'I don't give a shit about what happens to the tape,' Marlette retorted sharply, hoping he sounded convincing enough. 'I was hired by Nicole Auger to find her daughter. The kid's safety is my only concern.'

'How touching,' Chavez sneered. 'But then you and Auger were once more than just friends, weren't you?'

'How do you know about that?' Marlette demanded.

'We know a lot about you, Marlette,' she replied disdainfully.

Marlette stared coldly at her, then slowly nodded his head. 'Yeah, we had something going. Once. And that brings me to my own conditions for springing Ruiz from the safe house.'

'Conditions?' Miguel snorted contemptuously. 'I don't think you're in any position to be demanding any conditions from us.'

Chavez eyed Miguel sharply, then turned back to Marlette. 'Go on,' she said.

'After what happened at the orphanage tonight, you can be sure that by tomorrow morning my face will be on the front page of every newspaper across the country, probably with a large reward being offered for my capture. The police will be under a lot of pressure to bring me in as quickly as possible and, as they won't have any real leads to go on, they'll almost certainly put pressure on Nicole to tell them everything she knows about my movements since I first entered the country. They might even decide to charge her as an accessory to Coughlin's murder. I doubt whether they could make it stick, but I'm not prepared to take that chance. It's not just that though – if we are to find Michelle before Dennison's thugs can get to her, then she's going to need her mother more than ever after what she's been through.'

'So what you're saying is that you want the Auger woman brought here, is that it?' Chavez asked.

'That's right.'

'Where is she at the moment?' Chavez queried. 'We can arrange to have her picked up and brought here within the hour.'

'It's not that simple,' Marlette replied. 'She's at Dennison's guest-house in San Benito.'

'Forget it,' Miguel snorted. 'We wouldn't get near the place.'

'Miguel's right,' Chavez agreed. 'Dennison converted the house into a fortress after he bought it. It was even rumoured to have had a soundproofed basement where the death squads favoured by Dennison could take their prisoners for interrogation. It was said to have been especially popular with the UGB. It's probably still there, for all I know.'

'I'm just surprised that you've never heard about it, considering the close links you forged with the UGB when you were last out here,' Miguel snorted.

'I was a military adviser to the UGB, nothing more,' Marlette snapped back.

'And how many of our comrades died as a direct result of your so-called "military advice"?' Miguel hissed furiously.

'I was paid to do a job, just like the Russian and Cuban military advisers you had to train your people. There was no difference.'

'Except that none of them raped a twelve-year-old girl,' Miguel said disdainfully.

Marlette kicked back his chair angrily and crossed to the window where he folded his arms tightly across his chest and glared out into the darkness. He remained silent.

'You don't have an answer to that, do you, my friend?' Miguel sneered, then got to his feet and approached

Marlette from behind. 'So tell me, what was it like to fuck her?'

Marlette slammed his elbow into Miguel's midriff. As he doubled over, Marlette swung round and caught him with a hammering punch to the side of the head. Miguel stumbled backwards and dropped to his knees, one hand clamped over his stomach, the other clasped to his face. Struggling to his feet, his face still twisted in pain, he yanked his Colt .45 from its holster and levelled it at Marlette.

'Put the gun away,' Chavez ordered.

'You're going to regret doing that!' Miguel hissed through clenched teeth.

'I said put it away!' Chavez snarled furiously.

Miguel's breathing was ragged as he shifted uncomfortably on his feet, then he slowly lowered the pistol and banged it down angrily on the table. 'This is not over, my friend,' he warned Marlette.

'You're damn right it isn't,' Marlette replied icily, then turned back to Chavez. 'Either you agree to my terms or else you can get Ruiz out by yourselves. That's the deal. Take it or leave it.'

Chavez held Marlette's withering stare. 'I've told you already, we wouldn't get near the house.'

'I've got an idea of how we can get Nicole out of the house. I just hope we're not too late though. She may already have been taken away by the police for questioning.'

Chavez gestured to the chair opposite her. 'Sit down. If I think your plan will work, I'm prepared to consider it. If not, then she's on her own. That's the deal, Marlette. Take it or leave it.'

SEVEN

The guard jumped to his feet and grabbed his machine-pistol as the car swung into the driveway and came to a halt in front of the wrought-iron security gate. He emerged from his hut and approached the gate cautiously, his hand raised to his face to shield his eyes from the glare of the headlights.

The passenger door opened and a tall, clean-shaven man climbed out of the car. The guard's finger tightened around the trigger when he noticed the unmistakable bulge of a holstered weapon under the man's lightweight suit.

'Police,' the man announced brusquely, holding out his badge.

Satisfied that the badge was genuine, the guard lowered the machine-pistol. 'What do you want?'

'We're here to see a Ms Nicole Auger,' came the reply. 'I believe she's staying at this address.'

The guard frowned momentarily. 'There is a foreign woman staying at the house but I don't know her name. She is *Señor* Dennison's guest.'

'Would you open the gates, please?' The guard hesitated. 'I spoke to *Señor* Dennison on the phone before I came here,' the man assured him. 'He said he would call and explain the situation to you before we got here.'

'He hasn't called me,' came the reply.

The man cursed angrily then patted his pockets, found his notebook, and opened it to the relevant page and extended it through the gate. 'That's the number. Call him.'

The guard returned to the hut and rang the number on

the page. After a brief conversation, he replaced the handset and reached for the remote control, activating the gate.

The man climbed back into the car, which eased forward until the passenger window was in line with the hut door. 'We'd appreciate it if you'd call Ms Auger and tell her that we're on our way up there to see her.'

'I'll phone the housekeeper,' the guard said, reaching for the telephone again.

The passenger window closed and the car disappeared up the driveway.

'*Señora*, you must wake up,' Manuela insisted, shaking Nicole's shoulder. 'Please, *señora*, wake up.'

Nicole was awake in an instant and switched on the bedside lamp. 'What is it? What's wrong?'

'You must get dressed, *señora*,' Manuela told her. 'There is a policeman waiting downstairs to speak to you.'

'Is it about my daughter?' Nicole asked anxiously, grabbing Manuela's arm. 'Have they found her?'

'No, he wants to ask you some questions about Richard Marlette,' Manuela said, easing her arm from Nicole's grip. 'But he would not tell me any more than that.'

Nicole pulled back the sheets and swung her legs out of the bed. She was about to get to her feet when she looked up at Manuela, her eyebrows knitted in a frown. 'I thought you didn't speak English.'

'I speak English,' came the indifferent reply as if it was of little importance. 'I have already tried to call *Señor* Dennison at his house, but the number is engaged. I will try again while you are getting dressed.' With that Manuela left the room, closing the door behind her.

Nicole's mind was racing as she changed into a pair of jeans and a baggy sweater. Had something happened to Rick? Had he been arrested? Or injured? Or worse? No, she refused to believe that any harm could have come to him. She pulled on a pair of plimsolls, then headed for the door but, as she hurried down the stairs, she couldn't seem to shake off the sense of uncertainty and trepidation that continued to prey on her mind.

Manuela took Nicole's arm when she reached the foot of the stairs and guided her to one side. 'Do you know a priest called Coughlin?'

'No,' Nicole was quick to reply. Too damn quick, she chided herself angrily. It was obvious from the look on Manuela's face that she didn't believe her. 'Who is he?'

'He was an American missionary here in San Salvador. He was shot dead at his orphanage earlier this evening. The police believe your friend, Richard Marlette, may have been responsible for his murder. They seem to think that you might be able to help them with their investigation. You are to be taken to the station and questioned there.'

'Am I being arrested?' Nicole demanded, immediately going on to the offensive in a desperate attempt to mask her horror at the news of Coughlin's death.

'No. The police do not think you were involved in Father Coughlin's death. They just want to ask you some questions about Marlette. I still cannot get through to *Señor* Dennison, but the policeman said that his superior has already contacted both the American embassy and *Señor* Dennison on your behalf. The embassy has arranged for an English-speaking lawyer to be present at the station when the police question you.' Manuela indicated the man standing by the door. 'He does not speak any English. I will go with you to the police station to act as a translator until your lawyer arrives.'

Nicole followed Manuela from the house and across the portico to where the driver of the unmarked car was holding open the back door for them. He eyed Manuela suspiciously, but said nothing when she climbed into the back of the car. Nicole got in after her and the door was closed behind them. Folding her arms tightly across her chest, Nicole stared out of the window as the car pulled away from the house. There was no doubt in her mind that Rick was innocent of Coughlin's murder. What would he possibly have to gain by killing him? No, it was obvious he'd been framed. And it had worked, judging by the way the police had reacted. Assuming, of course, that they weren't also part of the conspiracy . . . She quickly dismissed that idea, though, given the history of ill-feeling which had existed for many years between the police and the military in El Salvador. She had a good idea who was behind Coughlin's murder – only she knew she could hardly go making wild accusations against Dennison without the necessary evidence to back them up. Her eyes flickered to Manuela. There was something distinctly military about her posture. Was she another of the ex-soldiers whom Dennison had recruited from the army? And why had Dennison told her that Manuela didn't understand English? It didn't make any sense. Or did it? She remembered now eager Manuela had been to unpack her suitcase and overnight bag when she'd first arrived at the house. At the time she'd been impressed rather than suspicious. But now the more she thought about it, the more she realized that Manuela had obviously been sifting through her belongings, looking for any clues which could have led Dennison to Rick. She felt distinctly unclean, as if she had been violated . . .

The car suddenly screeched to a shuddering halt and Nicole, who had been totally absorbed in her own thoughts, was thrown forward and cracked the side of her head painfully on the back of the passenger seat. She was still struggling to sit up when she realized why the driver had been forced to brake so violently. A car had shot out from a side street in front of them, blocking the deserted road. The three men who leapt from the car were armed with semi-automatic weapons, their faces hidden under black balaclavas. Two of them were dressed in T-shirts and scruffy jeans. The third wore an army flak jacket and camouflage trousers tucked into a pair of scuffed boots. Nicole looked round when she noticed the reflection of a pair of headlights in the rearview mirror, and saw to her horror that a second car had swung into view from another side street behind them. It stood motionless in the middle of the road, its engine idling. They were trapped.

The driver spoke anxiously to his partner, then said something to Manuela which Nicole didn't understand either.

'What did he say?' Nicole demanded when she saw the look of terror on Manuela's face.

'He thinks they are *un escuadrón de la muerte*,' she said, her eyes now riveted on the three men in the street. 'A death squad.'

'What do they want?' Nicole asked fearfully.

'I do not know. But if they demand money or jewellery from you, do not try and resist them. They will only kill you then take what they want from your body.'

Nicole shuddered.

The man in the flak jacket snapped his fingers, and the other two men took up positions on either side of the car, training their weapons on the driver and his partner. The man in the flak jacket gestured for them to get out of the car. The driver cast a despairing look at his colleague, then reluctantly activated the locks from a console on the dashboard but, before he could reach for the handle, the door was wrenched open from the outside and the barrel of a machine-pistol was pressed against the side of his neck. Both he and his colleague were quickly disarmed, then they were hauled from the car and marched towards a patch of dense undergrowth at the side of the road.

Nicole watched with a mounting sense of unease as the two men disappeared from view. A moment later the silence was shattered by a sharp burst of gunfire. Then silence. She looked at Manuela and saw the fear in her eyes. A mirror-image of her own emotions? The two masked men emerged from the undergrowth and returned to the car. Nicole shrank back against the seat when the door was wrenched open and a hand reached inside and grabbed Manuela's arm. Manuela tried to pull her arm free, but the man snapped furiously at her in Spanish, and prodded the barrel of the machine-pistol menacingly into her ribs. She stopped struggling and got out of the car. She was led across to the nearest car and bundled roughly into the back seat. The two men got in after her and the car drove off.

Nicole swallowed nervously as she stared at the lone figure still standing in front of the car. She could try and make a run for it, but how far would she get before he caught up with her? What was the alternative? She'd rather die than let him touch her. But what would become of Michelle if something were to happen to her? The thought of Michelle seemed to give her renewed confidence in herself, but that confidence was quickly put to the test when the man approached the back door. An idea flashed through her mind. It was a long shot, but she knew it was all she had. Desperate times call for desperate measures. And if it didn't work? She tried to push any negative thoughts from her mind, knowing that it was essential for her to play into his hands. She hugged her knees against her chest and cowered away from the open door, pretending to be in abject fear of him. She could feel her heart pounding frantically and she clamped her clammy hands together tightly in front of her knees to try and stop them from shaking. But how much of it was pretence and how much of it was real? It was only the thought of seeing her daughter again that seemed to be holding together what little bravado she had left. She knew she would have to time her move to perfection. One mistake and the element of surprise would be gone. And so would her chances of escaping. She waited apprehensively until the man reached the open door, then unleashed her legs like a coiled spring, slamming her heels savagely into his groin. She let out a yelp of delight when he cried out in agony and crumpled to the ground, then she scrambled across the seat, but he grabbed her ankle as she tried to flee the car. She tugged furiously at his vice-like grip, but when she couldn't free herself, she swung round on him, ready to lash out at him.

'Nicole, it's me, for Christ's sake,' came the anguished cry.

She had to check herself as she was about to follow through with her foot, then, dropping down on to her haunches, she pulled off the balaclava and found Marlette glowering at her through the pain. 'Rick, what are you doing here?' she asked in disbelief.

'Getting you away from Dennison,' he hissed through the pain. 'And this is the thanks I get for it.'

'I didn't realize it was you,' she replied anxiously.

'Obviously not,' Marlette retorted as he continued to draw short, sharp breaths of air through his clenched teeth. 'Jesus, Nicole, what the hell have you got in the soles of your shoes? Lead?'

'I said I was . . .' she trailed off abruptly then stood up and glared down at him, her eyes awash with anger. 'Why am I apologizing to you? You just had those two cops executed in cold blood. And why was Manuela taken away in that car? Or was that all part of the deal that you made with the "death squad"? You disgust me, Rick. You're no better than Dennison and his thugs.'

'Have you quite finished?' Marlette snapped, then eased himself gingerly to his feet and leaned back against the side of the car. 'For a start, nothing's going to happen to the woman. We didn't anticipate her coming with you, so we had to improvise as best we could. Secondly, I'm not in league with any "death squad", and lastly, those cops aren't cops and neither are they dead.'

'I heard the gunfire,' Nicole retorted, but already there was an edge of uncertainty in her voice.

'You shouldn't believe everything you hear,' Marlette

replied, then put two fingers to his mouth and whistled loudly. Moments later the two 'policemen' emerged from the undergrowth and gave him a thumbs-up sign. He then signalled to the driver of the car which was still idling at the end of the street. 'Satisfied now, or do you still think the worst of me?'

Nicole watched as the two men disappeared back into the undergrowth. 'I don't understand,' she said hesitantly.

'You will, once I've explained it to you. But right now we need to get the hell out of here before the real cops arrive.'

'Rick?' she said as the car pulled up beside them. 'I'm sorry about Father Coughlin.'

'Yeah, me too,' he said bitterly, then pulled open the back door for her. 'Get in.'

'So the two guys who came to the house were actually FMLN guerrillas?' Nicole said as she poured herself a coffee from the kettle on the stove once they'd returned to the FMLN safe house.

'Yeah,' Marlette said, pulling up a chair and sitting down. 'The FMLN often impersonated the police and the military during the civil war. That way they were able to gain access to restricted areas. The IDs were stolen and the photographs changed. That's how they were able to trick their way into the house.'

'But surely Dennison would have checked on their identities when the guard phoned him?' Nicole said.

Marlette sat back and allowed himself a faint smile of satisfaction. 'I said the guard phoned the number on the piece of paper. I never said he actually spoke to Dennison.'

'Then who . . .' She trailed off as the truth dawned on her. 'He spoke to you, didn't he?'

Marlette nodded. 'I'm the first to admit that Dennison's Spanish is a lot better than mine, but he still speaks it with an American accent. And to the locals, one American accent sounds very much like another. At least, that's what I was gambling on when the guard phoned me. Of course, I was more concerned that anyone inside the house, like the housekeeper, would have access to Dennison's home number, so shortly before the two phoney cops showed up at the house, I rang Dennison from a pay-phone in the city centre. When I didn't say anything, he hung up. I left the phone off the hook to block any incoming calls he may have got from the guest-house. That's why the housekeeper told you his number was engaged when she tried to reach him.'

'What will happen to Manuela?' Nicole asked as she reached for the packet of cigarettes that Miguel had left on the table.

'She'll be released unharmed in the morning.'

'So it was really just a straight swap?' she said, lighting a cigarette and discarding the match in the ashtray. 'The FMLN help you to get me away from Dennison, and in return you spring this Ruiz and bring him back here for them.'

Chavez appeared in the doorway behind Nicole before Marlette could answer. 'Are you ready?'

'Give me another few minutes,' Marlette replied.

Chavez's jaw hardened, but she said nothing. She disappeared back up the hallway.

'Can she be trusted?' Nicole asked, staring at the doorway.

'I'd trust her about as much as I'd trust Dennison,' came the reply.

'Then why did you team up with them?' Nicole asked.

'Because we need them.'

'*We?*' Nicole replied suspiciously.

Marlette sat forward and clasped his hands on the table in front of him. 'There's something I haven't told you yet, Nicole.'

'Why do I get the feeling it's bad news?' she said warily.

'Far from it. It's about Michelle.'

'What is it, Rick?' she replied excitedly, grabbing his hand. 'Do they know where she is? Do they?'

'According to Chavez, Kinnard made a deal with Ruiz the day before he was murdered. He agreed to give Ruiz a copy of the tape if, in return, Ruiz would hide Michelle until he was ready to leave the country. Only Ruiz wouldn't tell anyone where Michelle was, not even Chavez. Ruiz is the one person, apart from the guerrillas who are actually protecting her, who knows where Michelle is right now. I have to get to him if we're to have any chance of finding her.'

Nicole sat back slowly in her chair and cupped her hands over her nose and mouth as she took in what Marlette had just told her. When she finally lowered her hands, she smiled quickly at him through the tears which had welled up in her eyes. But she said nothing. What was there to say after everything she'd been through over the past few days?

'It's possible that Dennison may already know about the meeting,' Marlette said, breaking the lingering silence. 'It would certainly explain why he went to the lengths he did to keep Ruiz's abduction under wraps. Chavez insists that Ruiz would hold out under torture. I'm not so sure. Not if Jayson's been allowed to work on him. That's why it's imperative that I get him out tonight. I don't mean to sound pessimistic, but it is something we need to bear in mind all the same.'

'Always expect the worst; that way things can only get better,' Nicole said, sniffing back the tears. 'That's what my father used to say.'

'And they will, I promise,' Marlette said. He pushed back his chair and got to his feet. 'I'd better go and see Chavez. Will you be OK here?'

'Sure,' she replied.

Marlette put a reassuring hand on her shoulder as he

passed her on the way to the door, then made his way to an illuminated doorway further down the dimly lit hallway. The room contained a garish orange-coloured sofa which was wedged into the area directly beneath the spacious bay window; two threadbare armchairs, one green and one brown, were positioned against the two adjacent walls. Miguel was crouched beside the chipped cork table in the middle of the room, cleaning an old AK-47 assault rifle. Chavez, who was seated on the sofa, drew deeply on a hand-rolled cigarette, then gestured for Marlette to sit in the brown armchair. He eyed the armchair distastefully but sat down, careful to avoid the rusted spring which was protruding through the torn seat.

'My people got the weapons you requested,' Chavez said, and pointed to a battered hold-all at the side of the armchair. 'You'll find everything you had on your list in there, except for the night-vision goggles. But then I warned you that I didn't think they'd be able to get them.'

Marlette opened the hold-all. He rummaged through the contents: a Heckler & Koch MP5 sub-machine gun with three clips; four stun grenades and four smoke grenades. He nodded to himself, then looked across at her. 'Where did they get the gear from at such short notice?'

'That doesn't concern you,' she retorted sharply. 'But now that you have the weapons, I expect you to carry out your part of the deal as efficiently as my people procured these weapons for you. You'll go with the plan we agreed on before you left to get the woman.'

'I still say that we need a four-man team to spring Ruiz, especially as we won't know the strength of the opposition until we get there,' Marlette said, removing the sub-machine gun from the hold-all and checking the firing mechanism. 'Surely you must have at least two men that you can trust to keep their mouths shut until Ruiz is ready to show his face again in public?'

'We've already been through all that. You and Miguel

will go in alone.' Chavez checked her watch. 'Miguel, bring the car around to the front of the house.'

Miguel got to his feet and almost bumped into Nicole as he reached the door. He brushed past her and disappeared out into the hallway. Chavez stared coldly at Nicole as she hovered uncertainly in the doorway.

'She doesn't particularly like me, does she?' Nicole said, knowing that Chavez didn't understand English.

'You. Me. The world,' Marlette replied as he took a tube of camouflage cream from the hold-all. 'She's still stuck in her own little time-warp, and anyone who doesn't conform to her outmoded socialist ideologies is regarded at best as suspect, at worst as the enemy. I get the feeling that we fall somewhere in between the two.'

'Do you think she's planning to kill us once Ruiz is free?' Nicole asked.

'No,' Marlette was quick to reply. 'If there's one thing I learnt about the FMLN when I was last here, it was that they pride themselves on their fairness. You treat them right and they'll do the same. Double-cross them, then they'll kill you.'

Nicole sat down and the memories came flooding back to her as she watched Marlette cross to the cracked mirror behind the door where he streaked the camouflage cream liberally across his face. She could still remember the uncertainty that used to ball painfully in the pit of her stomach every time she watched him black up before going out on a night operation. The uncertainty of him ever returning. The uncertainty of ever seeing him again. She also recalled how he'd always try and reassure her with a wink and a smile. But she'd known that deep down he'd been as uncertain as she, and it was that element of human frailty which she'd found so appealing in him. She felt a knot of pain tighten in the pit of her stomach and realized that it was no longer a memory. Had it ever been a memory, or just a subconscious reminder of the past reflected in the nervous anxiety she was experiencing? She suddenly sensed that Marlette was watching her. When she met his eyes in the reflection of the mirror, he smiled gently at her. Then the wink. He knew. Was it that obvious? Not that it bothered her. She'd never felt uncomfortable around him. She smiled back, then took the packet of cigarettes from her pocket and lit one.

'Are you still in love with her?'

The question caught Marlette by surprise, and when he looked at Chavez he saw that she was smiling faintly at him. 'She'll always hold a special place in my heart,' he replied in Spanish. 'It's only natural after what we once had together.'

'It only takes a single spark to rekindle a fire,' Chavez said, then stood up and crossed to the door. 'I can see that she's already found the spark again.'

'You're a hell of an expert on someone you hardly know,' Marlette snorted.

'I don't have to know her. It's in her eyes. You obviously have a lot to learn about women, Marlette.'

Nicole watched Chavez leave the room. When she turned back to Marlette, she found that he was studying her intently. It was as though he were trying to read something in her eyes. 'Rick, what is it?' she asked with a nervous chuckle. 'What are you looking at?'

The sound of her voice startled him out of his trance-like state. 'Nothing,' he said quickly. 'Nothing at all.'

'You never could lie to me, could you?' she said, but held up a hand before he could say anything. 'Don't worry, it doesn't matter. Obviously something Chavez said to you.'

Marlette was about to lie again, but quickly dismissed the idea. It wouldn't do any good. She'd just see through his deception again. It had always bugged him that he could lie to anyone else and get away with it. But not with Nicole. It was almost as if he became completely transparent whenever he tried to lie to her. He shot another look in her direction, then shook his head sadly to himself. *It's in her eyes.* Well, if it was, he was damned if he could see it. Then again, he didn't even know what he was looking for. Perhaps Chavez was right – perhaps he did still have a lot to learn about woman. *Yeah,* him and every other man in the world. He pulled the olive-green bandanna from his pocket and began to shape it into a coiled headband.

'That's not the same one you used to wear in Africa, is it?' she asked, eyeing the offending article with disgust.

'The very same. I was wearing it the night we met, remember?'

'How could I forget?' she replied. 'I thought then that it was old and dirty. I hate to think what state it must be in by now.'

'Old, yes, but not dirty. It gets washed regularly. You know that,' he said defensively, then proceeded to secure it across his forehead before tying it at the back of his head.

'I still say it looks awful. You should treat yourself to a new one,' she said with a mock-reproving look.

'This bandanna's my lucky talisman. And you can't deny that it hasn't worked for me up to now.'

'True, but then it's not as if you even need one any more, not now that you've cut off all those flowing locks.'

He ran his hand over his cropped hair. 'Actually, I've got quite used to it like this. I reckon I'll keep it this way from now on.'

Chavez called out to him from the hallway. He picked up the hold-all and crossed to where Nicole was now standing by the door. She wet the tip of her thumb and wiped a smear of black cream from the corner of his mouth, then reached up and kissed him lightly on the lips. Their eyes met. Words would only have been a clumsy intrusion on the intensity of the moment. Then Chavez's voice echoed down the hall again, and the bond was broken. He turned away quickly and left the room.

Chavez stood by the front door, her hand resting on the handle. 'You have exactly ninety minutes to complete the operation.' She checked her watch. 'It's now three-twenty. You will be back here with Guillermo no later than four-fifty.'

'And if I'm late?' Marlette challenged.

'Then I'll kill the woman,' came the chilling reply.

Sensing it was no idle threat, Marlette levelled a finger of warning at her. 'You so much as harm –'

'Ninety minutes is more than enough time for you to carry out the operation,' she cut in quickly. 'You should be back here within an hour. That gives you an extra thirty minutes to deal with any unanticipated problems that may arise in that time.'

'Your generosity is overwhelming,' Marlette sniped.

'I don't trust you, Marlette,' she said matter-of-factly. 'I can imagine it could be very tempting for you to put a bullet in Miguel's back once the operation was over, then force Guillermo to tell you what you want to know about the girl. Then he would also have outlived his usefulness as well, wouldn't he?'

'I'm a professional, I've never reneged on a contract in my life,' Marlette snapped angrily, stung by the obvious implication to the contrary.

'I'm glad to hear it, but then the same can't be said for all foreign mercenaries, can it? I know that from bitter experience. So let's just say that this is my own way of making sure that you keep to your side of the deal. I'm sure you'd have done the same if the positions were reversed.'

Marlette contemplated the idea of trying to warn Nicole of Chavez's intentions. But warn her of what? The more he thought about it, the more he realized that her life would only be in danger if he failed to meet the deadline. The onus was on him to make sure he didn't fail her. In effect, her life was in his hands. He'd make damn sure he was back in time . . .

Chavez opened the door. 'Ninety minutes, Marlette.'

'Ninety minutes,' he agreed, then hurried to the waiting car.

Marlette didn't venture any small-talk to pass the time, preferring to concentrate on an imaginary spot on the windscreen, and although Miguel would occasionally shoot a glance in his direction, he was also silent. Not that Marlette was even consciously aware of Miguel as they made for their destination on the outskirts of San Salvador, so absorbed was he in his own world of thoughts.

Nicole. She was all he'd thought about ever since they'd left the house. Then again, not a single day had gone by in the last six years when he hadn't thought about her. Not that he'd ever admitted that to anyone. And he certainly wasn't about to admit it to her. Especially not to her. His thoughts had always seemed to centre on the little things which had occurred while they were together, many of them so insignificant that they hardly seemed worth remembering. And how often had he brooded for hours trying to recall the smallest of details as he'd painstakingly pieced together the emotional jigsaw he'd created in his mind? There had been times over the years when he'd despaired at himself for lingering so obsessively on the past. He'd become, in effect, a hopeless addict in those six years since she left him – a cerebral junkie, hooked on a quotidian fix of memories to help him get through the day. Some of the memories had been good. Some bad. It made no difference to him. He'd embraced them all, no matter how hurtful they'd turned out to be. And there were those which had left their scars. He'd known though that, without the full spectrum of emotions to guide him, he could never have learnt from his mistakes. But had he learnt anything constructive from it all, or was he just wallowing in the guilt and self-pity which is invariably left in the wake of a broken relationship? It was a question which had haunted him over the years, and one to which he still didn't have a conclusive answer. Or had he just been fooling himself into believing that? He didn't know . . .

It had been his favourite poet, Alfred Lord Tennyson, who'd once written: ''Tis better to have loved and lost, than never to have loved at all.' He'd obviously never loved and lost anyone like Nicole, Marlette thought ruefully to himself. There had been numerous times over the years when he'd cursed fate for ever having brought Nicole into his life. But then there were the other times – like the moment at the Rosewood when he'd looked up from the pool table to find her standing in front of him. Six years of pent-up memories had come flooding back to him in the blink of an eye. It had been one hell of a rush. Better than any shit he'd ever smoked. He had never realized that he had so many emotions inside him, all writhing about in the pit of his stomach, and it had taken all his nerve and self-discipline to appear unruffled by her sudden appearance. Then, once the initial rush was over, he'd quickly moved to isolate all the negative emotions inside him and used them as a buffer to keep her at a distance. It had worked, but only because she'd seemed even more uncertain of the situation than he was. Which was understandable. She had been on his turf, seeking his assistance, and that had automatically put her on the defensive. But what about her feelings? It had been impossible to tell whether she still felt anything for him. Well, not until tonight when she'd kissed him. It wasn't the kiss though. It was the look in her eyes. Not that he could explain it in words. A sudden thought came to him. Was this the 'spark' Chavez had mentioned? Yet, the more he thought about it, the more he realized that it actually threw up more questions than it did answers. She'd already had the courage to show her feelings, but he was still hiding behind the façade of defensive barriers which he'd built around himself since she'd left him. A protective screen, like a one-way mirror, which had allowed him to conceal his true emotions from the world. It had certainly worked, but the illusion would be shattered instantly if he were ever to drop his guard again. Perhaps friendship was the only realistic option open to them now. At least that way he couldn't get hurt again. The easy way out, he thought scornfully to himself. That wasn't in his character. He knew in his heart that he still loved Nicole. He always had. He always would. But was he ready to take the chance again, knowing there was no guarantee that the relationship would work any better the second time round?

'Are you ready?'

'I don't know!' Marlette shot back, then looked at Miguel who was frowning curiously at him. 'Sorry, I was miles away. Yes, I'm ready.'

Miguel eyed him suspiciously, then switched off the engine and reached for his AK-47 assault rifle which lay on the back seat of the car. 'We're parked about three hundred metres from the farmhouse. It won't be visible until the next bend in the road. We'll have to continue on foot from here.'

Marlette lifted the hold-all on to his lap and unzipped it. He removed a stun grenade and held it out towards Miguel. 'Have you ever used one of these before?'

Miguel took the oblong-shaped device gingerly from Marlette and shook his head as he turned it around slowly in his hand. 'No, but I've seen the National Guard use them. I was in another building at the time. I remember there was a loud bang followed by a blinding flash of light. I couldn't see for several seconds after it went off.'

Marlette took a second stun grenade from the hold-all and tapped the outer casing. 'Inside is a mixture of magnesium powder and fulminate of mercury which adds up to a very volatile cocktail indeed.' He pointed to the ring on top of the device. 'Pull this out and throw the grenade into the targeted area. Then look away. Fast. The mercury fulminate detonates and that causes the loud bang you heard. That, in turn, ignites the magnesium which produces the blinding flash. The combination of the two will cause temporary deafness and blindness to any person in the immediate vicinity of the explosion for anything up to a minute. That means total disorientation. The British SAS, who devised it, nicknamed it the "flash-bang". It's a very apt description of what it does.'

Miguel studied the device in his hand then held it out towards Marlette. 'You obviously know a lot more about them than I do. I still think it's best if we stick to the plan I proposed earlier at the house. You deal with the guards and let me concentrate on finding Guillermo.'

'And as I said earlier, who's to say the guards will all be conveniently located in one room? It's far more likely that they'll be situated in different parts of the building. Hang on to the stun grenade, you may yet need it.' Marlette noticed the look of anger which crossed Miguel's face as he attached the device to his belt. 'We've got more than enough problems as it is without the two of us working against each other as well. Either you accept the fact that I'm the one calling the shots here, or else we abort the operation now and return to the house. I don't think Chavez would be too pleased with your petulance, do you?'

Miguel glared sullenly at the AK-47 in his lap. 'I wasn't being petulant. I was just making a suggestion, that's all.'

'Your plan was discussed at length back at the house, and it was rejected on the grounds that it was too risky. The time for suggestions is over. We go with the plan that was agreed with Chavez. We first deal with the periphery guards, should we encounter any in the grounds, then you'll enter the building through the back door. I'll take the front door leading into the hall. Once inside the building we'll systematically search every room until we find

Ruiz. Then we use the smoke grenades to screen our escape.'

'You make it all sound so easy,' Miguel retorted.

'Far from it. It was never going to be easy with just the two of us, but we're going to have to adapt as best we can.' Marlette took a couple of two-way radios from the hold-all and gave one of them to Miguel. He attached a suppressor to the barrel of the machine-pistol then, snapping a clip into place, he released the safety catch. He stuffed the two spare clips into his pocket before removing the remaining stun grenades, as well as the smoke grenades, from the hold-all and dividing them equally between the two of them. 'Synchronize watches. I make it now . . . Three forty-two.'

'Check,' Miguel agreed.

'It's going to take me longer to get into place. If the area at the front of the building hasn't been altered since the original blueprints were drawn up, then I'm going to have to cross a clearing in order to reach the front door. It's the perfect killing ground. So it's imperative that you maintain complete radio silence until you hear from me. Is that understood?'

'Understood,' Miguel agreed, patting the two-way radio clipped to his belt.

'Let's go,' Marlette announced, reaching for the handle.

'Wait,' Miguel said, and took a key from his pocket. 'Anna told me to give you this. It's a spare key for the car in case anything should happen to me tonight.'

Marlette pocketed the key then got out of the car. He waited until Miguel had disappeared into the undergrowth, then, sticking close to the thick foliage which lined the road, he made his way to the wrought-iron gate at the foot of the driveway. It was obvious that the gate had once been electronically controlled, but now it was only secured with a chain and padlock. He crouched down and peered cautiously into the darkness beyond the gate. The driveway looked deserted. This was when the night-vision goggles would have proved invaluable. He quickly dismissed the thought. Improvise.

The perimeter wall was topped with shards of broken glass and coils of rusted barbed wire. He wasn't going to get in that way. That left the gate. He looked around apprehensively, then removed a Swiss Army knife from his pocket, selected a blade, and inserted it into the padlock. He bit his lip painfully as he tickled the tip of the blade inside the lock without any success. He paused to wipe his clammy hands on the front of his tunic then tried again. Just when he was beginning to despair that the tip of the blade wasn't fine enough to trigger the lock, he felt the padlock give and was able to ease the chain out from the bars. He winced when the rusted hinges squealed as he pushed open one of the gates. Slipping through the narrow aperture, he quickly looped the padlock between two of the links, careful not to lock it again. He knew he was taking a big risk by not securing the padlock behind him, but he had to chance it in case they needed to beat a hasty retreat.

No sooner had he ghosted into the shadows of a row of trees, than he heard the sound of approaching footsteps on the driveway. Had the sound of the hinges alerted one of the guards? Had he already been seen? He tightened his finger around the trigger of the sub-machine gun as he waited breathlessly for the footsteps to draw nearer. He instinctively shrank back further into the shadows when the figure loomed out of the darkness. The man was dressed in a pair of jeans and a denim jacket, and had a G-3 rifle slung over his shoulder, once the standard issue for soldiers in the National Guard. Marlette could see that the man was drunk. The guard paused a short distance from where Marlette was crouched and drained the last mouthful of cheap cane spirit from the bottle in his hand. He looked at the empty bottle, cursed angrily, and hurled it at the nearest tree. Marlette turned away sharply as the bottle shattered against the foot of the tree, and grimaced more out of irritation than pain when a sliver of glass sliced across the side of his face. He touched his cheek and could feel the blood on his fingers. He looked up to see the guard unzip his trousers and, as he moved unsteadily towards the trees to relieve himself, Marlette realized to his horror that he was heading straight towards him. His first reaction was to kill him. A single bullet through the heart. Death would be instantaneous. And silent. He was on the verge of firing when he suddenly pulled his finger off the trigger. No – the guy wasn't a threat either to him or to the operation. Jesus, he could hardly stand up.

Marlette turned the sub-machine gun around in his hand and straightened up just as the guard reached the tree. The guard didn't even have time to react before Marlette caught him on the side of the head with the butt of the weapon. Marlette grabbed him as his legs buckled underneath him but, no sooner had he propped the unconscious figure against the foot of the tree, than he slumped sideways to the ground. Marlette left him where he was, then ejected the magazine from the G-3 rifle and discarded both into the undergrowth. Not that the guard would be needing either of them again that night. He doubted whether he'd even wake before morning. But when he did eventually come round, he was going to have the kind of chronic hangover that could convert a man to total abstinence.

Marlette stuck to the trees as he followed the route of the driveway until it ended abruptly at the edge of the clearing. The farmhouse was now only fifty metres away from where he was crouched. He could see a single light emanating from behind a net curtain in a room adjacent to the front door. The other window facing out over the clearing was in darkness. He removed the bandanna from around his head, wiped his forearm across his sweating forehead, then replaced it before edging forward until he had a complete view of the clearing. No guards. Then he heard the sound of laughter coming from the illuminated room, and shrank back into the shadows when a man appeared at the window. The man pushed the net curtain aside and tossed a cigarette butt out on to the porch, but it was only when he leaned forward and spat through the open window that Marlette noticed the bottle of beer in his hand. The man stifled a yawn, then disappeared from view.

What the hell was going on? Marlette wondered. Dennison had a notorious reputation for being a strict disciplinarian with all his employees. Any misdemeanours and they were out. He never gave them a second chance. That's why it seemed totally out of character for him to let his men drink while on duty, especially when they were guarding such an important prisoner. Perhaps he didn't know anything about it. No, he couldn't believe that. Dennison had his spies everywhere. Not only that, his employees lived in constant fear of him. They wouldn't risk drinking behind his back. It made no sense at all. Then another fearful thought came to him. What if something had happened to Ruiz after he'd been abducted? What if he were already dead? But what use would a corpse be to Dennison? No, that didn't make any sense either. So many questions and not a single answer to put his mind at rest. It left Marlette feeling distinctly uneasy. But he knew at the same time that it would be that much easier to gain access into the building if the guards had been drinking. Well, it would in theory . . .

He checked the time. Miguel would be in place. He darted out from the trees and sprinted, doubled over, to the edge of the porch, where he crouched down behind a low hedge. The clearing was still deserted. Only one guard to patrol the area in front of the building? Perhaps the others had already passed out. The guard he'd encountered earlier certainly hadn't been far off it. Whatever the reasons, it was essential that he turn this lapse in security to his own advantage. He hoisted himself up on to the porch and made his way silently to the window, where he pressed himself flat against the wall before peering cautiously through the net curtain. There was a card table in the centre of the smoke-filled room with five chairs positioned around it. Five hands had been dealt. But there were only three players at the table. Two of the men had their backs to him. The third was sitting at an angle to the window. None of them could see him. It was obvious from the empty bottles scattered across the carpet that they'd also been drinking. But none of them looked drunk. He saw that their rifles were propped against the wall. Then his eyes went back to the two empty chairs. That meant there were at least two more guards unaccounted for. Was one of them the man he'd laid out near the main gate? Possibly, but he knew he couldn't afford to take that chance.

Marlette ducked down under the window, crawled across the porch, and looked through the window on the opposite side of the door. Although the room was in darkness, he could see that there was nobody inside. He jumped nimbly off the porch, crouched down in the darkness, and called up Miguel on his two-way radio.

'That's one more guard than I encountered,' Miguel replied once Marlette had briefed him. 'The kitchen light's on, but the room was empty when I last looked through the window. I've already checked the other windows, apart from the two at the front where you are, and all the rooms appear to be in darkness. Three of the rooms have their curtains drawn. It's my guess that Guillermo's in one of those. You concentrate on immobilizing the guards, and I'll check the rooms.'

'Remember, there are probably at least two other guards somewhere inside the house. They may even be in the room with Ruiz.'

'You just worry about yourself, Marlette,' Miguel retorted sharply.

Marlette bit back his anger. 'The moment you hear the bang from the stun grenade, you go in through the kitchen door. Understood?'

'Understood.' The connection went dead.

Marlette clipped the two-way radio back on to his belt and, satisfied that it was safe to emerge from the shadows, he hauled himself back up on to the porch and inched his way along the wall until he was standing beside the window. He was about to remove one of the stun grenades from his belt when he heard the sound of the front door being unlocked from inside the house. He swung the sub-machine gun on the doorway, waiting for the guard to appear.

'What the fuck are you doing now?' a voice called out irritably from the room.

'He said he was only going to be gone a couple of minutes,' came the muffled reply. 'It's been over ten minutes now. Where the hell is he?'

'We may as well play out this hand while we're waiting for him,' the voice said. 'Christ, the bastard's already taken all our money as it is.'

'I've already lost my next two weeks' wages to him,' a second voice retorted. 'Wait until my wife finds out about it.'

'He told us to wait for him in here,' the first voice called out from the room. 'And you know better than to cross him. Now get your ass back in here before he returns and finds out that you've disobeyed a direct order.'

The door suddenly swung open and a shadow fell across the porch. Marlette blinked as a drop of sweat seeped out from under the bandanna and trickled into the corner of his eye. His finger tightened around the trigger.

'Screw you,' the man snorted to himself. 'And screw you too, Dennison.' The door slammed shut.

Marlette exhaled deeply and leaned back against the wall. That had been close. He wiped the sweat from his eyes then shouldered the Heckler & Koch and took one of the stun grenades from his belt. He primed it, then, easing aside a corner of the net curtain, he tossed the device into the room. He immediately turned away, his eyes closed, and clamped his hands tightly over his ears. He heard the muffled bang through his hands and the floorboards shuddered momentarily under his feet. Unslinging the Heckler & Koch, Marlette kicked open the front door, then dropped down on to one knee and fanned the hall with the sub-machine gun. It was deserted. A figure appeared at the end of the hall, and for a moment their weapons locked on to each other. Miguel eyed Marlette coldly, then lowered his AK-47 and moved to the nearest door where he tried the handle. It was unlocked. Marlette watched him open the door and disappear inside before turning his attention to the three guards in the front room. One of the men lay unconscious on the floor, having struck his head on the edge of the mantelpiece. The other two were on their knees, their hands clutched tightly over their ears. The nearest man was whining pitifully to himself as he rocked from side to side, his eyes wide and staring. Marlette knew that the man couldn't see him. He stepped forward and struck him hard behind the ear with the butt of the Heckler & Koch. The man was already unconscious before he fell face forward on to the floor. Marlette dealt similarly with the second guard, and was about to remove the clips from the three rifles when he heard a noise behind him. He already had the sub-machine gun trained on the door when Miguel appeared in the doorway, his face flushed as he struggled to half carry, half drag the inert figure of Ruiz towards the front door.

'What's wrong with him?' Marlette asked anxiously, already fearing the worst.

'He's been drugged,' Miguel hissed breathlessly through gritted teeth.

'Let me carry him,' Marlette said, hurrying towards the door.

'No,' Miguel shot back. 'He's one of us. That makes him my responsibility.'

'I'm physically bigger and stronger than you are. We'll be able to get away a lot quicker if I carry him to the car.'

'I told you, he's my responsibility,' Miguel snapped.

'Before we left, Chavez gave me a deadline to get Ruiz back to the house. If we're not back in time, she's threatened to kill Nicole. And it's not a threat I'm about to take lightly. We don't have the time to start screwing around here while you struggle to drag Ruiz to the car. Look, you can tell Chavez that you carried him for all I care, but unless you let me carry him from here on, you won't be alive to tell Chavez anything. Do I make myself understood, *my friend*?'

Miguel's eyes went to the Heckler & Koch in Marlette's hand which was now aimed at his chest. 'Perhaps it would be best if you were to carry him,' Miguel conceded grudgingly.

Marlette placed the Heckler & Koch on the floor, then ducked underneath Ruiz's right arm and hoisted him up on to his shoulder. He pushed his right arm up between Ruiz's legs to hold him down on his back, then, securing his right arm against his right leg, he retrieved the submachine gun with his free hand and straightened up. 'Get the car and bring it round to the main gate,' he instructed.

'You'll need me to stay with you to watch your back,' Miguel replied smugly.

'I can watch my own back,' Marlette assured him.

'If anything should happen to Guillermo –'

'Just get the car!'

Miguel opened his mouth to argue, thought better of it, then moved to the door and scanned the surrounding area.

Satisfied that it was safe to venture outside, he zig-zagged his way across the clearing towards the trees. Marlette steadied his grip on Ruiz, then emerged on to the porch, down the stairs, and into the clearing. It had been years since he'd last carried anyone in a fireman's lift. And how he was feeling it. The sweat was now running freely down his face and neck, and he could feel it soaking the front of his tunic. But he was used to that kind of discomfort. What he wasn't used to – what he could never get used to – was being exposed in this kind of killing ground. On reflection, he knew he should have had Miguel watch his back, at least until he reached the sanctuary of the trees. But it was too late for that now. He was on his own. His eyes constantly flickered around him, ever vigilant for any movement that might signal the appearance of the missing guard. Or was it guards? As if it really mattered. One bullet was all it would take to put him down. A sobering thought. And a frightening one as well . . .

He was still some distance from the trees when he saw the man out of the corner of his eye as he darted out from behind the farmhouse. The jeans. The T-shirt. The G-3 rifle. His first reaction was to off-load Ruiz and drop to the ground. No time. He had to fire on the turn. But could he turn and fire accurately before the guard managed to squeeze the trigger? He knew the answer to that even before he started to swing the Heckler & Koch on the man, his body already braced as he waited for the inevitability of death . . .

The sharp burst of gunfire shattered the silence and Marlette gritted his teeth and almost stumbled off balance, expecting to feel that sharp, searing pain as the bullets thudded into him, a familiar pain he'd experienced in the past. Nothing happened. Then another movement caught his eye. The man's body was illuminated by the light streaming out from the front window; it spun grotesquely like some tortured dancer in the spotlight of death when the bullets ripped across his chest. Marlette turned towards the trees. Had the gunfire come from in there? Had Miguel saved his life? His heart was still pounding and his body tingling with relief as he tried to clear his thoughts. But it was useless to try and reason. There would be time for that later, once he was clear of this open space. At that moment his only priority was to get to the safety of the trees.

Tightening his grip on Ruiz, Marlette hurried to the sanctuary of the trees, where he paused to wipe his forearm across his sweating face. He looked back across at the farmhouse. Nothing moved in the eerie silence of the night. The guard's body lay close to the steps. There was something almost surreal about the way the light from the window illuminated the twisted body. It was like a scene from one of those pretentious pop videos on MTV. He almost expected to hear the director shout 'cut' and for the man to get up and dust himself off. Only this was real. The reality of death. With a last glance backwards, he threaded his way through the trees, still ever vigilant for the appearance of any more guards. He came across the intoxicated guard he'd left close to the main gates. The man was still out cold. Marlette continued on to the gates. The padlock and chain were lying on the ground and one of the gates was now standing open. As he emerged out on to the narrow sidewalk, a pair of headlights dissected the dark road in front of him. It was Miguel's battered Ford. The car pulled up beside him and Miguel jumped out and opened the back door. Between them they managed to slide Ruiz into the back seat and Miguel closed the door again behind him.

Marlette got into the passenger seat and replaced the sub-machine gun in the hold-all at his feet. Then, pulling off his sweat-soaked bandanna, he tossed it on to the dashboard as Miguel got back into the car. 'I owe you one. Thanks.'

Miguel's hand froze on the gearstick as he met Marlette's eyes. 'Owe me for what?'

'I wouldn't have thought that modesty was one of your strong points,' Marlette replied with a hint of sarcasm in his voice. 'For taking out the guard back there. I would never have nailed him if you hadn't hit him first.'

Miguel's eyes flickered momentarily, then he shrugged indifferently and put the car into gear before accelerating away from the gates.

A shadowy figure appeared at the gates moments after the car had sped away in a shriek of burning rubber. He held a mini-Uzi loosely in his gloved hand. Taking a portable telephone from his jacket pocket, he punched in a number which he'd already committed to memory. It was answered immediately at the other end.

'Dennison, it's Jayson. They've taken the bait.'

EIGHT

'Hi.'

'Hi,' Marlette replied when he saw Nicole in the reflection of the bathroom mirror. He was stripped to the waist, his face lathered in soap. He cupped his hands into the cold water in the washbasin and splashed it over his face.

She leaned against the jamb and folded her arms across her chest as she watched him. It was the first chance she'd had to speak to him alone since he'd returned to the house. He'd put on a few pounds since she'd last seen him without a shirt on. But he still looked damn good, she thought to herself, as she unashamedly appraised his muscular physique.

'Go on then, say it,' Marlette announced, breaking into her self-indulgent fantasy, then grabbed the towel which was draped over the side of the bath and dried his face. 'I've put on weight since you last saw me.'

Nicole felt herself blush when she realized that he'd been watching her. She put her fingers to her mouth as she chuckled to herself. 'It's not that obvious,' she said, trying to hide the lingering grin behind her hand.

'What's so funny?'

'Nothing,' she replied coyly.

'Come on, out with it,' he said, folding up the towel and replacing it carefully over the side of the bath.

She sat on the edge of the bath. 'Seeing you like this, well . . . it brought back a few old memories.'

'Good ones, I hope,' he said, then pulled on the T-shirt which Chavez had left out for him to wear.

'Something's bothering you, isn't it?' she said, her face now serious.

'What makes you say that?' he asked.

'The only times I ever knew you to replace a towel neatly like that were when you had something on your mind. I guess it was some kind of subconscious gesture on your part to try and organize your thoughts. I don't know.'

He found himself thinking about what she'd just said. It certainly wasn't something he'd ever done consciously. Perhaps she had a point, though he'd never been strong on psychology. But she was right – something was bothering him. And that's what made it so uncanny. He knew he could try and deny it, but she'd just see through the lie. She always did. It was like living under a microscope. But he knew she was obviously concerned about him, otherwise she wouldn't have mentioned it. It showed she cared and that felt good. He leaned back against the washbasin and folded his arms across his chest. 'You're right, there is something bothering me,' he admitted.

'Want to talk about it?' Nicole asked.

'Sure, if I knew what it was.'

'I don't understand,' she said hesitantly.

'The more I think about it, the more I'm inclined to believe that we were expected at the farmhouse tonight.'

'Why do you say that?'

Marlette explained briefly what had happened earlier at the farmhouse. 'It was almost as if we were allowed to walk in there and take Ruiz,' he concluded. 'It was just too damn easy.'

'Easy?' she shot back in surprise. 'You were almost killed.'

'That's because I don't think the guards were in on it,' he replied. 'That's obviously why they were plied with alcohol before we got there, which means that whoever was behind this little caper – and my money's on Dennison – must have been acting on inside information. How else could they have known that we were intending to spring Ruiz tonight?'

'Are you suggesting that either Chavez or the other guy, Miguel, is working for Dennison?' she asked.

'There were only the three of us who knew about the plan to spring Ruiz tonight, and I know I didn't tip off Dennison, or anyone else for that matter. Which leaves Chavez or Miguel.'

'It's all circumstantial, Rick. What if you're wrong?'

'I'm not wrong, Nicole,' he replied tersely.

'But you don't have any proof,' she retorted. 'This is a closely knit organization. You just can't go around making these kind of allegations unless you can back them up with solid evidence. You could do more harm than good if it were to backfire on you.'

'And that's exactly what's bothering me,' Marlette told her. 'Something wasn't right there tonight, Nicole. I must have been through the operation a dozen times already in my head, analysing every little detail, but I'm damned if I can figure out what it was. But I will, and when I do I'll have my informer.'

'Then you'll still have to try and convince the others.'

'You let me worry about that,' he said, then looked towards the door on hearing the sound of laughter coming from one of the rooms further down the hallway. 'I'd say Ruiz's made a full recovery from the effects of the sedative. Have you met him yet?'

'He's been in the lounge with Chavez and Miguel ever since he came round. I certainly wasn't about to go barging in on them uninvited. Not that it would have done much good. We wouldn't have been able to understand each other anyway.'

'Actually Ruiz speaks excellent English,' Marlette corrected her. 'He went to college in the States.'

'I was under the impression that these guerrillas came

from impoverished families who'd lived all their lives in the shanty towns,' Nicole said.

'On the whole they do. Ruiz is an exception though. He comes from a very wealthy family. His father owned one of the biggest coffee plantations in the country. He probably still does, for all I know. He was a staunch supporter of the anti-Communist regimes of the seventies and eighties. He publicly disowned his son when he found out that he'd become involved with the FMLN.'

'How come you know so much about Ruiz and his family?'

'The story broke when I was out here. As you can imagine, it made front-page news in every national newspaper. It also gave the FMLN a priceless propaganda coup at a time when they desperately needed it. Ruiz became a working-class hero overnight. His fluency in English made him the perfect spokesman for the cause, especially in their dealings with other left-wing organizations in Europe and the Middle East. He was given a senior position in the FMLN, which at the time was said to have caused a lot of resentment amongst some of the veterans who felt that he'd been appointed to the hierarchy just because he was an intellectual. When he was recruited, he had absolutely no field experience at all, and although he's since proved himself in the field, it was said that the resentment never really died. There's no question that he has his fair share of enemies within the organization, so when it was reported that he'd been killed in that military ambush, there were those who felt that certain old scores had been finally settled. Who knows.'

'Have you ever met him?'

'No, but from what I've heard he's supposed to be as charming as he is deceptive. Whether or not it's true, I don't know, but I'm sure we're about to find out.'

'I'm scared, Rick,' Nicole said as she stared at the floor, her arms wrapped tightly across her chest. 'What if it turns out that he doesn't know where Michelle is? Or what if Dennison has already got to her? And you know what Pruitt said about Jayson . . .'

'Ruiz made the deal with Kinnard, he has to know where she is,' Marlette was quick to assure her. 'As for Dennison, he's obviously still blundering about in the dark.'

'How can you be so sure?'

'Why else would we have been allowed to spring Ruiz, unless Dennison knew he could lead him to Michelle and the tape?'

'It makes sense, I guess,' she conceded in a hollow voice.

Marlette handed her a handkerchief. 'Wipe your eyes. You don't want to give Chavez the satisfaction of seeing that you've been crying.'

Nicole dabbed her eyes with the handkerchief, then splashed some cold water over her face. She dried her face then turned back to him. 'How do I look?'

'You look fine. Now come on.'

'I'm glad to see that you haven't lost your touch, Rick,' she said, managing a fleeting smile. 'You still know how to flatter a girl. That's where you and Bob were so different. He couldn't stop flattering me. At least he did when we were first married. I guess I should have realized something was wrong when the flattery suddenly dried up after the first few months.'

'Shallow words from a shallow guy,' Marlette said tersely, then held up his hand in apology. 'I'm sorry. I didn't mean that.'

'You always mean what you say, Rick. I know that only too well from bitter experience. You've always been blunt and to the point, even if it meant hurting someone's feelings in the process. You know something: you and my father were the only two men who could ever make me cry. He always used to say that real tears can only come from real love. I guess he was right.'

'And now the only person who can make you cry is

Michelle,' Marlette said, nodding thoughtfully to himself. 'Yeah, I guess he was right.'

She handed back his handkerchief. 'You know what I could really use right now? One of those hugs you used to give me whenever I was feeling down.'

For a moment he was undecided. He didn't want to be the one to initiate the contact. But why? Was it the fear of intimacy again after all these years? It was as if his head was ruling his heart. He wanted to hold her, reassure her, but there was still an intense negativity inside him. Don't let down those barriers. Not again. Keep your distance. Let her come to you. Don't initiate the contact. Don't . . .

Then the spell of self-doubt was broken. There was no going back. Not any more. He held her tightly against him, her slim body cocooned in his powerful arms as if he were trying to transfer his own inner strength to her. She laid her head against his chest and he could smell the scent of her freshly washed hair. Memories. So many damn memories. He was quick to push them from his mind. It wasn't the time for reminiscing. She needed to draw on his strength, not his sentiment. When he did reluctantly break the contact, she stepped away from him and took his hands in hers. 'You don't know how much I needed that.'

'You ready?' he said, gesturing to the door.

'As I'll ever be,' she replied, then took a deep breath and followed him out into the hallway.

They reached the closed lounge door. Marlette could hear Chavez's agitated voice emanating from inside the room, and he was about to put his ear to the door to listen when he heard footsteps on the wooden floorboards behind him. Both he and Nicole looked round simultaneously. Miguel stared back coldly at them, then, brushing past Nicole, he opened the door and gestured for them to enter.

Nicole's eyes went to Ruiz. She estimated him to be in his mid-thirties. His hair, which was still wet from his recent shower, had been combed back from his youthful face and tucked behind his ears. She also noticed the heart-shaped pendant on a gold-plated chain hanging around his neck. She thought it a strange accoutrement for someone like him to be wearing.

'I was wondering when the two of you were going to join us,' Ruiz announced, his accent still bearing the traces of his years spent in the States. He discarded the newspaper he'd been reading, then got to his feet and crossed to where they were standing. 'It seems I owe you a debt of gratitude, Marlette. Miguel told me what happened at the farmhouse tonight. Of course his version of the events was pretty colourful to say the least. But then he always tends to over-dramatize everything. I've learnt over the years how to weed out the facts from the fiction.'

'I couldn't have done it without him,' Marlette said matter-of-factly as he shook Ruiz's outstretched hand. 'In fact, he saved my life.'

'So he's told me. Several times.' Ruiz turned to Nicole and shook her hand. 'I'm sorry about Bob. He told me that the two of you didn't get on after the divorce, but I always found his company most enjoyable. He had a lot of good qualities in him.'

'Like abandoning his daughter in a strange country,' Nicole replied sarcastically, having decided even before entering the room to go straight on to the offensive, knowing it would help to mask the fear and the uncertainty which had been churning inside her stomach. But this was no façade. This was genuine anger – how could Ruiz defend Bob after what he'd done to Michelle?

'I can understand your bitterness, but Bob never abandoned her,' Ruiz said. 'He thought the world of Michelle. He'd never have done anything that would have put her life in any kind of danger. The arrangement was only supposed to have been for a night. He intended to pick her up the next morning and take her back to Washington with him.'

207

'You can defend him all you want, I really don't care,' Nicole retorted. 'My only concern right now is to find my daughter. You do know where she is?'

'Yes, and I also know that she's perfectly safe.'

'Where is she?' Nicole asked, unable to mask the anxiety in her voice. The façade was rapidly crumbling away.

'She's staying with a couple at a village in Chalatenango. It's a district in the north of the country. Chalatenango is a well-known FMLN stronghold, and there are areas that the military are reluctant to venture into for fear of being attacked. Michelle's in one of those areas.'

'Does this couple speak any English?' Nicole asked.

'Gustavo and I were at college together in the States. Like myself, he speaks English. His wife doesn't speak much English, but then Michelle will have spent most of her time with him anyway. It was important, given the circumstances, that Michelle was made to feel as comfortable as possible. That's why I asked Gustavo to look after her. Don't worry, she's in good hands.'

'Was she with Bob when you met him?' Nicole asked.

'No. I never actually saw her. I met with Bob at a hotel here in San Salvador. He told me that she was at the pool with the other kids. All I did was give him a telephone number where he could contact Gustavo once he arrived in San Salvador. I never saw Bob again after that.'

'When did you last speak to Gustavo?' Marlette asked.

'I managed to get through to him less than half an hour ago on the radio. He assured me that Michelle's fine. Whenever she's asked after her father, Gustavo told her that he'll be coming for her as soon as he's completed his business in the city. That always seemed to put her mind at ease.'

'Does Dennison know where she is?' Nicole asked fearfully.

'If he did, do you think he'd still be coordinating one of the biggest manhunts in the history of this country?' Ruiz replied, then took a packet of Camels from his pocket, drew one out, and extended it towards Nicole. She plucked it from the packet and bent forward to catch the flame of his lighter.

Marlette shook his head when Ruiz proffered the packet towards him. 'Weren't you interrogated about Michelle while you were being held at the farmhouse? I would have thought that was the whole reason why Dennison had you snatched in the first place.'

'Dennison doesn't know that I met with Bob,' Ruiz said after lighting a cigarette and handing it to Chavez, who was seated on the sofa behind him. He then lit one for himself and sat down beside her. 'My abduction had nothing to do with the girl or the tape.'

Marlette noticed Nicole's furtive glance in his direction, and knew exactly what she was thinking. He nodded in agreement. 'Yeah, that does kind of turn my theory on its head, doesn't it?'

Ruiz looked from Nicole to Marlette. 'Theory? I'm sorry, I'm not with you.'

'Forget it,' Marlette replied. 'It's not important. So if Dennison doesn't know about your meeting with Kinnard, why did he go to the lengths he did to have you abducted?'

Ruiz pondered the question for a few seconds. 'How much do you actually know about the coup d'état?'

'I've heard rumours, that's all,' Marlette replied with a quick shrug. 'Nothing definite though.'

'Well, it's definite all right,' Ruiz said, then leaned forward and rested his elbows on his knees. 'I overheard Dennison and Jayson discussing it at the farmhouse yesterday morning. I'd just regained consciousness, but I kept my eyes closed so as not to alert the guard who was in the room with me at the time. It was then I discovered the real reason why I'd been abducted. And as I said earlier, it had nothing to do with Bob Kinnard, the girl, or the missing videotape.'

'Go on,' Marlette prompted.

Ruiz rubbed his hands together in a gesture that Marlette could only interpret as being one of nervousness. 'I didn't hear everything they said, but I got the gist of it. The President is hosting a banquet at the Camino Real Hotel tomorrow night. Most of the cabinet will be there. That's when the assassination's going to take place.'

'Assassination?' Nicole said uncertainly.

'The target is to be the President. I don't know who's been hired to pull the trigger, but my money would be on Jayson. He's perfect for that kind of job. The soldiers who have been detailed to guard the hotel and the surrounding area will all be loyal to the coup, so the assassin would be able to slip away unnoticed in the ensuing confusion. Other detachments of soldiers will already have been deployed around the airport, the national radio station, and ANTEL, the state telecommunications company. They'll move in and take control of those strategic positions as soon as they know that the President's dead. By then the leader of the military junta will have taken charge at the hotel. Both Dennison and Amaya seemed confident that more of the military would desert to the cause once the new leader had made himself known on national radio.' Ruiz directed himself to Marlette. 'It's Ramon Vaquero.'

Marlette stared stony-faced at the floor. 'I can't say I'm surprised,' he said at length.

'Who's Ramon Vaquero?' Nicole asked.

'General Ramon Vaquero,' Marlette told her. 'He was head of the National Guard when I was out here. Personally, I found him arrogant and self-centred, but he always commanded the greatest respect from those under him. He was very popular, especially amongst the rank and file.'

'He's now the Defence Minister,' Ruiz added. 'He's still a committed fascist and it certainly came as a surprise to many of us when he was drafted into the cabinet. It's said that the President used him to appease the right of his party. I can believe it.'

'You still haven't explained why you were abducted,' Marlette said.

'I was to have been the "fall guy", as you Americans would say. It was their intention to leave my body next to the assassin's rifle. My fingerprints would have been on the weapon. It would have been claimed later that I'd been shot after I'd killed the President. That way Vaquero could have pointed a finger at the FMLN and claimed that he'd been totally justified in returning the country to martial rule. And who would disagree with him? The FMLN would have been ostracized. We'd have lost the popular support that we still have within the working classes. The leaders of the coup would have successfully killed two birds with one stone, so to speak. They're sure to come after me again. I'm still an integral part of their plans. That's why it's essential that I get the tape to the government as soon as possible.'

'How soon can we leave for the village?' Marlette asked.

'We can leave within the hour,' Ruiz replied, then spoke to Chavez, who got to her feet and followed Miguel from the room. Moments later came the sound of an engine starting up outside the house.

'What's that?' Marlette demanded suspiciously.

'It's only Miguel. He's got a few things to do. But don't worry, he'll be back to drive us to the village. He knows Chalatenango well. He grew up there.' Ruiz took the cigarettes from his pocket, lit one, and extended the packet towards Nicole. 'Take them. There's a fresh brew of hot coffee on the stove. I'd like to speak to Marlette alone.'

She took the cigarettes from Ruiz and left the room without a word, closing the door behind her.

'I like her,' Ruiz said with a smile. 'She's got guts. I admire that in a woman.'

'Let's cut the bullshit and get to the point,' Marlette

snapped. 'I don't know what the hell you were trying to pull just now, but I don't believe for a moment that you just happened to overhear Dennison and Jayson discussing the details of the coup at the farmhouse. It's all too damn convenient.'

Ruiz sat down slowly and inhaled deeply on the cigarette. 'I overheard them discussing the part I'd play in the coup. That much is true. The rest, well, I wanted to see how much you actually knew about the coup before I talked to you. And judging by your expression, I'd say you already knew everything I told you, bar the reason why I was abducted and taken to the farmhouse.' He sat forward, his elbows resting on his knees. 'I know we were once on opposite sides, but right now we need to work together if we're to have any chance of foiling this coup. That may mean going to the hotel to stop Jayson – or whoever's going to pull the trigger – from assassinating the President. I can't go. I'd be recognized before I got anywhere near the place. That leaves you, Marlette.'

'I didn't come here to get involved in the politics of your country, Ruiz,' Marlette told him. 'I'm here to find Nicole's daughter. And once I've found her, I'm getting them both out of the country. So don't try and rope me into your plans for personal glory.'

'This has nothing to do with personal glory!' Ruiz snapped indignantly. 'This is about preventing my country from sliding back into a state of civil war. But then I suppose I shouldn't be that surprised at your reluctance to get involved. After all, another conflict would only benefit you and your kind, wouldn't it?'

'They're not my kind,' Marlette retorted. 'Not any more. This is my last contract. After this I'm through.'

'Somehow I can't imagine you running a deli in downtown New York,' Ruiz said with a faint sneer. 'It's just not your style.' He got to his feet and crossed to the door. When he spoke again it was in Spanish. 'As I said just now,

I think you know as much about this coup as I do. Probably more. And believe me, you are going to help us stop the military from taking power in this country again.'

'Is that a fact?' Marlette said nonchalantly as he sat back and folded his arms across his chest. 'And if I refuse? No, let me guess. I'd be executed and dumped in some back street. Is that it?'

'You're no use to us dead, Marlette,' Ruiz said, then thrust his hands in his pockets and crossed to within a few feet of where Marlette was sitting. 'But the woman and the girl are of no practical use to us. I'm sure they could be used to persuade you to see the situation our way.'

Marlette leapt to his feet, grabbed the front of Ruiz's shirt, and slammed him against the wall. 'You harm Nicole or the girl and it'll be your body that will be dumped in some back street. Understood?'

'I wasn't actually sure of your true feelings towards Nicole, but now I am,' Ruiz said with a triumphant smile. 'I'd say that leaves me holding all the aces, wouldn't you?'

Marlette glared at Ruiz, then let go of his shirt and sat down on the edge of the sofa. He was furious with himself for playing straight into Ruiz's hands. Ruiz was right, he did hold the aces, but Marlette was still determined to play his remaining cards close to his chest, not to tell Ruiz any more than he already knew.

Ruiz smoothed down the front of his shirt. 'You were approached by the CIA in New York, weren't you?' he asked, reverting back to English.

'What are you talking about?' Marlette replied, affecting bewilderment, but desperately hoping that the uncertainty he was feeling hadn't filtered through to his voice.

'Let me be more specific. You and Nicole met with Alex Pruitt at your apartment the day before you flew out to Honduras. Of course we don't know what he said to you, but it can't have been that sensitive if he was able to talk in front of Nicole. What does interest us, though, is why

Pruitt returned to your apartment after Nicole had left. We need to know what he said to you then.'

Marlette rubbed his hands slowly over his face. There was no use in denying it. Ruiz obviously had inside information. But from whom? And how? 'Who's this *we*? It's certainly not the FMLN.'

'No, it's not,' Ruiz replied with a smile. 'I'm CIA. I have been ever since I was first recruited at college in the States. My brief was simple. Infiltrate the FMLN at the highest level. The rest you know.'

Marlette was more surprised by Ruiz's candour than by the actual revelation that he was working for the CIA. He certainly had no reason to disbelieve him. How else would he have known that Pruitt had been to the apartment? And how would he have known the details of the planned coup d'état unless Langley had given the information? No, Ruiz was on the level. Of that he was certain. And the more he thought about it, the more he realized just what an inspired move it had been by Langley to recruit him. Not only had he been a senior lieutenant at the very heart of the FMLN during those last turbulent years of the country's civil war, he'd also been in direct contact with senior operatives of other left-wing groups around the world. And all the time he would have been passing information back to his handler in Washington. Yes, an inspired move. So why had Ruiz blown his cover like this? The order must have come from his handler. Were the CIA running scared? It was something he intended to find out.

'Why are the CIA so interested in Pruitt? He's one of theirs. He was acting for them when he came to see me.'

'Alex Pruitt is currently the subject of an internal investigation at Langley. He doesn't know that, of course. He's been involved in several illegal operations over the past few years, and that's why it's imperative that we know what it was he wanted of you, in case it's linked to one of these operations.'

'Since when is it regarded as a crime within the CIA to carry out an illegal operation?' Marlette scoffed. 'The whole organization's riddled with sinister ginger groups out to undermine the opposition in any way possible. I saw enough of that when I was working in Africa.'

'I can't go into details, Marlette, simply because I don't know what he's done to merit this investigation. I'm on a need-to-know basis only. My handler's a very shrewd operative. Whatever you can tell me will be sent back to him for analysis. It's imperative that you level with me, Marlette. The very stability of this country's government is at stake here.'

'Did Kinnard know that you were with the CIA?'

'No, and I didn't know that he was with them either until my handler told me a few days ago. It certainly came as quite a shock, I can tell you. I was told to make contact with Bob and recover the tape. Only he didn't have it on him. The girl had it with her, but then I never came into contact with her. The only way I could be sure of getting the tape was by making a deal with Bob to ensure her safety. Then fate took a hand. First Bob was murdered, and then I was abducted by Dennison's men and taken to the farmhouse. The incidents were totally unrelated, but they still threatened to wreck my plans to recover the tape. But all's not lost if I can get to the girl before Dennison can.'

'And who ultimately gets the tape? Langley, or the Salvadorean government?'

'To be honest I don't actually know. Once I have the tape I'm to contact Langley for further instructions. Like I said, I'm on a need-to-know basis only.'

Marlette watched Ruiz as he inhaled deeply on his cigarette then exhaled the smoke slowly through his nose. Ruiz seemed totally unperturbed by all the events unfolding around him. Or was it all a façade? 'You're a cool one, Ruiz,' he said at length. 'If anyone in the FMLN ever found out that you were working for the CIA –'

'I'd wind up dead in a back street,' Ruiz cut in quickly. 'I know, but so far I've been lucky. Anna's nearly picked up on a couple of things, but it wasn't very difficult to gloss it over. In fact, it hasn't been very difficult to deceive her generally. She's totally infatuated with me, and that makes it all the easier to cover my tracks. I can do no wrong in her eyes. And that suits me just fine.'

'You don't feel anything for her, do you?'

'Nothing. I merely used her as a means of getting into the organization, and I've continued to use her to get the information I need to send back to Langley. I'm happy. She's happy. It's the perfect relationship as far as I'm concerned.' Ruiz fingered the heart-shaped locket around his neck. 'She gave me this for my last birthday. It contains a small picture of her. It's really kitsch, but she asked me never to take it off, so I wear it as a sign of my undying love for her.'

'And what's to stop me from telling her about your double life?'

Ruiz laughed heartily. 'You're really amusing, Marlette. Do you honestly think she'd believe you? She'd probably put a bullet in you for daring to make such an accusation against the man she loves. The only way she'd believe it is if she heard it from my lips. Why else do you think we've been speaking in English ever since I first mentioned the CIA?' He sat down again. 'So you see, Marlette, we're actually fighting on the same side.'

'No, we're not,' Marlette was quick to point out. 'Like any merc, I can be bought for the right price. But I've never sold out my country. Hell, I may not be much of a patriot but at least I'm not a traitor.'

Ruiz bit back his anger. 'The question still stands, Marlette. What did Pruitt want when he came back to see you after Nicole had left your apartment? I realize that you could spin some yarn and that I wouldn't be able to disprove it. But they'll know back at Langley whether you're on the level or not. I've been told to ensure your cooperation at all costs, so if it turns out that you're holding out on us, I'll take it out on Nicole and the girl. And don't think I wouldn't. So don't try and play head games with me, Marlette. I promise you it won't work.'

Marlette sat back and ran his fingers over his cropped hair. Ruiz had cast his line into very deep water. Now it was up to him to tug on the line and let Ruiz think he'd caught something. Sure he'd cooperate. He'd tell Ruiz what he thought he wanted to know. Nothing more. Nothing less. There was too much at stake to take any chances. Although ever conscious of protecting Nicole, he certainly didn't give a damn about the internal politics of the CIA, even though Pruitt had already given him a lucrative downpayment to carry out an assassination at the hotel the following night, and Richard Marlette had always prided himself on fulfilling a contract. Always . . .

'Hi,' Marlette said, peering round the kitchen door. 'Mind if I join you?'

'Sure,' Nicole said, beckoning him into the room. 'Do you want a coffee?'

'No, thanks,' he replied. 'That stuff should carry a government health warning.'

'So what was the big mystery all about, or shouldn't I ask?'

Marlette sat down. What to tell her? Should he tell her anything? You could be economical with the truth, he thought to himself. Give her a censored account of what had been discussed. After all, that's how he'd approached the barrage of questions which Ruiz had fired at him for the past twenty minutes. Ruiz had gone away seemingly satisfied. He'd also gone away with only part of the picture. But that was exactly how Marlette had intended to play him. He'd tugged on the line and let Ruiz think he'd landed the big one. Whether it would satisfy his handler at Langley was quite another matter, but at least it would give him the breathing space he needed to plan his next move.

'Rick?'

Marlette looked at her and grinned sheepishly. 'Sorry, I was miles away.'

'Are you OK?'

'Yeah, I'm just a bit tired, that's all,' he replied, stifling a yawn as if to stress the point. 'We had an interesting little chat, if nothing else. It certainly helped to clear the air.'

'And?' she prompted when he fell silent.

'And nothing,' he replied.

'I can take a hint,' she said with a knowing smile.

'It's nothing, Nicole. Trust me.' He put a hand lightly on her arm. 'You must be feeling pretty excited right now. In a few hours' time you'll be reunited with Michelle.'

Nicole held the cup between her hands as she stared thoughtfully at the opposite wall. 'I feel . . . I don't really know how to explain it. It's like a tingling sensation all over my body. Anticipation? Uncertainty? Relief? I don't know what it is, but it's strangely comforting all the same. It sure beats feeling numb with worry.'

She drained her cup, then crossed to the stove and poured herself another coffee. As she turned away she almost caught her foot on the AK-47 Miguel had propped against the wall beside the stove. 'These Kalashnikovs are so cumbersome. If it had been an Uzi or a Heckler & Koch he could have just put it away in a drawer and be done with it.'

Marlette looked up slowly at her as she reached the table. 'What did you just say?'

'What is it, Rick?' she asked as he stared unflinchingly at her. 'You're making me feel uneasy. Jesus, what is it?'

'An Uzi,' he said softly to himself, then banged his fist down on to the table. 'A fucking Uzi. Of course. How could I have been so stupid?'

'Rick, what are you talking about?' she pleaded.

Marlette kicked back his chair and grabbed the AK-47, then moved to the door where he paused to look back at her. 'Thanks.'

'For what?' he heard her call out after him, but he was already making his way down the corridor towards Ruiz's room. On reaching the room, he rapped sharply on the door. 'Ruiz, are you in there? Ruiz?'

A voice cursed furiously from inside the room, and a moment later the door was jerked open. Ruiz's eyes automatically went to the weapon in Marlette's hand. 'What do you want?'

'We need to talk. Now!'

Ruiz stared at Marlette then exhaled deeply. 'This better be good. Wait here.'

When Marlette was summoned into the room, he found Chavez sitting on the bed, a dressing gown wrapped around her body and a pillow propped between her back and the chipped headboard behind her. Her eyes went to the Kalashnikov in his hand, but she didn't say anything as she brushed the hair angrily from her face.

'OK, so what's so important that it couldn't wait until later this morning?' Ruiz hissed, then gestured to the AK-47 in Marlette's hand. 'And what the hell are you doing with that?'

'Miguel said he shot the guard at the farmhouse earlier tonight.'

'What of it?' Chavez snapped tersely.

'He couldn't have, not with this,' Marlette said, and tossed the AK-47 on to the bed. 'Because the guard was shot with an Uzi, not a Kalashnikov. I've had this uneasy feeling in the back of my mind ever since I left the farmhouse. I knew that something wasn't right but I couldn't put my finger on it. Then it came to me just now. Like any weapon, the Uzi and the Kalashnikov have a distinctive sound when fired. Distinctive, and different. I've been in this business long enough to recognize that difference. And the guard tonight was killed with an Uzi. I'd be prepared to stake my life on it.'

'If you're so sure, why has it taken you this long to realize it?' Chavez challenged.

'Because you don't always notice these little things in the heat of the moment. When I heard the gunfire from the trees, I automatically assumed that it was Miguel. I wasn't expecting anyone else to shoot the guard. The pitch of the gunfire obviously registered somewhere in the back of my mind, even though I wasn't conscious of it at the time. My only concern then was to get the hell out of there as quickly as possible.'

Chavez grabbed the Kalashnikov, ejected the magazine, and checked it. 'There are several bullets missing. That suggests to me that it's been fired.'

'Or removed to make it look as if it has been fired,' Marlette countered. 'I told you when Miguel and I first got back to the house that I thought it had all been too easy. It was almost as if we'd been allowed to spring Ruiz tonight. Now it's all beginning to make sense.'

Ruiz moved the Kalashnikov out of the way and sat down on the bed. 'Tell me everything that happened at the farmhouse tonight, Marlette.'

'You don't honestly believe that Miguel –'

'Let him speak!' Ruiz cut across Chavez's outburst. She was about to protest, thought better of it, then sat back and folded her arms tightly across her chest.

Marlette detailed the operation from the moment they arrived at the farmhouse up until the time Miguel drove away with the unconscious Ruiz safely in the back seat.

'You said just now that it was all beginning to make sense,' Ruiz said after Marlette had finished. 'What exactly did you mean by that?'

'It's a theory, that's all. One based on what happened. I could be wrong –'

'Let's hear it,' Ruiz interceded quickly.

'The first thing that struck me as odd was the drinking. You know as well as I do that Dennison wouldn't have allowed his men to drink while guarding a prisoner, especially one as important as you would have been to him. And I don't believe for a moment that they would have been drinking behind his back. They would have known what would have happened if he'd ever found out. Then there're the five hands which had been dealt at the table. There were three guards in the room at the time. The fourth player was almost certainly the guard who was shot as I was carrying you from the building.'

'And the fifth was the guard you incapacitated when you first entered the grounds,' Chavez concluded smugly.

'He was so drunk he could hardly stand up,' Marlette told her. 'He certainly wasn't in any condition to play cards. The others had been drinking, sure, but they weren't drunk. It's my guess that he'd been detailed to patrol the grounds. And the more he was given to drink, the easier it would be for us to sneak past him.'

'So who was this mysterious fifth player?' Chavez snorted.

'I think the answer to that lies in what I overheard the guards saying to each other. The hands had been specifically dealt on the instructions of one of the five players who'd also told them to stay in the room until he returned. And, judging by the way they were talking about him, it was obviously someone they feared. Only that player wasn't there. He'd conveniently left the room before I reached the porch. That's when one of the guards almost stumbled on to me when he opened the front door. He wanted to play the hand and was looking for the fifth player. Then, when one of his colleagues told him to come back to the room, I heard him say, "Screw you." At first I thought he was talking to his colleague. But then he added, "Screw you too, Dennison." That implied some kind of association with Dennison. And that's what really got me thinking. Who could have supplied liquor to the guards without them fearing any kind of retribution from Dennison? Someone who could have told them that he'd cleared it with Dennison to let them drink. There's only one person who fits the bill – Jayson. I believe Jayson was the fifth player there tonight. I think he also knew exactly when we were coming, and that's why he withdrew and gave specific orders that the guards stay in the room until he returned. It would be that much easier for us to deal with the guards if they were all together in a confined space. And there's only one way that he could possibly have known when we'd be arriving at the farmhouse. He already had that information.'

'Are you implying that Miguel was working in league with Jayson?' Chavez said furiously.

'If he wasn't, why was he so quick to take the credit for shooting the guard?'

'Because he did shoot him!' Chavez shot back in anger. 'Miguel and I grew up together in the same village. He's like a brother to me. In many ways I'm closer to him than I am to Guillermo. And for you to accuse him of collusion with the enemy . . .' She trailed off as she struggled to control her emotions. 'Get out of my room! Just get out!'

Ruiz held his hand up towards Chavez without taking his eyes off Marlette. 'OK, let's say for argument's sake that you are right and Miguel is working for Dennison – or the military, it doesn't really matter. Why go to all the trouble of having me kidnapped only to let the two of you walk in unhindered and free me again? It doesn't make any sense.'

'I think it makes perfect sense. You said yourself that your abduction had nothing to do with Michelle or the missing tape. They were going to frame you for the murder of the President tomorrow night. What if Dennison only found out from one of his contacts after you'd already been abducted that you could lead him to the tape? Dennison knew he couldn't risk torturing you for the simple reason he couldn't mark you, not if it had been his intention to use you as the fall guy. Any bruises would only have raised a lot of uncomfortable questions for the new government. That would leave him with only one alternative. To let you lead him to the tape. He wouldn't have needed to worry about tracking you, because Miguel would have done it for him. Then, once he had the tape, it would have been a simple matter for him to have you snatched again and still be able to implement his plan for tomorrow night.'

'You're overlooking one point. Anna knew about my meeting with Kinnard before I was kidnapped,' Ruiz said, and cast a sidelong look at Chavez. 'When exactly did you tell Miguel about it?'

'I told him . . .' She paused and wiped her hand nervously across her face.

'Anna, did you tell him about the meeting before or after I was kidnapped?' Ruiz demanded.

Chavez drew her knees up to her chest and clasped her arms around her legs. 'He was out of town that day. I didn't see him until he returned later that evening. By then I'd received word that your two bodyguards had been killed in an ambush and that you were missing.' Her eyes went to Marlette. 'But that doesn't prove anything. You still don't have a shred of evidence to back up these allegations. In fact, you seem to have all the answers. Perhaps you're Dennison's *oreja*.'

Marlette knew that *oreja*, the Spanish word for an ear, was the FMLN term for a spy. 'Except that I didn't approach you. You were the ones who came to me in the shanty town. How could Dennison have anticipated you'd be there if I was working for him?' Chavez remained silent. 'You said yourself that you'd made extensive enquiries about Ruiz once you knew he was missing and came up with nothing. Then suddenly Miguel announces that one of his contacts just happened to bump into a colleague who'd been involved in the kidnapping. This colleague even told him where Ruiz was being held. Didn't that strike you as being a bit strange after all your enquiries had drawn a blank?'

'Who was this contact?' Ruiz demanded.

'I . . . I didn't ask,' she replied guiltily, then reached over and grabbed Ruiz's arm. 'You don't actually believe any of this? You've known Miguel for years. Has he ever done anything to make you doubt his loyalty? You know he hasn't. He's not an *oreja*. He's one of us.'

Ruiz shrugged off her hand, then got to his feet and raked his fingers through his hair. 'Right now I don't know what to believe. My heart tells me that Miguel's loyalty has always been beyond reproach. But my head tells me not to be swayed by my personal feelings. And there's no question that Marlette's put forward a very convincing argument to prove his point.'

'Listen to you,' Chavez snarled. 'All Marlette's put forward so far are insinuations and innuendoes. And you've been taken in by it all.'

'I never said that.' Ruiz was quick to try and placate her.

'I know you, Guillermo, you've already condemned Miguel as a traitor.'

'And what if he is right?' Ruiz snapped. 'What if Miguel is an *oreja*? We have to face that possibility, no matter how improbable it may sound to you. We can't allow our personal feelings to get in the way. I have to take this seriously. If I didn't I'd be failing in my responsibilities as leader of this organization. He'll be suspended until a tribunal can be arranged to hear his defence.'

'And what good will that do?' Marlette said. 'He'll just deny everything. Wouldn't you if you were in his position?'

'The FMLN is a democratic organization, Marlette, and that means he'll be given every opportunity to answer the charges against him,' Ruiz replied.

'There is another way,' Marlette said. 'It would also determine once and for all whether Miguel is an *oreja*. Are you interested?'

Ruiz sat down slowly on the bed. 'I'm interested.'

'It's ingenious, if it works.'

Dennison knew it would work. There was no room for error. Not this time. His reputation was already damaged and he knew that any more mistakes wouldn't be tolerated under any circumstances. That had been made perfectly clear from the very start of the meeting. He lit a cheroot and looked slowly around him. The word 'inquisition' sprang to mind. He and Jayson were seated at a table in the centre of the room. Two trestle tables, which had been pushed together, were positioned on an elevated section of the floor in front of them. Both tables were covered with green baize. This was the meeting place of the Military Council, and had been ever since it was first convened to discuss the possibility of a coup d'état to return the military to power in El Salvador. Now the possibility was on the verge of becoming reality.

Of the twelve chairs behind the two tables, only seven were occupied. The five absentees had already made their apologies for not being able to attend. All were either prominent politicians or businessmen who hadn't been able to make it at such short notice. The seven men in attendance were all senior officers in the National Guard. Seated in the centre was the leader of the Military Council, General Ramon Vaquero. The black hair may have been thinning and the moustache flecked with grey, but Dennison was in no doubt that the mind was still as cunning and alert as ever. He shifted uncomfortably in his seat as he felt Vaquero staring at him from behind the dark glasses. But he knew that was impossible. Ramon Vaquero had been blinded after an attempt on his life by the FMLN in the last months of the civil war. He'd never been the type of person to allow himself to wallow in self-pity, though, and after resigning his post as commander-in-chief of the National Guard, he'd turned to politics, and in particular the right-wing Arena party which he'd supported since its inception in the early eighties. He'd campaigned tirelessly in the run-up to the first democratic elections in the country, held after the official ceasefire; and when the party was swept into power, he was rewarded with a position in the cabinet. There was only one portfolio he'd wanted from the start. Defence. He knew it was the perfect platform from which to plot the downfall of the government, while appearing to be toeing the party line on all the major issues. It had meant gritting his teeth while they cut the heart out of the armed forces and continually conceded ground to the left in a pitiful attempt to placate opposition politicians, many of whom had once been the sworn enemy of the state. But, as he'd already told the Military Council on several occasions since first bringing it together, he'd always known that his time would come.

Dennison's eyes flickered to Hector Amaya, seated on Vaquero's immediate right. Although Amaya had always denied it, Dennison knew that his position beside Vaquero was more than just a coincidence. Amaya was officially listed as the Military Council's secretary, whose job it was to take detailed minutes of every meeting, then have those minutes dictated on to a cassette which would be delivered to Vaquero's office. Dennison had a sneaking suspicion that Vaquero already had Amaya pencilled in for the powerful Defence portfolio once he announced his first cabinet. Dennison knew he would never be a part of Vaquero's cabinet. He wasn't even officially a part of the Military Council. He was still regarded as an outsider. His benefits would be purely financial: not only would his company be awarded all the lucrative government contacts once Vaquero took office, but he would also be able to provide the wealthy *patrónes* with the kind of security they would demand to protect their lands after the coup d'état. This would be the death blow for many of his rivals, who were already struggling for business; he'd make sure his own troubleshooters were circling around like ravenous vultures, waiting to buy them out for a fraction of their real worth. Just as it had been before the ceasefire.

Vaquero felt for the gavel in front of him and banged it once sharply on the table to officially end the meeting. 'Thank you for coming at such short notice, gentlemen,' he said, addressing the officers on either side of him. 'I'll keep you posted on any new developments, if and when they occur. Mr Dennison, would you remain behind, please, after the others have left. Colonel Amaya, I'd like you to stay as well.' He tilted his head slightly to catch the sound of Dennison's chair scraping on the wooden floor after the others had left the room. He smiled faintly when he sensed that Dennison was standing directly beneath him. 'We go back a long way, Peter, don't we?'

'A good ten years,' Dennison replied.

'I regard the others on the Military Council merely as colleagues,' Vaquero continued, 'but you I regard as a friend. I don't have to try and impress you. But I do have to impress them. I have to show them that I do have the necessary qualities needed to lead this country. That's why I'm so disappointed in you. You've let me down in front of them. You're my chief security adviser, Peter. I expect you to act the part and not leave a trail of tell-tale clues behind you wherever you go.'

'I've already explained —'

'Hear me out,' Vaquero cut in sharply, his finger raised in admonishment. 'You and Jayson screwed up badly in the shanty town last night, and it was only through Colonel Amaya's intervention that the damage was kept to a minimum. It could have been a lot worse had he not been there. We can't afford these slip-ups, Peter, not with the coup now only thirty-six hours away. I have to tell you that there has been some disquiet amongst some members of the Military Council about your role in the whole operation. There is definite resentment that an ex-CIA man should be in charge of security, but so far I've managed to assure them that you're the right man for the job. Don't let me down again, Peter.'

'There won't be any more screw-ups,' Dennison assured him.

'The plan you put forward was certainly ingenious. If you were to recover the tape and recapture Ruiz, it would go a long way towards silencing your critics. You say you already know from your informer where the girl's being held?'

'Yes. It's a village in Chalatenango. I've already dispatched a team to rendezvous with him. I'll be going to the village as soon as I leave here.'

'Take Jayson with you, he may come in useful,' Vaquero said. 'And make sure you keep him on a tight leash this time. I don't want him going around like some madman as he did in the shanty town last night. He may be a good soldier, I'm not denying that, but he's obviously no match for Marlette. If you can kill Marlette, so much the better, but just make sure that Jayson isn't allowed to cause havoc when you get there. Chalatenango is still rebel country. Get the tape, then get out. Anything else will be a bonus. Do I make myself clear?'

'Perfectly,' Dennison retorted through clenched teeth.

'Good. I look forward to receiving your report this afternoon.'

Dennison glanced uncertainly at Amaya, unsure whether that was meant to be his cue to exit. Amaya nodded and Dennison walked to the door. A small, nondescript man appeared suddenly in the doorway, and Dennison had to pull up sharply to avoid bumping into him. Dennison had been introduced to the man when he'd first met Ramon Vaquero, yet all he knew about him was his name: Jek. He didn't even know his first name. Jek was European, that much was obvious. But there was little else obvious about him. He never ventured any information about himself, so it had never been discovered why he'd come to El Salvador. Like the few who'd actually held some kind of dialogue with him, Dennison thought the accent Mediterranean, but it wasn't distinctive enough to pinpoint his nationality. He didn't smoke. He didn't drink. And although he hovered in the background whenever Vaquero attended a public function, Dennison had rarely seen him speak to anyone. There had been rumours over the years to the effect that he'd been Vaquero's personal hit-man during the civil war, dealing with any problem that fell outside the jurisdiction of the military. Except that Dennison had never seen him armed. That wasn't to say that he didn't carry a weapon. Jek was a complete enigma, and Dennison had long since given up trying to find out anything about him. He'd just come to accept Jek's presence whenever he was around Vaquero.

Jek did have one redeeming feature: his impeccable manners. He immediately stepped aside to allow Dennison to pass; his face remained totally expressionless as Dennison muttered a thank-you under his breath as he left the room.

Jek climbed the wooden steps leading up to the elevated section of floor and took up a position behind Vaquero, hands clasped behind his back, eyes staring at an imaginary spot in the distance.

'Ah, Jek. Good.' Vaquero turned his head towards where Amaya was sitting. 'I was very interested to read your report on Dennison's theory about the possibility of there being a mole in the Military Council,' he told Amaya. 'I thought it best not to mention it in front of the others. We don't want a mutiny on our hands, do we? I assume that you've already checked out this house where Marlette was staying prior to the fiasco at the orphanage last night? Is there any connection with the CIA?'

'None whatsoever,' Amaya replied. 'It's been vacant for the last six months. I spoke to the estate agents this morning. A man came into the office last week and asked to rent it for two months. He paid cash. I have a photocopy of the agreement, but I think we'll find that the name will turn out to be false. I certainly don't see any connection with the CIA. I could be wrong, of course.'

'You're not wrong, Hector,' Vaquero said, shaking his head. 'I just hope Dennison doesn't come up with any more of his little theories. His behaviour's been bizarre these last few days. He's beginning to worry me. We can't afford passengers. If he becomes a liability, he'll be of no use to us at all.'

'With all due respect, sir, I think you're being a bit hard on him. Granted, he made a mistake last night, but Jayson was just as much to blame for that. I think they've both learnt from it.'

'Dennison's lucky to have a friend like you,' Vaquero said. 'Thank you, Colonel. That's all.'

Amaya saluted and left. Vaquero waited until Amaya had left the room, then inclined his head slightly towards the figure standing motionless behind him. 'Jek, I want you to keep a close eye on Peter Dennison and report his every move back to me. I don't care how trivial it may seem to you, I want to know everything he does. And, should he become a liability, kill him.'

NINE

Dennison could sense the hostility around him when he got out of the car. It didn't surprise him. He was deep inside Chalatenango in an area regarded as one of the country's last remaining FMLN strongholds. He looked at the stony-faced villagers, who stared back at him with a venomous hatred from behind an armed cordon which had been set up in advance of his arrival by a handful of troops who now shifted uneasily in the morning heat, their eyes reflecting their anxiety as they cradled their rifles close to their chests. There was no room for complacency in this kind of volatile situation. He noticed the two soldiers positioned strategically on a water tower at the mouth of the single dirt road – the sole means of access into and out of the small village. Both men were down on one knee, scanning the outlying countryside through their high-powered telescopic sights. Dennison knew it would only take the slightest provocation from either side to ignite an already tense situation into a potential bloodbath. He'd already given strict instructions to the soldiers not to retaliate if provoked by the villagers. They were to hold their positions at all costs, and only resort to firepower as a last means of defence. Dennison dabbed a handkerchief over his sweating face. But it wasn't the heat that was making him sweat. It was fear. He knew there could be an enemy sniper secreted somewhere in the surrounding mountains, who already had him lined up in a telescopic sight. One shot. That's all it would take.

Although it was the first time that Dennison had ever

been that deep into Chalatenango, he knew his face would be known to the villagers. His photograph had appeared in many of the FMLN propaganda pamphlets during the latter days of the civil war. With his strong right-wing views, and close affiliation to the military, he'd long been regarded as a sworn enemy of the people. And to many of these villagers, the ceasefire had amounted to little more than a worthless piece of paper signed by traitors. For many, the struggle continued. Dennison glanced at Jayson, who'd climbed out of the car after him. He could see the uncertainty etched on his face. The driver closed the door behind them, quickly retreating behind the wheel and the protection of the opaque bulletproof windows and chassis which encased Dennison's white Mercedes.

Dennison crossed to where a soldier was standing guard in front of a shack close to the dirt road. He paused in the doorway, and noticed with a mounting sense of foreboding that the number of onlookers had swelled since he'd first arrived at the village. He entered the house, followed by Jayson, where he was met by a captain in the National Guard.

'Well?' Dennison demanded.

The officer shook his head. 'There's no sign of the girl, *patrón*. We've already searched the house and there's no evidence to suggest that she was ever here. The house belongs to an old woman. She's blind and partially deaf. Hardly the sort of person you'd leave in charge of a six-year-old who doesn't speak Spanish. Not only that, it seems that the woman lost her husband and two sons during the war. They were guerrilla sympathizers who were killed in skirmishes with the military.'

'We've been set up,' Jayson hissed.

'It's certainly beginning to look that way,' Dennison agreed. 'Where's the woman now?'

'Some neighbours took her away after I'd finished questioning her,' the officer replied. 'Do you want to speak to her?'

'No,' Dennison replied. 'Is *he* here?'

'*Sí, patrón*. He's waiting for you in the kitchen,' the officer said, gesturing to a door further down the hall.

'Tell your men to continue holding their ground. We won't be long in here.' Dennison put a hand lightly on the officer's arm. 'It's a powder-keg out there. All it needs is for one of your men to lose his head to ignite it all.'

'They have their orders,' the officer retorted sharply, bristling indignantly at the suggestion that there could be any question of indiscipline within the ranks.

'I hope so, Captain, or we might all be returning to San Salvador in body bags,' Dennison told him. 'Now wait outside. We'll call you if we need you.'

The captain saluted, then left. Dennison led the way to the kitchen. A faded orange curtain had been drawn over the single window, and a chair stood at an angle to the back door, its crown wedged underneath the handle. A man, his face concealed under a black balaclava, sat at the table, a cigarette held tightly between his thumb and forefinger. Several half-smoked cigarettes had already been ground out in the clay ashtray in front of him. A Tokarev pistol lay within reach of his other hand.

'Miguel!' Dennison snapped from the doorway.

The man grabbed the pistol and swung it on Dennison, who was quick to put a restraining hand on Jayson's arm as the Cockney reached for his own holstered automatic.

'It's not like you to be so jumpy, Miguel,' Dennison said as he entered the room.

Miguel slowly lowered the pistol. 'This is my village. I was born here. These are my people. If they knew I was a collaborator they would tear me apart with their bare hands and feed my limbs to the stray dogs that scavenge the bins at night.'

'I had no idea this was your home village,' Dennison

said. 'Someone certainly has a macabre sense of humour.'

'What do you mean?' Miguel asked, dragging anxiously on the cigarette.

'The girl was never here. We've been set up.'

'I . . . I don't understand what you mean,' Miguel said, tugging nervously at the edges of the balaclava.

'I think you do,' Dennison replied. 'Your cover's been blown. The FMLN know you're an *oreja*. Why else would they have sent you here?'

Miguel stubbed out the cigarette and immediately pulled another from the packet and lit it. 'The girl must have been here,' he said, desperation now seeping into his voice. 'She must have been moved when they heard the National Guard were coming here to the village.'

'*They?*' Dennison queried.

'The couple who've been hiding her.'

'There's no couple here. Only an old blind woman. Who sent you? Ruiz?'

Miguel nodded. 'He told me to go on ahead of them to scout the area for any signs of the military. I called you as soon as he gave me the location. That's what you told me to do.'

'You did right, only Ruiz is obviously on to you. I don't know how, but then that doesn't really matter any more. You're as useful to me now as you are to them.'

Miguel swallowed nervously. 'You will protect me, won't you? I've served you well over the years. You can't leave me here. You must help me.'

'We'll take care of you, don't worry,' Dennison replied with a consoling smile. 'It's the least I can do after all the information you've passed on to me since I first recruited you.'

The officer appeared in the doorway and cleared his throat to attract Dennison's attention. '*Patrón*, the crowd's getting increasingly restless. We must leave now, otherwise we're going to have a serious incident on our hands.'

'You can tell your men to prepare to move out, Captain,' Dennison said. 'We're on our way.'

'*Sí, patrón*,' the officer said.

Jayson took Dennison to one side after the captain had left the room. 'What are you going to do about Miguel?'

'Like I said, he's of no use to me any more,' Dennison replied.

'Do you want me to kill him?'

'No!' Dennison barked angrily.

'So what are you going to do with him?'

'You leave that to me,' Dennison replied, then gestured to Miguel. 'Let's go. It's time to get out of here.' Miguel stubbed out his cigarette, then stuffed the pistol into his belt. 'Do you want to incite trouble out there?' Dennison snapped. 'An informer armed with a weapon favoured by the guerrillas? They'd lynch you before you got anywhere near the car. Give me the gun.' Miguel hesitated, his hand hovering over the pistol. 'I said give it to me!'

Miguel reluctantly handed over the weapon, and Dennison tucked it into the back of his trousers, then smoothed down his jacket to conceal it. Dennison could feel the eyes on them as they crossed to the Mercedes, but the hatred he sensed from the crowd was reserved for the informer. The driver got out of the car and handed Dennison a brown manila envelope. Dennison extended it towards Miguel. 'That's the payment I promised you for finding the girl. I know we haven't found her yet, but let's just call it a gratuity for all the work you've done for me over the years. Go on, take it.'

'Not here, not in front of these people,' Miguel said nervously.

'What are you worried about? It's not as if they can see you.'

Miguel's avarice got the better of him, and quickly he plucked the envelope from Dennison's hand. He was about to rip it open and count the money, when Dennison put a restraining hand on his arm. 'Now that would be asking for trouble. There's more money in there than most of these people will make in a lifetime.'

The driver opened the back door, and Dennison indicated for Jayson to get inside. Dennison then put an arm around Miguel's shoulders and led him away from the car. 'You've been a good source of information to me over the years. Someone at the top of the FMLN hierarchy. I'll certainly miss that. But then I suppose all good things have to come to an end.' He ripped Miguel's balaclava off his head, and tossed it contemptuously to the ground.

Miguel's first instinct was to retrieve the balaclava, quickly pulling it back over his head. But the damage had already been done. His eyes were filled with terror as the villagers' initial disbelief at his identity turned to a fierce hatred. A stone caught him painfully in the small of the back as the crowd began slowly to close in on him. He ran after Dennison and grabbed his arm as he was about to get into the car. 'You can't leave me here,' he pleaded in a pathetic whine. 'Please take me with you, *patrón*. Please.'

'We'll need a distraction if we're to get out of here ourselves,' Dennison said disdainfully, then took the Tokarev pistol from the back of his trousers and tossed it on to the ground at Miguel's feet. 'You'll be able to take a few of them with you. I'm sure the dogs will feast well tonight.'

'*Patrón*, you can't leave me –'

'Get him off me,' Dennison snapped angrily at his driver as he struggled to release Miguel's vice-like grip on his arm.

The driver locked his arm around Miguel's neck and pulled him off Dennison. He threw him roughly to the ground, then closed the rear door behind Dennison and got back behind the wheel.

'Let's get the hell out of here,' Dennison ordered.

The driver didn't need any persuasion as he swung the wheel sharply and drove straight for the encroaching crowd. A barrage of stones rained down on the car before the villagers were forced to scramble out of its way.

Jayson looked through the back window. He could see Miguel waving the pistol around in abject desperation as the villagers closed in on him. He was struck from behind and Jayson lost sight of him as he stumbled off balance and disappeared under the furious blows of the incensed mob. Jayson opened the mini-bar in front of him and helped himself to a miniature bourbon, which he drank neat from the bottle. It went some way towards steadying his frayed nerves.

Once clear of the village, the driver handed Dennison an envelope over his shoulder. Dennison then activated the panel between the front and back seats and opened the envelope.

'What's that?' Jayson asked.

'It's the money I would have paid Miguel for finding the girl,' Dennison replied, slipping the envelope into the inside pocket of his jacket. He noticed the frown on Jayson's face. 'You don't think I was going to give it to him so that the rabble back there could have got their hands on it? That's why I brought two envelopes with me. The other envelope was filled with shredded newspaper. It pays to anticipate every eventuality.'

'Obviously,' Jayson retorted. 'So what happens now?'

'Ruiz may have managed to outsmart us this time,' Dennison said, lighting himself a cheroot. He drew deep on the stem and exhaled the smoke slowly. 'But as he's about to find out, the game's far from over.'

'How much further to go?'

'It's not far now,' Ruiz replied from the passenger seat. 'Four, five kilometres. That's all.'

Marlette glanced at Nicole who was seated in the back of the car with him, but her face registered no emotion in response to the news that they'd almost reached their destination. He wasn't even sure whether she'd heard Ruiz. She stared straight ahead, her hands clenched tightly in her lap, seemingly oblivious of her surroundings. She'd been like that for much of the journey, only speaking when fielding one of his questions. He'd quickly realized that she wasn't in the mood to talk, and left her to her own thoughts. The silence up front had been just as intense. Chavez hadn't uttered a word since they'd left San Salvador two hours earlier. She'd been furious with Ruiz for daring to question Miguel's loyalty to the cause, and the situation hadn't improved when he'd decided to go along with Marlette's plan of sending Miguel on ahead to a village in Chalatenango – not the one where Michelle was being hidden – on the pretext of having him reconnoitre the area in advance of their arrival. Marlette knew it would be the only way of finding out for certain whether he was in collusion either with Dennison or the military. It had been Ruiz's idea to send him back to his own village, knowing only too well the fate that would befall him there if Marlette's theory turned out to be right. They still had to receive word from the village, but Marlette was already convinced that Miguel had been turned. Although Ruiz hadn't admitted it in so many words, Marlette had a sneaking suspicion that he'd also resigned himself to the fact that Miguel was an *oreja*.

Marlette had mixed feelings about their progress through Chalatenango. Part of him felt secure in the knowledge that they were now deep inside rebel country, where there was little chance of them being challenged by the military. Yet another part of him felt distinctly uneasy that they hadn't encountered a single military patrol since leaving San Salvador. It was almost as if they were being allowed safe passage to the village. When he'd raised this theory, though, Ruiz had told him that he was reading too much into it. He'd added that, wherever possible, they'd purposely avoided travelling through the towns and villages, which was where the military would be concentrating their search for Michelle. Marlette had tried to convince himself that Ruiz was right and that he was probably overreacting, but he still couldn't seem to shake the feeling that something wasn't quite right. Were they being drawn into a trap? They hadn't been followed from San Salvador, of that he was certain, so how else could Dennison know where they were headed? It was a question which had haunted him for much of the journey – and one that still had no answer ...

The village, like so many in the Chalatenango district, was encircled by lush, verdant countryside which spanned out as far as the eye could see. It turned out to be little more than a couple of dozen houses – a few with thatched roofs but most with corrugated iron roofs, the rust of neglect evident through the faded paint – which were all clustered around a small chapel. A group of children were playing football with a plastic ball in the open space in front of the chapel when Ruiz pulled up behind the only other vehicle parked in the main street – a battered pick-up truck – and switched off the engine.

Marlette was the first out of the car, grateful to pull himself free of the sticky seat which had soaked the back of his shirt, and he used his damp handkerchief to wipe the sweat from his neck and face. The view was breathtaking. The cloudless azure sky contrasted vividly with the deep green of the trees which rustled gently in the afternoon breeze, and on the horizon he could make out the hazy outline of one of the country's many extinct volcanoes, which shimmered like a flickering mirage in the distance. He looked around slowly at the villagers who'd emerged warily from their homes on hearing the approaching car. He could see the mixture of suspicion and apprehension on their faces. He knew these were the kind of people – the illiterate peasants who lived in the secluded harmony of their own parochial world, so far removed from the restlessness of the big cities – who'd taken the brunt of the military's retribution during the country's bloody civil war. They'd been repeatedly punished for daring to support the FMLN, who'd striven to bring an end to the corruption and injustice of a country once ruled by the might of the ubiquitous military machine. For the first time since he'd returned to El Salvador, Marlette found himself feeling a sense of shame that he'd helped to train the soldiers who'd once swept through villages like this one, torching houses, raping women, murdering children, and all in the name of a continuing purge against Communism. Or had it been a continuing purge against freedom?

Nicole climbed out of the car and shielded her eyes from the intense rays of the sun as she scanned the group of children who'd now stopped their game to stare uncertainly at the newcomers. Michelle wasn't amongst them. Ruiz indicated a house with a thatched roof further down the road. 'That's Gustavo's house. I'll go and speak to him.'

'I'm coming with you,' Nicole announced.

'I think it's best if I speak –'

'Save it,' Nicole cut in. 'Let's go.'

Ruiz conceded with a shrug, then turned to Marlette. 'Wait here. We shouldn't be long. And I wouldn't advise trying to talk to Anna. She's in a filthy mood.'

'I'd never have guessed,' Marlette retorted facetiously.

Nicole had to force herself not to run ahead to the house. A single door was all that now separated her from Michelle. She could feel her heart pounding as she walked with Ruiz towards the house. Every step seemed like an eternity. And all the time she was expecting to see the door burst open and for Michelle to come running towards her, arms extended, the usual cheeky grin on her face. But the door remained closed. Suddenly her excitement was tinged with a faint sense of apprehension. Ruiz put a hand on her arm as they reached the porch and, although she had the desperate urge to push past him and run into the house, she wisely checked her emotions as Ruiz knocked on the door. It swung open and a woman appeared in the doorway. Nicole guessed they were of roughly the same age. Her eyes went to Nicole who was hovering anxiously at the foot of the steps, and in that instant Nicole knew Michelle wasn't there. That much was obvious from the look of sadness on the woman's face. The woman beckoned Nicole towards her. Ruiz stepped back as Nicole hurried up on to the porch and, although he hadn't understood the look, he knew better than to say anything.

'Where's Michelle?' Nicole asked anxiously. 'Is she safe?'

The woman smiled gently as she took Nicole's hands in hers. 'I . . . not speak much English,' she said, struggling to translate her thoughts into the little English she knew. 'You . . . Michelle mother?'

'Yes,' Nicole said. 'Where is she? Is she safe? Please, you have to tell me, is she safe?'

'She not here,' the woman said, shaking her head. 'But not trouble.'

Nicole looked despairingly at Ruiz. 'Where's Michelle? You've got to find out where she is.'

Ruiz took the woman to one side and they talked together in Spanish. Nicole looked round when she heard footsteps behind her, and Marlette bounded up the stairs and on to the porch. He put a reassuring arm around her shoulders as he listened to the conversation between Ruiz and the woman. Nicole tried to get him to translate each sentence, such was her desperation to find out where Michelle was, but he held up a hand to silence her without taking his eyes off Ruiz or the woman. It was only when Ruiz looked round grimly at him that he spoke. 'A patrol came to the village within the last hour. The woman says they looked like soldiers, but that they weren't in uniform. It sounds like it could have been Dennison's men. They'd been warned in advance that the patrol was on its way, so her husband drove Michelle to another village about ten kilometres north of here. It was a precaution, that's all. She's not in any danger though.'

Nicole felt the relief surge through her. Michelle was safe. That was all that mattered. If anything had happened to her . . . She quickly dismissed the idea as so much supposition. It hadn't happened and it wasn't going to happen. She was confident that she'd be reunited with her daughter within the next hour. The delay was a small price to pay for her safety.

The woman pointed to Marlette. 'You . . . husband?'

'No,' Nicole replied.

The woman's eyes went to Marlette's arm which was still around Nicole's shoulders, then she smiled. 'Michelle . . . pretty. She look like you.'

'Yes, I know,' Nicole said. 'I know I can never thank you or your husband for what you've done for Michelle. Without you, I . . .' She trailed off and quickly wiped a tear from the corner of her eye.

'I . . . also . . .' The woman paused, then turned to Marlette and continued in Spanish.

'She said, she knows what it's like to lose a child,' Marlette translated for her. 'She lost her own daughter in the war. That's why she was determined that nothing would happen to Michelle.'

'Thank you,' Nicole said in a barely audible voice.

Marlette and Ruiz withdrew discreetly to the foot of the stairs. 'Do you know how to get to the village?' Marlette asked.

'No, but Anna will know the way,' Ruiz replied.

It was then that Marlette noticed the woman shielding her eyes as she peered into the distance. When he followed her gaze, he saw a cloud of dust in the distance on the approach road into the village, but within seconds he noticed the vehicle which was throwing up the whirlpool in its wake.

'Who is that?' Ruiz called out to the woman, his hand

resting lightly on the AK-47 slung over his shoulder.

'That's Rafael,' she replied, then gestured vaguely towards a cluster of houses further down the street. 'He lives there with his mother. His father was killed by the National Guard. He now serves the cause.'

Marlette assumed she meant that he was with the FMLN, but didn't venture the question. The battered red and white Oldsmobile pulled up behind Ruiz's Ford and a youth leapt out of the car. He was clearly agitated. He was momentarily taken aback by the sight of Chavez when she climbed out of the Ford, not expecting to see the new commander-in-chief of the FMLN in his village, and he was about to speak to her when he noticed Marlette and Ruiz out of the corner of his eye. He eyes widened in amazement as he stared at Ruiz. 'It can't be,' he whispered, shaking his head in disbelief. 'They said you were dead . . .'

'They were wrong. As you can see, *compo*, I'm very much alive,' Ruiz replied. The word *compañero* – a friend or comrade – was used regularly within the confines of the FMLN as a means of addressing a fellow member. Ruiz had specifically chosen to use the shortened version of the word, regarded as a more affectionate term, to try and put the youth at ease.

Marlette noticed that several of the villagers had already congregated behind Ruiz, talking excitedly amongst themselves, some touching their faces as they debated whether it really was Ruiz without his trademark beard. One woman stepped forward and grabbed Ruiz's hand. He smiled at her. Then another approached him. Marlette could see the effect Ruiz's presence was having on them. Some reached out and touched him reverently, as if he were a messiah. Marlette knew that in many ways Ruiz *was* a messiah to these people. He was their one chance to be delivered from the poverty and hardship which had decimated the area. But Marlette realized that there was another side to it. Before he'd been kidnapped, Ruiz had obviously wanted to remain 'dead' until he was ready to approach the government with Kinnard's incriminating tape. So why the sudden change of heart?

It was Marlette's guess that Ruiz had wanted to be recognized once he reached the village. That way word would spread rapidly across Chalatenango that the messiah was still alive and ready to lead them to a better life, free of many of the injustices which still prevailed in the country. But Marlette knew it went deeper than that. Ruiz was also protecting himself. If he were recaptured, his arrest would come under the media spotlight, and that would make it impossible for Dennison, or the military for that matter, to use him as the fall guy for the assassination the following day. It was a clever strategy, but Marlette wasn't convinced it would necessarily work. He guessed that Ruiz would have the same doubts in his mind, although Marlette had to admit that he'd probably have done the same if he'd been in Ruiz's position.

Ruiz managed to extricate himself from the villagers who'd gathered around him and propelled the youth to one side. 'You drove here in a great hurry. Is there trouble?'

'*Sí, compañero*. The *Yanqui*'s soldiers are gathering in the next village. Twenty, maybe thirty. They are all armed with automatic rifles. And they are coming here.'

'How do you know they're coming here?' Marlette asked.

Ruiz noticed the youth glance suspiciously in Marlette's direction. 'It's OK, he's with us.'

'I overheard them talking. They're looking for the girl. The one who was in all the papers. They say they know that she's being shielded by our people, and have threatened to execute any *compañero* who is found to be hiding her. They've already sealed off the village so that nobody could come here to warn the *compañeros*. My car was parked in a field close to the village. That's how I was able to sneak away. But they will be here soon.'

'You say they were the *Yanqui*'s soldiers?' Marlette said. 'Do you mean Dennison?'

'*Sí*, Dennison.'

'How could they know we're here?' Ruiz asked.

'They're looking for the girl, not us,' Chavez cut in.

'Think about it, Anna, they searched this village less than an hour ago for the girl. They wouldn't come back again in those numbers unless they were expecting trouble. No, they obviously know we're here. Question is: how?'

'I agree with Ruiz,' Marlette said. 'I said to you before that I thought it was strange we hadn't encountered any military patrols on the roads. It was almost as if we were allowed to come here.'

'Just like you and Miguel were allowed to go to the farmhouse,' Ruiz concluded.

'Exactly, only this time Miguel couldn't have known we were coming here. There has to be another explanation.'

'I want you to take Marlette and Nicole and find the girl before the whole area's overrun with soldiers,' Ruiz said to Chavez. 'I'll remain behind to give you time to get clear of the village.'

'I'll stay with you,' Marlette said.

'No, you go with Nicole –'

'I'm staying,' Marlette snapped, then reached through the back window and removed the Heckler & Koch submachine gun from the seat. He then explained briefly to Nicole what was happening.

'What chance have the two of you got against thirty men? They'll kill you, Rick,' Nicole said, grabbing his arm. 'You've got to come with us. If we leave now we can make straight for the border as soon as we've picked up Michelle.'

'Sure, we'd be outnumbered, but we're not looking for a fight. We'd only resort to firepower as a last resort. But if it came to that, Ruiz wouldn't be able to hold out for very long. That's why I'll have to stay behind with him. It's essential that you get to Michelle before Dennison does.' Marlette could see the concern in her eyes. 'You should know better than to write me off so quickly. It'll take more than a bunch of Dennison's thugs to send me to an early grave. It was foreign mercs like me who helped to train those bastards in the first place and, like any good instructor, I made sure that I kept a few things back from them. And that's what gives me the edge.'

'You always were a stubborn son-of-a-bitch, Rick Marlette,' she said in frustration. 'You know we've got the chance to get across the border –'

'I was hired to do a job out here, and that's exactly what I intend to do,' Marlette cut in angrily.

'In other words, Michelle's just another contract to you?' Nicole snapped back. 'What a fool I was to think that you might actually care about what happened to her!'

'Part of the deal I made with Pruitt was to get you and Michelle safely out of the country. If I fail, I forfeit a percentage of the money that's still owed to me. It's got nothing to do with sentiment. This is business, Nicole, and you know damn well that I never renege on a contract.'

Ruiz heard the raised voices and approached the two of them cautiously. 'We've decided that the best plan of action would be to ditch my car in case Dennison's men already have a description of it. Rafael knows a place where it could remain undetected for months.' He gestured to the pick-up truck. 'It belongs to Rafael's uncle. He says his uncle will drive Anna and Nicole to the village where Michelle was taken earlier this afternoon.' He addressed himself to Nicole. 'We're arranging to get half a dozen of the locals to travel in the back of the truck with you. That way it'll look more innocuous should the truck be stopped by a patrol.'

'That's fine by me,' Nicole hissed, glaring at Marlette. 'When do we leave?'

'As soon as the locals are ready,' Ruiz told her.

'And what if the patrol wants to see their papers?' Marlette asked.

'That's a chance we've got to take. Anna will be armed in case there is any trouble. Rafael's leaving his car here for us to use once Dennison's men have left the village. I've got the keys with me,' Ruiz said, patting his pocket.

'I want to be armed as well,' Nicole told him. 'If there is trouble, she may not be able to handle the soldiers by herself.'

'It's best if you leave that side of things –'

'Nicole's father was an arms dealer,' Marlette was quick to cut in. 'She grew up around guns. She probably knows more about them than I do. She's also a damn good shot.'

'I didn't know that,' Ruiz admitted. 'But I still don't think it's a good idea. Nicole, you wouldn't be able to communicate with Anna and, if you were to act independently of her, it would only do more harm than good. No, I think it's best if you let Anna deal with any trouble. She knows the language and, perhaps more importantly, she also knows how these soldiers think. They can be very predictable at times.' He looked across as the first of the villagers reached the truck. 'Excuse me, I'd better go and see that they've all been briefed properly.'

'I'll come with you,' Nicole said, and went after him.

Marlette watched as Rafael manoeuvred the Ford out from behind the truck, then sped off down the dirt road. It was only then he noticed that Chavez was studying him closely, but her expression gave away nothing of what she was thinking. She pocketed the Tokarev pistol she'd taken from the glove compartment and walked over to him. 'I don't know what you were arguing about, but I could see from her eyes that your words hurt her deeply. Why do you hurt her when she obviously cares so much about you?'

The question caught Marlette by surprise. He'd been expecting Chavez to come out with some snide comment to try and provoke him into a reaction. He even had a sharp riposte lined up to rebuff her. Instead he looked across at Nicole who was standing beside the truck with her back to him. 'She wanted me to go with her to get Michelle. She's the kind of person who likes to get her own way and, if she doesn't, she'll try and badger you into submission. There wasn't time for that, not with Dennison's men already amassing in the next village. They could be here at any moment. I had to get her on the truck and, to be honest, it really didn't matter to me how I did it. I know she cares about me. How else do you think I managed to hurt her so easily? The closer you are to someone, the easier it is to wound them. You should know that.'

Chavez knew what he was implying, and her eyes went to Ruiz who was helping an elderly villager into the back of the truck. She smiled, and in that instant all the harshness and tension disappeared from her face. 'Guillermo and I will always have each other. Only God can separate us now.'

Marlette suddenly felt desperately sorry for her as he watched her cross to where Ruiz was standing. She had a word with him, then he helped her up into the back of the truck. She sat down beside Nicole, whose face was now partially obscured by the scarf she had pulled over her head. Marlette slung the Heckler & Koch over his shoulder and walked slowly towards the truck. Nicole stared resolutely at the rusted floor, refusing to look at him. The truck coughed into life. The engine spluttered then died. And again. Only on the third attempt did the engine catch. The accelerator was pressed to the floor. Marlette thought for a moment that the engine would be flooded but somehow the note held and slowly grew in strength, though it still sounded like a death rattle. Ruiz slapped the side of the van. It shuddered momentarily, but the driver managed to keep the engine running and it pulled away slowly from the small group of onlookers. Marlette stared after it, hoping

Nicole would look at him. Just once. She didn't. He wiped his forearm across his sweating forehead, and could feel the dust and grit scraping across his skin.

Ruiz beckoned the remaining villagers forward until they'd formed a semi-circle around him. 'You must go about your lives as if nothing's wrong. If the soldiers were to suspect that you were hiding us, they'd tear this whole village apart to find us. I don't have to tell you what animals they can be.'

'We have guns,' an elderly villager announced, proudly holding up a rusted carbine. 'We will fight them.'

Marlette winced at its desperate condition. It was likely to blow up in the old man's face if he were ever to pull the trigger. But he couldn't help but feel a powerful affinity with the spirit around him. They would die for Ruiz and the cause. And they would die, of that he had no doubt. Dated, rusting carbines against sub-machine guns. He'd seen it all before in Africa. Only then it was spears and machetes against AK-47s. Death before dishonour. He caught Ruiz's eye and shook his head. Ruiz understood what he was implying. 'You mustn't fight them, *compañero*. I know your heart is true, but your carbines would be no match against their weapons. To die for a cause is just, but there is no honour in dying needlessly. You are all good people and the day will come when you will fight for what you know is right, but this is not the day. We must avoid any unnecessary bloodshed. The *Yanqui* and I would only fight if we were cornered. But if we're to remain undetected, you must all carry on with your daily chores as if we weren't here. You must promise me that.'

The *cacique*, the village leader, looked around him as the others reluctantly muttered in agreement. 'We will do as you say, *compañero*.'

It was then that the woman who'd been hiding Michelle stepped forward, her arm around the shoulders of a boy Marlette estimated to be no older than ten. What disturbed him was the sight of the AK-47 the boy was carrying. As in so many of the Third World countries where he'd fought over the years, he'd come to realize that the innocence of youth was invariably sacrificed for the chance to recruit another pair of hands for the cause. How often had he seen children toting rifles that were bigger than themselves? Rifles supplied by their own parents. It was a grotesque travesty that a parent could deem their own child's life to be so unimportant. So cheap. So expendable. He'd seen it all, but he'd never been able to reconcile himself to those images.

'My son will take you to the chapel: it is the best place for you to hide,' the woman said after the boy had reluctantly handed over the AK-47 to the *cacique* in accordance with Ruiz's instructions. There was a sadness in her eyes when she looked across at the derelict chapel. 'It was damaged when the military planes bombed the village. We have no money to repair it. The government have promised to help us, but so far they have done nothing.'

'I'm sorry,' Marlette said, knowing just how important religion was in a country where over ninety per cent of the population professed to be Roman Catholics.

'We go to the church in La Reina now,' the woman told him. 'But we do not go as often as we should. The petrol is expensive.' She crossed herself as if she'd committed blasphemy by her admission, then patted her son on the shoulder. 'Take the *compañeros* to the chapel.'

'What's your name, *compito*?' Ruiz asked as they headed towards the church at the end of the street. He purposely used the diminutive of the word *compañero*, an affectionate term reserved for the younger recruits.

'Juan,' came the beaming reply, and the smile faltered as he looked up at Marlette. 'Why do you walk with the *Yanqui*? He is the enemy.'

'Not all the *Yanquis* are fighting against us. He's a *compañero*,' Ruiz replied. 'We walk as one.'

The boy raised a clenched fist at Marlette as a sign of respect. Marlette had to fight back the revulsion as he went through the hollow motions of returning the salute. A ten-year-old kid who regarded every American as a potential enemy. He blamed the likes of Ruiz and Chavez for that kind of blatant xenophobia. It came from all the emotive anti-American speeches that they, and other left-wing rebels, had delivered during the civil war, which would have influenced the boy's parents, and thousands of other parents across the country. Children taught to hate from an early age. He could see that Ruiz had noticed his anger, but neither man said anything as they reached the stone steps leading up to the front door of the chapel. Marlette was about to climb the steps when the boy tugged at his sleeve. 'The door is locked. Come, I will show you how to get inside.' They followed the boy around the side of the building where he pointed to a hole in the wall at ground level. The damage had obviously been caused by the bomb.

'Is this the only way in?' Ruiz asked.

'There is another door at the back,' the boy replied, 'but it is bolted on the inside.'

'*Soldados*,' a voice shouted excitedly, and Marlette immediately unslung his sub-machine gun as the man ran breathlessly towards them, gesturing wildly into the distance behind him.

'Get inside,' Marlette hissed at Ruiz. Ruiz didn't argue and crawled through the narrow aperture. Marlette scanned the approach road and saw the thick clouds of dust being thrown up by the approaching vehicles. They were coming in force. He crouched down in front of the boy. 'Go back to your house now.'

'I want to come with you,' the boy said.

'No,' Marlette replied and put his hand on the boy's shoulder. 'Your father would want you to make sure that nothing happened to your mother while the soldiers are here. Can you do that, *compañero*?'

'*Sí, Yanqui,*' the boy said with a grin, then ran off towards his house.

Marlette struggled through the opening and only got to his feet once he was inside the chapel. There was a gaping hole in the roof which had taken the brunt of the explosion. The rubble lay scattered across the floor; the altar, as well as a couple of the wooden pews, had been badly damaged by the blast. He noticed the jagged crack in the wall which ran from the ceiling to the main doors like a streak of lightning which had been miraculously frozen at the moment of impact. He could see too that the wall was dangerously unstable, which explained why the door had been bolted from inside the chapel. Marlette crossed to the nearest window and peered cautiously through one of the closed shutters as the first of the convoy rumbled into the village. It was a cream-coloured Land-Rover which bore the distinctive logo of Dennison's security company on its doors.

Marlette and Ruiz drew back from the window when the lead vehicle came to a halt beside the stone steps. They heard the sound of someone trying to force the front door. The wall shuddered and a loose beam was dislodged from the roof. Marlette had to scramble out of the way as it crashed to the floor. A shadow fell over the window as one of the men peered into the chapel before shouting to his colleagues that the door was locked from the inside. The footsteps retreated down the steps and a succession of orders were barked out to secure the area immediately around the chapel. Marlette waited a few seconds, then raised himself slowly until his eyes were level with the foot of the window. He pressed his eye to a small hole in the glass, and saw two men standing guard at the foot of the stairs with their backs to the door. Another two Land-Rovers were parked close to the chapel, and their occupants, all armed with M-16s, had already taken up strategic positions around the village. There was no escape. Then a fourth vehicle entered the village. A white Mercedes. He watched the driver get out of the car and open the back door. Dennison climbed out and slid a pair of dark glasses over his eyes. He smoothed down his white suit and slowly took in his surroundings. Jayson climbed out after him. He tugged a panama hat over his straggly blond hair, and shifted uncomfortably in the sweltering heat. It was noticeable that his face and arms were red and blotchy from the scorching rays of the unyielding sun.

'I could take the bastard out with one shot. He doesn't know how close he is to death,' Ruiz whispered, but he was quick to shake his head when Marlette glanced anxiously at him. 'These are my people. If I shot Dennison, his men would only take it out on them. They'd kill everyone then raze the village to the ground. Nothing would be left.'

They watched as Jayson beckoned an elderly woman towards him, gesturing around him as he spoke to her. She spat on the ground at his feet and shuffled away.

'I thought you told them not to provoke Dennison's men,' Marlette hissed.

'They're not,' Ruiz replied. 'She's only showing the contempt that all these people feel towards him and his kind.'

Marlette stared at Dennison who was now standing motionless in the road, his arms folded across his chest, a cold, supercilious look on his face. 'What the hell is he doing out there?' he asked in exasperation.

'He's gloating,' Ruiz replied.

'What?'

'I saw him do it once before, during a television interview with a foreign journalist at some fund-raising dinner in San Salvador. He was asked what had happened to the death squads after the ceasefire had been signed. He didn't say anything. He just stood exactly like that. He was gloating.'

'Why?' Marlette hissed.

'Because he'd hired most of them, and the journalist

didn't know that,' Ruiz retorted disdainfully. 'So if he's gloating, he obviously knows something we don't.'

'Wait,' Marlette whispered, and raised his hand as Dennison crossed to the nearest Land-Rover where he was handed a loud-hailer.

Dennison wiped his sleeve across the mouthpiece, then raised the loud-hailer to his lips. 'Ruiz, we know you're here,' he said in English, knowing that the locals wouldn't understand what he was saying. 'I'm not going to waste time by having my men search the village. These are your supporters, and they'll see to it that you avoid detection. It's understandable, but futile. I'll give you exactly two minutes to show yourself, otherwise we'll start shooting the villagers one by one for every minute that you refuse to surrender. You've got two minutes, Ruiz. After that their blood will be on your conscience.'

Ruiz slumped back against the wall and looked across anxiously at Marlette. 'He obviously knows I'm here. He wouldn't threaten to wipe out an entire village on the off-chance that I might be here.'

'He could also be calling your bluff,' Marlette said.

'No, not with the kind of support the FMLN have here in Chalate. It's exactly the sort of incident which could spark an uprising against the government. He wouldn't risk that unless he was absolutely sure I was here.' Ruiz noticed the look of uncertainty in Marlette's eyes. 'I may be a company spy, but I'm still a Salvadorean. And I know what would happen to this country if Vaquero's plan were to succeed tomorrow night.' He took the keys to Rafael's car from his pocket and held them out towards Marlette. 'It's obvious that Dennison doesn't know you're here, otherwise he'd have said something. It's up to you now to stop Vaquero.'

'I told you —'

'That Pruitt's already hired you to fulfil a contract,' Ruiz cut in. 'Yes, so you told me last night. Only you wouldn't tell me what that contract entailed. I just hope we're on the same side, otherwise this country's going to be plunged back into civil war. Mark my words, Marlette, if Vaquero's allowed to take power in El Salvador, the people will rise up again.'

'One minute, Ruiz,' Dennison's voice carried across the silence. 'After that we start killing a villager for every minute you continue to hold out.'

'Take the keys,' Ruiz said, wiping the sweat from his face. 'You're not doing this for me or my organization. You're doing it for the people of this country. People like these villagers. They risked their lives to protect Michelle. Don't you think you owe them something in return? It's time to make a stand, Marlette. Take the keys.'

Marlette wet his lips as he stared at the keys in Ruiz's hand. If he took them he would be morally obliged to carry out the hit the following night. He wouldn't be paid for it. Nor would he be thanked for it. And only the two of them would ever know the truth. He looked at his watch. Thirty seconds left. He closed his hand around the keys. Ruiz scrambled to his feet and crossed to the back door. Marlette followed him and took up a position to the side of the door, the Heckler & Koch gripped tightly in his hand. Ruiz drew back the bolt and eased open the door. There was no sign of any of Dennison's men. He paused to look round at Marlette. 'God be with you, *compo*.'

'And you,' Marlette replied softly but Ruiz had already disappeared through the doorway. Marlette was quick to bolt the door again behind him and, when he returned to his vigil at the window, he saw that Ruiz was now standing in front of the chapel, his hands clamped on his head, his AK-47 having been confiscated when he surrendered to the two guards at the foot of the steps. Dennison tossed the loud-hailer into the back of the Land-Rover, then climbed in beside the driver who drove him to where Ruiz was standing. Dennison got out and looked around slowly at the faces of the villagers who were steadily gathering in numbers behind the armed cordon on either side of the road. Marlette knew that behind the façade of victory, Dennison was just as uneasy as his men.

Although Marlette didn't hear everything that was said, he picked up enough of the conversation to be able to relate it to what followed.

'Is he clean?' Dennison asked of the two armed men standing on either side of Ruiz.

'*Sí, patrón*,' one of the men was quick to assure him.

Dennison leaned back against the side of the Land-Rover and folded his arms across his chest. 'I've got to give you credit for that little bit of deception earlier today, Ruiz. You certainly had us going for a while. Tell me, how did you know that Miguel was working for me?' Ruiz held Dennison's stare but said nothing. 'No matter, he's dead anyway. But it's ironic that even after his death he should be instrumental in leading us to you. In fact, if it wasn't for him, we wouldn't be having this little conversation right now.'

'It was very easy tracking you to here,' Jayson said with a contemptuous sneer.

'Show him,' Dennison said to Jayson.

Jayson took a small receiver, no larger than a cigarette packet, from his jacket pocket and held it up for Ruiz to see. 'It's tuned in to the miniature transmitter that you've been carrying on you ever since we let Marlette spring you from the farmhouse. We've known your every move to within a couple of hundred metres. There was no need to tail you from San Salvador today. We were able to keep tabs on you on this. And when your signal stopped moving, we were able to pinpoint your location and here we are. Simple really.'

Dennison allowed himself a faint smile of satisfaction. 'I realized when I first came up with the idea of planting the transmitter on you that I couldn't implant it under your skin because you'd be sure to notice the wound. It would also have been pointless to conceal it in any of your clothes. That's where Miguel came in. He told us the perfect place to secrete a transmitter without you ever suspecting it was there. What's the only thing you keep on you irrespective of where you go or what you do? That locket around your neck. The one Chavez made you promise you'd never remove for as long as the two of you were together. I placed the transmitter behind the miniature photograph of Chavez that you keep in the locket.'

'We know you came here with Marlette and the Auger woman,' Jayson said. 'Where are they?'

Ruiz said nothing.

'You're only delaying the inevitable, Ruiz,' Dennison told him. 'The whole area's now swarming with my men. It won't be long before we find them. Cooperate with us, and I guarantee you that Nicole Auger and her daughter will be released unharmed.' Still silence.

'I'll get him to talk,' Jayson hissed, and moved menacingly towards Ruiz.

'Leave him!' Dennison snapped. He grabbed Jayson's arm and took him to one side. 'These villagers are guerrilla sympathizers. You touch Ruiz in front of them and we'd have a bloodbath on our hands.' He turned back to Ruiz. 'We know that if they aren't here in this village, then they certainly can't be far away. So you'll be saving these villagers a lot of trouble and anguish if you tell us now where they are. If not, we'll tear this village apart in our search for them. And I have the President's authorization to do just that if I think these people are hiding Marlette. He's a wanted fugitive, and I've been given strict instructions to apprehend him at all costs. Bear that in mind, Ruiz, before you condemn these people to a great deal of unnecessary suffering.' He reached into the back of the Land-Rover for the loud-hailer, then noticed that the villagers were already beginning to push against the armed cordon not twenty metres away from where he was standing. It was obvious that his men were heavily outnumbered, and the uncertainty of the situation was evident on their faces as they struggled to contain the crowd as it became ever more volatile. He knew he had to do something fast. 'Listen to me,' he boomed through the loud-hailer. 'Listen to me!'

The jostling subsided and the angry voices became whispers as all eyes turned on him. He felt the sweat seeping down the side of his face, but he made no move to wipe it away. It could be misconstrued as fear, and he knew that it would inevitably be seen as a sign of weakness amongst these people. And it wasn't the time for weakness.

'We have no quarrel with you,' he told them, 'and to prove this, I'm prepared to pay the sum of fifty thousand American dollars, the equivalent of three hundred and fifty thousand colónes, to anyone with information leading to the arrest of the *Yanqui*, Richard Marlette. We know he came here with Ruiz. Three hundred and fifty thousand colónes for his capture.'

'And where's this money?' a sceptical voice called out from the crowd.

'In my car,' Dennison replied, and snapped his fingers at his driver, who retrieved an attaché case from the back seat of the Mercedes and handed it to him. Dennison flicked open the locks, lifted the lid, and held the case at an angle for the crowd to see. 'Fifty thousand American dollars. It's yours if you tell us where to find the *Yanqui*.'

A silence descended across the crowd as they stared at the layers of fifty-dollar notes lining the case. It was the kind of money they'd only ever seen in the Hollywood movies which regularly played at the cinema in La Reina. Money that could be used to rebuild the chapel. Educate their children. Bring fresh running water to the village. They didn't owe the *Yanqui* anything. He wasn't one of them. The whispering began as they sought to reach a decision amongst themselves.

'I would speak with you,' the *cacique* announced, and Dennison gestured for him to be allowed through the cordon. 'You give us the money, and agree to release the *compo* unharmed,' he paused to gesture in Ruiz's direction, 'and we will give you the *Yanqui*.'

'No!' Ruiz screamed in fury, but when he tried to step forward his path was quickly barred by the two guards on either side of him. One of the guards glanced across at Dennison, unsure whether to silence Ruiz, but Dennison shook his head, knowing that any force now would only work against him.

Ruiz glared at the *cacique*, then turned on the villagers. 'I can't believe that you would accept the money from these men. They are our enemies. Where is your honour?'

'We can use the money for our village,' the *cacique* said, and there was a general murmur of agreement from the crowd.

'Then take their blood money!' Ruiz snarled. 'But don't use me to try and justify your actions. You betray the *Yanqui* and you shame yourselves before God and your country. I would rather die than be part of that shame.'

Dennison sensed the unease in the crowd as Ruiz's emotive words cut deep into their consciences. A movement caught Dennison's eye and he was still turning when a stone caught him painfully on the shoulder. He stumbled forward and the attaché case fell to the ground. The thick bundles of blank paper, each secured with an elastic band and topped with a genuine fifty-dollar note to cover the deception, spilled out across the road.

Juan, the boy who had thrown the stone at Dennison, picked up one of the bundles which had come to rest at his feet and held it out for the other villagers to see. One of the guards swung his machine gun on the boy, but Ruiz shoulder-charged him before he could fire. The second guard caught Ruiz across the back of the head with the butt of his rifle, and Ruiz crumpled unconscious to the ground.

'Get him into the Land-Rover,' Dennison yelled above the vitriolic shouting which had erupted around him once the deception had been revealed. The two guards dragged Ruiz to the Land-Rover, their eyes darting nervously towards their colleagues who were struggling to contain the angry crowd now trying to break through the cordon. They'd barely managed to bundle Ruiz into the back of the Land-Rover when a shot rang out from the chapel. The bullet took one of the guards in the back. Dennison ordered his men to return fire, then clambered after Jayson into the back of the Mercedes and banged sharply on the glass partition between the front and back seats. Stones and rocks peppered the Mercedes as it ran the gauntlet of enraged villagers, and only when they were clear of the missiles did Dennison look behind him, relieved to see that the Land-Rover which contained the unconscious Ruiz was following closely. He sat back in his seat, then reached for the telephone to call in reinforcements for the impending journey back to San Salvador.

Marlette had seen the boy break away from the edge of the crowd, but he hadn't seen the stone in his hand. It had been uncannily accurate and, had it been higher, it could easily have done a lot more damage. It was then he knew that the simmering tension had reached boiling point. He'd seen the guard turn his rifle on the boy, but before he could react Ruiz had shoved the man off balance, almost certainly saving the boy's life in the process. Then Ruiz had gone down under the savage blow and Marlette had tried to get in a shot at the two guards as they dragged Ruiz towards the Land-Rover. It had been too risky, though; he might hit Ruiz by mistake. It was only when Ruiz was dumped unceremoniously into the back of the Land-Rover that he finally had a clear shot. He'd taken out the nearest guard with a single shot.

He barely heard Dennison's order above the incessant clamour of the voices, but he'd managed to fling himself sideways in the split second before a fusillade of bullets ripped through the shutters, spraying glass and wood across him as he lay face down on the floor. He scrambled to his feet and ran to the temporary sanctuary of an upturned pew. Crouching down behind it, he'd listened with growing dismay to the sounds of violence which had erupted outside the chapel. Then suddenly the shutters were ripped aside and the barrel of a G-3 rifle appeared through the shattered windows. Marlette dropped to the floor as a row of bullets chewed across the back wall. Whoever was out there obviously couldn't see him, just as he couldn't see them. Then the barrel disappeared from view and, seconds later, he heard the sound of a boot being kicked against the front door. The wall shuddered under the impact, and chunks of masonry fell to the floor, throwing up clouds of dust directly in front of the door. The boot made contact again. And again. And all the time the masonry continued to fall as the wall swayed precariously on its damaged foundations.

The pounding stopped as suddenly as it had started. Marlette's eyes flickered from the door to the window. He was still trying to determine what was happening when he heard a loud thump behind him. Someone was now trying to kick down the back door. Then the pounding started up again on the front door. Double jeopardy. He scrambled to his feet and pressed himself up against the back wall. He wasn't as close to the door as he would have liked, but he couldn't risk getting any closing for fear of being seen from the front window. Now all he could do was wait for the first of the intruders to break through into the chapel.

The front door was the first to give way. He heard the sound of splintering wood as one of the hinges was ripped away from the wooden frame. The next blow broke the inside bolt, and the door was kicked open with such savagery that it slammed back against the wall. He never knew whether it was the shuddering vibration as the door struck the wall, or whether it was the sustained hammering leading up to it, but the wall collapsed as if it had been dynamited. The man in the doorway simply disappeared, his body crushed beneath the devastating avalanche of bricks and mortar which cascaded down on him. A brick slammed into the wall close to where Marlette was standing and, in his desperation to scramble clear, he caught his foot on a pew and fell heavily to the floor. The Heckler & Koch spun from his hands and skidded underneath one of the upturned pews. He leapt to his feet again. As he darted towards the bench he heard the sound of splintering wood. The back door had been kicked open. He was still clawing frantically underneath the pew for his fallen weapon when he heard the footsteps on the wooden floorboards behind him. He looked round in desperation and found himself staring down the barrel of an M-3 rifle. Marlette knew he could never retrieve the sub-machine gun in time.

It was then he saw, out of the corner of his eye, Juan scrambling over the rubble in the front of the chapel, a brick clenched tightly in his hand. The guard followed Marlette's horrified stare, snorting in disgust as he pumped several rounds into the small body. In his fury Marlette ripped the pew aside with one hand, grabbed the Heckler & Koch in the other, and dived to the floor as the guard swung the rifle back on him. The guard was still trying to line up the rolling target when Marlette opened fire, scything a row of bullets across his chest. The guard stumbled backwards, the surprise still mirrored on his face, and Marlette raised himself on to one knee and emptied the rest of the magazine into him. Discarding the spent clip, he snapped a fresh one into place, then sprinted over to where the boy lay. He went through the motions of checking for a pulse, even though he already knew the boy was dead.

A shadow loomed over Marlette and he swung the Heckler & Koch towards the figure, his finger already curled around the trigger. The *cacique* looked from Marlette to the boy, but when he tried to reach down to pick up the lifeless body, Marlette jabbed the barrel of the Heckler & Koch menacingly into his stomach. The *cacique* stepped back, and it was then Marlette became aware of the other villagers who had already congregated at the foot of the steps. Nobody spoke. The onlookers parted to allow the boy's mother through, and she was quick to shrug off the *cacique*'s consoling hand as she climbed the steps to where Marlette was crouched over her son.

'I'm so sorry,' Marlette said softly. 'If I'd only been able . . .' His voice trailed off as he realized just how hollow his self-recriminations must have sounded. He could never undo what had happened. The boy was dead, and he knew the guilt would haunt him for the rest of his life. Another innocent face to torment those dark hours of sleep . . .

The woman made no attempt to wipe away the tears that streamed down her cheeks as she crouched down and cradled her son's head in her arms. When she finally looked at Marlette there was no anger or bitterness in her eyes. Only regret. 'His father taught him from an early age that all Americans should be regarded as the enemy. I knew it was wrong to raise a child with such hatred in his heart, but he never listened to me when I tried to reason with him. He worshipped his father and he always believed the propaganda that my husband, and others in the village, were always drumming into him. But today he discovered for the first time that maybe not all Americans are the enemy. He realized that he could trust you, and trust is the most cherished gift any adult can give to a child.'

'And I betrayed that trust when he needed me most,'

Marlette said despairingly. 'If only I could have got to my weapon quicker . . .'

'I know in my heart that you would have done everything possible to protect my son,' she said, then placed a hand lightly on his arm. 'There is nothing more you can do for him. He is with God now. You must go to your woman. She needs you.' She lifted the lifeless body to her chest and carried it slowly to the altar, placing it gently in front of the towering statue of the Virgin Mary.

Marlette slung his Heckler & Koch over his shoulder and, with a last glance in the direction of the woman who was now kneeling in prayer before the hallowed statue, he picked his way carefully through the rubble and paused on the steps to take in the carnage spread out before him. He counted over a dozen bodies scattered across the dry, barren ground. He estimated at least half of them to be Dennison's men, but was quick to remind himself that these were only the bodies he could see. There would certainly be others lying behind houses or in the surrounding forest. The injured were being taken to the shade of an over-hanging tree, where a couple of women were treating them with a motley collection of bandages, plasters and lotions contained in a battered camouflage rucksack. He was about to make his way across to the tree to give some assistance when a hand grabbed his arm from behind. He looked round to see the *cacique* shaking his head, having already anticipated what Marlette had in mind.

'I can help,' Marlette told him. 'Hell, I'm no doctor, but I do know a few things about first aid. In my profession you learn how to treat your own wounds when you're in the bush.'

'We don't want you here,' the *cacique* said brusquely. 'You have brought much suffering to my village. Go.'

Marlette was about to defend his presence but, realizing the futility of it, snapped his mouth shut and took the car keys from his pocket.

'You cannot use the car,' the *cacique* told him. 'Not now. You can be sure that word will have already reached the military about what happened here. The soldiers will be out in force, stopping all cars across Chalate and checking everyone's papers. You would not get far.'

'Do you have any other means of transport?' Marlette asked.

'There are some horses. I will have one of my sons ride with you to the village where your woman went earlier. He will see to it that you are not stopped by any of the army patrols.'

Marlette watched the *cacique* walk back to the chapel where he spoke to a youth in his twenties. They both looked across at Marlette, then the *cacique* climbed the steps and disappeared into the chapel. The youth beckoned Marlette towards him and gestured with a sweep of his arm in the general direction of where the horses were stabled. Marlette cast a last look over his shoulder at the village, then followed the youth as he made for the trees.

TEN

Nicole heard the distant gunfire as the truck wound its way carefully through the narrow mountain col. Although she couldn't be sure of exactly where it had originated from, she automatically feared the worst. There was a lot of excited talk and animated gesturing amongst the others; her frustration at not understanding what they were saying only added to the anxiety which was building in the pit of her stomach. Up until then her thoughts had been concentrated solely on Michelle. Now she found herself thinking about Rick. Was he all right? What if he was captured? What if he was tortured? Or worse, what if . . .

No, she refused even to contemplate that. This was Rick Marlette, the last of the survivors. Although the uncertainty continued to linger on in her mind, she found she was able to temper her angst by constantly reminding herself of their flare-up back at the village. Had he been showing his true colours? Had he really become so devoid of feeling that he regarded Michelle simply as a means of fulfilling a contract? That wasn't the Rick she knew; even after six years apart, she still believed she knew him better than anyone else. He'd certainly become more wary of letting his emotions show, and she knew she was partly to blame for that, but she reminded herself that he'd rarely shown his real feelings when they'd been together anyway. She'd dismissed the idea that he was under some kind of pressure and hadn't meant what he'd said. He'd always been at his best under pressure, and it had been obvious from the cold, cynical tone of his voice that he'd meant every word he'd said. And that's what had upset her so much. She realized now she'd been naïve to have believed there was ever a realistic chance that they could get back together again. She still loved him and she'd been sure that the feelings had been mutual. But obviously she'd been wrong. He knew just how much Michelle meant to her, yet he'd made her out to be little more than a means of collecting the balance of the money that was still owed to him on his return to the States. She would never jeopardize that special bond she shared with her daughter for any man. But it wasn't just the intensity of their love that made the relationship so special. They also shared a unique friendship she'd rarely encountered in other mother–daughter relationships. If Rick couldn't accept Michelle as an integral part of any future they might have together, then he could go to hell as far as she was concerned. And he could take his money with him . . .

The sound of the agitated voices brought her out of her reverie, and when she followed the gaze of the anxious faces around her she saw to her horror that a cream-coloured Land-Rover was coming up behind them. It bore the logo of Dennison's security company. These were the kind of men, according to Ruiz, who regarded themselves as being above the law, especially while operating within the rebel strongholds in the north of the country. The driver barked out an order over the roof-speaker, and Nicole's heart sank when the truck pulled over to the side of the road and the engine switched off. The Land-Rover drew up behind the truck; two men got out while the driver remained behind the wheel. One of the men went to speak to the driver. His colleague remained at the back of the truck and snapped out an order in Spanish. The flap was lowered. Nicole instinctively tugged the scarf down further over her forehead, looking down at her feet as she felt his eyes on her. He gave another order; Chavez jabbed her elbow into Nicole's ribs and indicated with her eyes the ID papers she had in her hand. Nicole took from her pocket the papers she'd been given at the village. Chavez plucked them hastily from her fingers and handed them to the woman beside her, who added her papers and passed them down the line. The man shouted angrily when he realized what was happening and indicated that the papers be returned to their owners. It was exactly what Nicole had been dreading. The papers she was carrying belonged to a woman in the village: it had been hoped that if the truck was stopped she could get away by presenting everybody's papers together. It was a chance she'd had to take but now it had backfired. The papers were to be checked individually. She was trapped. If she presented the papers, she'd be arrested. If she didn't, she'd be arrested. She knew Chavez wouldn't hesitate to use the automatic concealed under her poncho, but that would only be a short-term solution. Once Dennison found out that his men had been bush-whacked, he'd send in reinforcements to track down their killers. She knew Ruiz had insisted Chavez use the automatic only as a last resort, but now that seemed the only choice left open to her. She noticed that Chavez was holding her papers in one hand; her other hand was already tucked underneath the poncho.

The second man reappeared and, after a brief word with his colleague, signalled to the woman beside Chavez to show him her papers. Nicole could feel Chavez's body tense beside her as the man returned the papers and beckoned to Chavez to pass him hers. Nicole was next. She could feel the sweat on her palms as she watched the man carefully check through Chavez's dog-eared papers. Ruiz had told her earlier that they were false – as were the papers of all the senior FMLN guerrillas – but they were such good forgeries that she'd been using them without incident for the past few years. Satisfied they were in order, the man handed them to one of the women to return to Chavez.

Then he snapped his fingers at Nicole and gestured for her to pass him her papers.

She felt Chavez's arm bump against her; in that instant Nicole realized she was about to draw her automatic from under the poncho. Desperate to avoid a confrontation, she grabbed Chavez's wrist and gave her papers to the next woman to hand to the man. She knew that the odds were stacked heavily against her, but it was worth the risk to avoid any unnecessary bloodshed, which would only bring more of Dennison's men into the area. And if her deception was uncovered, then Chavez could make her move. She could sense the tension in Chavez's body, although whether it was due to the uncertainty of what might happen, or the fact that Nicole still had a vice-like grip on her wrist she couldn't be sure. They both watched apprehensively as the papers were passed from hand to hand down the line towards the man.

The papers finally reached the last pair of hands, and the man was about to take them when a gunshot echoed across the silence. Nicole looked up, sensing the shot had originated from one of the mountains overlooking the pass. Chavez jerked her hand free of Nicole's grip, but she made no move to draw her weapon on the two men who were now crouched down, both facing in opposite directions, their rifles trained on the mountains. Neither man fired. It was impossible for them to pinpoint the sniper's position amongst the dense foliage. A second shot rang out, then a third. Each shot had come from a different direction. A bullet slammed into the ground in front of one of the men. He fired blindly in the general direction from which the shot had originated, then ran, doubled over, to the Land-Rover, ducking down behind it. Another bullet slammed into the side of the Land-Rover close to where the man crouched. He looked round in desperation, his eyes wide and fearful, then beckoned his colleague towards the vehicle as the driver struggled to start up the engine.

As more bullets rained down from the mountains, most peppering into the ground around the Land-Rover, Nicole began to realize that the concealed snipers weren't out to kill, or even to injure the men. They could have done that with their first three bullets – they were obviously intent on scaring, rather than harming, their targets. It also explained why Chavez had been reluctant to draw her weapon when she'd had the chance.

The driver started the engine and slewed the Land-Rover sideways in an ungainly one-hundred-and-eighty-degree turn. A derisive cheer went up when the vehicle clipped a large boulder, ripping off the front fender. The driver managed to regain control of the vehicle and, as it sped away, the villagers celebrated its ignominious retreat by singing and dancing in the back of the truck. Nicole had never experienced anything like it before and, although she'd initially remained seated as the others danced around her, she was quickly pulled to her feet and found herself joining in the celebrations until Chavez grabbed her arm and pointed to a figure silhouetted on the mountainside above them. Dressed in olive-green fatigues, and with a red bandanna secured over the lower part of his face, the figure was brandishing an AK-47 victoriously in the air. Chavez greeted her comrade with a closed-fist salute and, after returning the gesture, the figure disappeared back into the undergrowth.

The driver got out of the cab and had a word with Chavez, who drew her pistol and fired a single shot into the air. It had the desired effect of bringing the celebrations to an abrupt halt. She gestured for the villagers to sit down. Nicole now found herself squashed up against the back of the cab, but considered it a small price to pay, considering what could have happened had the guerrillas not intervened when they did. It was almost as if the gods had finally decided to smile on her. The truck shuddered into life once more, and she clenched her fists in frustration as it pulled away slowly and trundled leisurely towards the first bend in the road. Why couldn't the damn contraption go any faster? She would have been willing to run barefoot across broken glass if it had meant reaching Michelle any quicker. How much further before they *did* reach the village? Her impatience got the better of her and in desperation she put the question to Chavez. It was understandably met with a puzzled frown.

'Village,' Nicole said, pointing despairingly into the distance. 'How far? How many kilometres?'

'*Kilómetro?*' Chavez replied, picking up on the one word she thought she'd understood. '*Aldea?*'

Nicole shrugged helplessly. 'Michelle? How far?'

'Michelle?' Chavez said, indicating with her hand the height of a small child.

Nicole nodded and pointed into the distance again, hoping Chavez had understood what she was trying to say.

Chavez scanned the road then tugged Nicole's sleeve and gestured towards a swathe of trees ahead of them. For a moment Nicole thought they were still on a different wavelength, then, as the truck rounded another bend in the road, she suddenly saw what Chavez had been trying to point out to her. A settlement, which until then had been obscured by the trees, spread out across the verdant slopes of one of the country's many extinct volcanoes.

'Michelle,' Chavez announced.

Nicole broke into a wide grin, then, discarding the shawl, she got to her feet and vaulted over the side of the truck. She almost lost her balance as she landed on the ground, but she quickly found her footing and began to run towards the village. Chavez smiled to herself at the sight of the amazed faces around her, then went after Nicole. She was already breathless when she caught up with Nicole and, although she managed to stay with her for another hundred metres, she finally had to stop, her hands on her knees, as she gasped for air. Nicole cut through the trees, and when she emerged from the undergrowth she found herself on the edge of the village. Only then did she pause for breath.

Brushing her hair back from her sweating face, she looked around her, desperately hoping to see Michelle amongst the startled villagers who were staring back suspiciously at her. She wasn't there. Nicole winced as a sharp pain shot through her side. She was a regular jogger back home, but the sheer pace of the run had taken its toll. Ignoring the pain, she walked towards the main street. The village was marginally bigger than the last one and, being concealed in the protective shadow of the volcano, there was something strangely innocent about the unblemished beauty of the surrounding countryside. She thought it fitting that Michelle should have been brought there.

Nicole heard a scuffing sound behind her and, when she looked round, saw Chavez, hands on hips, gulping down mouthfuls of air as she struggled to catch her breath. Chavez coughed violently and shook her head despairingly, then gestured for Nicole to follow her as she made her way towards a group of women sitting by the side of the road. They were weaving baskets which would be sold to passing traders for resale to the tourists in the south of the country. Nicole watched as Chavez approached the women and engaged them in conversation. *Come on*, Nicole urged Chavez silently. *All you have to do is ask them if they know where to find Michelle. If not, then find someone who does . . .*

'Mrs Kinnard?'

The voice startled Nicole, and with it came the terrifying thought that either the military, or worse, Dennison's thugs, had tailed them to the village. But she was damned if she would surrender without a fight. She'd rather die than let those bastards anywhere near Michelle. Slowly, anxiously, she turned around. The man was in his early forties, although his thinning hair made him look older. He had a red bandanna tied loosely around his neck, but she derived little comfort from the knowledge that it was widely regarded as an integral part of the FMLN's uniform. It would be the first accoutrement any undercover man would have on his person. She was hoping that Chavez might know the man, but saw that she was still in conversation with the women. Nicole decided to let the man take the initiative . . .

'You are Nicole Kinnard?' he asked, pronouncing each word carefully in his thick Salvadorean accent. 'My name is Gustavo. I have been . . . caring for your daughter.'

'Michelle?' Nicole blurted out anxiously. 'Where is she? Please, you must take me to her.'

Chavez swung round, alerted by Nicole's outburst, her hand already resting on the pistol in her belt. She let her hand drop, then hurried across to the man and embraced him warmly.

Nicole shifted restlessly from one foot to the other as she watched them talking and laughing together. Finally her patience snapped and she stepped between them and shoved Chavez aside. 'You can reminisce all you want just as soon as you've taken me to my daughter. Where is she?'

'I will take you to her,' the man said.

Nicole was barely able to conceal her excitement as she followed the man to a house in a narrow side street off the main road. He gave a coded knock on the door, then came the sound of a heavy bolt being drawn back on the inside of the house. The door was opened and they were beckoned inside. He spoke briefly to the woman, then led Nicole to a door further down the hallway. 'She is in there,' he told her.

Nicole stared at the closed door after the man had withdrawn. It was the moment she'd been praying for every second of every day, ever since she'd first heard that Michelle was missing. The reunion. She was about to get her little girl back. She reached out towards the handle, then jerked her hand back and dug a handkerchief from the pocket of her jeans, using it to wipe the sweat and grime from her face. Then she ran her hands through her hair and brushed the dust off the front of her T-shirt. She smiled sheepishly to herself when she realized that she was acting as if she was about to meet a date. Well, she was – the most special date she'd ever had in her life. You've got to be strong for Michelle, she reminded herself. And that meant no tears. Then, taking a deep breath, she pushed down the handle and opened the door.

Michelle was sitting cross-legged on the floor in front of a portable black and white television set. She had her back to the door and was so engrossed in the Tom and Jerry cartoon on the screen that she didn't even hear her mother enter the room. So far, so good, Nicole said to herself. No tears. Then Michelle suddenly got a fit of the giggles as Jerry dished out another dose of violent retribution to the hapless Tom. The tears streamed down Nicole's face, but she made no attempt to wipe them away. So much for being strong. But when she tried to speak, no sound came from her throat. She tried again. 'Michelle?' came the croaked attempt.

Michelle looked round, and for a moment she stared in disbelief at her mother. Then a wide grin flashed across her face and she leapt excitedly to her feet. Nicole crouched down, arms extended, and Michelle ran into her loving embrace. She wrapped her arms around Michelle like a protective cloak, holding her tightly against her own trembling body. She never wanted to let her go. Then nothing, and nobody, would ever be able to harm her . . .

'Mommy, you're hurting me.'

The small, muffled voice startled Nicole, and she pulled away from her daughter as if she'd just received a sharp electric shock. She took Michelle's hands gently in hers. 'I'm sorry, sweetheart, I didn't mean to hurt you.'

'Why are you crying, Mommy?'

Nicole smiled bravely through the tears as she traced her

hand lightly down the side of Michelle's face. She couldn't tell her the truth. One day, perhaps, when she was older. But as she stared into Michelle's pale blue eyes, all she could see was a child's innocence. She would never take that away from her. She wiped away the tears from her cheeks, then reached out and hugged Michelle again. 'I'm just glad to see you, sweetheart,' she said, knowing how lame it sounded. But what else could she say without drawing Michelle into the harsh reality of her own personal anguish?

'Where's Daddy?'

It was the question she'd been dreading ever since she'd first been told of Bob's death. She knew she would have to tell her the truth eventually, but this was neither the time nor the place for it. She brushed her fingertips across her eyelids as she felt her eyes well up with tears again. But they weren't tears for Bob. They were for Michelle. She managed to get a grip on her emotions, then drew away from Michelle and held her at arm's length. 'Daddy had to go away, sweetheart. That's why I came out here to take you home.'

'When is he coming back?'

'I don't know,' Nicole replied softly.

'I'm glad you came, Mommy. We always have lots of fun together when we fly on an aeroplane.'

'I know,' Nicole said, brushing a loose strand of hair from Michelle's face. 'I promise you we'll have lots of fun when we fly back to Chicago.'

'When can we go?' Michelle asked excitedly.

'Soon,' Nicole told her, then took out her grimy handkerchief and wiped it across her cheeks.

Michelle screwed up her nose and shook her head. 'Your face is still dirty, Mommy. You look like the bag lady who's always hanging around the back of the restaurant. I don't think she ever washes her face.'

Nicole chuckled to herself. 'Gee, thanks, Michelle. She

must be all of eighty if she's a day. And you think I look like her?'

'You look just like her, Mommy,' Michelle said, giggling delightedly to herself.

'Then I guess I'd better go and wash.'

Michelle reached out and grabbed her mother's hands before she could stand up. 'Eskimo kiss first, Mommy.'

Michelle had seen a couple giving each other an Eskimo kiss on the children's cable network a few weeks earlier, and ever since then she had pestered Nicole for an Eskimo kiss at least once a day. But she would only do it with her mother. Nicole remembered the time when Carole, her partner at the restaurant, had wanted to give Michelle an Eskimo kiss, only to have Michelle refuse with a stern shake of her head. And Michelle was closer to Carole than she was to any of Nicole's other friends. It was an affection-ate gesture reserved only for her mother. Some gesture, Nicole thought to herself as she went through the ritual of rubbing noses with her daughter. Why couldn't she just get a normal kiss like any other mother? But she knew Michelle was so much like her that it was often like looking into a mirror and seeing an exact reflection of herself at that age. It was uncanny, but strangely reassuring at the same time. That's why she could relate to the Eskimo kiss and all the other unconventional personality traits Michelle seemed to have inherited from her. It only served to bring them even closer together with every passing day . . .

Michelle wrapped her arms around Nicole's neck. 'I love you, Mommy.'

'I love you too, sweetheart,' Nicole replied, hugging her tightly, 'more than you can ever imagine.' She reluctantly eased Michelle's arms from around her neck, then got to her feet. 'Where's the bathroom, do you know?'

'You'll have to get the water from a tank out in the yard. It's the same at Uncle Gustavo's house.'

'Uncle Gustavo?' Nicole said in surprise.

Michelle pointed to the door. Nicole looked round and found the man who'd brought her to the house standing in the doorway. He gave her a placatory smile. 'I thought it important to make Michelle feel at home while she was staying with my family. That is why I asked her to call me Uncle Gustavo. I hope you are not offended.'

'No, not at all,' Nicole replied with a quick shrug. 'I guess I hadn't really thought about what she called you.'

'I heard you say you wanted to wash,' he said, breaking the silence. 'Most of the villages here in Chalate — Chalatenango — do not have running water. The water must be drawn every morning from a well or a river. There is plenty of water stored in the tank at the back of the house. Water is the one commodity we do not have a shortage of here in Chalate. In this weather most of us prefer to use cold water, but I can arrange to have it heated for you if you wish.'

'Cold's fine,' Nicole replied, then looked at Michelle. 'Do you want to come with me, sweetheart?'

'Can I stay and watch cartoons?' Michelle asked, pointing to the television set.

'Of course you can,' Nicole replied, kissing Michelle on the forehead. Normally Michelle was very wary of strangers, especially men, but it was obvious that she was suffering no psychological ill-effects from staying with 'Uncle Gustavo' and his family for the past few days. But she knew Bob would have prepared Michelle for it by sitting her down and carefully explaining the situation to her. And if he'd told her that the family were his friends, she would have believed him. She'd always trusted Bob, and Nicole knew she'd have walked through fire for him if he'd assured her she'd be safe. Then again, it reminded her so much of the trust she'd placed in her own father when she was growing up in Africa. Like mother, like daughter . . .

Chavez waited until Nicole had disappeared out into the backyard before entering the room. Michelle gave her a cursory glance, then returned her attention to the television screen.

'Ask her about the tape,' Chavez urged Gustavo.

'I think we should wait until her mother gets back.'

'We've fulfilled our part of the deal. I want the tape. Ask her for it.'

'I still say –'

'Do it!' Chavez snarled.

Gustavo sat down on the edge of a chair beside the television set. 'Michelle, did your daddy give you a video-tape before you came to stay with me?'

Michelle said nothing.

'I think he did. Will you give it to me?'

'No,' came the sharp riposte.

'Why not?'

Michelle fidgeted with the hem of her T-shirt. 'Daddy told me to keep it for him. He said I wasn't to give it to anyone else.'

'You can give it to me, I'm your daddy's friend,' Gustavo said with a friendly smile, but when he tried to put a reassuring hand on her shoulder, she drew back sharply from him.

'I won't give it to you,' she said bluntly. 'I'll only give it to my daddy.'

Chavez demanded to know what was being said, and cursed angrily when she heard that Michelle had refused to hand over the tape. 'Ask her again.'

'It won't do any good,' Gustavo told her. 'Wait until her mother's here. She'll be able to reason with the child.'

'I want that tape now!' Chavez snarled.

Michelle eyed Chavez nervously, then scrambled to her feet and headed for the door, deciding she would be safer with her mother. Chavez grabbed her arm roughly as she reached the door, forcing Michelle to look at Gustavo. 'Now ask her!'

278

'Please give me the tape, Michelle,' Gustavo pleaded with her.

'No,' Michelle retorted as she struggled furiously to try and free herself from the vice-like grip Chavez had on her arm. 'Let me go!' she cried in terror.

Chavez heard the pounding footsteps, and was still turning towards the door when Nicole grabbed her from behind, spun her round, and slammed her back against the wall. Nicole's finger was trembling with rage as she levelled it at Chavez's face, and her voice was soft and menacing when she finally spoke. 'You ever touch my little girl again and I'll tear your heart out with my bare hands.' She grabbed the lapels of Chavez's flak jacket and thumped her back painfully against the wall. 'Do I make myself clear, *compita*?'

Although Chavez hadn't understood any of what Nicole had said to her, the harsh tone of her voice and the fury in her eyes was enough not to warrant a translation. Nicole shoved Chavez away from her, then crouched down and hugged a tearful Michelle tightly to her. She stroked her hair gently, comforting her until the sobbing had stopped.

Michelle pulled back from her mother and wiped the tears from her eyes. 'Daddy made me promise to keep the tape for him until he came back. He said I wasn't to give it to anyone else. He said he would be very angry with me if I didn't obey him. I don't want Daddy to be cross with me, Mommy.'

Nicole's fury switched from Chavez to Kinnard. *The callous, insensitive bastard*, she thought bitterly to herself; but it was so typical of him. He'd had more feelings for some goddamn story that would have given him the spurious respect of his peers than for a little girl who loved him.

'Are you cross with me, Mommy?' Michelle asked anxiously, noticing the look of anger flash across her mother's face.

'Of course I'm not cross with you, sweetheart,' Nicole was quick to reassure her.

'I am sorry if Anna frightened Michelle,' Gustavo said behind Nicole. 'She did not mean her any harm.'

'Why do I find that so hard to believe?' Nicole retorted bitterly.

'Just give us the tape,' Gustavo said tersely.

'I'm surprised that you haven't already forced Michelle to hand it over,' Nicole snapped.

'I did not know the tape even existed until Anna told me about it a few minutes ago,' Gustavo replied. 'And even if I had known about it, I would not have put any pressure on Michelle to reveal its whereabouts. It is not our way. We made a deal with Kinnard, and we pride ourselves on always honouring our side of a deal. And we have kept our word by reuniting you with your daughter. We would now expect you to do the same.'

Nicole sat down in the nearest chair and took Michelle's hand in hers. 'Sweetheart, where's the tape Daddy gave you to keep for him?'

'Daddy made me promise not to give it to anyone,' Michelle replied.

'Not even me?' Nicole asked.

Michelle stared at her feet. 'I guess . . .' She trailed off with an uncertain shrug.

'You guess?' Nicole said with a bemused smile. 'Look, sweetheart, Daddy promised to give the tape to that man – Uncle Gustavo – when he came back here. But Daddy couldn't make it. That's why I'm here. We're going to fly back to Chicago together, but first we have to give the man the tape that Daddy promised him. Do you understand what I'm saying, Michelle?'

'Daddy won't be cross with me, will he?' Michelle asked anxiously.

'I promise he won't,' Nicole told her.

'Cross your heart?'

'And hope to die,' Nicole said, drawing her finger across her throat — another of Michelle's macabre little rituals that she'd picked up from some tacky television programme. She suddenly grinned at Michelle. 'I'll tell you what. I'll swap you for the tape. I've got something I know you'll really want.'

'What is it, Mommy?' Michelle asked excitedly. 'What is it?'

'I'll show you,' Nicole said, getting to her feet. 'I've got it in my hold-all.'

'Where is it?' Michelle asked, pulling on her mother's hand.

Nicole looked across at Gustavo. 'Is my bag still in the truck?'

'Anna had it brought into the house. It is in the hall.'

Nicole retrieved her hold-all, then took Michelle's hand and led her into a room further down the hall. A hold-all and a pink suitcase stood by the window. The hold-all was the same colour and make as her mother's, only smaller, and the pink suitcase, now somewhat scarred and battered from years of use and abuse, had been a birthday present from Bob Kinnard's parents. Michelle took the key for the suitcase from around her neck and opened it. Inside was a VHS-C cassette, compatible with the Camcorder which Kinnard had bought for himself shortly after they were married. Michelle handed the tape to her mother, and a mischievous grin tugged at the corners of her mouth as her eyes went to the larger of the two hold-alls on the bed. Nicole made a theatrical sweep of her arm before pulling Kermit out of her hold-all. Michelle gave a yelp of delight and clutched the soft toy tightly to her chest.

'I was surprised that you'd left him behind,' Nicole said.

'I thought I'd packed him in my bag,' Michelle replied, nuzzling the toy with obvious affection. 'Thanks for bringing him, Mommy.'

Nicole smiled and followed Michelle out into the hall.

She was about to return to the lounge with Michelle, when she noticed Chavez and Gustavo talking animatedly to a youth out in the street. He was wearing olive-green fatigues and had a red bandanna tied around his neck. She heard Chavez shout something, then gesture angrily towards the surrounding forest. When Gustavo tried to placate her, she just shrugged off his hand. Nicole told Michelle to go into the lounge, then made her way to the front door. The youth saw her and immediately stopped talking. Gustavo followed his suspicious gaze and hurried across to where Nicole was standing.

'What is it?' she asked suspiciously.

'There has been some trouble in my village.'

'The gunfire?' Nicole asked.

'You heard it?'

'I could hardly have missed it,' Nicole replied. 'What happened?'

'At the moment we only know what has been picked up over the radio. We monitor all military communications in the area. According to the reports, a group of Dennison's men were ambushed when they arrived in the village. We know that Guillermo Ruiz was captured during the subsequent fighting. He is being taken back to San Salvador.'

'And Rick?' Nicole asked anxiously. 'Is there any news of him?'

'The American, Marlette?'

'Yes,' Nicole replied. 'Is he all right?'

'There has been no word of him in any of the reports, so we can only assume that he has not been caught. But he could be among the casualties. We do not know the exact number of casualties yet, but the reports say that several of the villagers were killed. It was inevitable. The young men are fighting in the mountains. They have the modern weapons. There were only a few old carbines in the village. What good would they have been against Dennison's men armed with machine guns?'

'Oh God, your wife's still there, isn't she?' Nicole said in horror.

'And my boy, Juan.' Gustavo gazed out towards the trees on the edge of the village. 'I am worried for them. Juan is only ten but he is very headstrong. He is very much like his father.'

'I'm sure they'll be all right,' Nicole said, and realized just how hollow her words sounded. *Just shut up, Nicole*, she chided herself.

'I must go back to see if my family are safe, but Anna does not understand that.' Gustavo smiled sadly as he looked at Chavez, who was still engaged in a heated discussion with the youth. 'She has always believed that the organization must come first. It is easy for her, she has no family. She wants me and several of our comrades to go with her to San Salvador to try and free Guillermo. I will not go with her. Not until I have been back to my village.'

'Wouldn't the military arrest you if you were to go back there now?'

'It is a chance I must take. I am sure you understand. You took many personal risks to come here and get your daughter.'

'Yes, I do understand,' Nicole replied. 'When will you leave?'

'Very soon. I am just waiting for transport. And I will ask about Marlette when I get there. But I am sure he is safe. He is one of the most wanted men in El Salvador right now. If he had been among the casualties, then you can be sure it would have been reported on the radio. The military take great pleasure in boasting of their achievements. Perhaps it is because they are so few in number.'

'Good luck,' she said, extending her hand towards him.

'And you,' he said, gripping her hand firmly.

'I know I can never begin to repay you for everything you and your wife have done for Michelle these last couple of days, but you can be sure that I'll never forget it. Thank you.'

'We did not know Michelle for long, but she will always have a special place in our hearts. She is very . . . gutsy, is that the right word?'

'She's gutsy all right,' Nicole replied with a smile.

Gustavo looked round on hearing the sound of an approaching engine. It was the same battered pick-up truck which had brought Nicole to the village earlier. 'This is my ride,' he announced, and waved an acknowledgement to the driver.

Chavez challenged him as soon as he made his way across to the truck and, although Nicole didn't understand what had been said, she could guess by the sudden flash of anger in Gustavo's eyes that it had something to do with his loyalties. Gustavo climbed into the passenger seat, slamming the door again behind him, and Chavez stepped out of the way as the pick-up pulled away from in front of the house, watching until it finally disappeared from view. When she turned away she found Nicole staring at her.

'There will always be things more important than the cause, no matter how much you may believe in that cause,' Nicole said to her, even though she knew Chavez wouldn't understand her. 'I just hope for your sake that you come to realize that one day.'

For a moment Nicole thought she saw a flicker of recognition in Chavez's eyes. It was as if Chavez had understood the sentiment of what she was saying, if not the words. No, that was impossible. She had to be mistaken. Or was she? Then the moment was gone and Chavez walked off. Nicole stared after the retreating figure, then shrugged to herself and went back into the house.

When Ruiz came round he found himself lying on the ridged metal floor in the back of a Land-Rover. He had no idea how he'd got there. His last recollection was being struck on the back of the head when he'd tried to prevent one of Dennison's men from shooting Gustavo's boy at the village. Then everything had gone black. What had happened to the boy? To the villagers? To Marlette? So many unanswered questions. The Land-Rover hit a pothole in the road and he grunted in pain as he cracked his head painfully against the floor, but when he tried to sit up he found that his feet had been manacled to one of the support stanchions and his hands cuffed in front of him.

'Looks like someone's awake,' a voice jeered above him, and Ruiz winced as the tip of a boot thudded into his exposed ribs.

Ruiz eased himself over on to his back. The canvas awning had been secured over the back of the vehicle, and the only aperture was the flap at the rear. From where he lay, Ruiz could see the vast expanse of mountains behind them. They were obviously still in Chalate; it was the only district in the country that could boast that kind of breathtaking view.

'Your *compañeros* can't save you now,' the voice sneered, and again the boot caught him painfully in the ribs.

'Jayson said he wasn't to be marked!' a second voice hissed sharply. 'Leave him alone.'

Ruiz looked at the two guards on either side of him. They were seated on wooden benches, which he knew from past experience were hard and uncomfortable, and both were armed with G-3 rifles which they held across their laps. The one who'd kicked him – a burly, unshaven character with long, unwashed hair – glared back at him. The other man, also unshaven but younger than his colleague, stared at his scuffed boots as his body rocked with the jarring rhythm of the vehicle as it twisted and turned through the narrow mountain pass.

'You got a cigarette?' Ruiz asked, directing his question

to no one in particular, as he struggled to sit up against the back of the driver's seat. The reinforced metal bars dug into his back, but it was still more comfortable than lying on the floor within range of a metal-tipped boot.

'Don't smoke,' the younger man muttered without looking up.

His colleague took a packet of cigarettes from his sweaty tunic pocket, placed one between his lips, and lit it. Then, without taking his cold eyes off Ruiz, he slipped the packet back into his pocket and purposely exhaled the smoke in Ruiz's direction. He sniggered to himself and spat on to the floor close to Ruiz's feet.

'I see you're easily amused by little things,' Ruiz said as he held the man's icy stare. 'I guess it runs in the family. Your wife must be amused by little things if she lets you screw her.'

The younger man grabbed his colleague's arm as he was about to lunge at Ruiz. 'Just let it go,' he snapped as his colleague struggled to break free of his grip.

The driver laughed heartily as he glanced at the burly man in the reflection of the rearview mirror. 'Hey, Rodriguez, if you can't satisfy your wife, you just tell her to come over to my place any time. She won't go away disappointed.'

'Shut it and drive,' Rodriguez snapped, shrugging off his colleague's arm and slumping back against the metal stanchion behind him. He glowered at Ruiz. 'You open your mouth again and you'll be wearing my boot for braces.'

'What would Jayson say?' Ruiz taunted.

'Fuck Jayson,' came the contemptuous retort.

'What about Dennison?'

Rodriguez shifted uneasily on the wooden bench but didn't reply. It never ceased to amaze Ruiz just how terrified Dennison's men were of their employer. Men twice the size of Dennison would visibly shake at the very mention of his name. But then he'd heard rumours, and they were only rumours, that over the past few years several insubordinate employees had simply disappeared. No trace of them had ever been found. Whether it was true or not was immaterial, but it obviously had the desired effect. Dennison ruled his domain by fear, and yet there were said to be thousands of applicants on the company's waiting lists. Most were ex-soldiers. Part of it was certainly the prestige that went with the job. The other part was the wages. Dennison was reputed to pay his employees handsomely, but in return he expected complete loyalty, total commitment and absolute respect. And by all accounts, that's exactly what he got.

The driver dropped a packet of cigarettes over his shoulder, which landed on the floor close to Ruiz. ' "I see you're easily amused by little things," ' he said, still chuckling softly to himself. 'That's funny, Ruiz, that's really funny. Take a cigarette. You earned it.'

Ruiz struggled to lift the packet off the floor. He managed to ease out a cigarette far enough for him to catch it between his lips. 'I need a light,' he said, dropping the packet back on to the floor.

'Give him a light,' the younger man said.

Rodriguez cursed under his breath, then took a lighter from his pocket and reluctantly lit Ruiz's cigarette for him. Ruiz inhaled deeply on the cigarette and craned his neck to see through the flap. Although the narrow road was constantly twisting and turning through the mountains, he estimated there were another three or four Land-Rovers behind them. Two of them were open at the back, and he could see the gunners, their eyes hidden behind goggles, their faces glistening with sweat, as they manned the general-purpose machine guns mounted directly behind the driver's seat, the barrels glinting in the fierce overhead sun as they constantly swept the surrounding mountains for any sign of an impending ambush. Then, as the

Land-Rover was about to turn into another bend, Ruiz thought he saw an armoured vehicle bringing up the rear. But he couldn't be sure as the tail of the convoy abruptly disappeared again from sight.

He slumped back against the reinforced metal bars, then drew deeply on the cigarette as he contemplated the stark reality of his current predicament. Was it still the Military Council's intention to frame him for the President's assassination the following night? It certainly looked that way in the light of Jayson's strict orders to the guards not to mark him. Orders that would have come directly from Dennison. But at the same time he knew that word of his 'miraculous resurrection' would already be spreading through Chalate, and would be front-page news across the country by the morning. That meant the Military Council would have to rethink their strategy. This time his capture would have to be made official, and that could only work in his favour. Yet the more he thought about it, the more doubt and uncertainty began to creep into his mind. He was too valuable to the Military Council for them to give him up that easily. If, in fact, they ever intended to hand him over to the proper authorities on reaching San Salvador. What if they already had some kind of backup plan to cover themselves for this kind of eventuality? He knew he'd have had one if he were in Vaquero's shoes. What if Dennison were to claim the convoy was ambushed by guerrilla forces en route to San Salvador, which had resulted in their prisoner escaping? It certainly made sense. That way they could hold him without the authorities being any the wiser. And he knew there was no chance of escape. No Marlette to bail him out this time.

It was at that moment he realized he was going to die. Yet that didn't seem to frighten him. Perhaps it was right, some kind of poetic justice for having deceived so many for so long. His fate now lay in his own hands. And he intended to take full advantage of that . . .

He tapped the ash off the tip of his cigarette and peered out through the open flap again. It was then he noticed the sheer drop on one side of the road. How many wrecked military vehicles now lay rusting at the bottom of the ravines that were such a dominant feature of Chalatenango's rugged terrain? It was then that a plan began to take shape in his mind. It was going to be very risky, but what option did he have? He took another drag on the cigarette then addressed himself to the younger guard. 'How big's the convoy?'

'Big enough,' came the terse reply.

'Big enough for what?' Ruiz asked.

'You were told to shut up!' Rodriguez snarled, levelling a finger at Ruiz.

'Big enough to repel any kind of attack your comrades might be planning to try and free you,' the driver announced, smirking to himself as he glanced in the rear-view mirror.

'Where's Dennison? I don't see his Merc behind us.'

'He's riding up ahead with Jayson,' the driver replied.

'Just tell him everything, why don't you?' Rodriguez snarled at the driver.

The driver tossed the butt of his cigarette out of the window. 'What harm can it do? It's not as if he can do anything with that kind of information.'

'Unless I was to try and communicate it telepathically to my comrades up in the mountains,' Ruiz said facetiously.

The driver instinctively glanced up at the dark, menacing façade of sheer rockface bordering one side of the road. 'We're totally exposed down here,' he hissed. 'All they'd have to do is topple a couple of boulders over the edge of one of these mountains to start an avalanche. We wouldn't stand a chance.'

Ruiz took comfort in their discomfort, but he knew there would be no ambush. Not in daylight on what he guessed was a heavily armed convoy of at least a dozen vehicles.

Dennison had obviously done his homework by ensuring there was additional armed back up to accompany the convoy through the potentially treacherous mountain roads of Chalate. Ruiz had noticed that one of the Land-Rovers behind them also had its awning drawn up over the back of the vehicle. He assumed several other Land-Rovers in the convoy were similarly covered. It would be impossible for any *compañero* monitoring the convoy from the mountains to know exactly which vehicle was carrying him. Although Dennison must have known the chances of an attack on the convoy were minimal, he still wasn't taking any risks.

But Dennison had overlooked one crucial factor. The chance of a suicide mission, from within the heart of the convoy. If Dennison had considered it, Ruiz knew he would still be unconscious on the floor and not planning his own death. It was an eerie, macabre feeling, but it was tempered by the satisfaction of knowing that Dennison would have a lot of explaining to do when the news was broken to the Military Council. He only wished he could have been there to see Dennison try to weasel his way out of that one. But first his plan had to work . . .

'I need to take a piss,' he announced.

'Forget it,' Rodriguez retorted between puffs on his cigarette.

'Then I'll just piss on the floor,' Ruiz retorted with a quick shrug. 'It makes no difference to me.'

'You try that and you know exactly where my boot will go,' Rodriguez snorted in disgust.

'Just remember, any marks on me and Dennison will be roasting your balls over an open fire,' Ruiz countered.

Rodriguez inhaled angrily through his teeth but said nothing.

'The convoy won't stop just so that you can take a piss,' the driver called out over his shoulder.

'I know the drill. You carry a plastic container under the

passenger seat whenever you're travelling through guerrilla territory because you're all too shit-scared to stop and relieve yourselves by the side of the road.' Ruiz noticed the look of surprise on the guards' faces. 'I've had the pleasure of travelling in one of these before. That's how I know about the container you keep under the seat. Now, do I get it, or do I piss on the floor?'

'Give him the fucking bottle,' Rodriguez snarled at the driver, then pointed a finger at Ruiz. 'One wrong move –'

'Sure, with my hands and feet manacled like this,' Ruiz cut in sarcastically. 'I'm not Harry Houdini.'

Rodriguez frowned: the name meant nothing to him. He turned the rifle around in his lap so that the butt was now directed at Ruiz. His colleague reached out and took the empty container from the driver. He placed it carefully on the bench, unscrewed the top, then sat down again, his fingers curled tightly around the stock of the rifle.

'Can I stand up?' Ruiz asked, knowing it was an essential part of his plan.

Rodriguez closed over the flap, then nodded to Ruiz who struggled to his feet. He had to stoop, shoulders hunched, to prevent his head from coming into contact with the canvas awning. He was now directly behind the driver. This was it. His one chance. He leaned over the container and his eyes flickered towards the cab. He was confident he could reach the steering wheel from where he was standing. But he would have to distract the driver first. And he knew exactly how to do that. He plucked the cigarette from his lips, then, gripping it tightly in his fingers, he stabbed the glowing tip into the side of the driver's neck. The driver howled in pain and instinctively reached up a hand to protect his neck, leaving only one hand on the wheel. Ruiz then caught him painfully above the ear with his elbow, knocking him sideways, and for a second both his hands were off the wheel. It was all the time Ruiz needed; he lunged across the back of the driver's seat and twisted the wheel violently, veering the Land-Rover towards the flimsy wooden barrier, the only protection between the road and the sheer drop into the ravine below. A rifle butt slammed viciously into his back, then an arm locked around his throat, but he clung resolutely to the steering wheel. The driver, still stunned by the sharp blow to his temple, was desperately trying to feel for the brake pedal with his foot when the Land-Rover smashed through the barrier and plunged into the ravine.

Dennison's driver slammed on the brakes the moment he saw the Land-Rover veer out of control in the reflection of the rearview mirror. Both Dennison and Jayson could only watch in horror as the Land-Rover ploughed through the barrier and disappeared from sight. Dennison threw open the back door and leapt out of the car. He ran over to the broken barrier and, standing perilously close to the edge of the road, peered down into the ravine. The drop was over five hundred metres to a narrow river which threaded its way through the picturesque gulley below. A swirl of dense smoke and dust spiralled upwards from the ground around the twisted remains of the Land-Rover which had come to rest on its roof close to the water's edge.

'*Patrón*, it is dangerous for you to be out here,' a voice said anxiously beside him. 'These mountains are teeming with terrorists. You must go back to your car.'

Dennison turned his head slowly to look at the man – a former officer in the National Guard, and now one of his most trusted lieutenants – but there was no recognition in his eyes. 'He knew,' Dennison said in a soft, hollow tone as he subconsciously voiced his thought out aloud. 'Somehow the son-of-a-bitch knew he'd never come out of this alive. That's why he did it.'

'*Patrón?*' the man queried, the language completely lost on him, but when he got no response he reached out and tentatively touched Dennison on the arm.

The contact was enough to snap Dennison out of his subliminal state. 'I want you to take a team down there and make sure that Ruiz is dead.'

'Nobody could have survived that,' the man said.

'We can't afford to take any chances. Ruiz has already cheated death once before. Find him, dead or alive, and bring him to my guest-house in San Benito. It's imperative this whole incident is kept tightly under wraps until the relevant authorities have been notified. I want all these men sworn to silence until further notice. And if anyone disobeys my orders, I'll personally cut out his tongue and feed it to my dogs. Do I make myself clear?'

'*Sí, patrón.*' The man swallowed nervously as he struggled to pluck up the courage to question Dennison's orders. '*Patrón*, this is rebel country,' he stammered. 'We will be exposed to their snipers if we go down there.'

'Then I suggest you take some extra men with you,' Dennison shot back contemptuously. 'There are three gun-ships on standby at the company airfield in San Salvador. Use them as additional backup. That's what they're there for. I don't care about the other bodies. Just find Ruiz, because the one thing we don't need right now is a dead martyr on our hands. And that's exactly what we'd have if these terrorists were to get hold of the body before the authorities had a chance to decide on how best to deal with the situation.'

'I'll get on to it right away, *patrón*.'

'And remember, you're in overall command of this oper-ation. That means you have all the company resources at your disposal. And if anyone doesn't like that, you tell them to call me.'

'*Gracias, patrón.*'

Dennison grabbed the man's arm as he turned away.

'Fail me on this, and it won't *just* be your tongue I'll feed to my dogs.'

Suddenly one of the 20-mm cannons opened up from the back of an open-top Land-Rover. Dennison dismissed the man's insistence that he return to the safety of the Mercedes, and followed the aim of the cannon's barrel. He saw the bullets scything through a patch of thick foliage on the other side of the gully, then the firing stopped, and the gunner grinned triumphantly at a colleague. The grin vanished when he realized Dennison was watching him.

'Well?' Dennison called out to him.

'A sniper, *patrón*,' the gunner replied nervously.

'Did you get him?'

'*Sí, patrón*,' came the stiff reply.

Dennison gave the man a thumbs-up sign before returning to the Mercedes. He got in beside Jayson, and the door was closed again behind him.

'What was all that about?' Jayson asked. 'You don't honestly think that Ruiz is still alive, do you?'

'He survived my ambush last year. I just want to be sure this time.'

'What are you going to tell Vaquero?' Jayson asked. 'He's going to crucify us. We don't have the tape and now we don't have Ruiz either. This has thrown everything into disarray. What are we going to do?'

'For a start we don't tell Vaquero about what happened here this afternoon. Why do you think I had the men sworn to silence? I'm buying myself time.'

'For what? The Military Council are bound to find out sooner or later. It's best if we come clean with them once we get back to San Salvador. They'll realize it wasn't our fault once we've explained what happened. Ruiz must have jumped the driver –'

'Ruiz was our prisoner,' Dennison cut in sharply. 'That meant he was our responsibility. We've already been up in front of the Military Council to explain our handling of the events at the orphanage last night. We lost Marlette last night. Now we've lost Ruiz. Do you honestly think Vaquero is going to buy our excuses? We've got to redress the balance before we tell him. Get him the tape and another fall guy for the assassination tomorrow night. That way, when we do come to break the news to him that Ruiz is dead, assuming that he *is* dead, then we'll have a stronger hand to play.'

'I assume you already have this "fall guy" in mind?'

'Who's most likely to have Kinnard's tape now?' Dennison asked, lighting himself a cheroot.

'Marlette,' Jayson replied after a moment's thought.

'Find Marlette and we'll have the tape and our fall guy,' Dennison said, then gave the order for the convoy to continue on to San Salvador.

ELEVEN

'Marlette.'

'Rick's here?' Nicole asked.

Chavez pointed towards the window. 'Marlette. *Exterior.*'

'Thank you,' Nicole said, hoping she understood what Chavez was trying to say. '*Gracias.*'

'*De nada,*' Chavez replied as she left.

'What is it, Mommy?' Michelle asked.

'You remember I told you about that friend of mine who came over here to help me out with the language?' Nicole replied. 'I think he's here. I'd better go and check.'

'Can I come too?' Michelle asked excitedly.

'No, I want you to stay here, sweetheart,' Nicole replied. The grin abruptly vanished from Michelle's face. 'I need to talk to him about something first. OK?' Nicole said softly.

'You mean "grown-up" talk?' Michelle said, referring to the name Nicole had given to the numerous conversations between herself and Bob from which Michelle had been excluded. Usually bitter, acrimonious conversations that Nicole hadn't wanted her daughter to hear.

'Yes, "grown-up" talk. But I'll bring him back here as soon as we're through. I promise.'

'Cross your heart?'

'And hope to die,' Nicole replied, drawing her finger across her throat, then left the room and hurried down the hall and out on to the porch. She was momentarily taken aback by the sight of Marlette holding the reins of a sweating horse which was busy scuffing the dry ground with one of its front hooves. Chavez was standing beside him, talking to a youth who was holding the reins of a second horse. It was only when she alighted from the porch that Marlette noticed her. She inhaled sharply when she saw the matted blood on his neck.

'Hi,' he said as she approached him. 'You OK?'

'Better than you by the looks of it,' she replied, struggling with her conflicting emotions. Part of her wanted to throw her arms around him, such was her relief that he was safe, but another part of her couldn't forget what he'd said about Michelle. Don't push it, she warned herself. It's not worth it. Nothing and nobody's worth damaging that special relationship with Michelle . . .

'It's the wound I picked up at the orphanage,' he said, touching his neck gingerly. 'It opened up again during the firefight. I assume you heard the gunfire?' No reply. 'Anyway, it's only a superficial cut. You've seen me a lot worse than this before. Broken ribs. Gunshot wounds. Hell, this is nothing.'

'You're right, it's nothing,' she shot back. 'Where's Ruiz?'

'It's a long story,' Marlette replied. 'I'll tell you all about it later. How's Michelle?'

'Fine. She seems to think this is one big holiday,' Nicole said, her voice softening. She smiled to herself as she glanced back at the house. 'And I'm only too glad to play along with that right now. The less she knows about what's really happening out here, the better it will be for her. I'll go to any lengths to protect her from the truth, Rick. Any lengths.'

'Is that a dig at me?' Marlette said defensively. 'Because if it is, it's completely unfounded. What do you think I'm going to do? Tell her all the gory details of the last couple of days?'

'All I'm saying is, just bear in mind what you do say

when you're in front of her.' Nicole gestured to the house. 'She's inside. I told her you were an old friend who could speak Spanish. That's why you came, to help me with the language.'

'That's fine. What about my neck though? How do we explain that?'

'We'll say that you cut yourself when you fell off your horse on your way over to the village.'

'Nicole?' he said as she turned away from him. 'About what I said to you earlier.'

'Forget it,' she replied with a dismissive flick of her hand. 'It's really not important.'

'It is to me,' he called out after her as she began to walk back towards the house. 'At least hear me out. Please.'

She paused at the foot of the steps. Again her emotions were tearing her apart. Why should she bother listening to him try and peddle some lame excuse to her? He never could get away with lying to her. And if he tried to lie to her now, that would really piss her off. No, walk away. Limit the damage. Let it go.

'Nicole?'

Walk away, she urged herself, but her conscience – the voice of reason – was telling her to hear what he had to say. Didn't she at least owe him that much?

'I didn't mean those things I said about Michelle,' Marlette told her, quickly putting up a hand before she could reply. 'Yeah, I know, you'd have known if I'd been lying. But in a way I was. When I first took on the contract I did see it merely as a means of paying off my debts and getting out of this business once and for all. And part of the contract included Michelle. Hell, I admit that. But things have changed in the past few days. I've come to realize that there's so much more to this than just the money. In the past I've always managed to distance myself from the emotions of the civilians around me. Men, women, kids. It didn't matter. You learn to do that in this business, otherwise you'll get sucked into their world. That's when you let down your guard and you wind up going home in a body bag. It's kill or be killed. Those are the options. There's no place for sentiment in this game.'

He rubbed his hands over his unshaven cheeks as he tried to marshal his thoughts. 'I guess I thought I could be the same with you. But I was fooling myself. When you care about someone you can't just look away when they're in pain. Their pain becomes a part of you as well. I said what I did because I still care about you. I had to get you away from the village before Dennison's goons arrived. But you'd got it into your head that you weren't going anywhere unless I went with you. And I know that stubborn streak of yours only too well. You're like a bull terrier when you've got your mind set on something. You just don't know when to let go. That's why I said what I did. I knew it would hurt you and you'd back off. It was the only way, Nicole.'

She said nothing. What could she say? One moment she'd been ready to pour scorn and derision over whatever lamentable excuse he was going to come up with to try and appease her – the next she was burdened with a deep sense of guilt for ever having doubted the sincerity of the feelings she'd always suspected he still harboured for her. Bob had been the one with the fancy talk and the slick charm. Rick was the complete opposite. He could lie if the need arose, but unlike most men she knew, he'd never actually been comfortable straying from the truth. And she knew that sense of unease had gone a long way to explaining why she could tell whenever he'd been lying to her. He liked to call it as he saw it. He could be brutally frank in his appraisal of a situation, especially when he was fraternizing with his fellow mercenaries; then there were the other times, usually when he was more relaxed around those he regarded as his few close friends, when there was an almost childlike naïveté to his honesty. But you always knew where you stood with Rick Marlette. No frills. No bullshit. Just the truth. And more than anything else, it was the single quality which she still loved most about him . . .

'Are you going to say something?'

'You're a bastard,' she retorted, but there was no malice in her voice.

'So the other mercs keep telling me,' he replied with a wry grin.

'When you said those things about Michelle I thought . . .' She threw up her hands despairingly in the air. 'Oh, forget it. Come on, Michelle's waiting to meet you.'

They went into the house and he placed his Heckler & Koch behind the door before following her to the lounge. Michelle jumped to her feet when her mother entered the room, then gasped in fright when she caught sight of the dirty and bloodied Marlette in the doorway behind her. She instinctively shrank against her mother as she stared at Marlette with wide and uncertain eyes.

'Don't be scared, sweetheart,' Nicole said gently. 'This is Rick Marlette.' She took Michelle's hand and led her across to where Marlette was standing. 'I'm sure he won't mind if you call him Uncle Rick.'

'Sure I mind,' Marlette countered as he crouched down in front of Michelle. 'You don't have to call me "uncle",' he said, screwing up his face as if he'd just swallowed a mouthful of lemon juice. 'Your mommy calls me Rick. My other friends call me Rich or Richie. You take your pick, Michelle. What's it going to be? Rick, Rich or Richie?'

Michelle glanced up at her mother, the unease still apparent on her face. 'Rick,' she said softly, then looked down shyly at her feet as she clung resolutely to her mother's hand.

'And who's this over here?' Marlette said, deciding on a different approach in his attempt to break the ice, and gestured to the stuffed toy perched on the chair behind him. 'It looks like Kermit the Frog to me.'

'It's Kermit the Pirate,' Michelle corrected him firmly.

'Ah, right,' Marlette replied as he crouched down in front of the toy. 'Well, Kermit the Pirate, you certainly look like you've been in the wars. Tell me, what happened to your eye?'

'He can't talk,' Michelle said with a matter-of-fact innocence, and shook her head when Marlette looked round at her.

'You got me there,' Marlette conceded with a sheepish grin. 'So what did happen to his eye? And his hand? My God, and all those stitches.' Michelle inhaled sharply and clamped her hand to her mouth. 'What is it?' Marlette asked uncertainly as he looked to Nicole for guidance.

'You took the Lord's name in vain,' Nicole chided him gently, and gestured towards Michelle with a nod of her head. '*We* don't think that's right.'

'Sorry,' Marlette said, and gave Michelle an apologetic smile. 'Slip of the tongue. It won't happen again. Do you forgive me?'

Michelle nodded, then picked up the toy and extended it towards Marlette. 'A dog got into our apartment and chewed him. Mommy sewed him together again for me.'

Marlette turned the toy around slowly in his hands, whistling softly to himself. 'There're a lot of stitches there. He must have been in quite a mess when you found him.'

'What happened to your neck?' Michelle asked, abruptly changing the subject, as befits an inquisitive mind of that age.

'I fell off my horse on the way over here,' Marlette replied.

'Why?'

'You'll have to ask the horse,' Marlette replied. 'It was his fault.'

'Does it hurt?'

'A bit,' Marlette replied, then raised his finger as if suddenly overcome by a brilliant idea. 'Perhaps I should get your mommy to stitch it up for me. She did a good job patching up Kermit.'

'No,' Michelle said with a smile. 'You need a doctor.'

'But doctors cost money,' Marlette replied. He brushed his fingers lightly across Michelle's ear as he spoke, and when he opened his hand there was a shiny quarter in his palm. 'Do you think that's enough to pay for a doctor?'

'No,' Michelle replied, giggling delightedly as she put her hand to her ear in amazement, dumbfounded as to how the money could possibly have come to appear in his hand.

'Wait a minute,' he said, magically plucking a second quarter from behind her other ear. 'Fifty cents. Is that going to be enough?'

'No,' Michelle replied, grinning up at her mother. 'Where did the quarters come from, Mommy?'

'Behind your ear,' Nicole replied, poker-faced, and put her hand to her mouth to hide her smile at Michelle's puzzled expression.

'Well, if it's not going to be enough to pay for a doctor, then you'd better have your money back,' Marlette said, placing the two quarters in Michelle's hand.

'Can I keep them, Mommy?' Michelle asked excitedly, looking up at her mother.

'They are yours, sweetheart,' Nicole told her, keeping up the pretence.

Michelle stepped away quickly from the door when Chavez appeared. To Nicole's surprise, she took refuge behind Marlette. His eyes narrowed angrily when he noticed the fear on Michelle's face, and he grabbed Chavez's arm before she had a chance to speak, propelling her out into the hall. 'What the hell's going on?' he hissed furiously. 'Why's the girl so frightened of you? What did you do to her?'

'It's nothing,' Chavez replied tersely, tugging her arm free of Marlette's grasp. 'I've no interest in the child now. I have the tape. I came to tell you that I'm leaving for Tejutla. It's a city about fifteen kilometres north of here. I have already arranged with a sympathizer there to use his video recorder to check the authenticity of Kinnard's tape. I should be back later this evening.'

'The roads will be swarming with soldiers after what happened earlier today,' Marlette told her.

'Your concern is touching, but I can look after myself,' Chavez retorted. 'I'll see you later.'

Marlette watched her stride briskly down the hall and disappear out into the street. He returned to the lounge and took Nicole to one side. 'What happened between her and Michelle?'

'It was nothing,' Nicole said with a dismissive flick of her hand.

'Strange, that's exactly what Chavez said when I asked her. Only I saw the look on Michelle's face when Chavez entered the room. Something happened earlier when I wasn't here, didn't it?'

'Yes, and I dealt with it myself,' she told him. 'Now let's just drop it, OK?'

'OK,' Marlette replied. 'Sorry I asked.'

'*Señor?*' a voice called out from the open window.

Marlette moved to the window. The youth who'd accompanied him from the neighbouring village was standing out on the porch. They talked briefly then the youth hurried away.

'Is anything wrong?' Nicole asked anxiously, making sure she was out of earshot of Michelle.

'Hardly,' Marlette replied, quick to allay her fears. 'He just asked whether we wanted a bath. I know I need one. I said you'd probably want one as well. He's gone off to arrange it.'

'Arrange it?' Nicole replied suspiciously.

'I assume you know there's no running water in these villages?' Marlette said.

'Yes, they store the water in open tanks at the back of the houses,' Nicole replied. A look of uncertainty crept over her face. 'You don't mean that we're going to have to bath out there, do you?'

'No,' he replied with a smile. 'You and Michelle can bath in here. The tin baths are large enough to accommodate at least two adults. Bathing's regarded in most villages as something of a communal pastime, especially amongst the women. They seem to regard it as a way of catching up on all the latest gossip. It's a daily ritual out here. Salvadoreans generally take great pride in their personal hygiene.'

'But there's no privacy here,' Nicole said, gesturing towards the window. 'There are people walking past the house all the time.'

'These aren't the sleazy streets of Chicago or New York, Nicole. Believe me, nobody will even give you a second glance. But it's essential that you follow their customs when you bathe, otherwise you'll offend them. Bare breasts are acceptable, but most women still prefer to bathe in their underwear. And when you've finished bathing you wrap a towel tightly around your body and wriggle out of your wet underwear, then wriggle into your dry clothes. Whatever you do, don't discard the towel until you've finished changing. That is guaranteed to offend.'

'I think I can live with that,' Nicole replied with obvious relief. 'What about Michelle? Does she have to go through the same procedure as well?'

'Yes,' Marlette replied. 'But if she's had a bath since she came to Chalate, then she'll already know the drill.'

The tin bath duly arrived and was placed in the centre of the room. The cold water was brought in ceramic bowls by two middle-aged women, and poured into the bath until it was half full. A bar of soap and two brightly coloured towels were left beside the bath, then the women smiled politely at Nicole and withdrew discreetly from the room.

'Well, I suppose I'd better find out where I'm bathing,' Marlette announced, crossing to the door. 'See you guys later.'

'Bye,' Michelle said softly but Marlette had already left the room.

'You like Rick, don't you?' Nicole said.

Michelle nodded. 'Is he your new boyfriend?'

'No, he's not my *new* boyfriend,' Nicole said with a mock-reproving look. 'I told you, he's just a friend. Now come on, Little Miss Cupid, let's go and get some clean clothes from the other room, then we can have our bath.'

'Knock, knock.'

'Come in, Rick,' Nicole called out.

Marlette pushed open the flimsy plywood door and stepped into the room. He was dressed in a white vest, blue shorts and a pair of loose-fitting sandals, all of which he'd borrowed from one of the villagers while his own clothes were being washed at the river. 'Who's this pretty young lady here?' he demanded, gesturing towards Michelle. 'Where's Michelle? What have you done with her?'

'I am Michelle,' came the giggled response.

'No way,' Marlette said. 'When I last saw Michelle she was wearing a scruffy old tracksuit and her hair was in a pigtail. You're much too pretty to be the same little girl.'

'I am, I am,' Michelle insisted.

'There's only one way to be sure,' Marlette said, crouching down in front of her and reaching out behind her ear. When he opened his hand again there was a quarter in the centre of his palm. 'I guess you are Michelle after all,' he conceded, placing the coin in her hand.

She grinned at him as she clutched the quarter to her chest. Then she stepped closer to him and pointed to his arm. 'What's that?'

305

'It's a tattoo,' Marlette replied. 'Have you ever seen one before?'

Michelle shook her head and traced a finger lightly across the tattoo. 'It's a picture of a gun. Did you draw it?'

'No, a friend of mine in New York did it.'

'Can you rub it out with an eraser and draw another picture?' Michelle asked.

'No, sweetheart,' Nicole said from the chair by the window. She smiled gently to herself at Michelle's innocence, discarded the towel she'd been using to dry her hair and got to her feet. 'It's a special drawing. You can't just rub it out.'

'Why not?' Michelle asked.

'It's a special pen with special ink,' Marlette replied, coming to Nicole's rescue. 'It would hurt if I tried to rub it off.'

'Are you a soldier?'

'I was a long time ago,' he replied, glancing at Nicole. His vague answer was met with a nod of approval.

One of the women who'd brought the towels earlier appeared in the doorway and announced in Spanish that Chavez had asked her to prepare some extra food which she'd left in the kitchen for them.

'*Muchas gracias*,' Marlette said, then stood up and clapped his hands together. 'Food's up, you guys.'

'Great, I'm starved,' Nicole said, grateful to have moved the subject away from Marlette's past. 'Come on, let's go and eat.'

They followed the woman to the kitchen, then she withdrew and closed the back door behind her.

'What is it?' Nicole said, indicating the three plates which had been laid out neatly on the table. 'It certainly smells delicious.'

'Let's see what we've got here,' Marlette said, inspecting the nearest plate. 'It's just your basic bean and meat stew, that's all. I used to live on . . .' He stopped when he realized he was about to mention his previous visit to El Salvador. He glanced across at Michelle and saw to his relief that she hadn't heard him.

'How do we eat it?' Nicole asked, looking around forlornly for some kind of utensil.

'With the tortillas,' Marlette told her, pointing to the pile of thin cornmeal pancakes which had been piled up on a separate plate. 'You break off a section and use it as a spoon to scoop up some of the stew. You eat that, then break off another section, and so on until you're finished.'

'I'll show you, Mommy,' Michelle said, removing the top tortilla from the pile. She broke off a piece from the edge of the pancake, scooped it into the stew, then pushed the lot into her mouth. She grinned at her mother's startled expression. 'Uncle Gustavo showed me when I was staying at his house.'

'I hope he also didn't show you how to talk with your mouth full,' Nicole said, taking a plate and a couple of tortillas and sitting down in one of the wicker chairs.

'So what do you think of it?' Marlette asked, watching as Nicole tucked ravenously into her food.

'I think I want the recipe for the restaurant,' Nicole replied between mouthfuls. 'And these tortillas are divine. They're not doughy like the ones you get back home.'

'You can keep your haute cuisine as far as I'm concerned; I still say the simple food's the best,' Marlette declared. He smiled when he caught sight of Nicole's good-humoured scowl. 'And there goes my invitation to dine at your restaurant.'

'Are you going to come to the restaurant?' Michelle asked. 'You must come. Please say you'll come.'

'Only if you'll be there?'

'Can I, Mommy?' Michelle asked.

'I'm sure we can arrange something, as long as it's not on a school night. Maybe during your next vacation.'

'I'm going to see Daddy on my next vacation,' Michelle said.

The smile faltered on Nicole's face, but she quickly regained her composure. 'Of course you are, sweetheart. Silly me for not remembering. Don't worry, we'll invite Rick up to Chicago sometime and show him around.'

'Can he stay at the apartment?' Michelle asked.

'I think you've just found yourself a new friend,' Nicole said to Marlette.

'Nonsense, we're already old friends,' Marlette said, grinning at Michelle. 'Right?'

'Right,' came the gleeful reply. 'Where do you live?'

Again the abrupt change in conversation caught Marlette by surprise. 'New York,' he told her.

'Do you have any children?' Michelle continued.

'Michelle,' Nicole said, and gestured to the plate in her daughter's lap. 'I'm sure I can hear your stomach saying a little more food and a little less talk, thank you very much.'

'No wife, no children,' Marlette said. 'But I do have a sister. She has a couple of children.'

'Does she live in New York too?' Michelle asked, then glanced across at her mother, expecting to be told off for talking again.

Nicole said nothing. She was more interested to hear what Rick was going to say about his family. She knew about the deep rift which had existed between him and his family. Even though it had been six years since he'd last spoken to her about it, she doubted whether there would have been any kind of reconciliation in that time. Not after what happened.

'No, they still live in Alabama. That's where I was born. Have you ever heard of Alabama?' Michelle shook her head. 'It's a state next to Florida. You've heard of Florida?' A nod in the affirmative. 'My mother lives there as well.'

'And your daddy?'

'My daddy died a long time ago,' Marlette replied as he

placed his empty plate on the table. Then he leaned forward, his arms resting on his knees. 'My daddy was a preacher. He was tall, even taller than me, with eyes like burning coals and a voice that sounded like a deep rumble of thunder. And he had white hair. White, like newly fallen snow. I can remember everything about him as if I'd only seen him yesterday. Yeah, I remember him all right.'

Nicole realized that this was the first time she'd ever heard him speak of his father without being vehemently critical of him. She knew only too well how much he'd hated and despised his father while he'd been alive. And the bitterness hadn't diminished with his death. But it was a bitterness she could understand. Wallace Marlette had been a strict disciplinarian who'd forced his son from a very early age to learn lengthy passages of text from the Bible then recite them, parrot-fashion, before going to bed. Any mistakes would be punished by a single lash of the thick leather strop which hung in the bathroom. There were many nights when he'd lain awake in bed, unable to sleep because of the severity of the beating he'd received at the hands of his father.

His mother had never once stood up for him, and his younger sister, who'd always been the apple of her father's eye, had never once been punished for making mistakes while reciting her allotted text. Nicole could understand how the seeds of hatred could have been sown in his mind from that early age. He'd finally rebelled against his father's martinetism when he'd reached his mid-teens; after several brushes with the law he'd run away to New York shortly before his eighteenth birthday. It had been four years later, while serving with the French Foreign Legion in Africa, that he'd received word of his father's death. He'd contacted his sister to arrange to fly back to the States for the funeral, but had been told bluntly that neither she nor her mother wanted him there. Unknown to him at the time, his father, on first learning that he'd joined the Legion, had been so ashamed that he'd announced to all his friends that his son was dead, and the family had vowed to respect his wishes, even after his death. That had been twelve years ago. As far as Nicole knew, Rick hadn't had any contact with his family since then . . .

She realized he'd been watching her, and sensed he knew what she'd been thinking. He smiled sadly at her, then got to his feet and opened the back door. 'I'd say we were due some rain in the next hour,' he declared after scanning the night sky. 'It'll only be a shower though. They always are at this time of the year.'

Nicole noticed that Michelle had only consumed part of her food. A half-eaten tortilla lay on top of the remainder of the stew. 'Have you had enough to eat, sweetheart?'

'There was too much food, Mommy,' Michelle replied. 'I couldn't eat it all.'

'You've done fine,' Nicole said, taking the plate from Michelle and placing it on the table. She looked at her watch. 'Well, it's already gone seven-thirty. Time for you to get ready for bed.'

'Can't I just stay up a little longer?' Michelle pleaded.

'No,' Nicole replied firmly. 'Now say goodnight to Rick.'

'Goodnight, *Mister* Soldier,' Michelle said with a cheeky grin.

'Goodnight, Miss Ragamuffin,' Marlette replied from the door.

'What's a "raga-muffin", Mommy?' Michelle asked hesitantly.

'I'll tell you when you're in bed,' Nicole said, following Michelle from the room.

Marlette made his way down the hall and out on to the front porch. A light wind had sprung up within the past few minutes, another sign that the impending rain was imminent, and he sat down on the top step and tilted back his head, allowing the breeze to caress his neck. It was a sticky, humid evening, and the refreshing wind was a welcome friend. He leaned back against one of the wooden pillars which were supporting the thatch roof. The street was almost deserted, save for the occasional shadow as someone flitted between the collection of mud huts opposite him. He could smell the aroma of freshly brewed coffee coming from an assortment of metal containers which were being heated over numerous open fires around the village. Yet none of it seemed to rekindle the memories of the last time he'd been amongst the villages of northern El Salvador. Or was his memory preventing him from remembering by subconsciously blacking out those images? Only then he hadn't been sitting peacefully on a porch, enjoying the tranquil serenity around him. Then the sky had been on fire and the air filled with the petrified screams of women and children as they fled their burning homes in terror, many of them gunned down mercilessly by the contingent of National Guard soldiers under his command. He'd never participated in the slaughter, always remaining at a discreet distance, usually in the passenger seat of an army jeep, and although the atrocities had repeatedly horrified him, he'd never once tried to prevent them. It hadn't been his war.

But then they never were his wars. He'd been around long enough, he'd known the rules: a mercenary never allowed himself to become emotionally involved in the politics of somebody else's war. You fought for whoever was prepared to pay you the most pieces of silver. It had been just another contract to him. No more, no less. But then there came a time, he couldn't say exactly when, when he'd come to realize that he couldn't remain neutral to the brutality of the conflicts around him any more. Yet he'd known if he'd ever said anything he'd have been labelled a troublemaker. And in mercenary parlance, that would have made him unemployable. There was no place for conscience in his line of work. Either you accepted the rules of the game, or you got out. And he'd known for the past couple of years that it was time to get out. It had just been a question of choosing the right moment . . .

'I'd forgotten about that.'

Marlette looked round at Nicole who was standing in the doorway. 'Sorry, what did you say?'

'I said I'd forgotten you still had that tattoo,' she replied, lighting a cigarette. 'I thought you might have had it removed after we split up.'

Marlette looked at the tattoo on his arm. It depicted a rose with its stem weaved around an intricately detailed drawing of an FA MAS automatic rifle, standard issue of the French Foreign Legion, and carefully inserted in the length of the barrel was the word *Nicole*. 'Yeah, it is an embarrassment these days,' he said, nodding in agreement.

'Thanks,' she retorted, drawing on the cigarette.

'Come on, you know I only use Heckler & Koch gear now,' he said with a smile.

She exhaled on the cigarette then looked at the tattoo again. 'I'll always remember the day you came back to the apartment after you'd had that done. You thought it was really neat. I couldn't believe it. Any other guy would have had a heart tattooed on his arm with his girl's name inside it. But not you. Oh no. You had to put my name on a gun.'

'Hearts are boring,' he replied with a shrug. 'This was different. More distinctive.'

'And so much more romantic,' she added with a hint of gentle sarcasm in her voice.

'Is Michelle in bed?' Marlette asked.

'Well, if you can call a blanket on the ground bed,' Nicole replied. 'I can remember the nights when I had to sleep on a hard floor, sometimes not even with a blanket for warmth, when my father took me to some remote village to negotiate yet another arms deal. It always took me ages to get to sleep. But it doesn't seem to bother Michelle. How many kids back home would have thrown a tantrum if they didn't have the luxury of a soft mattress to sleep on? She never ceases to amaze me.'

'She's a great kid,' Marlette said, then looked up as the first spots of rain began to patter on the hard ground.

'I knew you'd like her. And she's obviously taken quite a shine to you as well. She's normally very reserved around men. But you two seemed to have hit it off almost right away. That trick with the quarters certainly helped. Where did you learn that?'

'I picked it up from a Dutch merc when I was over in Armenia.'

'Hidden talents,' she said, then leaned against him, the back of her head on his shoulder. It just seemed so natural at that moment. 'This reminds me of the first night we met at that bar in Bardai up in northern Chad. What a dive! Remember we sat outside on a porch like this listening to the rain? It didn't let up till daybreak.'

'What I can still remember is the sound of the rain drumming on the old corrugated iron roof,' he said.

'Which was leaking everywhere,' she added with a thoughtful smile. 'I wonder if the bar's still there?'

'God knows,' he snorted, then put a hand on her shoulder. 'Sorry, no blaspheming.'

'It's something Michelle was taught at school,' Nicole replied, resting her hand lightly on his. 'I'm more than happy to go along with it, although I've got a horrible feeling it won't be long before she starts picking up the wrong kind of words from the other kids. And there sure are some rough kids at her school. Little thugs with the kind of bad attitude and abusive language which can only get them into a lot of trouble when they get older.'

'Michelle will be OK,' he said. 'She takes after her mother.'

'And her father,' Nicole added softly.

'Since when did Bob Kinnard have any redeeming virtues?' Marlette snorted. She sat up sharply and tossed her cigarette out into the rain. 'I'm sorry, Nicole, that was well out of order.'

'It's not that.' She got to her feet and moved to the other side of the porch, where she took another cigarette from the packet and lit it with trembling fingers.

'What is it? What's wrong?' he asked, scrambling to his feet.

Nicole folded her arms tightly across her chest and stared out across the wet, deserted street. When she spoke her voice was soft and emotional. 'Bob's not Michelle's father.'

'What?' he shot back in amazement, then nodded to himself when he guessed what she was doing. 'I know you must be feeling a lot of resentment towards Bob right now, but to deny that the guy –'

'Bob isn't Michelle's father,' Nicole hissed sharply. 'Don't make this any harder for me than it already is.'

'Then who . . . ?' He stopped abruptly as a look of startled disbelief came over his face and he slumped down on to the wooden chair behind him. 'Are you saying . . . you mean that . . .' He stammered helplessly, unable to comprehend what was going through his mind at that moment, let alone what he was trying to say.

'Michelle's your daughter, Rick.'

He opened his mouth to speak but found that he couldn't say anything. He knew what he wanted to say. Or did he? What could he possibly say that would make any kind of sense of his jumbled thoughts? He finally managed to utter a single word. 'Cigarette.'

'I thought you'd quit smoking?' she said, but handed him the packet anyway.

He pushed a cigarette between his lips and grabbed the lighter from her outstretched hand. She watched as he tried several times without success to spark the flint, then she reached down and gently removed the lighter from his fingers and lit the cigarette for him. He took several long drags on the butt, then shook his head in disgust at the odious taste and tossed it out into the rain. Then silence.

'Say something, Rick,' she pleaded. 'Just speak to me. Let me inside. I want to know what you're thinking.'

'Right now I don't know what I'm thinking.' He leaned forward and rested his arms on his knees. 'I'm numb. It's like I'm just coming round from an anaesthetic. There're so many things going on in my head. I guess I just need time to sort them all out.'

'I had my reasons for not telling you, Rick,' she said. 'You must believe that.'

'Did Kinnard know?'

'No. Nobody knew except me. It was the only way.'

'Not even your father?' Marlette asked.

'Especially not my father,' she replied quickly. 'You know how fond he was of you. If I'd told him the truth about Michelle he'd have been devastated. As it is, I know he never really forgave me for leaving you.'

'He's probably saying a few choice things right now,' Marlette said, gesturing up at the night sky.

'I bet he is,' she replied with a sad smile.

'Did you know you were pregnant before we split up?'

'Yes.'

'How long?'

'I left the same day I got my results back from the hospital,' she replied.

'Jesus, Nicole, the same day!' he shot back.

'The relationship was already over,' she said defensively. 'You know that as well as I do. By then we were just going through the motions. My being pregnant was the final incentive to get out.'

'And I had no say in the matter?'

'It was my life, Rick.'

'It was our child,' he countered. 'Or didn't that count for anything?'

'Not at the time, no,' she replied bluntly. She tossed her half-smoked cigarette into a puddle in the road, but immediately lit up another one. She stared at the discarded cigarette bobbing in the water as she struggled to collect her thoughts. 'When we first met in Africa I was a real tearaway. A wild child. You know that. And it was that Nicole Auger who fell in love with you. I guess it was only natural that I would fall for a merc. I certainly had enough dealings with them while I was growing up. But you were different. You respected me for who I was, but you were also quick to put me in my place whenever I stepped out of line. At the time it's exactly what I needed. I learnt so much about life from you, especially when I went back to New York with you. It was like a whole new world for me there. I had so much to discover, not only about life, but about myself as well. I think that's when we first began to drift apart. I came to realize that to get ahead in America, you couldn't depend on others. You had to look out for yourself. I had to grow up. It was a big step for me, and I know I could never have done it without you. I suppose in a way I was the little caterpillar who turned into a butterfly. And when I became the butterfly, I wanted to spread my wings and fly away. I wanted to be free of my past. And you were part of that past. I was also finding it increasingly difficult to reconcile myself with you constantly going off to fight someone else's war. But that was your choice and I respected you for it.

'Then, when I discovered I was pregnant, I realized I didn't want my child to grow up in the knowledge that its father was a mercenary who went off for months at a time to kill people he didn't even know. I didn't want a house bought with blood-money. But perhaps more important than all of that, I didn't want my child to have the kind of cynical, streetwise childhood that I had when I was growing up in Africa. Children should be allowed to cherish those few years of innocence before they have to learn the truth about the real world. And that's all I ever wanted for Michelle. To give her the innocence I never had. I don't know if you can understand that, Rick, but that's the real reason why I walked out on you that day.'

'Why didn't you tell me all this at the time?' he asked.

'What good would it have done? It would have sounded like an ultimatum, wouldn't it? Give up your career or you'll never see either me or your child again. I couldn't do that to you, Rick. I think one of the relationship's greatest strengths was that we always respected each other's independence. I also know how much your career meant to you at that time. And even if you had given it all up to be a father, who's to say you wouldn't have regretted it later and taken your resentment out on me? Or worse, on Michelle.'

'You know me better than that, Nicole. I would never have laid a finger on either of you.'

'I know you wouldn't, but there are more ways to hurt someone than with your fists,' she said.

'Don't I know,' he said, looking straight at her.

'*Touché*,' she conceded.

He got to his feet and moved to the railing. 'So why tell me now? Wouldn't it have been simpler not to have said anything at all?'

'Nothing in life's simple, Rick,' she replied. 'Why tell you? Because we've both changed since those crazy years we spent together. I've mellowed since I became a mother. And you're not the same Rick Marlette I walked out on six years ago. You were much harder and more cynical in those days. I guess age has mellowed you as well. But I think more than anything else it was seeing the two of you together that made me realize it was something I had to tell you. Frankly, I was amazed when she took to you so quickly but, in retrospect, perhaps it's not so surprising after all. The bond between you was already there. As I said just now, she's got a lot of your traits as well.'

'Will you ever tell *her* the truth?'

'It's something I've thought long and hard about over

the years, but I've always decided against it to protect her, more than anything else, especially as she already had a close relationship with Bob. I'm dreading having to break the news to her about Bob's death. I know she's going to take it badly. It's only natural. So if I were ever to tell her the truth, it wouldn't be until she's older. At the moment she's just too young for something like that, especially on the back of Bob's death.'

'I want you to promise me something, Nicole,' he said. 'That you'll let me be there if you do ever tell her.'

'I wouldn't have it any other way,' she replied. 'So, what does it feel like to know you're a father?'

'I think I'm still recovering from that anaesthetic,' he replied with a smile. 'But the hardest part of this is going to be knowing, when she doesn't.'

'Rick, it's in her own best interests that she doesn't know, at least not yet.'

'I agree with you. I'm not about to rock the boat. I'm just saying it's going to be tough for me, that's all.'

'I know,' she said softly.

'It's stopped raining,' he said, breaking the sudden silence. 'I told you it would only be a quick shower. Smell the air. It's so refreshing.'

'And so peaceful,' she added. 'I could live in a place like this and never tire of it.'

'Enjoy it while you can.'

'Until a military patrol or a group of Dennison's goons arrive to tear the village apart,' she said.

'There won't be any raids tonight. There are only two roads in and out of the village. Both are narrow mountain passes which are guarded every night by bands of heavily-armed guerrillas. No patrol would stand a chance if they were caught in an ambush. Even a chopper wouldn't risk flying over the area. The guerrillas have surface-to-air missiles. The ravines up here are littered with the remains of army choppers shot down during the civil war. No, don't worry, we're quite safe here tonight. But you can be sure they'll come in the morning.'

'We'll be safely over the border by then.' She waited for confirmation of what she'd said. Only silence. 'We will be safely over the border by the morning, won't we?'

'I'll talk to Chavez about that when she gets back from Tejutla. She can arrange for you and Michelle to be taken across the border before dawn.'

'You're not coming with us?'

'I can't,' he replied. 'Don't ask me to explain, Nicole. It's better if you don't know any more than that.'

She crossed the porch angrily, then swung round on him. 'And that's it? Oh, by the way, I won't be coming with you tomorrow but don't ask me why because I *won't* tell you. I can't believe it, Rick. I've just bared my soul to you. I've just told you the truth about Michelle because I thought you'd changed. Now I discover that you're shutting me out again, just like you did in the old days. But what hurts most of all is that I had to find this for out myself. You weren't even going to tell me that you weren't coming back with us.'

'I would have told you,' Marlette shot back defensively. 'At the right time, I would have told you.'

'At the right time?' she snorted facetiously. 'That's really big of you, Rick. And when exactly were you planning to spring this little surprise on me? Later tonight over a romantic candlelit dinner?'

'I would have told you,' he repeated, stung by her biting sarcasm.

She sat down on the top step and took the cigarettes from her pocket but didn't open the packet. She finally looked up at him. 'This has something to do with the coup, hasn't it?'

'I told you, I can't tell you anything.'

'You're a part of it, aren't you?'

'If I was part of it, do you think they'd have been hunting

me down like some animal for the past two days? Do you think Jayson would have tried to kill me at the orphanage, or perhaps you think this is just make-up?' Marlette snapped, indicating the wound on his neck.

'So why are you staying behind?' she demanded, then threw up her hands in exasperation. 'What's the use? And you say I'm stubborn.'

'I was hired by Pruitt to carry out a hit at the hotel tomorrow night,' Marlette said as he sat down beside her.

'Money, I should have guessed.'

'I don't give a damn about the money, Nicole. All I'm worried about is the contract that's been haunting me for the past five years.'

'There's a contract out on you?'

He watched as an emaciated dog darted out from behind one of the mud huts. Moments later the door was flung open and a woman hurled a bucket of cold water over it. The dog yelped in fright and scampered into the adjacent shadows. The woman noticed Marlette watching, and stepped back into the hut, slamming the door shut. 'I guess it's my turn to reveal a skeleton in my cupboard,' he announced, then leaned back against the wooden pillar and drew one knee up to his chest. 'I was accused of having raped and murdered a twelve-year-old kid when I was last out here. But then you know that already. You said the American Ambassador couldn't wait to tell you about it when you first arrived. You can't blame the guy. It's the official story. Why should he know any different?

'But it's not the truth. As far as I'm aware, there are only four people who know what really happened that night.' He rested his arm lightly on his knee and fiddled absently with his sandal as he struggled to collect his scattered thoughts into a cohesive and coherent pattern. 'Her name was Marisa. She was a decent kid. Shy, reserved and real smart. Her family was a founder member of the "oligarchy". The "oligarchy" was the name given to the original thirteen families who ran the coffee industry here in El Salvador. Every one of them wealthy, powerful and corrupt. By the eighties the "oligarchy", through inter-marriage over the years, had grown to about two hundred families in all. And they were still wealthy, powerful and corrupt. I first met her father at a function in San Salvador, when he asked me if I'd be interested in training the Nica-raguan and Guatemalan mercs he was using to protect his estate. The money he was offering was too good to refuse. What I didn't know at the time was that he had a couple of ex-Marines working on the estate as well. They took an instant dislike to me because I was, in effect, their superior. I should have walked away then but of course I didn't. Not for that kind of money.

'On the night in question I was invited to a party at the mansion. When I got there I realized the guest list read like a *Who's Who* of Salvadorean high society. Well, you know me, I'm not into rubbing shoulders with those kind of people. So I grabbed a beer and went for a walk in the garden. Marisa was there. We talked for a couple of minutes, then went our separate ways. I carried on walking until I reached a pond at the foot of the garden. That's when I heard the scream. It had come from a barn not far from the pond. Naturally I went to investigate. The doors were closed but not locked. I pulled open one of the doors.' He stopped abruptly and sat forward, his head in his hands. He remained that way for several seconds before looking up at Nicole. 'The two Marines had her pinned down, one on each arm, and a third man was crouched over her. He had his back to me so I couldn't see what he was doing. Then one of the mercs saw me and went for his gun. I was carrying as well. Force of habit, I guess. I shot him. It was self-defence. At that moment the man looked round at me. I guess it was a combination of the surprise on seeing who it was together with the sheer dis-gust of what he was doing to the kid that caused me to freeze. Jesus, Nicole, the bastard had a broken bottle in his hand. I don't think I have to spell out what he was doing to her, do I?'

'Oh God,' Nicole gasped, and clasped her hands to her mouth, the nauseating vision in her mind mirrored by the revulsion in her eyes.

'That's when the second merc jumped me. I shot him as well. By then I was in a rage. I just wanted to get my hands on the guy and tear him limb from limb. I was still getting to my feet when he caught me on the back of the head with what I found later was a shovel. I blacked out. When I came round I was lying outside the barn. The police were there and that's when I learnt that Marisa was dead. She'd been shot with my gun. I had her blood on my clothes and that automatically put me in the frame for her murder. Nobody believed me when I tried to explain what had really happened. I was taken to the police station and charged with the kid's murder. That's when Dennison came to my cell and told me the authorities were reluctant to press charges because they feared my connection with the death squads would come out in court. I was to be quietly deported. He even had my deportation orders with him, which had already been signed by General Ramon Vaquero. The same man who'd brutalized and murdered the girl in the barn. I realized then why I was being deported. It had nothing to do with the death squads – he couldn't risk having me stand up in court and tell the truth. Even if I hadn't been believed, it would still have damaged his credibility. As it was, he was the acclaimed hero of the moment. He just inverted the roles by making out that he'd come across me and the two mercs in the barn. There were no witnesses. And who would a jury believe? Some foreign merc with a drink problem, or one of the most decorated military officers in the country's history? As it was, I was lucky not to have been put up in front of a firing squad. It was only the intervention of the American embassy that saved my butt. That's obviously how Dennison got involved in the first place. Vaquero was a personal friend, so he made sure Dennison got to handle the deportation.

'Dennison escorted me to the airport. That's when he first told me about the contract. Vaquero and Dennison had come up with it themselves. Nobody else knew of its existence. The bottom line was they would implement the contract if I ever revealed the truth of what happened in the barn. Of course I knew I could never say anything. I told Coughlin the truth one night when I was drunk and I've regretted it ever since. But he was the only one. I couldn't even tell Brad. He always said he never believed I did it, but it's always bothered me that maybe somewhere in the back of his mind he may have had his doubts. Now I'll never know.'

'I'm sorry, Rick,' Nicole said softly. 'You've had to carry that burden around with you all this time. It must have been awful.'

'It has been, but not in the way you think,' he replied. 'They threatened to put out the contract on you, not me.'

She stared at him, hardly able to comprehend what he'd just said. 'Me? I . . . I don't understand.'

'They knew a threat like that against me wouldn't carry much weight. I'm a merc. When you're confronted with as much death as we are, life tends to become cheap after a while. Even your own. So to make sure I wasn't going to rock the boat, they threatened to kill the one person I've ever cared about in this godforsaken world. You. They knew I'd never do anything to put your life at risk.'

'You've carried that burden around with you for the last five years just to protect me?'

'If I'd opened my mouth they'd have had no qualms about having you killed. I've no doubt of that.'

'And if you carry out this assassination tomorrow night, then they'll lift the contract, is that it?' she asked.

'No, Vaquero will never lift the contract,' he said grimly.

'He knows he's safe as long as I don't talk. And I won't talk as long as the contract's in place. In effect, it's become a stalemate.'

'So if it's not that, what is it?'

He got to his feet and leaned his arms on the railing. 'Pruitt came to see me after he'd taken you back to your hotel. He had a proposition for me. A hundred thousand dollars to assassinate the President of El Salvador.'

'The President? That would be playing straight into Vaquero's hands.'

'That's obviously what he wants,' Marlette agreed. 'I don't know why, and he wasn't about to tell me either. I'm only the hired help. His people would get me into the building opposite the hotel. They would also provide the sniper's rifle. I'd have one shot. But Pruitt was concerned that, as Vaquero will be arriving with the President at the hotel tomorrow night, I might be tempted to put the bullet in him instead. That's when he told me he knew about the contract. I don't know how he knew, but he was certainly well informed about it, right down to the last gory detail.'

'So if you were to shoot Vaquero, Pruitt would make sure the contract was carried out,' Nicole deduced. 'But if you do as you're told, you're a hundred grand richer and I'll be off the hook. Right?'

'Right,' Marlette replied. 'At the time I thought he was crazy. For a hundred grand I could easily keep my personal feelings under control. But after the events of the past couple of days, I'm not so sure any more.'

'I should think so,' Nicole retorted. 'If you assassinate the President everything this country's worked so hard for since the ceasefire will have been for nothing. Martial law would be imposed, and with it would come the resurgence of the death squads. Is that what you want, Rick?'

'If I take out Vaquero, Pruitt will have you killed,' Marlette replied.

'I'll take my chances,' Nicole shot back, then crossed to

the chair in the corner of the porch and sat down. She lit a cigarette. 'Look around you, Rick. What do you see? I know what I see. A country that's finally coming to terms with its freedom. No more fighting. No more fear. Forget about Ruiz and Chavez and their little band of Merry Men, they're living in the clouds. They'll fall in line when they finally come to realize that Marxism's alive now in name only. The people are just starting to rebuild their lives again after decades of oppression. And you'd be prepared to take that away from them for your own personal greed?'

'I told you, it's got nothing to do with the money,' he said.

'Don't say you're doing it for me,' she countered. 'Do you honestly think I could live with myself knowing I was responsible in some way for all the bloodshed that would inevitably follow this coup?' She took a long drag on the cigarette as she stared out into the darkness. 'I'd heard of El Salvador before I came here, but I certainly couldn't have placed it on a map. It was a name to me, that's all. Now it's a part of me. I can never forget what these people did for Michelle. She wasn't one of their own, yet they risked their lives to make sure no harm came to her. If it wasn't for them, I'd probably never have seen her again. No, Rick, don't use me as an excuse for any doubts you may still be harbouring in your mind. If you go ahead and assassinate the President tomorrow night, you'll be doing it for the money. And if you do, don't ever come near me or Michelle again.'

'Now that's the Nicole Auger I remember,' he said with a wry smile. 'If I do hit Vaquero tomorrow night, then it's essential that you and Michelle are given every protection against any possible backlash. Before I left New York I put the details of the deal I made with Pruitt on a cassette tape. At the time I did it as a safeguard against Pruitt trying to double-cross me after the hit. I sent a copy to him at CIA headquarters in Langley, and a copy to you at your restaurant. I included a letter for you with instructions to release the tape anonymously to the media should anything happen to me. Well, now we can turn that around to your advantage. If Chavez can get you into one of the neighbouring states, you can contact Amnesty International, or one of those organizations, and explain the situation to them. You'll get so much publicity that Pruitt wouldn't dare carry out his threat, especially if he knows the tape would be sent to the newspapers if anything were to happen to either of you.'

'This is all hypothetical, Rick,' Nicole reminded him.

'If I had a foolproof plan don't you think I'd use it?' he retorted. 'We've got to use what we have at our disposal. This is the CIA we're up against here, Nicole. There are no rules. You survive on instinct in their world. Sure it could backfire, but that's the chance you've got to take.'

'What about you?'

'You let me worry about that,' he told her firmly.

Nicole saw the approaching headlights and jumped to her feet as she peered anxiously into the distance. 'Rick, you don't think . . .'

'I told you, the military won't come here at night,' he replied.

It was only when the car pulled up in front of the house that they saw Chavez in the passenger seat. She climbed out and slammed the door behind her. The car drove off. She climbed the steps and tossed the video cassette on to the porch. '*Blanco*,' she snapped at Marlette.

'What's wrong?' Nicole asked.

'She says the tape's blank,' Marlette replied.

'That doesn't make any sense,' Nicole said.

'This is all we need right now,' Marlette said in despair. 'Are you sure this is the tape Kinnard gave to Michelle?'

'How many tapes do you think Michelle's got with her?' Nicole responded caustically. 'Of course it's the tape.'

'Check,' Marlette said, and saw the anger in her eyes.

'Please, Nicole. Just do it.' He waited until she'd disappeared into the house before turning to Chavez. 'Did you check the whole tape?'

'Don't patronize me,' Chavez hissed. 'The tape's been wiped clean. So either Kinnard switched them and gave the girl a blank tape, or else your girlfriend's holding out on us.'

'Nicole doesn't care about the tape. She only came out here to find her daughter. But I can buy the idea of Kinnard switching the tapes. It's exactly the sort of thing he'd do.'

Chavez banged her fist down angrily on the railing. 'All this time we've been protecting the girl and for what? A blank tape.'

Nicole appeared in the doorway, Michelle's pink case in her hand. 'Rick, can I see you for a minute?'

'Have you found something?' he asked.

'Yes, and it's not good.'

'What is it?'

Nicole handed him the suitcase. 'Look inside. Top pocket.'

Marlette opened the case and pulled back the elastic string protecting the mouth of the pocket. 'Oh shit,' he exclaimed.

Chavez grabbed the case from him and looked inside. She cursed furiously and shoved it back into Nicole's hands.

'Where the hell did she get that from?' Marlette asked.

'It's an industrial magnet Bob picked up when he was doing a series of articles on American factories last year. I don't remember it being there when I packed the case. Michelle must have put it in afterwards.'

'And over the last few days the magnet's erased everything from the tape,' Marlette concluded. 'Well, Vaquero's likely to give her a medal for that.'

'And just what's that supposed to mean?' Nicole snapped, rounding on Marlette. 'She's a six-year-old child.

327

How could she be expected to know the magnet would damage the tape?'

'There's nothing more I can do here,' Chavez told Marlette. 'I'll be leaving for San Salvador later tonight. I'm going to have to kill Vaquero myself. It's the only way to stop the coup now.'

'You wouldn't stand a chance,' Marlette replied. 'The hotel will be swarming with security personnel.'

'I can't stand by and do nothing, not with the future of my country at stake,' she said, then walked to the steps.

'I'll kill him,' Marlette called out after her.

She paused at the foot of the steps and looked round at him. 'And what chance would you have? At least I have the contacts –'

'So do I,' Marlette cut in quickly. 'And they can get me within range of Vaquero when he arrives at the hotel. It's already been set up.'

Michelle appeared in the doorway and rubbed her eyes sleepily as she stepped out on to the porch. 'You woke me up, Mommy. You were shouting.'

'I'm sorry, sweetheart,' Nicole said, hugging Michelle to her. 'Come on, I'll tuck you in again.'

'Nicole, I've got a few things I need to discuss with Chavez. I'll see you later.'

'Sure,' Nicole replied, then took Michelle's hand and led her back into the house.

'We need to talk,' he said to Chavez.

'Yes, we do,' she agreed. 'There's an empty hut where we can talk. I brought some *aguardiente* back with me from Tejutla. I could certainly do with a drink right now.'

Aguardiente. Marlette hadn't tasted the stuff since he was last in El Salvador. A potent fire-water made from sugar cane with a high alcohol content which had left him nursing some of the worst hangovers he'd ever experienced in his life. Not that he'd be drinking it in those quantities again, he reminded himself as he hurried after Chavez.

An hour later he emerged from the hut. He'd only had a couple of shots of *aguardiente* but they'd gone straight to his head. Chavez had drunk twice as much as him but without any obvious ill-effects. *You're just getting old*, he said ruefully to himself as he made his way back towards the house.

It had been a constructive discussion. Frank. Honest. Open. On both sides. It had been the only way. He'd realized from the start that he would have to tell Chavez about Pruitt and the contract, if only to protect Nicole and Michelle. It had been a big gamble but it seemed to have paid off. Chavez had discounted the idea of taking them across the border the next day. She'd learnt in Tejutla that the border was swarming with Dennison's men, waiting for them to make a move. She'd admitted that it was possible they might be able to evade capture, but it wasn't a risk worth taking. She would rather take Nicole and Michelle south again, something Dennison and his men wouldn't be expecting. It had been agreed she would take them to La Puerta del Diablo and rendezvous with the helicopter the following evening. But that was still playing into Pruitt's hands. The pilot would be one of Pruitt's men, with orders to take them to a prearranged destination where either Pruitt or one of his lieutenants would be waiting for them. The only alternative was to force the pilot to land elsewhere. In another country if possible. Marlette knew he could force the pilot to change course once they were airborne. But they would still need a flight plan. And that would require permission from the relevant authorities. Chavez had the connections in neighbouring Honduras. She'd said she would try and make the necessary arrangements. They'd both realized it was a long shot, but it was all they had left now. . .

Marlette climbed the steps on to the porch and entered the house. He went to the bedroom and found Nicole and Michelle huddled together under a single blanket on the ground. Neither stirred when he entered the room. He was about to reach down to lift the blanket up over Nicole's shoulder when he checked himself. He didn't want to risk waking her. She looked so peaceful beside Michelle. What he had to say to her could wait until morning.

He sat down in the chair in the corner of the room. It was the first time he'd had the chance to look on Michelle not as Nicole's daughter, but as *their* daughter. *His* daughter. He wanted to say it over and over to himself. The words had such a wonderfully warm feeling to them. All his adult life had been spent killing and maiming for profit. There was no honour in that. His had been a particularly destructive life and yet here was this little ragamuffin, *his* little ragamuffin, the very antithesis of everything he'd believed in for the last twenty years, who represented the one true light in that eternal darkness. Nicole had been right to walk out on him when she did. The preservation of innocence. Although he felt ashamed of all that killing, not only for Michelle but also for himself, he found himself wondering whether her very existence was some kind of reparation for all his past misdemeanours. He now realized he'd finally reached the point of no return. The future, whatever it held for them, either collectively or as individuals, was all that mattered to him now. He'd never bring shame on his daughter again. Never . . .

He felt something touch his cheek. He quickly brushed his hand across his face and found, to his surprise, that the tips of his fingers were wet. He rubbed his moist eyes and smiled ruefully to himself. He hadn't cried since . . . hell, he couldn't remember the last time he'd cried.

'Sleep tight,' he said softly, then got to his feet and left the room.

TWELVE

'Your hunch may have been right after all; it's possible Marlette is working for the CIA.'

Dennison stood by the window of his luxurious penthouse office, slowly taking in the breathtaking panoramic landscape that was San Salvador; a sprawling city dwarfed by the rugged, untamed terrain of the surrounding mountains and volcanoes. It was a view he never tired of, and certainly one few locals would ever witness. But then wealth had its own aesthetic privileges. He tapped the ash off the end of his cheroot, then turned to Hector Amaya who was helping himself to a bourbon from the drinks cabinet. 'That's a turnaround. Last night you were scoffing at the idea.'

'Last night I was scoffing at the idea that there might be a mole in the Military Council,' Amaya corrected him. 'But to put my own mind at rest I had three of my most trusted aides check out each member of the Military Council for any possible links with the CIA, or any other foreign intelligence service for that matter. As I expected, they came up with nothing.'

'Who checked you out?' Dennison asked, easing himself into the padded leather chair behind his desk.

'You did,' Amaya said. 'I also have my contacts at Langley, Peter. I heard you'd been making some enquiries of your own. I assume I passed the test?'

'I wouldn't be talking to you if you hadn't,' Dennison replied. 'So what did you learn about Marlette? All my enquiries at Langley drew a blank.'

'I didn't get my information from Langley,' Amaya told him. 'I received a tip-off from a reliable contact about an employee who works at the government building opposite the Camino Real Hotel. What my contact couldn't have known was that this same person used to run errands for the CIA here in San Salvador a few years back.'

'Would I have known him from the embassy?'

'No, you'd already left by then. At the time we kept an eye on him, but he was a small fish so we just left him to it. You understand I can't divulge the name of my source or what he told me but, acting on his information, I had this employee picked up and brought in for questioning. He's a divisional manager which gives him access to the whole building. It didn't take long to break him. It turns out his orders were to get Marlette into the building later this afternoon and hide him in an empty storeroom on the top floor until all the staff had left. He was also told to hand over duplicate keys for several of the offices overlooking the hotel. Presumably Marlette would have carried out the hit from one of those offices. We don't know how he would have come by the gun. Perhaps another contact would have left it in the building for him, I don't know.'

'Who was his intended target? Vaquero?'

'I hardly think it would be the President, do you?' Amaya snorted.

'Which means Langley already know about the coup,' Dennison concluded. 'What if they've already alerted the President?'

'Don't you think I'd have known if they'd alerted the President? I am the head of his security team. It was obviously Langley's intention to use Marlette to do their dirty work for them, then claim the credit for thwarting the coup. No, Langley have already played their hand. They won't be a problem now.'

'Have you told Vaquero yet?'

'I thought you'd want to be the first to hear the good

news,' Amaya said. 'I'm going to see him after I leave here.'

'This might just take the sting out of his anger after what happened to Ruiz earlier today,' Dennison said.

'I wouldn't count on it,' Amaya said. 'He's well pissed off with you right now. As I said to you earlier on the phone, it's just as well you weren't there when I broke the news to him about Ruiz's death. He really flew off the handle.'

'I'll just be glad when all this is over, so we can get back to some kind of normality here again. Do you know how much business I've lost in these last couple of days with so many of my men out of circulation?'

'Just think of all the government contracts you'll get once Vaquero's in power,' Amaya reminded him.

'That's all that's keeping me going, believe me,' Dennison replied, stubbing out his cheroot. 'So what are we going to do about Marlette? Do you want me to deal with him?'

'No,' Amaya replied quickly. 'Let me handle it.'

'What are you going to do?'

'Nothing, at least not until he's safely inside the building. And by the time he realizes he's walked into a trap, it'll be too late for him to do anything about it.'

'I only wish I could be there to see it,' Dennison sneered, and watched Amaya cross to the door. 'Keep me posted.'

'You can count on it,' Amaya called out over his shoulder as he left the room.

The two main international hotels in San Salvador are the Sheraton and the Camino Real. The Sheraton, which is generally regarded as the more classy of the two, is frequented by visiting diplomats and a variety of foreign intelligence operatives, and was a particular favourite of the CIA during the civil war. The Camino Real has a more friendly ambience, and is a regular haunt of foreign journalists and travelling businessmen alike.

Although he'd never stayed at either hotel, Marlette had always had a preference for socializing at the Camino Real, and had rarely missed a Sunday brunch where, for the price of a few drinks, he'd regularly traded information with the foreign journalists. They'd wanted to know about military manoeuvres in the restricted areas of the country, and in return they'd kept him abreast on all the latest developments in the world's trouble spots. It had been a fair exchange, he thought to himself as he stood on the Boulevard los Heroes looking up at the hotel's white and brown façade. Little had changed since he'd last seen it.

He waited until the traffic lights had changed to red, then darted across the dual carriageway. As he walked towards the hotel entrance he was intercepted by an eager taxi-driver who pointed towards the cluster of yellow cabs in the adjacent parking lot. Marlette just shook his head, then looked back at the grey and black building on the opposite side of the street. How many times had he been to the hotel during those months in San Salvador and never once had he even noticed the building? Not that he knew much more about it now. All he'd been told was that it was a government office where the general public could go to pay their electricity bills. He stepped under the portico and crossed to the main glass doors. A doorman darted forward to open one of the doors for him. He paused to look back at the building again and was alarmed to see that now only the first two floors were visible from where he stood; roughly the same spot where the dignitaries would alight from their limousines later that evening. He was under no illusion – it was going to be a very difficult shot.

He entered the hotel foyer and glanced at his watch. He was due to meet his contact at three o'clock. That left him with twenty minutes to kill. Perhaps not the best choice of words under the circumstances, he thought to himself, then made his way across the foyer to the Lobby Bar. He ordered himself a Coke at the bar and sat down at one of the empty tables.

It hadn't been easy breaking the news to Nicole that it would be too dangerous for the FMLN to try and smuggle her and Michelle into one of the neighbouring states, not with the recent build-up of Dennison's men along the border. Not that she'd taken it badly; it was almost as if she'd been expecting another setback. He'd explained to her that Chavez would take them to La Puerta del Diablo in plenty of time to meet the helicopter later that evening. It wasn't the ideal solution, but it was still the one realistic chance left open to them to get out of the country. What happened to them after they were safely across the border depended on the plan that he and Chavez had discussed over the *aguardiente* the previous evening. Although Nicole hadn't said anything at the time, it had been obvious she'd had her doubts about whether the plan would work. She wasn't the only one with reservations about it, but it was all they could come up with at such short notice. Not that they would need the plan if he assassinated the President. Forget it, he chided himself angrily. But he knew he couldn't forget it. There was still that lingering doubt in the back of his mind. Kill the President and it would totally alienate him from Nicole. He would never see Michelle again. But at least that way he could be certain they would both be safe. But was it really worth the sacrifice? On the other hand, if he killed Vaquero, Pruitt wouldn't hesitate to carry out his threat; unless Nicole could make enough noise to scare him off once she reached a neutral country. But first she had to get there. So many options with so many consequences. What to do? Nobody could tell him that. It was now down to him. Two targets. One bullet. No mistakes.

He drank down the last of the Coke and looked at his watch. Two fifty-two. Eight minutes. He got to his feet. As he left the bar he noticed a guest by the elevator with a copy of *La Prensa* in his hand. The words written in bold letters across the front page made Marlette shudder: *Mercenario Asesino*. Mercenary Murderer. Under the headline was a black-and-white photograph of him. The one consolation was that the picture had been taken when he'd last been in El Salvador. His hair was still long and he hadn't shaved for several days. It was an eerie feeling – he had the same photograph in his apartment. He suddenly sensed the man staring at him, and for a worrying moment he thought he'd been recognized. Then the elevator doors parted and the man stepped inside, the doors closing again behind him. Marlette cursed himself for letting his nerves get the better of him. It wasn't like him to get jittery. But this whole operation was unlike any other he'd ever undertaken. There was so much at stake. He bowed his head as he crossed the foyer. On emerging from the hotel he saw that most of the taxi-drivers sitting on the grass verge adjacent to the parking lot were also reading copies of *La Prensa*. One of them was reading a morning edition of the other leading national newspaper, *Diario de Hoy*. It carried the same picture on its front page. Slipping on the sunglasses he'd borrowed from Ruiz, he strode briskly down the drive and darted between the flowing traffic to get to the other side of the road.

He was sweating. He wiped his forearm across his face and considered the idea of buying himself a peaked cap from one of the shops in the Metrocentro which was situated close to the government building. After all, most Salvadoreans wore hats of some kind. And baseball caps seemed to be the most fashionable. He checked his watch, decided he just had enough time to buy a cap, and went to the Metrocentro where he found a sports shop. He ignored the tourist caps and bought one with 'Mets' written across it. Tugging it down firmly over his head, he walked casually through the main gates and up the concrete path towards the steps which led into the foyer. He mounted the steps and was about to push one of the doors when it swung open from the inside and an armed policeman emerged on to the steps. He held the door and Marlette was about to slip past him when a second policeman appeared in the doorway. Marlette quickly stepped aside when the policeman snapped at him to get out of his way. They moved down the steps. Marlette stepped into the foyer. Two armed guards stood by the door but, to Marlette's relief, both were in conversation with a stunningly attractive woman in her early twenties who had the kind of figure to shame a catwalk model. He knew there were hundreds of women in El Salvador who were just as slim and beautiful as her, yet the tragic irony of it all was that many of these women, who would have been worshipped for their looks in Europe, lived in the abject poverty of the shanty towns, without work and without hope.

Pruitt had told him his contact would make the first move. With this in mind, Marlette reluctantly removed his peaked cap and slipped the sunglasses into the breast pocket of his open-necked shirt. The plan was that his contact would introduce himself with one phrase and Marlette would counter with a phrase of his own. All very cloak-and-dagger stuff, but it beat trying to spot the man with a carnation in his lapel carrying yesterday's edition of the *New York Times*. Assuming his contact was a man. It could just as easily be a woman. His eyes instinctively went to the woman who was still talking to the two guards. Some chance! He looked at his watch. It was a minute to three. He was beginning to feel distinctly uneasy standing around idly in the foyer, especially with so many copies of *La Prensa* and *Diario de Hoy* in circulation. It was as if his face was staring back accusingly at him from every angle. Just act naturally. It was the only way he was going to get through this . . .

'Excuse me, could you tell when the next 406 bus leaves for Santa Ana?' a voice said behind him.

The phrase. His contact. 'I'm afraid the 406 doesn't go to . . .' Marlette stopped abruptly when Hector Amaya stepped into view.

'It's good to see you again, Marlette,' Amaya said with an icy smile.

Marlette's mind was racing. Was Amaya his contact? Or had he been set up? He suddenly remembered that Pruitt had a mole in the Military Council. But Amaya? He was the last person he'd have suspected. No, it couldn't be. Not Amaya. It had to be a set-up.

Amaya's eyes flickered past Marlette to the two armed guards who were now standing only a few metres away from them. 'There are two of my men behind you. Another two are standing by the elevator behind me. I'm sure you can see them. I don't want any trouble here, Marlette, but if you resist arrest you'll certainly regret it.'

Marlette glanced behind him and noticed the same two men who had been speaking to the woman. He had been set up. But how could he have known he was walking into a trap? The thought was scant consolation considering his predicament. One of the men began to disperse a gaggle of onlookers who were hovering uncertainly around them. His colleague moved forward and prodded his machine pistol into the small of Marlette's back as he quickly frisked him. Amaya unholstered his automatic, stepped back, and gestured to the floor. Marlette looked around despairingly but there was no way out. He knew if he tried to run now, he'd be shot.

The butt of the machine pistol caught him painfully in the back and, as he stumbled forward, he was grabbed from behind and forced to the floor. A knee was pressed agonizingly into the small of his back, his arms were twisted roughly behind his back and a pair of handcuffs were snapped over his wrists. He was then hauled to his feet and marched from the building. The two men who'd been standing at the elevator flanked Amaya as he followed the struggling Marlette to a waiting car. Marlette was bundled into the back seat. Amaya got into the passenger seat and waited until the driver had started up the engine and pulled the car away from the kerb, then he looked round at Marlette who was still struggling violently with his captors. 'Sedate him,' he snapped. 'We can't have any bruises.'

One of the men pinned Marlette against the back seat while the other produced a tranquillizer gun and, pressing it against Marlette's neck, squeezed the trigger. Marlette felt a sharp stinging sensation as the needle penetrated his skin. Within seconds the sedative had begun to take effect; he shook his head furiously, trying desperately to fight off the claustrophobic drowsiness which seemed to be closing in on him. But he knew he was just delaying the inevitable. He couldn't beat it. He glared at Amaya, whose face was already beginning to swim before his eyes. Everything began to blur. He heard Amaya's contemptuous laugh as his chin dropped on to his chest. He tried to lift his head but there was now no feeling in his neck muscles. He couldn't move. He felt as if he'd been paralysed. Then everything went black.

When Marlette regained consciousness he found himself lying on a cold, hard concrete floor. He struggled into a sitting position but found his movements were severely restricted by the length of chain which had been looped through the handcuffs and attached to a rusted hook protruding from the ceiling. His neck ached but he assumed that was more from the position he'd lain on the floor than from any after-effects of the tranquillizer. The fact that he didn't seem to feel any the worse for wear certainly surprised him. He'd have expected at least to have had a headache. But there was no discomfort whatsoever. It was as if he'd just woken up from a deep sleep.

He looked around him slowly, trying to work out exactly where he was. The room was windowless and the only source of light was the naked bulb above him. The room was empty except for an elongated table in the shadows against the far wall, with what appeared to be a tarpaulin tossed over it. Was there something under the tarpaulin? He couldn't be sure, not from that distance. The stone steps beside the table led up to a solid wooden door. A closed-circuit camera mounted on the wall by the door was trained on him. It could be a police cell, but the more he thought about it, the more inclined he was to think he was in a cellar. Then he noticed the spotlights secured to the ceiling. They were directed to different areas of the room but only two of them had bulbs. No, this wasn't a police cell. So where exactly was he?

His thoughts were interrupted by the sound of the door opening. The familiar figure of Stuart Jayson appeared at the top of the steps. He closed the door behind him and slowly descended the steps. He paused at the foot of the steps and stared disdainfully at Marlette. 'Sleep well?' he sneered sarcastically.

'Where the hell am I?' Marlette snapped angrily.

'I thought you'd have figured that out for yourself,' Jayson retorted, easing himself down on to the bottom step. 'You're at Dennison's guest-house in San Benito.'

'Of course,' Marlette muttered, looking around him again. *La Muerte Sótano*. The Death Cellar. 'I heard rumours about this place but I never knew it actually existed. It doesn't look much though, does it?'

'The room was stripped after the ceasefire,' Jayson said. 'Although I'm told when it was operational back in the eighties the death squads used to regularly bring their more valuable prisoners here for interrogation. The walls are soundproofed so they could do what the fuck they wanted to them and nobody could hear their screams. I believe Dennison even used to hold dinner parties upstairs while the prisoners were being tortured in here. That's quite something, isn't it?'

'My admiration knows no bounds,' Marlette shot back in disgust. 'Is our congenial host here at the moment?'

'He'll be down shortly.'

'What am I doing here?'

'You'll find out soon enough,' Jayson said, gingerly touching the strip of plaster protecting the stitches on his cheek.

'And how's the face?' Marlette asked contemptuously.

'The glass cut through to the bone,' Jayson replied with a dismissive shrug. 'It'll leave a scar, but then a lot of women seem to go for that sort of thing, don't they?'

'For the right price, whores will go for anything,' Marlette retorted. 'But then you already know that, don't you? It's the only way you ever get laid.'

'I don't need to make it with any whores,' Jayson shot back. 'I have a wife back in Guatemala City.'

'I hope you're paying her enough to keep up the pretence, otherwise she'll just go back to doing ten-buck tricks on the side when you're not around.'

Jayson leapt to his feet and pulled his automatic from his shoulder-holster. He levelled it at Marlette's head. 'I don't have to take that shit from you, Marlette.'

'Put the gun away!' Dennison barked furiously from the top of the steps.

'Not before he apologizes,' Jayson hissed without taking his eyes off Marlette.

Dennison hurried down the steps and snatched the automatic out of Jayson's hand. 'If he can rile you that easily, then maybe there's some truth in what he said after all. Now go upstairs and wait for me in the lounge.'

'I'm going to enjoy killing you,' Jayson hissed furiously at Marlette. He plucked the automatic from Dennison's hand and left the room.

'You must be slipping, Dennison,' Marlette said. 'You've got all that money at your disposal, yet the best you can do is hire a psychopath like Jayson.'

'He's good at what he does, as you'll find out in a few hours' time,' Dennison replied coldly.

'Is this after you've let him torture me in some futile attempt to try and make me reveal the whereabouts of Kinnard's tape?'

'The tape's not important at this stage of the operation,' Dennison said.

'So why was I brought here?'

'You're the last piece of the jigsaw,' Dennison told him. 'There's going to be an outcry at the UN once the military seize power again here in El Salvador. It's inevitable. But if it was made to look as if the military only took the action to stabilize the country after the assassination of the civilian President, then it would certainly help to dilute any backlash from the UN. As I'm sure you already know, we were going to use Ruiz as the patsy. But unfortunately things haven't gone according to plan. That's why we've had to revert to our backup plan. We needed to find another patsy, and who better than an international mercenary who's been known to be associating with the FMLN since his arrival in El Salvador? By the time the investigation into the President's death has been completed, there will be irrefutable proof to show that you'd been hired by the FMLN to assassinate the President. So with the FMLN in disgrace, it can only strengthen the military's grip on the reins of power.'

'What happened to Ruiz?'

Dennison activated one of the spotlights from a wall-mounted board, then crossed to the table and lifted back a corner of the tarpaulin. Marlette fought back the rising bile in his throat as he stared at Ruiz's grotesquely disfigured face.

'What did you do to him?' Marlette asked in disgust.

'Nothing,' Dennison replied, replacing the tarpaulin. 'The Land-Rover he was travelling in went off the road and into a ravine. As there were no survivors, we can only assume he somehow managed to grab the wheel and force it off the road.'

'Suicide?' Marlette replied in surprise.

'We'll never know for sure, but it looks that way. He'd probably guessed what was going to happen to him, so he decided to take his own life. A martyr for the cause. Very admirable, but unfortunately his little plan backfired because nobody in the FMLN even knows he's dead. And we intend to keep it that way. That's why I went to the lengths I did to have the body recovered. I actually lost eight of my men in the process, picked off by terrorist snipers as they were searching through the wreckage. But that's not important; they can easily be replaced. What is important is that the body's here now.'

'Vaquero must be well pissed off with your incompetence by now,' Marlette snorted. 'You've blundered from start to finish, haven't you?'

'I've made a couple of mistakes these last few days, but then again I'm not the one in handcuffs with only a few hours left to live, am I?'

Jayson appeared in the doorway. 'You've got a call on your scrambler line. It's Vaquero.'

'What does he want now?' Dennison said irritably.

'He didn't say. Just that he wanted to speak to you.'

'Tell him I'm on my way,' Dennison replied.

'Before you go, answer me one last question,' Marlette said after Jayson had left.

'The condemned man's last question. Go ahead, ask.'

'Why was Brad Casey murdered?'

'I heard he'd been shot in New York. Nicole told me,' Dennison replied. 'But it certainly wasn't orchestrated from this end if that's what you're implying.'

'What harm can it do now to tell me the truth?' Marlette

countered angrily. 'Brad was my best friend. I want to know the truth, Dennison. Why was he killed?'

'If I knew, I'd tell you,' Dennison assured him.

'There's a witness who claims the assassin spoke with a Cockney accent. I think it's a bit too much of a coincidence for it not to be Jayson, don't you?'

'When exactly was this?' Dennison asked.

'Four days ago.'

'Then it wasn't Jayson,' Dennison replied. 'He's only been out of the country once in the last six weeks, and then it was just to see his wife in Guatemala City. I'd say you've been set up, Marlette. It's a pity you'll never find out who was behind it.'

Marlette found himself believing Dennison. He had no reason to lie. Not after everything he'd already told him. Was Dennison right? Had he been set up? But by whom? And why? The only name that came to mind was Pruitt. After all, he had been the one who'd first broken the news about Brad's murder to him. Had Brad stumbled on to something to link Pruitt with the coup? But how could Brad have known about the coup, unless he also had a source inside the Military Council? No, that was crazy. None of it made any sense. There had to be another explanation. But he was damned if he knew what it was . . .

He suddenly sensed Dennison behind him, but before he could react he felt a sharp pain in the side of his neck. He knew what it was even before he saw the tranquillizer gun in Dennison's hand.

'It'll take a few seconds for the sedative to get to work in your bloodstream,' Dennison announced. 'After that you'll just fall into a deep sleep. This way you won't be any more trouble to us.'

Marlette tugged furiously at the handcuffs as the first effects of the drug began to take hold. 'Don't fight it, Marlette. Just let it happen,' he heard Dennison say, and he blinked his eyes rapidly to try and clear his vision as the room began to swim around him. Again he heard Dennison's voice, but now it seemed to be a distant echo originating from somewhere deep inside his head. 'As I said ... Jayson's very good ...' Words melted into words like some psychedelic mirage in his mind. '... clean kill ... heart ... needn't concern you ... won't feel anything ...'

A last, despairing thought flashed through the hazy, distorted parameters of his mind before he finally passed out: *You're never going to wake up ...*

Jayson took a last drag on the cigarette, stubbed it out on the sole of his boot, then dropped the butt carefully into a paper bag on the desk in front of him. It was imperative that he leave no clues behind of his ever having been there. He looked at his watch. 7 p.m. The President was due at the hotel in thirty minutes. It was a sticky, humid evening, and his hands were sweating under the gloves. Although he'd already contemplated the idea of removing them to wipe his palms on the front of his shirt, he'd resisted the temptation. There couldn't be any slip-ups. One misplaced fingerprint could ruin everything. He was about to reach for the cigarettes on the table, decided against it, then pushed back the swivel chair and got to his feet.

He was in an office on the first floor of the government building opposite the Camino Real Hotel. Dog-eared folders were strewn across the two desks, with dozens more stacked on the floor around them. Several of the cupboard doors were ajar, revealing hundreds more folders piled up inside. Judging by the VDUs and the numerous ledgers on both desks, he'd already come to the conclusion he was in the accounts department. Not that it mattered. He crossed to where he'd already set up the Maadi-Griffin sniper rifle by the window. Although it wouldn't have been his first choice – he would have gone for the Finnish Sako TRG

21 – it was still a damn good sniper rifle and perfect for the job. The opaque window was open, as were the Venetian blinds in front of it. The tip of the barrel, which was bound with masking tape to prevent its reflection from being caught in the dying rays of the setting sun, protruded through two of the horizontal blinds. He crouched down and peered through the MeOpta scope which he already had trained on the hotel's portico. A red carpet had been laid out from the main doors to the edge of the kerb, and although none of the guests had arrived as yet, there was still plenty of activity as security men and hotel staff alike made sure everything would run smoothly once the first of the chauffeur-driven vehicles pulled up under the portico.

He could see several soldiers with high-powered rifles patrolling the hotel roof, but he knew he had nothing to fear from them. All were members of an élite National Guard anti-terrorist unit who were completely loyal to the coup. Others from the unit were stationed in the hotel grounds, their sole job to act as a heavily armed bodyguard for Vaquero once he'd seized power. The hotel would become a virtual fortress until reinforcements arrived from the army barracks to escort Vaquero to the national radio station – which would already have been seized by forces loyal to the coup – where he would formally declare his intention to return the country to military rule. By then ANTEL, the telecommunications company, would also be in military hands, as would the airport tower and all border posts. And all this would come about once he'd assassinated the President. One shot. A difficult shot, granted, but there was no room for mistakes.

He looked at his watch again: 7.08 p.m. Marlette was due to be brought to the office at 7.15. He had to admit, albeit grudgingly, that he'd always respected Marlette as a merc. The guy was good at what he did. Too damn good. How many times over the years had they ended up on opposite sides, and yet never once had he managed to outwit Marlette in battle. Yeah, a lot of old scores would finally be settled when he killed Marlette.

'He's coming round.'

The words sounded distant and hollow, as if trapped somewhere in the deepest recesses of his mind. Thoughts? Memories? No, not possible. Why not? Don't know. Can't comprehend . . .

He was suddenly aware of being shaken roughly. More voices. Different voices. This time they seemed closer. More resonant. His mind was clearing. But there was something about the voices, and it took him another few seconds to realize what it was. The voices were Spanish. He didn't think in Spanish. These voices weren't in his mind. He forced open his eyelids but everything still seemed blurred. Like a picture out of focus on a cinema screen. He blinked his eyes rapidly, as if trying to adjust the projector. Better. Clearer now. Almost focused. He tried to put his hands to his face to rub his eyes, clean the lens, but found that his hands were restricted. Manacled. Then it all began to come back to him . . .

'Marlette?'

A face loomed over him. The eyes were cold and insensitive. A tongue flicked out to wet the fat lips, brushing across the neatly trimmed pencil moustache. Hector Amaya. The mouth tugged in a faint smile on noticing the recognition on Marlette's face.

'One thing's for sure: if I am dead, this isn't heaven,' Marlette said. 'Not if you're here.'

'I never did understand humour in adversity, Marlette, but I'm told it helps to cloak the fear of death,' Amaya said. He snapped his fingers. 'Get him on his feet.'

Two men hauled Marlette to his feet. The corridor was dimly lit and Marlette could hear the sound of dripping water somewhere in the background. A batch of thick, unsightly pipes, many corroded from years of use, ran the lengths of the unpainted, windowless walls, and he could see what looked like some kind of power-generator in the distance. The air was pungent with the acrid smell of diesel and oil fumes.

'Where the hell are we?' he asked.

'*You're* exactly where I want you,' Amaya replied, then walked towards a service elevator further down the corridor.

Marlette was grabbed and propelled after Amaya. 'We're in the building opposite the hotel, aren't we?' he called out as Amaya pressed the button for the elevator. No reply. 'I was under the impression that I was still to be sedated at this stage. Why the sudden change of plan?'

'You'll see,' was all Amaya would venture before he disappeared into the elevator.

Marlette was bundled roughly into the elevator after him. The two men followed him into the cage, then Amaya pressed the button for the first floor. Marlette noticed that the two men were armed with holstered automatics on their belts. Both had short hair and were wearing grey flannels and short-sleeved white shirts, open at the neck. These weren't a couple of Dennison's goons. Two of the élite Presidential bodyguard? It seemed the most likely explanation. Amaya was dressed in a loose-fitting suit, the perfect cut to conceal a shoulder-holster. When the elevator stopped, the door drew back slowly and Amaya stepped out into the corridor, looked around, then beckoned to his men. Again Marlette was led to a door further down the deserted corridor. Amaya gave a coded knock, then came the sound of a key being turned in the lock and the door was opened.

Jayson's eyes went straight to Marlette. 'He's supposed to be sedated. What's going on?'

'Can we come in?' Amaya asked.

Jayson opened the door wider and stepped aside to allow the two men to haul Marlette into the office. Amaya entered the room behind them, but remained by the door. 'Wait for me downstairs,' he told his men, then locked the door again behind them.

'What's going on?' Jayson snapped, gesturing to Marlette. 'Dennison said he'd still be sedated when you brought him here.'

'That was Dennison's idea,' Amaya replied. 'But I know how much you've always despised Marlette, and I thought you'd want to look him in the eye as the trigger was pulled.'

A slow smile crossed Jayson's red, blotchy face. 'Yeah, I like that idea. Look into his eyes as I pull the trigger. You got the gun?' Amaya removed a Smith & Wesson from his shoulder-holster and affixed a suppressor to the barrel. Jayson's eyes went to Marlette, who was looking around anxiously in a last, desperate attempt to try and save himself. 'There's nowhere to go, Marlette. I guess you could try throwing yourself against one of the windows, but they're all made of laminated glass. You wouldn't make any impression on it. And anyway, you'd be dead long before you got there.' He snapped his fingers irritably at Amaya and gestured to the gun in his hand. 'Let's get this over with. Give it to me.'

'Prophetic last words,' Amaya said, and shot Jayson through the heart.

The force of the bullet knocked Jayson backwards. He caught his foot on a pile of folders, lost his balance, and crashed to the floor. Marlette's mind was racing as he watched Amaya cross to where Jayson now lay motionless on the carpet, a layer of blood-streaked folders scattered around him. He was still too surprised to be able to evaluate the situation logically. Why had Amaya killed Jayson? Was he going to turn the gun on him next? His eyes went to the door. It was locked. The window. Shout for help? Would anyone even hear him? Would he be shot by one of the soldiers Pruitt had told him would be on the hotel roof?

'Dead,' Amaya announced after checking Jayson's carotid artery for any signs of a pulse. He straightened up without taking his eyes off Marlette. 'Turn round,' he ordered.

'Why, so you can shoot me in the back?' Marlette retorted defiantly.

'So I can unlock the handcuffs,' Amaya said, holding up the key. He lowered the gun and, crossing to where Marlette was standing, removed his handcuffs. Then he pulled a pair of gloves from his pocket and tossed them to Marlette. 'Put those on.'

Marlette slipped on the gloves, massaged his wrists, then sat down on the nearest swivel chair. 'I think you owe me some answers.'

'Didn't Alex Pruitt tell you about me?' Amaya said, switching back to Spanish.

'So you are Pruitt's man after all?'

'That's right. I was told to keep an eye on you. I guess you could say I've been your guardian angel while you've been out here.'

'I'm touched,' Marlette retorted facetiously.

Amaya looked at his watch. 'The President's due to arrive at the hotel in less than ten minutes' time. Jayson's already set up the sniper rifle by the window. It's a Maadi-Griffin. That's the model you told Pruitt you wanted for the hit.' He dug into his pocket and withdrew a bullet which he handed to Marlette. 'Soft-nosed for maximum damage on impact. One shot. One hundred thousand dollars. Make it count, Marlette.'

Marlette got to his feet and crossed to where the sniper rifle was resting on the tripod. He crouched down and fed the bullet into the breech, then looked across at Jayson's lifeless body. 'I can understand why you would need another fall guy now that Ruiz's dead, but why Jayson? He's one of yours.'

'He's one of Dennison's,' Amaya corrected him. 'And Dennison isn't one of us.'

'What does that mean?'

'He's an outsider. And he's more radical than most of the members of the Military Council. He's also a narrow-minded bigot with pretensions to power, and that's what worries most of us on the Military Council. Not because he could ever hope to be brought into the government, but because he has the kind of money behind him to finance his own coup when Vaquero refuses to bring him in as his adviser. I say *when* because Dennison's already made overtures to Vaquero about it. He's a very dangerous man with delusions of grandeur. So what better way to damage his credibility than to discredit him like this? It'll destroy his reputation. And that's exactly what Vaquero wants.'

'Why not just kill him?'

'He's not without influence. It comes from being one of the richest men in El Salvador. Killing him would only create an atmosphere of unease and suspicion, and it's imperative for Vaquero to have the complete support of the wealthy coffee barons for this coup to be successful. The same coffee barons who are also Dennison's closest allies.'

Marlette peered through the sights and readjusted the focus fractionally to suit his own specifications. 'You didn't need me for this. You could have let Jayson make the hit, then killed him. You could even have done it yourself.'

'Pruitt thought differently. And he's right. I'm no sniper and Jayson's too unreliable for a shot like this. There's no room for mistakes. You've got something of a reputation as one of the best marksmen in the business. That's why you were brought in.'

'Is that also why Pruitt had Brad Casey killed?' Marlette asked. 'To make sure I'd come out here, looking for revenge?'

'I heard that Casey had been shot, but I've no idea who

was behind it,' Amaya said, looking down and checking his watch. 'Seven minutes to go. And you can be sure that the President will be on time. He's always punctual.'

'How do I know you're not going to put a bullet in me once I've made the hit? It makes sense from your perspective.'

'You made a deal with Alex Pruitt. He always keeps his word.'

'Why don't I feel reassured?' Marlette retorted.

'Alex Pruitt always repays loyalty. That's how he's managed to build up such a wide network of contacts around the world. You see him right, and he'll see you right. It's that simple. You do your job tonight, Marlette, and you're on your way to rendezvous with the helicopter at La Puerta del Diablo. There's a car parked out back. My orders are to take you there myself. You'll be back in the States by the morning, a hundred grand the richer for your troubles.' Amaya opened a second window fractionally, then took a slimline night scope from the inside pocket of his jacket and scanned the hotel portico below. 'But screw this up and I will kill you. And both the woman and her daughter would be hit within twenty-four hours of their returning to Chicago. But then you know that already. As I said, Alex Pruitt always keeps his word.'

'Believe me, I'd like nothing better than to put a bullet in Vaquero for what he's put me through these past five years. But at what cost? No, he can have his coup for all I care. This isn't my country. It isn't my fight.'

'That's very sensible,' Amaya said absently as he continued to scan the area with the night scope.

'Who knows, perhaps another time?'

'Perhaps we'll even hire you to do it,' Amaya replied, lowering the night scope.

'You're saying that Vaquero won't be President for long?'

'I'm saying it's seven twenty-five,' Amaya said evasively.

'Five minutes before the President's due to arrive. The convoy will consist of six black Lincoln Continentals escorted by two police motorcyclists. They started out from the Presidential Palace, so they'll be approaching the hotel from our left. The two motorcycles will carry on past the hotel. The first two Lincolns will turn into the hotel and stop in the car park. The third and fourth cars will pull up under the portico. The President and his wife will be in the third car. Vaquero and Guaverra, the Finance Minister, will be in the fourth car. The idea being that the President and his two most senior ministers will be on hand to greet the guests as they arrive at the hotel.'

'Inside or outside?'

'Inside. They'll be in the foyer. I did several dummy runs with my men earlier this week, and I estimated that from the moment the President alights from the back of the car until he enters the foyer, you'll have at most ten seconds to get in a shot. And with the area around the hotel already sealed off, he won't be able to give his customary wave to his adoring public, which means it could be even less than ten seconds.'

'I only need a second to get his head in my sights and pull the trigger.'

'You just make sure it's the right head,' Amaya said coldly.

'I've already told you —'

'Spare me the protestations, Marlette,' Amaya cut in sharply. 'And just in case you think that by killing Vaquero you'd prevent the coup from going ahead, you'd be wrong. If Vaquero were killed, I would then go down there and set the wheels in motion myself. One way or another, there will be a new government in power tonight. Whether you live to see it depends entirely on you.'

'You almost make it sound as if you want me to kill Vaquero,' Marlette said, casting a sidelong glance at Amaya.

'Not tonight,' Amaya replied without lowering the night scope. 'Definitely not tonight.'

Marlette wiped his sleeve across his forehead, then pulled his bandanna from his pocket and secured it firmly around his head. His mind was in complete turmoil. That morning he'd been prepared to kill Vaquero and to hell with the consequences. Now, even if he were to assassinate Vaquero, the coup would still go ahead. He had one shot. Take out Vaquero and he'd never leave the room alive. And what about Nicole and Michelle? Sure, he'd agreed with Nicole the previous night that what was important was to stop Vaquero, but at the time he'd thought she was the sole target of the contract. That's what Pruitt had told him back in New York, but Amaya had made it clear that Michelle would be killed as well. How could he sacrifice his own daughter? He knew he couldn't . . . and even if he were never to see either of them again, as Nicole had threatened if he went ahead and assassinated the President, at least he'd know they were both safe. That was all that mattered to him. Or was it? A hundred thousand dollars to sell out a nation. Blood-money, every last dollar of it. The dollar – the currency of democracy. But mercenaries didn't have principles, he told himself. Money was money in any currency. To hell with democracy.

He could have believed that a year ago. Even six months ago. But not any more. Sure, he wanted the money, but not at the price of losing Nicole and Michelle. He'd lost Nicole once. Never again. And Michelle? How could he even contemplate ever giving up a part of himself? Which brought him full circle. Assassinate Vaquero and to hell with the consequences. The coup would still go ahead and he'd be dead. So would his family. *His* family? He'd never thought of it that way before. And they *were* his family. The mother of his daughter. And his daughter. What to do? It was time to face up to the responsibilities and make a decision, one way or another . . .

'The convoy's coming into view,' Amaya said excitedly.

Marlette shifted uneasily. He was still sweating. A cold, clammy sweat. For the first time in his life he was experiencing real fear because he knew whatever he did in the next couple of minutes would be wrong. And he would have to live with that guilt. If he lived, he reminded himself. He put his eye to the sights and followed the convoy by slowly manoeuvring the rifle on the axis of the tripod. The two motorbikes overshot the hotel entrance as the first of the glistening black Lincoln Continentals swung up the ramp before turning sharply into the vacant car park. The second car followed it in; a cluster of sombre-suited men alighted from the vehicles and hurried across to the portico where the President's car had stopped. Marlette wet his dry lips and touched his finger lightly against the trigger as the fourth car pulled up behind it. The back doors of both cars were opened simultaneously, and for a moment the rifle wavered between the two cars. A woman got out from the back of the lead car. She was refined and elegant in an imported evening gown. Marlette assumed she was the President's wife. The President would emerge next.

His attention was suddenly directed to the other car. Vaquero emerged from the back and allowed one of the security team to lead him a couple of paces away from the door. There he paused and tilted his head slightly, almost as if he were anticipating the inevitability of the shot. Suddenly all the memories of that night five years ago came flooding back, and he reached up to tweak the sights fractionally until he had a clear view of Vaquero's head in the cross hairs. His finger tightened on the trigger. Just do it, he said to himself. A drop of sweat seeped out from under the bandanna, trickled down the side of his face and into the corner of his eye. He drew away sharply from the sights and quickly rubbed it away. It was then he noticed Amaya watching him, the suppressed Smith & Wesson now clutched tightly in his hand. It was as if he were anticipating trouble. Marlette slowly put his eye to the sights again as the President stepped out on to the portico. The President reached out a hand and touched Vaquero on the arm. He said something to him, and for a moment the two men were framed together in the cross hairs. The seconds were ticking by. He had to decide. For Nicole. For Michelle. For himself. He had to make the decision. The right decision.

It was then he finally knew what he had to do.

THIRTEEN

La Puerta del Diablo. The Devil's Door. Two towering boulders standing over thirteen hundred metres high, said once to have been a single rock formation, framing a breathtaking view of the rugged, verdant valley spread out below. The boulders are separated by a sharp drop into a deep, rocky gorge and this chasm is known as the 'door'.

Not that Nicole had seen much of the view, as it was already dark by the time they reached La Puerta del Diablo. There was a spacious parking area to cater for the tourist trade, but Chavez chose instead to conceal the car in an area of patchy undergrowth out of sight of the approach road. With twenty-five minutes still to go before the helicopter was due to arrive, Nicole decided to take a closer look at the gorge to help pass the time. Michelle insisted on going with her, not wanting to stay alone in the car with Chavez. With only the car's headlights to guide her, she'd made her way across the empty car park and stood silently between the two boulders, Michelle's small hand clutched tightly in hers. As she looked out over the vista, illuminated only by the sporadic flickering lights of the tiny settlements in the valley below, she found herself thinking back to what Rick had said about the gorge having once been a dumping ground for the bodies of those who'd dared to oppose the repressive rule of the gun. Men. Women. Children. It had made no difference. With hands tied behind their backs, they'd been dispatched by a single bullet to the back of the head and their bodies had been tossed like unwanted garbage into the gorge. But they weren't gone. Or forgotten. Was it her imagination, or could she sense a presence around her? Voices whispering in the light breeze as it brushed lightly across her sweating face, invisible fingers teasing her hair and gently caressing her moist skin. She felt humbled as she stood in her own private Arcadia, at one with the spirit, and it was only Michelle's hand tugging anxiously at her jeans which finally brought her out of her reverie. Only then did she realize that it had begun to rain. They hurried back to the car.

Fifteen minutes on and the rain was still drumming incessantly on the roof. Nobody spoke. Nicole was sitting in the back with Michelle, who was staring at the rain as it splashed abstract patterns across the windscreen. Nicole couldn't tell what was going through her daughter's mind, but she wasn't about to intrude on her silence. She'd explained to Michelle about the helicopter before they'd left the village. Michelle had been excited at the prospect of flying in a helicopter, especially when she'd learnt that Rick would be going with them. Michelle had never taken to anyone as quickly as she had to Rick. Normally she was very reserved with strangers, but Nicole knew it shouldn't have surprised her. An invisible bond between father and daughter. She'd tried not to think about Rick, but it hadn't been easy, stuck as they were in the car for much of the day. There wasn't much else to occupy the mind. Michelle's prolonged games of 'I-spy' usually exhausted her, but this time she'd been grateful for the distraction and had tried to draw out the games for as long as possible. Not only had it taken her mind off Rick, but it had also helped to relax Michelle, who'd always suffered from car sickness. There had been the inevitable pit-stops along the way, but in general Michelle's stomach had held up well.

Her eyes went to the hold-all at her feet which Chavez had picked up at a house in San Salvador earlier in the evening. At the time she'd told Michelle the hold-all belonged to Rick and that she was to leave it alone. It had seemed to do the trick. She'd only looked inside the hold-all once herself. It contained a battered biscuit tin which had been carefully packed with a block of plastic explosive and a detonator cap. The transmitter was in her pocket. The device was similar in design to those her father sold to the warring factions in Africa and, although it had been made up to resemble the real thing, it was actually quite harmless. The dummy transmitter had no internal components. It was part of the plan Rick and Chavez had devised the previous evening and, although she had her reservations, she also knew it was their one chance of coming out of this alive . . .

'*Helicóptero,*' Chavez announced, gesturing into the distance.

Nicole couldn't see anything through the rain-streaked windscreen, and it was Michelle who first drew her attention to the intermittent light flashing on the approaching helicopter's underbelly. Although Nicole could only make out the vague silhouette of the helicopter in the distance, she knew it was a Bell Huey by the distinctive chopping sound of its rotors. The two ex-Vietnam vets who'd flown regularly for her father had both sworn by the Huey because of its reliability. How many times had she sat harnessed in the open cabin doorway, the wind billowing through her hair, as the Huey flew low over the arid landscape, its menacing shadow scattering the magnificent herds of impalas and zebras in its wake? The rhythm of African skies. Those were good memories.

Nicole watched Chavez take a flare from the glove compartment before scrambling out of the car, where she lit it and tossed it on to the ground, suddenly illuminating the dark, forbidding cliffs directly ahead of them. Michelle hugged herself tightly against her mother as the sound of the helicopter's engine grew closer and she pointed excitedly at the Huey when it loomed out from behind one of the boulders. The helicopter hovered momentarily like some ferocious predator, waiting for the kill, then it slowly edged forward until it was clear of the rock. Then, as if dangling on an invisible web, it began slowly to descend towards the ground.

Nicole looked at her watch. The helicopter was seven minutes behind schedule. So where was Rick? He should have been here by now. He knew the deal — the helicopter wouldn't wait for him. She had to give him more time. Stall the pilot. She grabbed the hold-all and pushed open the back door. The deafening sound of the helicopter's engine burst into the car and, grimacing against the noise, she took Michelle's hand and ran across to the helicopter. The door was already open and she hooked her hands under Michelle's arms and lifted her carefully into the empty cabin. She caught sight of the helmeted pilot who was peering anxiously over his shoulder, his features obscured by the opaque visor over his face. He gestured for her to get in, then banged his two fists together to signal for them to fasten their seatbelts.

'Wait here for me, sweetheart,' Nicole said, sitting Michelle down on a bench which ran the length of the cabin wall.

'Where are you going, Mommy?' Michelle asked anxiously, grabbing her mother's arm.

'I'm going to wait for Rick,' Nicole replied, snapping the harness securely over her daughter's waist. 'Promise me you'll wait here.'

'What if the helicopter leaves without you?' Michelle asked fearfully.

'It won't, sweetheart,' Nicole said gently, and kissed Michelle on the forehead. 'I promise you it won't leave without me.' Michelle's eyes mirrored her uncertainty. 'Have I ever lied to you?' Michelle shook her head. 'Now promise me you'll stay here. Promise me, Michelle.'

'Cross my heart and hope to die,' Michelle said softly.

Nicole hugged her tightly, then jumped back out of the cabin and hurried round to the cockpit door. The pilot stabbed his finger angrily over his shoulder towards the cabin, but she shook her head and gestured for him to open the door. After a moment's hesitation he reluctantly unlocked the door and thrust it open. 'Rick Marlette's not here yet and we're not leaving without him,' she shouted above the noise of the engine.

'Like hell we're not,' he yelled back at her. 'You know the drill. I put down, pick up whoever's here, then get the hell out of here. I'm risking my neck every second I'm down here on the ground.'

'We wait,' she shouted, then opened the hold-all. Her hand hovered momentarily over the biscuit tin, but she knew the device was only to be used once they were airborne. Instead she plucked the videotape from the hold-all and held it up for the pilot to see. 'This is what Pruitt's really after. You go back empty-handed and you're going to have a lot of explaining to do, aren't you?'

The pilot glowered furiously at her. She was right. That's what made it so damn hard to swallow. His orders had been made very clear before he took off from the secret base in southern Guatemala earlier that evening. Retrieve the tape at all costs. He looked at his watch. 'Five minutes,' he barked, and held up five fingers. 'Then I'm leaving, with or without you.'

Nicole didn't reply as she backed away from the door, her body doubled over to avoid the whirring rotors above her. The approach road was obscured by one of the boulders, and she had to move away from the helicopter before it came into view. Chavez was standing in the centre of the clearing, a faded peaked cap now tugged over her head, an AK-47 clenched tightly in her hand. Nicole wiped her hand over her wet face, then brushed her matted hair back over her head. Where the hell was Rick? Had something happened at the hotel? She knew it was possible, especially

361

if he'd killed Vaquero. Yet she was still confident he could outsmart the likes of Dennison and Amaya. She looked at her watch. *Come on, Rick*, she urged him, her eyes riveted to the approach road. She knew the pilot wouldn't wait beyond the five minutes. She'd already pushed his patience to the limit. She also had to think of Michelle. The longer they remained on the ground, the more likely they were to be detected. She struggled to push any negative thoughts from her mind as she glanced back at the helicopter. She couldn't see Michelle from where she was standing. Just as well. At least she had the peace of mind of knowing Michelle would stay in the helicopter. Michelle would never disobey her. Her eyes went to the cockpit. The pilot tapped his watch impatiently and held up two fingers. Nicole checked her own watch again. She shuddered. Only two minutes left. *Come on, Rick. Come on . . .*

Chavez touched Nicole on the arm and shook her head. Nicole knew she had to face up to reality. Think of Michelle. Get out while you still can. She cast a last, despairing look towards the approach road. Still nothing. *Face it, Nicole, he's not coming*. Time to cut loose. Let it go. She hurried back towards the helicopter.

'*Carro!*' Chavez shouted. Nicole swung round, her gaze desperately following Chavez's pointing finger. '*Carro. Automóvil!*'

Headlights on the approach road. Nicole could barely conceal her excitement and, ignoring the pilot's protestations which were all but lost above the roar of the engine, she ran back to where Chavez was now crouched down on one knee, the AK-47 trained on the approaching vehicle. The Audi sped across the open ground and skidded to a halt ten metres in front of them. She couldn't see anything behind the glare of the headlights, and Chavez swung the Kalashnikov on the figure who leapt out from behind the wheel.

'Rick!' Nicole exclaimed in relief, then ran forward and

hugged him fiercely. 'I thought you weren't going to make it. Are you all right?'

'Yeah,' Marlette replied, casting an anxious glance over his shoulder. 'I know I've been followed. We've got to get the hell out of here.'

'I'm with you on that,' Nicole said. 'What happened at the hotel? Is Vaquero dead?'

'I'll tell you about that later,' he replied, looking across at the helicopter.

'Come on, the pilot won't wait any longer,' she urged.

'You go on, I'll catch you up,' Marlette told her. 'I've got to talk with Chavez.'

'The pilot won't wait, Rick,' she pleaded.

'He'll wait,' Marlette assured her, then turned to Chavez. 'I know Dennison saw me as I left the building. He can't be far behind.'

'Leave him to me,' Chavez said.

'If he's already called up reinforcements . . .'

'I can hold them off long enough for you to get away.' Chavez grabbed Marlette's arm as he was about to turn away. 'Vaquero?' Marlette just nodded. 'And Guillermo?'

'Dead,' Marlette shouted above the helicopter engine. 'I'm sorry.'

Chavez said nothing, but ran to the car and climbed inside. She started up the engine, swung the wheel violently and headed towards the approach road. Marlette was still crossing towards the helicopter when he caught sight of the headlights which had suddenly appeared on the approach road. The headlights were stationary. Whoever it was must have had a damn good reason for stopping there. A burst of gunfire suddenly shattered his thoughts. It was Chavez, firing from the driver's window as she bore down on the stationary vehicle.

'Rick, come on,' Nicole yelled from the cabin doorway. 'Come on.'

A blinding flash originated from behind the headlights,

and Chavez's car was ripped apart by a deafening explosion. Flaming debris was hurled up into the night sky. Marlette lost his footing and fell awkwardly as he tried to dodge the searing fragments of twisted metal as they rained down over the clearing. Nicole leapt out of the helicopter and ran to where he was still struggling to get to his feet.

'Get the hell out of here,' he screamed at her when she tried to help him up. 'That was a rocket-propelled missile. I'll try and stall them to give you time to get clear.'

'They'll kill you if you stay behind.'

'And they'll kill us all if I don't,' Marlette shouted back. 'The helicopter won't stand a chance once it's airborne. I've got to distract them. Now get out of here while you still can.' He looked round on hearing the sound of a car's engine and saw Dennison's white Mercedes parked close to the gorge, now in sight of the helicopter. It was obvious to him that Dennison was going to take out the helicopter even before it could lift off. 'Go, Nicole. Get out of here. Now!'

She turned and ran back to the helicopter, clambering awkwardly into the cabin. Marlette gestured to the pilot to lift off, then sprinted to where the Audi was parked. With time running out fast, he only had one option left to him now. He secured the safety belt across his chest and started the engine. Then, pressing his foot down on the pedal, he drove straight at the Mercedes.

Although he was still unsure of what exactly had happened at the hotel, Dennison had been in no doubt that the planned coup d'état had gone horribly wrong. But he knew he could limit the damage by destroying Kinnard's tape, the one incriminating piece of evidence which could still link him to the Military Council. They may have failed in their attempt to seize power, but he wasn't about to go down without a fight.

It had been his driver who'd first spotted the low-flying

helicopter in the distance. Dennison had subsequently monitored its progress with a pair of high-power night-vision binoculars which he always kept in the car. An unmarked Huey. And obviously heading for La Puerta del Diablo. That made sense. It was one of the few options open to Marlette on that particular stretch of road. It had to be Marlette's escape route.

That's when he'd first come up with the idea of using the surface-to-air missile system which was in the trunk. The portable 'Blowpipe' system had originally been destined for the soldiers on the roof of the hotel, to guard against any attempt by troops loyal to the President to try and storm the building from the air. But with the attempted coup d'état now in tatters, the missile systems hadn't been deployed. He'd ordered his driver to switch off the headlights on their approach to La Puerta del Diablo. That way they could lie in wait on the approach road for the helicopter to lift off. Although he doubted there would have been any artillery on the helicopter, it still made sense not to take any unnecessary risks. One surface-to-air missile to take out the helicopter. That had been the idea before Chavez had picked out the Mercedes in her headlights. Then she'd opened fire. Although the chassis was bullet-proof, Dennison knew he couldn't manoeuvre the Blow-pipe with bullets thudding into the bodywork around him. The confrontation had been inevitable. He'd reluctantly turned the Blowpipe on Chavez's car, knowing it would only waste valuable time when he came to reload the system again. After identifying the approaching target through the monocular sight, he'd released the safety catch and squeezed the trigger. The radio-controlled missile, which he'd guided on to the target by moving the thumb-controlled joystick on the aiming unit, had detonated on impact, disintegrating the car in a searing inferno. Ruiz dead. Chavez dead. Two more nails in the FMLN coffin. Perhaps it had been worth it after all . . .

The helicopter was out of sight now behind one of the boulders. When Dennison got back into the Mercedes he ordered his driver to take him to within visual range of the target. The driver accelerated the car across the clearing and pulled up close to the gorge. With the car now straddled lengthwise to the helicopter, it was exactly the protection Dennison needed from which to launch the second missile. He crouched down behind the car and quickly unclipped the empty missile canister before reaching on to the back seat for a fresh one. His eyes constantly flickered towards the helicopter as he expertly reassembled the system; although he couldn't see Marlette or Nicole, he heard Marlette shout something and saw Nicole run back to the helicopter and climb into the cabin. Then the helicopter began to rise slowly off the ground.

'Patrón!'

Dennison followed his driver's pointing finger and saw Marlette getting into the Audi. He realized then that Marlette was going to try and ram the Mercedes. Dennison glanced across at the helicopter. It was already lifting off the ground. Although the missile system had an effective range of three kilometres, he didn't want to risk losing the helicopter in the surrounding mountains. He had to bring it down while it was still in view.

'Kill him!' Dennison yelled, then raised the Blowpipe to his shoulder and trained the monocular sight on the helicopter. He had a lock-on. He released the safety catch and tightened his finger around the trigger . . .

Marlette saw the mini-Uzi in the split second before the driver fired. He'd ducked down low behind the steering wheel as the bullets thudded into the windscreen, showering him in a fine spray of splintered glass. He could feel the blood trickling down the back of his neck as he peered cautiously through the myriad cracks which now dissected the shattered windscreen like some monstrous glass web.

He was less than thirty metres away from the stationary Mercedes. But he couldn't see Dennison and that worried him. How close was Dennison to launching the second missile? The disturbing thought was still lingering in the back of his mind when the mini-Uzi reappeared at the driver's window. He ducked down again, expecting a second volley to be directed at the windscreen, but this time a fusillade of bullets raked across the radiator. A bullet punctured one of the front tyres and he fought desperately to regain control of the wheel as the Audi slewed sideways and skidded helplessly towards the Mercedes. He clamped his hands protectively over his head when he realized that collision was inevitable, and braced himself for the impact. The Audi slammed into the side of the Mercedes and the momentum whipped his body sideways. He cried out in pain as he was jerked back abruptly in his seat by the safety belt, which was still secured tightly across his chest. He was struggling to clear his groggy head when he noticed that the Audi was still moving sideways; he saw to his horror that the two vehicles had become locked together on impact. The Mercedes had been shunted forward by the sheer force of the collision, and was now swaying on the edge of the chasm. Marlette knew that if the Mercedes slid over the edge the Audi would almost certainly be dragged after it and, as he fumbled desperately for the buckle to release the safety belt, he knew it would only be a matter of seconds before the Mercedes toppled over into the chasm. The release clip was jammed. Suddenly the soft, macerated ground gave way under the weight of the Mercedes; Marlette was still struggling with the spring as the Audi was dragged ever closer to the chasm. The Mercedes tilted sharply to the side and there was a grinding of metal on metal as it ripped free of its anchor and plunged down the slope. But the separation had come too late for the Audi, which was now balanced precariously with only two wheels still on the ground. For a brief moment Marlette was caught in a fearful dilemma. If he continued to struggle with the safety belt the movement could be enough to tilt the car off the road, but if he remained motionless the car could still topple into the chasm. He had to take the risk to try and free himself.

The ground shuddered violently when the Mercedes exploded, and he felt the Audi jolt sharply as a piece of debris hammered into its undercarriage. It was enough to dislodge the Audi from its delicate axis, and he tugged frantically at the buckle as the car slid helplessly down the grassy slope. Suddenly the buckle came free but, as he was reaching for the door, he felt the car going over on to its side. He threw up his hands protectively as he was flung forward towards the windscreen.

Blackness engulfed him.

Dennison heard the second explosion as he was searching frantically for the missile system which he'd dropped in his haste to get clear of the doomed Mercedes. He couldn't see it anywhere, and he knew then that it had obviously been lost over the gorge. He looked up despairingly at the helicopter which was already banking away from La Puerta del Diablo, heading due north. He watched until it finally disappeared from view behind the nearest mountain, then moved to the edge of the clearing and stared despondently at the twisted remains of the Audi which was burning fiercely at the foot of the gorge. He gained little comfort from the thought that Marlette was dead because, even in death, Marlette had still won.

It was only then that he looked down at his leg. In his haste to jump clear he'd caught it on the back of the Mercedes and he could see the deep gash through the jagged tear in his trousers. The blood was streaming down his leg and soaking into his sock. Not that it hurt. The pain would come later. In more ways than one, he thought bitterly to himself. It was then he heard the sound of a car engine.

When he looked round he saw a pair of headlights on the approach road. The car pulled up in front of him. The engine was switched off but the headlights remained trained on him. When the driver's door opened a familiar, albeit surprising, figure got out.

'Jek?' Dennison said in amazement. Vaquero's right-hand man was the last person he'd expected to see. 'What are you doing here?'

Jek brushed the first few spots of rain off the front of his tuxedo, then stepped away from the car. 'You failed, Mr Dennison,' he said in his clipped voice.

'We all failed,' Dennison retorted.

'General Vaquero gave me instructions to cover for this eventuality.'

'What instructions?' Dennison demanded.

'To execute you,' Jek replied, then pulled a Heckler & Koch P7 automatic from the concealed shoulder-holster under his tuxedo.

Dennison raised his hands in terror. 'Wait. Listen to me, Jek. It's not over. I've still got a lot of money behind me. We can start again.'

'I've always prided myself on carrying out my orders, Mr Dennison.'

'Do you want money?' Dennison whined pitifully. 'Is that it? I can give you whatever you want. One million? Two million? Just name your price, Jek. Name it. It's yours. But please, don't kill me.'

Jek raised the automatic and shot Dennison through the heart. Dennison stumbled backwards, his hand clutched to his chest. He could feel the blood seeping through his fingers. His legs felt like lead. He couldn't move them any more. A second bullet slammed into his chest and he was already dead when he fell backwards into the mud. A trickle of blood seeped from the corner of his mouth; it was quickly washed away by the rain. Jek used his shoe to roll Dennison over on to his back, shooting him once more through the back of the head. He glanced up irritably at the firmament as he returned to the car, and was about to get back in when he noticed a streak of mud on the tip of his polished shoe. He removed a handkerchief from his breast pocket and carefully wiped the offending mark off his toecap. Then, pocketing the handkerchief again, he got back behind the wheel and started the engine.

Nicole was crouched motionless by the open cabin door, her hand looped through an overhanging strap, when the pilot gently banked the helicopter away from La Puerta del Diablo, heading due north-west. The horrific images were still vivid in her mind, playing out like some cleverly orchestrated cellular illusion. The Audi slewing out of control and crashing into the side of the Mercedes. The Mercedes tumbling down the gorge, dragging the Audi after it. Then, as the Audi had teetered precariously on the edge of the embankment, she'd seen Rick's shadowy silhouette behind the wheel as he'd tugged frantically – desperately – at the safety belt which was still strapped across his chest. In an iniquitous twist of fate, what should have protected him had ultimately cost him his life. She'd watched, transfixed, as the Audi had rolled down the embankment, save for a couple of seconds where it had disappeared from sight behind one of the towering boulders. Tumbling, tumbling, as it gained momentum before exploding in a searing fireball at the foot of the gorge.

It was then that the tears had come. Slowly trickling from the corners of her eyes, only to be lost on the contours of her cheeks in the fine droplets of rain teasing lightly across her face.

'Don't cry, Mommy. Please don't cry.'

The tiny voice was almost lost in the roar of the helicopter's engine and the rhythmic whirring of the overhead rotors. But she heard it. Frail and tearful. Quickly she turned to where Michelle was sitting, sobbing uncontrollably to herself, her arms clasped tightly across her chest, her cheeks streaked with tears. Nicole reached out her free hand and slammed the cabin door shut, as if to cut herself off from what had happened. Michelle needed her now. She unwound her hand from the overhead strap and knelt down in front of Michelle, who wrapped her arms fiercely around her mother's neck.

'I'm scared, Mommy,' the tiny voice whimpered tearfully.

'I'm here, sweetheart,' Nicole assured her, pulling Michelle closer to her. 'You don't need to be scared any more.'

'I heard all those loud bangs outside.'

'They can't hurt you,' Nicole said, drawing away from Michelle and tracing her finger lightly over her daughter's wet cheeks. 'Nothing will ever hurt you when I'm here. You know I'd never let anything happen to you.'

'Where's Rick?' Michelle asked between sobs. 'You said he was coming with us.'

'He had to stay behind.'

'You're crying because you like him very much, aren't you, Mommy?'

'I guess I am,' Nicole admitted with a sheepish chuckle, wiping her hand across her cheeks.

'I like him too. When will he be coming to see us in Chicago?'

'I don't know, sweetheart,' Nicole replied, sniffing back the tears.

'I hope he comes real soon because then you won't be sad any more,' Michelle said softly.

Nicole smiled gently, running her fingers lightly through Michelle's hair. She was about to get off her haunches and sit on the bench beside her when she noticed the hold-all on the cabin floor. She'd completely forgotten about the dummy bomb. Rick was to have dealt with that, had he been there. Now it was up to her. What if the pilot called her bluff? She knew Rick would have had that maniacal edge to convince the pilot he was just desperate enough to blow up the helicopter if his demands weren't met. Now it was up to her to do the same. If she failed, they would almost certainly be killed on Pruitt's orders. It didn't matter about herself. But she would never let anything happen to Michelle.

Quickly she wiped her cheeks and grabbed the hold-all. 'Do you want to ride up front with the pilot?'

Michelle nodded eagerly through the tears, but Nicole swiftly prevented her from unbuckling her safety belt. 'I've got to clear it with him first. It's best if I talk to him alone. If he agrees, we'll go and sit up front. OK?' Michelle nodded. Nicole touched her affectionately on the cheek, then made her way to the cockpit. She reached over the back of the passenger seat and placed the hold-all beside the pilot.

'What the hell do you want?' he snapped. 'Go back and sit with your kid. I'll let you know when we're about to land.'

You arrogant son-of-a-bitch, Nicole thought angrily to herself. *Keep it up. It can only work in my favour.* 'And just exactly where are we supposed to be landing?' she demanded.

'Guatemala,' came the sharp riposte.

'Wrong,' Nicole said, taking a piece of paper from her pocket and extending it towards him. 'These are your new coordinates.'

'What is this, some kind of fucking joke?' he snarled, pushing the paper out of the way. 'Go and sit down.' He ignored Nicole as she unzipped the hold-all and lifted the lid off the biscuit tin. She tugged sharply on his sleeve to get his attention, then gestured to the tin.

'Jesus Christ,' the pilot hissed, drawing back in horror from the hold-all as if it were about to attack him. 'Are you crazy? That's a fucking bomb.'

'And I've got the remote control here to detonate it,' Nicole said, patting the pocket of her jacket. She noticed him glance towards the box again. Don't give him any ideas, she reminded herself, and she replaced the lid. 'I should warn you it's been booby-trapped, in case you were thinking about trying to disarm it by pulling out the wires. Pull them out in the wrong sequence and it'll go off.'

The pilot swallowed nervously, then removed his Dolphins peaked cap and wiped the sweat from his forehead. 'Look, lady, I'm just a flyer, that's all. My orders were to take you to an airbase in Guatemala.'

'Not any more.' Nicole held out the sheet of paper again. This time the pilot took it from her. 'Those are your new coordinates. It's a private airstrip in Honduras. A flight plan's already been cleared with the Honduran air traffic control. All you have to do is get us there.'

'Honduras?' the pilot shot back sharply. 'You're fucking crazy. I'm not going to Honduras.'

Nicole took the transmitter from her pocket, flicked back the protective cap, then caressed her thumb lightly over the red detonator button. 'Do you want to call my bluff?' she said menacingly. 'Well, do you?'

'For Christ's sake, take it easy with that thing,' he pleaded, his eyes flickering between the detonator and the instrument panel in front of him. 'If we hit any turbulence now you'll blow us all to hell.'

The plan was working. She could sense his fear. Keep on the offensive. Let him sweat. Force him to compromise. 'I'll put it away just as soon as we've changed course for Honduras.'

'You press that button and you'd kill your own kid. I don't believe you'd do it,' the pilot snapped, but there was little bravado left in his voice.

'In case you didn't know, the coup failed. And that means Pruitt's going to be real pissed off. Part of his twisted deal was that he'd have my daughter and me killed if Rick didn't go along with his little scheme. So you see, I've got nothing to lose. And neither has Michelle. I'd rather she died here with me now than let that bastard, Pruitt, get his hands on her.' Her savage outburst had even surprised her. She hadn't needed to sound convincing because her anger was now genuine. Straight from the heart. She knew she could make this guy do anything. The act was over.

'You are fucking crazy,' the pilot said, but there was no more fight left in his voice. She knew she'd finally broken his resolve. He slowly unfolded the paper and read the new coordinates. 'OK, I'll do as you say. I'm setting a new course for Honduras. Just put that thing away before we have an accident none of us will live to regret.'

She grabbed the hold-all off the seat, then stood directly behind him so that he couldn't see what she was doing. She slid the dummy transmitter back into her pocket. When she leaned over the passenger seat again she kept her hand in her pocket. 'And in case you might still be thinking about going to Guatemala, hoping I wouldn't know the difference, I've been told to look out for several landmarks on our approach to the airfield. So if I don't see them before we land, I'll blow us all to hell. So I'd think long and hard about it if I were you, before you try and be a hero.'

'I'm no fucking hero, lady. Like I said, I'm just a flyer. I've got a wife and three kids back in Miami. Right now my only concern is to see them again.'

'Do you swear like this in front of them as well?'

'What?' he said in bewilderment.

Nicole gave Michelle a thumbs-up sign, and beckoned her towards the cockpit. 'It's just that, as I'll need to keep an eye on you from now on, my daughter and I will be sitting up front for the rest of the journey. Your swearing doesn't bother me, but I'd prefer you to watch your language in front of her.'

'Shit,' the pilot muttered, rubbing his thumb and fore-finger over the bridge of his nose.

'And one other thing. She doesn't know anything about the bomb. Let's keep it that way, shall we?'

'Whatever you say, lady,' the pilot replied with a resigned sigh. 'Whatever you say.'

FOURTEEN

It was the perfect location for a safe house. Situated on top of a steep hill, and hidden from view by a dense forest of bristling pine trees, the house had only one approach road – a bumpy, potholed dirt road – which was virtually impossible to negotiate unless with a sturdy four-wheel-drive vehicle and a very reliable suspension system. For this reason air transportation had become the favoured means of travelling to and from the house; thus, soon after acquiring the property, the CIA had cleared an area of forest and built a helipad.

The rotors whipped up the scattered pine-cones from the helipad as the helicopter slowly descended towards the yellow circle in the centre of the concrete structure. A man, armed with a sub-machine gun, hurried to the helicopter when the skids touched down on the helipad, and pulled open the passenger door. A lone figure got out, an attaché case in one hand, the other hand clamped over his white hair. The two men bent double as they crossed to the steps which led to a tiled patio at the front of the house. The man who'd disembarked from the helicopter descended the stairs. The front door was opened before he reached the patio.

'Morning, sir,' a bespectacled man said as he gestured the man into the house, closing the door again quickly behind him.

'Morning, McCrain,' came the gruff reply as the man smoothed down his hair. 'Damn things make such a noise. I can never get used to them.'

McCrain smiled politely, then gestured down the hall. 'This way, sir,' he said, leading the way to the kitchen.

The white-haired man paused in the doorway and looked at the figure seated at the table tucking into a plate of bacon, eggs and sausages. 'For a corpse, you've certainly got a healthy appetite.'

Richard Marlette looked up slowly from his food. He was unshaven and there were several bruises on his face; the most noticeable a dark, discoloured welt under his left eye. A jagged cut ran from the bridge of his nose down to his upper lip. 'Hail to the Chief,' he said sarcastically, and sat back in his chair.

'So you know who I am?'

'Warren van Horn, the new Director at Langley,' Marlette replied. 'I thought you handled yourself well on "Face the Nation" last month. It can't be easy trying to convince an already sceptical American public that the CIA are actually the good guys, especially when you've got the likes of Alex Pruitt working for you.'

'Alex Pruitt no longer works for the CIA,' van Horn said tersely, then crossed to the table and sat down. He indicated the plate in front of Marlette. 'Please, don't let me stop you.'

Marlette sat forward, his elbows resting on the table. 'I think it's time for some answers, don't you?'

Van Horn nodded to McCrain. 'I'll call if I need you.' He waited until McCrain had left the room and closed the door behind him before continuing. 'What has McCrain told you?'

'Only what he's been authorized to tell me,' Marlette said disdainfully. 'That the coup d'état failed and that all the members of the "Military Council" have since been arrested and charged with treason. He also told me Dennison's dead. Only I didn't kill him.'

'I know that,' van Horn said. 'Do you know where you are?'

'A CIA safe house in Illinois, about forty kilometres east of Chicago. I've been here for the past two days. I assume McCrain rang you when I regained consciousness last night?'

'Yes, he did.' Van Horn got to his feet and poured himself a coffee from the percolator. 'I assume you also know Ms Auger and her daughter are now safely back in Chicago?'

'It's the first thing I asked when I came round. McCrain said they would be under a constant twenty-four-hour guard until Pruitt's contract had been lifted.'

'It was lifted after Pruitt was arrested,' van Horn assured him as he retook his seat. 'As it turns out, the contract was to have been carried out by the same man who killed your friend, Brad Casey.' He waited for a reaction. There wasn't one. 'You don't seem surprised. Didn't you think Jayson was behind the hit on Casey?'

'I did at first, but then I realized it couldn't have been Jayson. Which left Pruitt. Who else could it have been?'

'Do you know why Pruitt had Casey murdered?'

'I can guess. He thought I might not want to go back to El Salvador, even for the kind of money he was offering, so he had Brad killed and made it look as if Jayson was responsible. He knew if I wanted to avenge Brad's death, I'd have to go back there to confront Jayson. Am I right?' Van Horn just nodded. 'I realize now I should have seen through it at the time. Whatever else you want to say about Jayson, he was a professional. And that meant he wouldn't have said anything at the scene of the crime, not with that distinctive Cockney accent of his. It would have been a dead giveaway. But I guess it was the only way Pruitt could link Jayson to the murder. And I fell for it.' Marlette pushed his plate away from him. 'What I still don't understand is what Pruitt had to gain by backing the coup.'

'He was motivated purely by the promise of financial gain. As you already know, Amaya was Pruitt's mole in the

Military Council. And, according to what Amaya's already told the Salvadorean authorities since his arrest, he was to have been given the powerful Defence portfolio in the new administration. One of his jobs would have been to strengthen the military, which has been considerably weakened since the end of the civil war. Pruitt had close links with several of the leading European weapons manufacturers, and he'd have seen to it that they won the contracts to re-arm the Salvadorean militia. These would have amounted to multi-million-dollar deals, had they come off, and Pruitt would have been in line to receive a substantial commission from each of the manufacturers for services rendered. Where do you think he got the money from to pay you? What's two hundred thousand dollars against a possible thirty or forty million? It's worth it for these companies to take the risk, especially as the money's already been written off as a bad debt. Weapons are still big business, Marlette. Very big business.' Van Horn took a sip of coffee. 'I'm still intrigued by your actions at the hotel though. As far as I could see, you only had two options open to you. Kill the President, and walk away with a hundred grand. Or kill Vaquero and prevent the coup from taking place. Yet instead you turned the gun on Amaya. Why?'

Marlette thought for a moment before answering. 'I only had one bullet in the chamber. I had to make it count. If I took out the President, I'd plunge the country back into civil war. If I hit Vaquero, Amaya would have killed me and Pruitt would have put a contract out on Nicole and Michelle. I had both Vaquero and the President in my sights when I suddenly remembered Amaya saying that, even if I were to kill Vaquero, he would have taken charge of the coup himself. After killing me. That's why I turned the rifle on him. Survival. Common sense. Hell, call it what you want. It just seemed the most logical thing to do at the time. He didn't even have time to react. Unfortunately

I only winged him. I slugged him to keep him quiet and handcuffed him to the radiator before making my escape.'

'And you think you actually thwarted the coup?' van Horn asked, peering at Marlette over the rim of his cup.

'All I know is there wasn't a coup. I guess I must have done something right.'

'You did,' van Horn assured him with a contented smile. 'You sent Pruitt a tape detailing the two meetings you had with him at your apartment.'

'How do you know about the tape?' Marlette demanded.

Van Horn moved to the window where he gazed out over the tree-lined horizon. 'Alex Pruitt has been the subject of an internal investigation at Langley.'

'So Ruiz told me. Your man, I believe?'

'Yes. I've been his handler ever since he was first recruited at Notre Dame. It's a pity about what happened to him. He was a useful informer.' Van Horn gave a quick shrug to dismiss the subject. 'For the last month Pruitt's been shadowed and all his mail has been intercepted and read before it reached him. That's how I first found out about the tape. It certainly made interesting listening. Not that he ever received it though. We couldn't risk frightening him off. Not at that delicate stage of the investigation.'

'So you knew I was going to be at the hotel that night?' Marlette said suspiciously.

'Of course I knew,' van Horn replied. 'That's why I instigated my own plan to counter anything which may have happened as a result of your little escapade. We have several high-ranking National Guard officers working for us and, by collaborating with them, I was able to neutralize the coup without Pruitt knowing. The soldiers on the hotel roof were supposed to have been élite troops loyal to Vaquero, only they were isolated before they reached the hotel. The soldiers who took their place were loyal to the President. And wherever Vaquero had troops waiting to move into action on his command, we'd already taken measures to counter them. Jamming radio signals, confining certain units to barracks at the last possible moment so as not to alert Vaquero or any of his conspirators, and replacing them with troops loyal to the President. So you see, Marlette, it really didn't matter what you did. It was already out of your hands.'

'If the President knew that a coup was imminent, why didn't he act sooner and have the conspirators arrested?' Marlette asked. 'And why show up at the hotel, knowing there was a chance he might be assassinated? It doesn't make any sense.'

'Who said the President knew about the coup?' van Horn replied, turning away from the window. 'There would have been the inevitable rumours of a coup, but then there always are in countries like El Salvador. That's why he had a head of security to investigate the rumours. Of course, Amaya just passed them off as another false alarm and, as the President had no reason to doubt him, he naturally took no action.'

'You actually *wanted* me to kill the President, didn't you?'

'It would have been the final nail in Pruitt's coffin,' van Horn agreed. 'But as it is, we've already got more than enough evidence to bury him.'

'And this is the new face of the CIA?' Marlette said in disgust. 'You'd have stood by while a foreign leader was assassinated just to tie up a few loose ends in your case against Pruitt?'

'That's rich coming from you, Marlette,' van Horn retorted indignantly. 'You were prepared to assassinate the President for a hundred thousand dollars. It's only the principle that's the difference here.'

'Except I wasn't the one preaching about the declining morals of our country, or about a new era of openness at Langley on "Face the Nation" last month,' Marlette countered contemptuously.

'And what do you think this is all about?' van Horn thundered, banging his fist down angrily on the windowsill. The door opened and McCrain peered anxiously into the room. Van Horn dismissed him with a curt flick of his hand, then crossed to the table and looked down at Marlette. 'The Central Intelligence Agency has taken some appalling criticism over the years, which has led the American people to see Langley as little more than a corrupt, secretive organization which seems to regard itself as above the law. When I took over as Director I vowed publicly to weed out the corruption, and to make the organization more answerable to the public. And that's exactly what I intend to do. Starting at the top. Alex Pruitt is going to stand trial and he's going to go to jail. That I can promise you now.'

'And you'd have been prepared to topple a foreign government just to achieve that end?'

'I don't give a damn about the internal politics of some ineffective Third World country,' van Horn snorted contemptuously. 'My only concern is for the future of this country. The American people are rightly fed up with a succession of lacklustre governments who've promised so much at the hustings then gone back on their word once they got into power. And the Central Intelligence Agency is an integral part of every government. It's time to stand up and be counted. I don't care how unpopular I become with my colleagues: heads are going to roll.'

'It'll certainly help to boost your ratings when you do decide to run for the White House,' Marlette said. 'I assume that's what this is really all about?'

'Who knows, perhaps one day,' van Horn replied with a knowing smile.

'And I suppose I'm going to be expected to bolster your credibility further by testifying against Pruitt when he does go on trial?'

'I hardly think that's going to be possible, do you?' van

Horn said, retaking his seat. 'What's that saying? Dead men don't tell tales?'

'And just what the hell's that supposed to mean?'

Van Horn stared at Marlette. 'You really don't know, do you?'

'What are you talking about?' Marlette demanded.

'You're dead,' van Horn replied matter-of-factly. 'Who do you think found you after you'd been thrown clear of the car at the Devil's Door? Who do you think smuggled you across the border into Honduras, then flew you back here to the States?' He could see the confusion on Marlette's face. 'My people did, that's who. They were at the Devil's Door. They saw everything that happened there. They got you away before the Salvadorean military arrived on the scene. What do you think would have happened to you if the Salvadoreans had found you? You certainly wouldn't be here, that's for sure. You'd be languishing in some prison cell awaiting trial after having a confession beaten out of you.'

'Your people were at La Puerta del Diablo all the time and they didn't even lift a finger –'

'Be realistic, for God's sake,' van Horn cut in sharply. 'What could they do? What if one of them had been killed? A dead Langley spook found in El Salvador! Can you imagine what the world's press would have made of that, especially on the night of an attempted coup? They were only there as observers. And it's just as well they were there, for your sake.'

'Who told them about La Puerta del Diablo?' Marlette asked.

'You did, on the tape you sent to Pruitt. Dates, times, locations. It was certainly very thorough.' Van Horn sat forward, his hands clasped on the table. 'I've already been in touch with a senior politician in El Salvador who, shall we say, owes me a few favours. He's had a story put out that the body of Dennison's driver which was recovered from the wreckage was, in fact, you. The body was so badly burnt it could only have been identified by dental records. Your death certificate's already been signed. So now you're officially dead.'

'And what if I don't want to be "dead"?' Marlette shot back angrily.

'We could hardly take credit for thwarting the coup, so you were posthumously accredited with it. It's made you something of a hero over there. Of course, not everybody was pleased with the outcome, especially several of the wealthy coffee barons who were said to have been the money behind the coup. So if they were ever to get wind that you were still alive, you can be sure there would be several lucrative contracts put out on your life. Of course, if you want to risk it that's entirely up to you.'

Marlette's mind was still reeling as he struggled to take everything in – but what really pissed him off was that he knew van Horn was right. If he were ever to show his face around any of his old haunts again, word would quickly filter back to the 'oligarchy' that he was still alive. Lucrative contracts? That was an understatement. There wouldn't be a shortage of offers for that kind of money. Professionals and amateurs alike would be queuing up to take shots at him. He'd be hounded relentlessly for the rest of his life – and he had a feeling it would be a very short life indeed anyway. Richard Marlette was better off 'dead'. At least it gave him a chance for the future. But that still didn't explain why van Horn's men had gone to all the trouble and the personal risk of smuggling him out of the country then flying him back to the States. They could just have shot him and nobody would have been any the wiser. What did van Horn have to gain by keeping him alive? Unless . . .

'Now I see what this is all about,' Marlette hissed angrily. 'You give me a new identity, relocate me wherever you need me, and I end up working as some shadowy assassin for Langley.'

'You'd be relocated in a country of your own choice outside the United States, guaranteed a reputable job as a cover, and any work you did for me would be well rewarded. In cash, of course.'

'Fuck you,' Marlette snarled, kicking back the chair as he jumped to his feet. The door swung open and McCrain burst into the room. 'Get out!' Marlette yelled at him.

'It's OK,' van Horn assured McCrain, and gestured towards the door with a nod of his head.

Marlette waited until McCrain had left and closed the door behind him before speaking. 'You hypocritical son-of-a-bitch. You've just finished telling me that you're cleansing the CIA of corruption, but at the same time you're quite prepared to use me for your own dirty work. When it comes down to it, there's really no difference between you and Pruitt, is there?'

'On the contrary,' van Horn replied. 'Pruitt was motivated by financial greed. My only motivation is for the good of my country. I'd say there was a substantial difference.'

'Yeah, you can always buy off greed. But patriotism's like religion. It has no price. And that's what makes them both so dangerous.'

'I wouldn't expect you to understand; your only loyalty was to whoever offered you more money for your services.'

Marlette picked up the chair and placed it back on its feet. 'I'm through with killing, van Horn.'

'It's all you know, Marlette,' van Horn replied. 'And you're damn good at it as well. You're a specialist in your field. I need that kind of expertise on my team.'

'And I told you, I'm through with killing.'

'I don't see you have much choice in the matter, do you?' van Horn said with a contented smile. 'You're officially dead now. You don't actually exist any more. You don't even have any documentation to prove who you are. Frankly, we're all you've got. I realize, of course, that you still have the money Pruitt gave to you as an advance on the deal. That could certainly buy you a new identity and a ticket out of here. But I'd think twice about that. I really would. I'd hate anything to happen to Nicole Auger and her little girl.'

'You so much as touch them . . .' Marlette snarled, levelling a finger at van Horn.

'Actually, I'd prefer them to go with you,' van Horn said. 'It would provide you with a better cover. Why else do you think you were brought to this safe house? It's only a short distance by helicopter to O'Hare Airport. We could easily arrange for them to be "killed" in an auto accident. Their death certificates could be signed the same day, so the three of you would be officially dead. That way you'd be able to make a new start. You go along with this deal, Marlette, and I'll arrange for you both to get new passports, all the necessary travel documents to whatever country you choose, as well as the balance of the money owing to you. It is your money, after all. So what do you say?' Marlette said nothing. 'I can understand you not wanting to involve Nicole Auger or her daughter, but if they were to go with you, they needn't ever know you were working for us. As I said, you'd have a legitimate job. We could easily arrange to get Ms Auger a job as well.'

'And just what exactly would I be doing for you?'

'The occasional assassination, that's all. And you'd be paid handsomely for it, that I can promise you. You certainly wouldn't be running errands for us or anything menial like that. You think it over and let McCrain know your decision in the next few days. He'll be staying on here as your liaison officer. And should you decide you want to see Ms Auger again, let McCrain know and he'll arrange for the helicopter to pick you up to take you through to Chicago. Well, if you'll excuse me, I've got a plane to catch to take me back to Washington.' Van Horn got to his feet. 'We won't be meeting again. All communications will go through McCrain from now on. In the meantime, please enjoy our hospitality. I'm sure you'll find the house and its facilities most relaxing.'

Marlette ignored van Horn's extended hand. 'Hopefully one day the CIA will put a contract on you – for the good of the country,' he said grimly.

Van Horn smiled, then left the room. Marlette poured himself another coffee and watched as van Horn crossed the helipad and climbed into the helicopter. He turned away from the window when the pilot started up the engine and sat down at the table. His emotions were tearing him apart as he struggled with his burdened conscience. What was he to do about Nicole and Michelle? He desperately wanted to be reunited with them again – his family – but he knew he just wasn't being realistic. His heart was ruling his head. How could he possibly expect Nicole to leave behind everything she'd made for herself in Chicago – the apartment, the restaurant, her friends – to start a new life with him in some foreign land? A new life with no guarantees. It wouldn't be fair to put her in that kind of predicament. Yet at the same time he knew there was always the chance that she would go with him. Could he live with himself if he didn't at least offer her that chance?

He was just being damn selfish and he knew it. He had to make a clean break of it. That meant never seeing her again. Never seeing Michelle again. All his instincts told him that was what he had to do. If you love her, let her go. He knew it made sense. It was the only way. Yet still the doubt lingered in his mind . . .

He flung the mug against the wall. His anguished howl was drowned out by the sound of the helicopter as it lifted off the helipad.

'I'll lock up tonight.'

'Don't be silly, Nicole, you go on home. I'll do it.'

'I said I'll lock up!' Nicole snapped, then gave her partner an apologetic smile. 'I'm sorry, Carole, it's just that I've been cooped up in the apartment ever since I got back to Chicago. This is my first night back at the restaurant. I need to throw myself back into the work again. It all helps me to forget . . .'

'Are you OK?' Carole asked when Nicole paused mid-sentence.

'Sure,' Nicole said, putting a reassuring hand lightly on Carole's arm. 'Don't worry, I'm not about to break down into floods of tears. I've cried enough for Rick. It's time for me to get on with my life.'

'You really loved him, didn't you?'

'I don't think I ever stopped loving him.'

'Tell me something I don't know,' Carole said with a gentle smile.

'My father used to say you only ever fall in love once in your life. Perhaps he was right.'

'In your case, I know he was,' Carole said, holding up the restaurant keys. 'Are you sure you want to lock up?'

'Sure I'm sure,' Nicole said, plucking the keys deftly from Carole's hand. 'You've got a very patient and loving husband waiting for you at home, and I know he'd like to see a bit more of you these days. Now go on, get out of here. I'll see you tomorrow.'

'It's already tomorrow,' Carole said, tapping her watch.

'Go home,' Nicole said with a mock-reproachful look.

'See you in the morning,' Carole said. She opened the front door and disappeared out into the cold Chicago night.

Nicole locked the door behind her. She took a reading from the computerized till, removed the cash-drawer, then switched off the restaurant and bar lights before making her way up the stairs and along the corridor to her office. She placed the cash-drawer on her desk, lit herself a cigarette and switched on the compact-disc player on the shelf behind her. A selection of CDs were layered neatly in a rack beside the system. It was an odd mixture of music:

classical and heavy metal. Bartók, Debussy and Tchaikovsky interspersed with Black Sabbath, Iron Maiden and Led Zeppelin. She smiled to herself as she touched several of the heavy metal discs, each with its own private memory. Her finger finally settled on one disc: Judas Priest's *Defenders of the Faith*. Rick's favourite album by his favourite band. Judas Priest had been the first live band he'd taken her to see in New York. She could still picture him in his black leather jacket and his skin-tight jeans, his hair plastered to his sweating face, lost in the electrifying ambience of the mind-numbing music. That was one gig she'd never forget. Taking the disc from the case, she placed it carefully on the tray and programmed the remote control to play the track she'd always associated with him: 'Rock Hard, Ride Free'.

She started to count out the float, but quickly found that her mind was wandering as the music invaded her thoughts. She reached for the remote control to switch off the music but realized she couldn't do it, at least not that particular track. She replaced the remote control on the desk and sat back in her chair, her eyes closed, a sad smile on her lips.

'You're playing my song. You must have been expecting me.'

Nicole's body froze and she felt her heart pounding frantically against her chest. She was so sure the voice had been in her head that, like some cherished dream, she didn't want to open her eyes for fear of losing it altogether. Reluctantly, almost fearfully, she slowly opened her eyes and stared in disbelief at the figure standing in the doorway.

'Hi,' Marlette said with a lopsided grin. 'I'd have called, but you know how it is.'

Suddenly Nicole was out of her chair and running towards him. She threw her arms around his neck, sniffing back her unashamed tears of joy as she kissed him, quickly drawing back from him when he grunted in pain as her elbow caught him painfully in the ribs.

'I cracked a couple of ribs,' he said in reply to her worried frown, gingerly touching the bandages secured tightly around his chest.

'And your face,' she said, wincing as she indicated the laceration across his nose.

'A few cuts, a few bruises and a couple of cracked ribs. Hell, I'll settle for that, considering I should be dead right now.'

'How did you get out of the car?'

'I don't know. All I remember is managing to unclip the seatbelt as the car went over on its roof. Then nothing. The doctor who patched me up said that judging by the bruising on my back, I was probably thrown backwards through the windscreen when I was already unconscious. Whatever happened, I'm incredibly lucky to still be alive.' He sat down on the leather sofa opposite her desk. 'How's Michelle?'

'It's been pretty rough on her but I think she's beginning to get over the worst of it now. She couldn't sleep by herself for the first couple of days after we got back to the apartment. I thought about taking her to a child psychologist but my own doctor said she'd get over it by herself in the next few weeks. The main thing is that she never actually saw anything. That would only have made it so much worse. My doctor gave me some sedatives for her. They've been working a treat. She sleeps right through the night now. That's why I decided to come back to work again.' Nicole smiled gently. 'I told her you'd had to stay behind when we left El Salvador. Now she's always asking after you. If anything, she seems to talk more about you than she does about Bob. You've got yourself a big fan there, Rick. A real big fan.'

'Yeah,' he muttered, knowing there was every chance he'd never even see her again. But it was something he'd already geared himself up to accept if Nicole did decide to stay on in Chicago. Well, as geared up as he could be under the circumstances . . .

'Who found you?' Nicole asked. 'And how did you get back to the States? Tell me everything, Rick. Everything.'

Marlette moved to the desk and used the remote control to switch off the CD player. This was the part he'd been dreading. What to tell her. What not to tell her. When he turned back to her his face was grim. 'My being alive has a price, Nicole. A very heavy price.'

'What do you mean?' she asked, sitting forward, her eyes now riveted on his face. 'Rick, what is it?'

'Officially, Richard Marlette's dead,' he said, clasping his hands around the edges of the desk on either side of him. 'I can never go back to New York. In fact, I'm going to have to leave the country. And the sooner I leave, the safer it'll be for me.'

Nicole remained silent, waiting for him to continue in his own time. She could see the anguish on his face and, although she desperately wanted to go to him, to be with him, she stayed seated on the sofa, her hands clenched tightly together.

He went on to explain the situation to her, but decided against mentioning the threat van Horn had made against her and Michelle if he tried to double-cross Langley. She didn't need to know about that, seeing that he'd already decided to go along with van Horn's proposal. It wasn't as if he'd ever really had much choice in the matter. When he finished he took a passport from his pocket and handed it to her. 'That's who I am now.'

'Frank Leonard,' she said, reading the name on the passport. Opening the book, she looked at the photograph. There were no marks on his face. 'When was this taken?'

'A couple of days back,' he replied. 'The guy who took the photo concealed the cut and the bruises with a bit of foundation and powder. He did a good job.'

'Where is this safe house?' she asked, handing the passport back to him.

'I don't know its exact location, other than that it's somewhere here in Illinois.' He smiled to himself. 'It's got everything though. Cable TV, a gymnasium, a jacuzzi, and the food there's something else. They've got this Cuban woman who's the housekeeper-cum-cook. She lives on the property. Her husband was killed by Castro's secret police. Understandably she's radical in her views about her country, but I get on fine with her, especially as I can talk to her in her own language. Hell, they've even got a pool table there. I've been shooting pool most of the time with the guards. And then there's McCrain. He's my liaison officer.'

'John McCrain. Curly hair. Glasses. Talks a lot.'

'Yeah, that's McCrain. How do you know him?' Marlette asked in surprise.

'He was at the airport to meet us when we flew in from Honduras. He arranged for us to have round-the-clock protection until the CIA were satisfied Pruitt's contract had been lifted. He must have been to the apartment half a dozen times, but he never mentioned anything about you. But then I guess that's understandable, given the circumstances.'

'Van Horn thought it best that I decide for myself whether I wanted you to know that I was still alive. I've hardly slept these last few days trying to make up my mind whether to come here or not. I still don't know whether I've made the right decision.'

'You did, and I think you know that otherwise you wouldn't have come,' Nicole said. She got to her feet, crossed to where he was standing, and took his hands in hers. Her mouth was dry and it took her some time to find her voice. 'Rick, about what you said just now. You know, about Michelle and me going away with you when you leave . . .'

'You don't have to say it, Nicole,' he said. 'I realize now I should never have mentioned it. I was just being selfish.'

'No, you weren't,' she said, squeezing his hands. 'If this was six years ago in New York, I'd have jumped at the chance to go with you. But things have changed since then. I've got responsibilities here. The restaurant. The apartment. And most importantly, I've got to think of what's best for Michelle. It would mean giving up everything here, and just when I finally seemed to have got my life together. So if anyone's being selfish around here, it's me.' She paused as her simmering emotions threatened to surface. 'It goes deeper than that though. Remember what I said when I told you why I'd walked out on you after I discovered I was pregnant? I didn't want my child growing up knowing that its father was a mercenary. I know you wanted to put that life behind you when you got back from El Salvador, but it hasn't turned out that way, has it? I know these are circumstances beyond your control, and that the CIA have got you over a barrel, but the fact still remains you'd be working as some kind of freelance assassin for them. I know that Michelle need never have known you were working for Langley, but I could never have reconciled myself with that kind of deceit, and that would only have led to friction between us. What if the relationship broke down? Where could Michelle and I have gone after that? We certainly couldn't come back here, not if we were already supposed to be dead. We'd be stuck in no man's land, and Michelle would be the one to suffer most. I would never do that to her, Rick.'

'She's a lucky kid to have a mother like you,' Marlette said.

'Her father's not that bad either.'

'Yeah, maybe,' he replied with a shrug. 'I guess I'd better be going. McCrain's parked out in the alley. I told him I wouldn't be long, so if I don't show my face soon he'll be getting ideas that I've tried to make a run for it.'

'It's an idea at that,' Nicole said thoughtfully.

'It has crossed my mind, but for the moment I think it's best if I just play it by ear.' He gestured to the door. 'I'll leave the way I came.'

'You know, I didn't even ask you how you got in here,' she said with a sheepish chuckle.

'I used a credit card to unlatch one of the kitchen windows after all the staff had gone. I noticed you've got a pretty sophisticated security set-up here. Obviously it's not activated at the moment, but I'd still have the windows checked if I were you. It really wasn't that difficult to get in.'

'I will,' she replied. 'When will you be leaving the safe house?'

'I'm not sure, but I'd guess some time in the next few days. There's nothing left for me here any more.'

'Will I see you again before you leave?' she asked.

'No, I think it's best if we don't see each other again. I'm already endangering your life just by being here. If it were ever discovered I was still alive, certain interested parties wouldn't hesitate to use you or Michelle to try and get at me.'

She picked up the framed photograph of Michelle from her desk and extended it towards him. 'It was taken by a professional photographer at his studio earlier this year. I want you to have it.'

'But that's your favourite photo of her,' he said, hesitating to take the photograph from her.

'That's why I want you to have it,' she replied.

He took the photograph, then pulled her to him and wrapped his arms tightly around her. 'You take care of yourself,' he whispered. 'And you take special care of the little ragamuffin.'

'I will,' she said softly.

He tilted her head up towards him and kissed her lightly on the lips before reluctantly easing himself from her arms and heading for the door.

'Rick?' she called out after him. He paused in the doorway to look back at her. 'I love you.'

He turned away quickly before she could read anything into his expression, and disappeared out into the corridor. There was a part of her that willed him to come back, desperately wanting to feel his arms around her for one last time. But she knew he wouldn't be coming back. He could only look ahead from now on, and that meant he would have to bury the past for ever. And she represented an integral part of his past. But just knowing he was alive would make it that much easier finally to let go. She also had to look to the future. She had a daughter to raise and she was determined not to let anything, or anyone, get in the way of that . . .

She sat down slowly behind her desk and looked across at the doorway as an inkling of doubt flickered through her mind. Had she dismissed Rick's proposal too hastily? No, she chided herself angrily. Her decision had been based on what would be best for Michelle's future. That was all that mattered to her. Quickly pushing any lingering doubts from her mind, she reached for a cigarette on the desk, but when she lit it she noticed her hands were trembling. She returned her attention to the cash-drawer and tried again to count the float but found she couldn't concentrate as the doubts slowly crept back into her subconscious thoughts.

In frustration she threw down the notes she'd been counting and slumped back in her chair, having already resigned herself to the inevitability of the long, sleepless night she knew lay ahead of her.

FIFTEEN

'Wait in here.'

Marlette stepped tentatively into the room. It was sparsely furnished with only a filing cabinet, a table and a couple of uncomfortable-looking wooden chairs. The whitewashed walls were windowless and there was a faint scent of antiseptic in the air. He looked round at McCrain who was hovering in the doorway behind him. 'What the hell is this place?'

'It's used by the custom officials for strip-searches,' McCrain replied. 'Drugs, contraband, that sort of stuff.'

'So what are we doing here?'

'You'll find out soon enough. I won't be long.'

'Look, I want to know . . .' Marlette threw up his hands in frustration when McCrain left the room, closing the door again behind him. He dumped his hold-all on the table, then pulled out one of the chairs and sat down. They were as uncomfortable as they looked. He already had his boarding pass and his suitcase had been checked through to London Heathrow. He glanced at his watch. The flight would be called in the next twenty minutes. So where had McCrain gone? And why was he being so secretive? Had there been some last-minute hitch? He knew better than to start speculating. All he could do was wait until McCrain returned . . .

It had been three days since he'd seen Nicole at the restaurant and in that time she'd rarely been out of his thoughts. He'd been tempted to call her several times from the safe house but he'd known it would only have done more harm than good. Nicole had made her decision based on what would have been best for Michelle and, much as he was loath to admit it, he knew she'd been right. It was time for him finally to break with the past. A new identity. A new country. A new beginning . . .

He looked up sharply when the door opened, but it wasn't McCrain who entered the room. 'Nicole?' he said in amazement, his voice reflecting the look of disbelief on his face.

'Not any more,' she replied. 'My name's now Catherine Toure. Well, that's what it says on my passport.'

'You mean . . . you're coming with me?' he said incredulously, still struggling to believe any of this was actually happening to him.

'Not just me.'

'Where is Michelle?' he asked, his eyes flickering to McCrain who was now standing by the door.

'There's a supervised crèche close to the departure lounge,' Nicole told him. 'I left her there. I thought it best if I came here alone.'

'Does she know I'm here?'

'Yes. I told her we're going away on a long vacation with you. She's really excited about it, especially as you're coming as well.'

'I still can't believe any of this,' Marlette said. 'When I saw you at the restaurant you were adamant you wouldn't come with me. What made you change your mind?'

'I thought it was a woman's prerogative to change her mind without having to explain herself,' she replied with a smile. 'I'll tell you about it once we're airborne. Let's just say it was to be a surprise.'

'It's certainly that all right,' Marlette conceded.

'Ms Auger rang me the day after you'd been to see her,' McCrain said. 'She invited me to the restaurant for a meal that evening. That's when she asked me to make the arrangements so that she and her daughter could go with you. I was sworn to silence and, after such a delicious meal, how could I refuse?'

'Mr McCrain, would you mind giving Rick ... sorry, Frank and me a few minutes alone before we fetch my daughter from the crèche?' Nicole asked.

'I was about to leave anyway,' McCrain replied. 'There's still the little matter of arranging a road accident later this afternoon. I believe my colleague already has the keys to your car? We'll see to it the local press gets the news by this evening. You and your daughter will officially be "dead" by the time you reach London.' He took a travel wallet from his pocket and handed it to her. 'It contains your flight tickets, your boarding passes, as well as confirmation of your hotel reservation in London. One of our people will contact you there in the next couple of days.'

'Thanks for all your help,' she said, shaking his hand.

McCrain crossed to where Marlette was standing and led him out of earshot of Nicole. 'We've kept to our side of the bargain. Now it's up to you to keep to yours. I realize with the money you got from Pruitt in New York you might be tempted to try and make a break for it once you get to London. I really wouldn't advise it. All we'd have to do is put out the word that Richard Marlette is still alive. You'd be on the run for the rest of your lives, looking over your shoulder at every turn. That would hardly be fair on the kid, would it?'

'You're all heart, McCrain,' Marlette retorted disdainfully.

'You work for us now, Marlette. Don't ever forget that.'

Nicole waited until McCrain had left the room, then led Marlette away from the door. 'We need to talk, Rick. That's why I asked McCrain to give us some time alone.'

'Yeah, we do,' he replied, pulling out one of the chairs and sitting down. 'You wouldn't have changed your mind unless you'd had a damn good reason for doing so. You've obviously concocted some elaborate scheme to try and outwit Langley. Well, whatever it is, it's not going to work, Nicole. We're not dealing with a bunch of amateurs here.'

'You could at least hear me out before you jump down my throat,' she shot back.

'I don't need to hear you out, it won't work. These bastards have got me by the balls and there's nothing I can do about it without putting . . .' He trailed off and banged his fist down angrily on the table, realizing he'd already said too much.

'Without putting our lives in danger,' she said, finishing the sentence for him. 'That's what you were going to say, wasn't it?'

'I should never have come to the restaurant –'

'It's a bit late for that now, isn't it?' she cut in. 'You told me everything van Horn said to you at the safe house, except how he'd ensure your loyalty once you'd left the country. It's obvious. He used Michelle and me as the carrot, didn't he? Step out of line and we'd suffer the consequences. Am I right?' Although he didn't say anything she could see by his expression that she was right. 'You've spent the last six years protecting me. Enough's enough, Rick. I couldn't live with myself knowing Michelle and I were being used as pawns by Langley to keep you in line. I care too much about you to ever let that happen again.' She held up a finger before he could say anything. 'At least hear me out.'

'I'm listening,' was all he said in a less than convincing tone.

'I spun McCrain the story about wanting to surprise you here today. The real reason I didn't want you to know in advance was because I wasn't even sure whether we'd make it.' She unzipped an inside pocket of her overnight bag and removed two passports which she tossed on to the table in front of him. 'I got these this morning. It was touch and go whether they'd be ready in time.'

Marlette picked up the two passports. Both were American. One was in the name of Nicole Devereaux; the other Richard Tyler. He opened the Tyler passport and, as he leafed through it he found it contained several authentic entry and departure stamps. But what really impressed him was the professionalism of the forgery. It was certainly on a par with the Langley passport he had in his pocket. Closing it over, he looked up quizzically at Nicole. 'Where the hell did you get this from?'

'The best passport forger in Chicago,' she replied as if it was really no big deal. 'They cost a bit, but that was because they had to be done at such short notice.'

'And how do you come to know the best passport forger in Chicago?'

'I don't,' she replied. 'I'd heard about him through one of our regular customers at the restaurant. I made a few discreet enquiries of my own, and that's how I managed to get in touch with him.'

'Where did you get the photo of me from?'

'You remember you had to renew your passport while we were living in New York? For some reason the excess photos ended up in the back of my photo album. You haven't changed much in the last six years, apart from the hair, but I had the passport backdated a couple of years anyway just to be on the safe side.'

'Ingenious. And I suppose we use these passports when we go on the run, is that it?'

'We're not going on the run,' she corrected him. 'I thought about settling somewhere in France. You speak the language fluently from your years in the Foreign Legion, and I've been teaching Michelle to speak French from a very early age. I remember my father taking me to the Bordeaux region as a child. I loved it. And there're a lot of small family restaurants around there. One of them would be perfect for us.'

'This is all very cosy, Nicole, but you can bet Langley

would find us soon enough and then we'd be right back to square one again. So why all this deception?'

'Because Langley wouldn't be looking for us,' she replied. 'It was the tape you made for Pruitt which first gave me the idea. You make another tape once we reach London, only this time about van Horn, detailing everything that's happened to you ever since you first met with Pruitt.'

'I've got nothing concrete on van Horn. Certainly nothing he couldn't weasel out of if it were ever made public.'

She took a boxed audio mini-cassette from her overnight bag. 'He won't be able to weasel out of it with this as backup.'

'What is it?' Marlette asked, taking it from her.

'The conversation I had with McCrain at the restaurant,' Nicole replied. 'We've got a couple of secluded booths at the restaurant for customers who want a bit of privacy while they eat. It's the showbiz types who normally use them. McCrain and I used one of the booths so we could talk without being overheard. I played the naïve girlfriend, and that way I was able to coax things out of him he wouldn't have mentioned himself. There's no major revelation on the tape. It's more what's implied that would do the most damage to van Horn's credibility, especially as McCrain admitted quite freely that he's one of van Horn's closest aides. Any good journalist would be able to make one hell of a story from it.'

'And you're suggesting we send a copy of the tape to van Horn and threaten to make it public as a means of keeping him off our backs?'

'No, it's best if van Horn's left in the dark. You send a copy of the two tapes, together with a handwritten letter, to the American Ambassador in London. In the letter you'd explain that all you want is to be allowed to carry on your life without having Langley breathing down your neck, but that if anything were ever to happen to any of us, the original tapes and the false CIA passports would be forwarded on to one of the major news networks here in the States. You can bet the Ambassador would have the tapes on their way to the White House in the next diplomatic bag. The President would soon realize just how damaging these revelations would be to him and his administration if they were ever made public. After all, he appointed van Horn when he took office. So if anything were to happen to us and this story were to break, the President would find himself in a very awkward position. If he claimed he didn't know what van Horn was doing, it would make him look incompetent. If he tried to back him, it would make him look corrupt. In a nutshell, van Horn would become a serious liability to the administration. The only way the President could distance himself from van Horn's damaging jingoism would be to force him out of office. And that would also almost certainly put paid to any chance van Horn might have had of running for the White House one day.'

Marlette turned the mini-cassette around in his hand. 'And what if van Horn puts out the word I'm still alive after he's been forced out of office?'

'He wouldn't dare if you'd already fingered him as your paymaster,' Nicole replied. 'He could deny it all he wants, but he'd be as good as dead if it were ever made public. The first rule of journalism: never let the truth get in the way of a good story. Bob taught me that. It's time to play van Horn at his own game. It's the only way we're going to beat him.'

'It's still a risk —'

'Sure it's a risk, but what's the alternative?' she cut in angrily. 'Letting van Horn and his successors manipulate you for the rest of your life just so that Michelle and I won't come to any harm? Forget it, Rick. I don't care what happens to me, but the hell I'm going to let those bastards use Michelle like that. And I would hope you'd feel the same way about your own daughter.'

'A little restaurant in Bordeaux, you say?' Marlette said at length. 'Yeah, I think I could live with that.' He handed her the mini-cassette, then got to his feet. 'You've got this all worked out down to the last detail, haven't you?'

'Someone's got to do the thinking around here, especially with our daughter's future at stake,' she replied with gentle sarcasm. 'There is only one problem. We're going to need to use some of Pruitt's money to pay for this little business venture. Where is the money? New York?'

'Right here,' Marlette said, patting the hold-all on the table.

'What?' Nicole shot back in amazement.

'Two hundred thousand dollars in cash. McCrain wanted to send it on to London for me to pick up there but I wasn't about to let it out of my sight that easily. So he agreed to let me take it with me on the plane. He cleared it with customs before we left the safe house. He told me I wouldn't be stopped at Heathrow either. It's certainly saved me the hassle of trying to get it out of the country by myself.'

'So McCrain has his uses after all,' she said, slipping her arms around his waist. 'You know, I could really come to like a man carrying around a couple of hundred grand in cash.'

'I bet you say that to all the guys,' Marlette replied with a grin.

'How did you guess?' she purred, then reached up on tiptoe and kissed him. 'Well, Rockefeller, we'd better go and get our daughter before the flight's called.'

'I'm with you there,' he said, grabbing the hold-all off the table.

They left the room and made their way to the crèche. Michelle had her back to them and was playing with a couple of girls of her own age.

'Well, aren't you going to go in and get her?' Nicole asked.

'In there?' he retorted, staring at the dozens of screaming children running around excitedly behind the perspex façade.

'You can survive for weeks in the jungle with all its persistent dangers, but you can't even go into a room full of kids to fetch your own daughter,' Nicole said, shaking her head in despair.

'Given that choice, I think you'd find most guys would rather take their chances in the jungle.'

'My hero,' she muttered, ducking out from under his arm.

Marlette watched as she dodged the flailing arms and feet with the experience of a seasoned running back to reach Michelle. She pointed towards him, and a wide grin spread across Michelle's face. She ran ahead of her mother to the exit. Marlette crouched down as she emerged from the crèche. 'Hey, ragamuffin,' he said, and inhaled sharply when she clattered against his injured ribs as she threw her arms excitedly around his neck. 'What's this?' he said, reaching behind her ear, and when he opened his hand there was a quarter in his palm.

Michelle plucked the quarter from his palm and grinned at her mother. Her face suddenly became serious when she turned back to Marlette. 'Are you Mommy's boyfriend?'

The question took him by surprise. 'Well . . . I don't . . .' he stammered, but when he looked to Nicole for help she just folded her arms across her chest, a faint smile on her lips.

'Mommy doesn't have a boyfriend,' Michelle said earnestly, 'and all her friends keep telling her that she should have a boyfriend. Because when you get old you look like a bag lady and then nobody thinks you're pretty any more.'

Marlette chuckled at Nicole's bemused expression, then

took Michelle's hands gently in his. 'Do you want me to be your mommy's boyfriend?'

Michelle nodded her head vigorously. 'Yes, and when you love Mommy enough you can marry her and be my other daddy.'

Marlette hugged Michelle tightly to him. 'I'd like that.'

'Me too,' Michelle said, then picked up her pink suitcase and looked up excitedly at her mother. 'Can we go on the plane now?'

'Soon, sweetheart,' Nicole assured her. 'Let's go and wait in the departure lounge for it to be called.'

Michelle grabbed Marlette's hand, and grinned when he looked down at her in surprise. He winked at her, then led her towards the departure lounge. Nicole was about to pick up her overnight bag when she noticed McCrain standing further down the corridor. He was staring directly at her. His mouth twitched in a half-smile of acknowledgement, but his eyes remained cold. What was he doing there? A sudden fear gripped her — what if he'd overheard them talking? *You're overreacting*, she chided herself.

'Mommy, are you coming?'

The voice startled her. She looked round at Michelle who was beckoning her towards them. Rick hadn't seen McCrain. When she looked again McCrain had gone. With a lingering sense of unease she picked up her overnight bag and went after them.

The excitement continues in

ALISTAIR MACLEAN'S
RENDEZVOUS
by Alastair MacNeill

A blockbuster author in his own right,
Alastair MacNeill is also the author of seven
bestselling novels based on screenplays left after
Alistair MacLean's death.

The following pages contain the prologue
to *Alistair Maclean's Rendezvous*,
Alastair MacNeill's latest work, a gripping
novelization of a short story by Alistair MacLean.

NOW AVAILABLE IN HARDBACK

PROLOGUE

'. . . Earth to earth, ashes to ashes, dust to dust; in the sure
and certain hope of the Resurrection to eternal life, through
our Lord Jesus Christ. Amen.'

The minister's eulogy was followed by a murmured
'Amen' from the small congregation of mourners who were
huddled under an array of black umbrellas around the
open grave on that cold, bleak Glaswegian morning. James
McIndoe stepped out from under the protection of an
umbrella and felt the light drizzle caressing his face as he
reached down to scoop up a handful of soil which he tossed
over the top of his father's casket. He stood motionless at
the lip of the open grave, his head bowed respectfully in
silent thought, his eyes lingering on the name which was
embossed on the brass plaque on the coffin lid: *Samuel
Donald McIndoe, 1914–1995.*

He stepped back and took the umbrella from his wife,
Heather, who slipped her hand into his and squeezed it
tightly. He watched as their two children each took it in
turns to drop a handful of soil over their grandfather's
coffin. Nineteen-year-old Isobel, who'd inherited her
mother's beauty, was in her first year of a journalism degree
at Glasgow University. The third generation of McIndoe
to attend the prestigious university. And fifteen-year-old
James – or Jamie as he'd been known ever since he was a
toddler – who wanted to follow in his father's footsteps
and become a mathematics teacher once he'd finished

school. James McIndoe was fiercely proud of both his children. And he knew that their grandfather had been as well.

A hand touched his arm, startling him, and when he looked round he found one of his father's friends standing behind him. The man gripped McIndoe's hand tightly, muttered his condolences, then moved off towards the row of cars which were parked outside the cemetery gate. The procession of mourners then dutifully filed past James and Heather McIndoe to offer their sympathies to the family on their recent bereavement.

'Who's that over there?' Jamie asked when the last of the mourners had left, pointing to an elderly man dressed in a raincoat and a trilby who was standing in a cluster of trees at the edge of the cemetery. 'He's been there for the past twenty minutes. Do you know who he is?'

James McIndoe shook his head. 'Can't say I do. He could have been someone your grandpa knew in the old days.'

'I don't recognize him,' Heather said, looking across at the man.

'I'll go and see what he wants,' McIndoe said.

Heather grabbed her husband's arm as he turned to go. 'Leave him. He's not doing any harm. If he wants to talk to us, he'll come over.'

'We'll see.' With that James McIndoe walked over to the man and introduced himself.

'My condolences to you and your family on your bereavement,' the man said in a clipped German accent.

'Thank you. Did you know father?'

'Not personally, no,' came the reply. 'Samuel, that was his name?'

'Sam. Nobody called him Samuel,' McIndoe replied.

'I spoke with your father on the telephone last week,' the man told him. 'We had agreed to meet at his house today, but when I arrived I was told by a neighbour that he had died of a heart attack at the weekend.'

'What exactly was it that you wanted to see my father about?' McIndoe asked, removing his rain-spattered glasses and wiping them on his handkerchief. 'Perhaps I could be of help?'

'It was not so much me wanting to see your father as him wanting to see me,' the German replied. 'He has no doubt told you about the operations he carried out for the British SOE during the last war.'

'Yes, many times,' McIndoe replied with a wistful smile. 'I used to sit on his knee as a child and listen to his stories over and over again. I never tired of hearing them.'

'Then you will no doubt have heard about the covert operation in Sicily. February, 1942.'

'That was the one operation my father recounted to me more than any other,' McIndoe said in surprise. 'I heard it so many times that it got to a point where I almost felt as if I'd been there myself.'

'Then you will know there was always one elusive piece of the jigsaw which would have put the whole operation into perspective for him and, perhaps more importantly, also have put his mind at rest. And from what he told me when we spoke on the telephone, finding it had become something of an obsession for him since the end of the war.'

James McIndoe knew exactly what the German meant. He could still vividly remember as a young child over-hearing the vitriolic arguments between his parents – before his father's successful career as a respected author of Roman military history could sustain what had ultimately become a fifty year obsession – which were always centred on the same subject: his father wanting to dip into the precious family finances to pay some dubious informer who claimed to have the vital information he'd been searching for; and his mother yelling at him to start acting like a reliable parent and stop chasing after ghosts from his past. Her reasoning, however sound, never had any effect on

411

him. It was an obsession he'd finally taken to the grave with him.

'And you have that last piece of the jigsaw?' James McIndoe asked suspiciously, recalling only too well those perfidious deals his father had struck with a succession of dubious con-men which had never brought him any closer to the truth.

The German nodded.

'Had he agreed to pay you for this information?'

The German's eyes narrowed angrily. 'How dare you suggest that I am in this for financial gain. I was a highly respected officer in the West German intelligence service for thirty-seven years. Your father insisted on paying for my plane ticket and for my accommodation while I was here in Glasgow. But any question of him paying me for this information . . .' He paused to wipe his hand across his mouth as if to remove the disgust he felt at such an accusation. '. . . I regard that as an insult.'

James McIndoe realized he'd touched a nerve and was quick to make reparations for his blunder. 'I'm very sorry, I didn't mean to infer anything by that. It's just that over the years there have been those who've tried, and in many cases succeeded in ripping off my father by giving him false and misleading information.'

'I am not one of them,' came the sharp retort.

'No, of course not.' McIndoe cast a despairing look up at the dark, overcast sky. 'We're getting soaked out here. Would you care to come back to the house? We can discuss this further there.'

'Thank you. I have a hired car parked nearby,' the German informed him. 'I will follow you to your house.'

McIndoe gestured towards the main gate. 'That's settled then. Shall we go?'

ALISTAIR MACLEAN'S

Night Watch
Alastair MacNeill

After lengthy negotiations the Rijksmuseum in Amsterdam agrees to send its priceless Rembrandt, 'Night Watch', on a tour of the world's art galleries. Security is intensive. Even so, when the painting arrives in New York it is discovered to be a fake.

The United Nations Anti-Crime Organization, UNACO, is immediately called into action. Agents Mike Graham, C.W. Whitlock and Sabrina Carver must find out who is responsible for the brilliant forgery and, most important, who now has the original in his private collection.

Speed and secrecy are vital. The hunt leads them to Rio de Janeiro at Carnival time, where their quarry is secure in his mountain fortress, high above the sea . . .

ISBN 0 00 617743 3

Alistair MacLean's Code Breaker

Alastair MacNeill

It begins a couple of days before Christmas on the tarmac at Lisbon airport. Sergei Kolchinsky, Deputy Director of the world's most secret and effective anti-terrorist organization, UNACO, is heading home in the company of his colleague Abe Silverman, a world authority on codes. In a sudden, terrifying attack, Kolchinsky is shot and Silverman, along with coded documents of unmeasurable value, is captured.

It may be the holiday season, but UNACO's Strike Force Three must respond to the incident immediately. Liasing with the Portuguese Special Forces, the UNACO team sets about tracking down the vital secrets.

Before long they realize they are dealing with one of the most successful and dangerous military minds of the former Soviet Union – and, worse still, they are under threat at home from an investigative journalist determined to blow their cover.

A pulsating story that builds to a nail-biting climax, *Alistair MacLean's Code Breaker* is a thriller worthy of the master himself.

ISBN 0 00 647622 8

The Heart of Danger

Gerald Seymour

'Unmissable' *The Times*

In a wrecked Croat village, a mass grave is uncovered and the mutilated body of a young Englishwoman, Dorrie Mowat, is exhumed.

Her mother, who loathed Dorrie in life, becomes obsessed by the need to find out about her death. But with civil war tearing apart the former Yugoslavia, none of the authorities there or in Britain are interested in a 'minor' war crime.

So she turns to Bill Penn, private investigator, MI5 reject. For him this looks like a quick trip to safe Zagreb, the writing of a useless report and a good fee at the end of it. But once there he finds himself drawn inexorably towards the killing ground behind the lines, to find the truth of the young woman's death and, perhaps, the truth of himself.

Penn's search for evidence that could, one day, convict a war criminal in a court of law becomes an epic journey into a merciless war where the odds are stacked high against him.

'It's impossible to find fault with this book, which builds relentlessly to its climax. It has an intense feeling of authenticity and it's well written'

NICHOLAS FLEMING, *Spectator*

'Vivid stuff. I write a fortnight after finishing the book and some of the scenes of pursuit and mindless cruelty still return to me'   DOUGLAS HURD, *Daily Telegraph*

ISBN 0 00 649033 6